TAINTED IDOL

RUINED ROCKSTARS BOOK FIVE

HEATHER ASHLEY

The way your fingers fit in mine, it's five plus five, not rocket science.

FLORIDA GEORGIA LINE

BOOKS BY HEATHER ASHLEY

RUINED ROCKSTARS:

STEAMY ROCKSTAR ROMANCE

DEVIANT ROCKERS
FALLEN STAR
DIRTY LEGEND
BROKEN PLAYER
VICIOUS ICON
TAINTED IDOL
WICKED GOD

HOLLYWOOD GUARDIANS:

DARK BODYGUARD ROMANCE

CAPTIVE
CHASED
HOSTILE
DECEIT

TWISTED SOUL MAGIC:

MAGICAL REVERSE HAREM ROMANCE

CROSSED SOULS
BOUND SOULS

EMERALD HILLS ELITE:

ACADEMY REVERSE HAREM ROMANCE

TWISTED LITTLE GAMES

RULES WERE MEANT TO BE BROKEN...

ONE
GRIFFIN

"Where the hell's my latte?" Wynter shrieked while she stomped her foot, and I cringed. For some reason, she was always like this now. I almost couldn't remember the girl she'd been when we first met, even if it was only a few months ago.

Her blue eyes landed on me, and her scowl turned into a pout as she sauntered over, throwing her arms around my neck. "Ross is so useless, Griff," she whined, and I sighed. What did she expect me to do about her weaselly assistant?

"I know," I cooed, patting her back, and she stepped back a half step, focusing her shrewd gaze on my face, then something over my shoulder, before lifting on her toes to press her lips to mine. As I returned her kiss—because annoying she was, I still had a dick—she turned us to a different angle. That was also something she did all the time, taking advantage of the photographers who followed us constantly and trying to get the best angle.

I pulled away from her, and she scowled at me, but I was not feeling her bullshit. Wynter was gorgeous, old-Hollywood stunning with ruby red lips and strawberry blonde hair that never had even a strand out of place.

When we met six months ago at a stuffy industry party, she caught my attention across the room, but she didn't wait for me to make the first move. She marched right up to me and demanded I take her on a date. I grinned at the memory.

With all the guys in the band settling down, I hated being by myself. Wynter inserted herself in my life, and it worked. I had a date to every function and never had to worry about being the annoying little brother just tagging along.

I brushed her hair out of her face and she swatted my hand away. She hated when I messed up her hair or makeup. "How 'bout we go to that sushi place you like for dinner?"

She squealed and clapped her hands together. "Yes, that sounds *amazing*! I need a new outfit." She bit her lip, and her eyes went far off like she was picturing said outfit. I looked down at myself, planning to wear the jeans and t-shirt I had on.

I checked my watch. "I've got a meeting with the band and then some promo stuff, but I'll pick you up at eight." I leaned down and pressed a kiss to her cheek as she pouted up at me.

"What kind of promo stuff?"

Wynter liked to tag along to as many band events as she possibly could. She was supportive like that. "I'm not sure yet. Harrison's going over it with us at the meeting."

"Make sure to text me and let me know," she murmured, leaning in to kiss me again as I wrapped my arms around her one last time before I had to go. She was always asking me to let her know the specifics of what was going on with the band, what kind of promo we'd be doing, stuff like that, but I figured she just liked knowing what I was up to.

I'd never had a girlfriend before, but that seemed to be pretty standard girlfriend behavior if TV was in any way accurate.

Out of the corner of my eye, I watched Ross bustle up behind Wynter with her to-go coffee cup gripped in his hand as he watched us with pursed lips. I stepped back and let her go, nodding over her shoulder at Ross. He glared at me in return, but that wasn't new. The dude was always a prick to me, no matter how nice I was to him.

At this point, it was a game to see how much I could piss him off by being extra nice. So far, I'd managed to get him to turn a weird red-purple color and shake with rage. Next, I wanted to see if I could get him to actually explode like a volcano.

My dad always told me it was important to have goals.

I snorted to myself as Wynter eyed me curiously before letting me go and turning her ire on her unfortunate assistant. For some reason, no matter how awful she was to him, he stuck to her like glue. I didn't understand their dynamic, but I didn't have to. It wasn't my place to tell her how to build her career as long as she stayed out of how I built mine.

I took a few steps backward before calling out a promise to text her later and made my way to my car. A few paps followed me, snapping some last-minute pictures, but when I slipped behind the wheel of my truck, they wandered back to Wynter.

I still wasn't used to LA traffic. Back home in Texas, when I drove into Houston, the traffic could be shitty, but for the most part, it was nothing like it was out here. There was no *rush hour*, just a constant standstill on the interstate. Lucky for me, I was already downtown, so the trip to meet up with the band at our publicist's office didn't take long.

Stepping off the elevator, I smiled and greeted the receptionist before I walked into the conference room. People loved me—I always made sure I had a lazy smile on my face and remembered small details about their lives. I'd always needed to be the most-liked person in the room. It was a compulsion.

I was the first to show up, so I pulled out a chair in the middle of one of the long sides of the glass table and sat down, stretching out my legs and crossing them at the ankle. I pulled out my phone, scrolling through social media to pass the time. Wynter had tagged me in a couple of pictures she'd taken of us on the sidewalk earlier. I raked my hand through my hair, closing out of the app, and pocketing my phone.

Sometimes I wished she didn't have to share everything so publicly. Sure, I liked people, but I didn't need my entire life plastered everywhere for people to comment on, *like*, or judge. I shook off my clouded thoughts when Harrison pushed into the room, looking as put together as always.

I'd never seen him out of a suit, but my brother swore that he liked to surf with True and actually put on swim trunks to do it. I wasn't sure I believed him. "Hey, Harr… ison," I recovered, almost slipping up and calling him *Harry* to his face, which the guys all did behind his back, but I knew he hated.

He narrowed his bright blue eyes at me before his expression smoothed into one of calm with just a little bit of arrogance. "Griffin."

He dropped his tablet onto the tabletop and pulled out the chair at the head of the table, unbuttoning the single closed button on his jacket before sinking into the chair, and I chuckled. "Don't you get tired of always being so buttoned-up?"

He eyed me warily. "Honestly, mate? Sometimes, but at this point, it's like a second skin. I forget I'm even wearing it most of the time until I get home and undo this bloody tie." He reached up and loosened it a fraction, almost as if it were cutting off his air supply.

"Your secret's safe with me," I promised with a laugh as he closed his eyes and took a breath. The echoes of the rest of the guys in the band laughing in the lobby announced their arrival before I could see them. I watched as Harrison straightened up and fixed his tie.

Maddox moved into the room first and strode over to me, ruffling my hair with a smirk. I swatted at his hands, but secretly I loved it. I'd always wished for a sibling growing up, so when I found out I had a big brother a year and a half ago, I was beyond excited. It was a no-brainer to move to LA to be closer to him.

The fact he was in one of my favorite bands of all time? Un-fucking-believable.

And now I somehow found myself in the band, too. I still didn't quite trust that I wouldn't wake up one morning back in my crappy apartment in Texas and find that this had all been a dream. But for now, I was more than happy to go along for the ride. If nothing else, someday it would be a kick-ass memory.

"What's up, baby bro?" Maddox asked as he dropped into the seat next to me. Zen and True took the seats on the other side of the table from us.

"Just excited to see what's up with this tour," I admitted. The guys weren't new to touring. They'd done it so many times I doubted they gave much of a shit about it at this point, but playing music for a living had been a far off fantasy until Maddox came along and changed everything for me.

"Aww, junior's first tour," Zen teased in the voice he used to talk to his son, Nico, and True chuckled beside him. I should have probably glared at them or something, but I didn't have it in me. I was too damn excited and didn't even care if I let them see it.

"We're just waiting on Montana," Harrison explained, interrupting the guys giving me shit. He hadn't even finished his sentence when the telltale sound of heels clicking on marble announced her arrival, and she pushed through the door, bringing a whole lot of fiery attitude with her that matched her bright red hair.

"Boys," she greeted us as she breezed into the room and took the chair at the other end of the long table from Harrison. She dropped her bag down onto the surface with a loud *thunk* and rooted around inside, plucking out her iPad. "Ready to talk tour details?"

We all nodded and turned toward her. "Good. I've been planning this tour—the *Wild Ride* tour—since you first started recording the album. It's not going to be worldwide for now since you're financing it yourselves through Phoenix Records. I've got fourteen stops as of right now with venues reserved across the US, but we need to hire a tour manager."

"I've already got interviews set up after this meeting with a dozen or so music bloggers to announce the tour in the other conference room," Harrison added, nodding his head in the direction of a room similar to this one across the floor of his office. "I figured since we've got the whole indie label thing going for us, we'd do some grassroots promo while we're at it."

"I like that," Zen agreed, and I found myself nodding along.

"Everything sounds perfect so far. I think I can speak for all of us when I say we trust you to hire a competent manager," True assured her. "My only stipulation is that there be enough room on the bus for Amara and Phoenix to come along."

"And Kennedy and Nico. Oh, and Jericho, and you know he's not going anywhere without Moon and the baby," Zen told her with a grin.

Montana pinched the bridge of her nose and took a deep breath before letting it out. "Jesus. While we're at it, let's just rent a fucking school bus and drive a goddamn caravan. We can become a fucking traveling family band complete with a convoy of fucking minivans," she mocked, waving her hands around animatedly as she paced.

I bit my lip to keep from laughing at her ridiculous spiel. Shadow

Phoenix had most definitely tamed their wild rockstar ways over the past couple of years. As the youngest member, I sort of figured it was up to me to uphold the crazy traditions like getting stupid drunk and trashing dressing rooms and shit.

Maddox chimed in mid-tirade. "Ryan's coming, too."

Montana snorted and honed her attention in on me. "What about you and that attention whore you call a girlfriend?"

I recoiled a little at the venom behind her words and scowled at her. It wasn't like I was in love with Wynter or anything, but she was still my girlfriend. I couldn't let Montana talk about her like that, could I? "Don't call her that."

"Dude, that's what she is," Maddox added, and I cut my glare his way.

"You guys don't know her like I do."

Zen snorted. "We're not new, kiddo." I hated when he fucking called me that, which he'd taken to doing basically all the time. "You don't think we've seen more than our fair share of women trying to get their claws in us and take advantage?"

True was nodding along. "My high school girlfriend tried to pin her baby on me right when we were starting to gain a little traction with the band. We all have stories like that, bud. He's not trying to piss you off. You're one of us now, and we watch out for our own. That girl…"

"Is a low-rent social media influencer wannabe," my brother finished.

"What he said," True agreed, and my jaw clenched. I didn't care if they were watching out for me, they had no idea what my relationship with Wynter was like, and it was messed up that they were ganging up on me.

"You're lucky Jericho's not here," Zen remarked, tapping his tattooed fingers on the tabletop. "He hates her the most."

I rolled my eyes and looked at Harrison, who wasn't paying attention at all. He had his face buried in his phone, and his eyebrows furrowed. I wasn't getting any help from him, not that I thought he would defend Wynter, but I thought he might at least understand where she was coming from. "You guys have made your point, but she's not taking advantage of me. She's just ambitious."

Zen snorted, and Maddox tried to cover the fact he'd just cough-yelled *bitch* with a hacking cough that sounded ridiculous. I pounded him on the back harder than necessary, taking out a little bit of my irritation on him. He deserved it for being an asshole.

Montana clapped her hands, making me jump, and we all turned our focus back on her. "If you're done, let's talk about the tour manager. The guy we used last time got almost everything set up but had an emergency and had to quit. I've got to find a last-minute replacement. Do you all have any preference? If not, I'm going to post the job and start wading through resumes."

The guys all exchanged glances, and Zen flicked his eyes over to me. "We tend to prefer hiring people with little to no experience fresh out of school. They usually have new ideas and good energy. It's worked out well for us so far. You good with that?"

I appreciated that he was asking for my opinion. The guys were cool like that—they always tried to include me in decisions even though I was new. I nodded, and Zen turned back to Montana. Clearly, he was the leader here now that Jericho wasn't involved in the day-to-day band stuff.

"Find us someone fresh. I think with the new label and the new album, we need a different perspective on our tour," he decided, and Montana made a note on her iPad before flipping the cover closed and shoving it back in her bag.

"My job here is done. I'll let you know when I find someone. I hope you're ready because this tour is going to be insane; I can already tell. You've got two weeks, boys."

We all said our thanks, and when she left, Harrison finally put his phone down. The dude looked tired. Not just tired but *weary*, like he hadn't slept in a month and was also carrying the weight of the entire planet on his shoulders. "You lot better be up for some promo interviews about the album and the tour because I've arranged an hour of video chatting. You've got fifteen minutes to familiarize yourself with all of this," he said, sliding a thick stack of papers to each of us, "before we start."

Maddox flipped through his next to me and then looked back up at Harrison. "Isn't there a summary sheet or anything? This is a fuck ton of information for fifteen minutes."

I had to agree, and we all turned back to Harrison, who sighed. "Just look over the setlists you gave Montana in there and the list of venues. The rest you'll have to figure out as you go."

He stood up and left, face buried back in his phone, to give us time to read the mountain of paperwork. My phone had been vibrating in my pocket for the entire meeting, but I'd been ignoring it. I glanced down, worried that something could be seriously wrong because why else would someone call me repeatedly like that?

I cringed when I saw Wynter's name and hit *ignore*. I forgot to text her what was going on, but she could get over it. I didn't owe her an explanation or play-by-play for every second of my life. We weren't serious like that. Maddox had been watching me instead of reading his info packet. "What?"

"She is not getting anywhere near our tour, bro. Don't even think about it."

I chuckled. "And if I want her to come along?"

"The girls fucking hate her, dude, and they don't hate anyone. If she comes along, she's going to make everyone miserable."

Was Wynter really that bad? I didn't think so, but looking at the three guys in this room and hearing their opinions, I wasn't sure what to think. I trusted them. They'd never steered me wrong, and they'd been through some shit before I ever met them. Finally, I decided it just wasn't worth the fight to bring her along. She could deal with me being gone for a couple of months. "I won't bring her," I conceded, and True shot me a grateful look while the other guys went back to reading.

I'd just flipped to the second page when the sound of high heels clicking on the tile sounded again, and I looked up to see Wynter, followed by Ross, the weasel, stomping through the office straight for the conference room. "Fuck," I muttered, and Maddox looked up, glaring at the woman approaching.

"You've got to be fucking kidding me," he hissed.

True and Zen turned around, and Zen turned back, shooting me a look that said, *see?* True rolled his eyes and went back to studying.

Wynter pushed inside the conference room without waiting for anyone to invite her in and not bothering to hold the door open for Ross, so it swung back and hit him in the face. He turned pink but pushed it open and stumbled in behind her. If I weren't so irritated, I probably would have laughed my ass off.

She looked pissed with her hands on her hips and tapping one high-heeled foot on the tile, making a steady *click-click-click* noise that was grating. "Why weren't you answering my calls?" she snapped, and before I could answer, she asked, "And why haven't you texted me to tell me what kind of promo you were going to do today?"

"Maybe because it's none of your fucking business?" Maddox drawled without ever looking up, and I kicked him under the table before I stood up and walked around to her. I grabbed her hand and pulled her out of the conference room.

"Are you going to let him talk to me like that?" Wynter practically shrieked.

"I'll talk to him, but you can't just barge in here when I've got band stuff going on," I scolded, and her whole demeanor changed. She crumpled in front of me, her eyes welling with tears, and I felt like a gigantic asshole.

She sniffled quietly. "You don't want me here?"

I rubbed her arms gently, hating that she was upset with me. That whole needing everyone to like me thing was a real bitch sometimes. "Of course I want you here, but sometimes I also need to have a little space to do my job."

She nodded, and Harrison walked past us, stopping to take in the scene before his knowing blue gaze settled on me. "It's time. Live streams wait for no one." He moved past me to get the other guys, and I turned back to Wynter, who no longer looked upset. Instead, excitement filled her eyes.

"You're doing live streams? I should totally come along! Could you imagine how much people would eat it up if we did them together? Everyone loves a good love story!" She was practically vibrating with excitement, and her voice had gone into that high-pitched range that made most men's balls want to shrivel up and fall off, mine included.

The guys filed out of the conference room, and I didn't know what to say to tell her she couldn't be a part of what I was about to do without pissing her off again. I looked at the guys, pleading for their help, and finally, Harrison took pity on me.

"Listen, you…" he closed his eyes and took a calming breath before snapping them both open. I'd noticed Wynter had that effect on a lot of people. "If you step one toe into that conference room, I'll have security escort you out of this office, and if you so desperately want to be on the band's feed, I'll live stream the whole bloody thing," he promised, and Wynter paled.

She gathered herself, pushing her nose up into the air, and spun on her heel with Ross following closely behind. I didn't know if that meant she was pissed off at me or not, but I wasn't sure I really cared. What'd she been thinking showing up here? Maybe the guys were right, and I needed to take a closer look at her motivations in this relationship.

Maybe I was trying too hard to fit in with all the couples in the band, not wanting to be by myself, and because of that, I'd jumped into a relationship with someone who wasn't in it for the right reasons. My chest hurt at the thought, and I hoped I was wrong. Being used never felt good, and if that's what this was, it wouldn't be the first time.

Hopefully, this time, I was wrong.

TWO
MAGNOLIA

It was the whimpering that caught my attention first. I whipped my head around at the sound, looking for its source. It sounded distressed, like whatever was making it was sad down to their very soul. The pain resonated within me, and I couldn't just pass it by like all the other people going about their day, bustling in and out of the grocery store's automatic doors.

Of all the people going by, not one of them stopped to investigate.

I knew what it felt like to be in pain and be passed by; my agony ignored, my suffering brushed aside. Even if I was the only one who paid attention, who connected with the misery of other beings because my experiences allowed me to feel their pain as if it were my own, at least *someone* was paying attention and willing to step up and help.

I would always be that someone for those who needed it.

I shuddered as memories tried to suck me under, but I pushed them away. Now was not the time to focus on that. My eyes scanned the busy sidewalk in front of the store before landing on a tattered old cardboard box that'd been shoved between a concrete pillar and a bike rack. If I hadn't been staring at it, I wouldn't have noticed the shaking.

I moved quickly, avoiding everyone around me with practiced ease. Kneeling in front of the box, I peeled back the flaps, and my breath caught. A pair of bright blue eyes stared back up at me, and the fluffiest puppy I'd ever seen was huddled in the corner of the box, trembling and eyeing me warily.

"What kind of a monster would leave you here?" I cooed, reaching into the box slowly with gentle hands to lift the ball of fluff into my arms and snuggling it close. When the tiny puppy stopped shaking, I held it out from my body so I could look into its eyes. I also sneaked a little peek at whether it was a boy or a girl.

"I'm gonna take you home, so I hope you don't mind crappy motels," I explained even though I was sure there was no way the little guy could understand a word I was saying. He looked up at me and blinked slowly, suddenly looking exhausted and relieved all at once. I briefly wondered how long he'd been sitting in that box before I stumbled across him and made a mental note to swing by a vet's office on my way home.

Standing up, I scanned the area, studying the faces of everyone walking past me before I let out a heavy sigh of relief. I didn't used to be like this, but this new me? She was born of necessity and a survival instinct so strong, no one would ever get the better of me again.

In one hand, I held my new puppy against my chest, and in the other, my fingers were wrapped around my car keys so I could get in quickly and not leave myself vulnerable. When I stepped up beside my beat-up old Honda, I glanced into the back seat first before I unlocked the door and slipped inside, shutting the door and locking it behind me before I set the puppy in my lap and started the car.

"I'm gonna call you Lucky," I murmured, stroking between his ears as he curled up, resting his chin on my thigh with a contented huff as his eyelids drooped.

I needed groceries, but I could pick them up later after getting the little guy settled back in my room. After a quick stop at the vet for shots and a checkup, I took my new healthy pup home with me.

Home was a generous word for the cheap motel I was staying at. Over the past year, I hadn't wanted to stay anywhere more than a couple of weeks, so I moved from one sketchy cash-only motel to another. Looking over my shoulder constantly was exhausting, but things were changing.

My business management degree was finally in my hands, and the plan

I'd been working my butt off for the last couple of years was coming together. I was going to permanently escape my past and carve out a future I'd been dreaming about and holding onto for the past three years even if it killed me.

Some days, plans for the future were the only thing that held me together and got me through.

I looped the end of Lucky's new leash around my wrist and set him down on the concrete after I'd climbed out of the car. He stared up at me. "Don't look at me like that. I can't carry you everywhere," I scolded, grabbing the bag of puppy food and supplies off the passenger seat. I walked slowly, balancing the bag in one arm and tugging gently on the leash to get Lucky to follow. He stubbornly sat his fluffy butt on the ground and yawned, looking up at me as if he'd made his move and wanted to see what I'd do.

"You're not gettin' me to carry you. I'll wait all day," I threatened. We stared at each other before he finally huffed and trotted along beside me, waiting while I unlocked the door before bounding inside. I set the bag down on the tiny table that doubled as a desk and pulled my vibrating phone out of the back pocket of my jeans.

"Hello?" I winced when I realized I hadn't checked the caller ID before answering. I'd blame it on the puppy distracting me.

"Miss Johnson?"

The tension in my muscles relaxed just a little at the sound of a woman's voice using my made-up name. "Yes, ma'am, that's me. What can I do for you?"

"I'm calling because I'd like to talk to you about your ad." Right, the ad I'd placed on the local neighborhood group online. Because of Winston, I couldn't get a traditional job—at least not the kind where I'd be in the same place for any long period of time. It would take him next to no time to find me if I did, and then I'd have to start all over. It was better to get paid in cash and move around on my own. If I never set down roots, I couldn't be upset when I had to pack up in the middle of the night and go somewhere new to stay safe.

When I was a kid, my Grammy gave me her old camera. In the days when I felt most disconnected from the world as something *other*, a taint on me that made me a pariah with the other kids as if being an orphan was contagious, I'd lose myself in capturing the beauty around me. If I could've made a career out of photography, I would have, but for now, it was enough to take cash for any sessions that came in to get by until I could start my career.

"Sure, what can I do for you, ma'am?" I inquired, shifting my phone so it rested between my shoulder and my face while I untangled Lucky from his leash as he used his needle-sharp teeth to gnaw on it.

"My son's going to be a senior this year, and he needs his photos done. We had a photographer set up, but she backed out last minute. Are you available this afternoon?"

I eyed Lucky as he eyed me right back. He definitely had an attitude and made himself comfortable fast considering he'd been abandoned in a cardboard box, but I could relate. "Sure, as long as you don't mind me bringin' my puppy along." No way could I leave him in here. He'd pee on everything and probably chew some stuff up, too.

"Great, we planned on doing the shoot at Centennial Park. Are you familiar with it?"

"Sure." I totally wasn't, but then again, my phone had Google Maps. "What time?"

"At two." She sounded apologetic, like she knew that was hardly any time. Lucky for her, I didn't have anything going on and really needed the money.

"I'll be there," I agreed and hung up after going over payment details with her. My Grammy did a lot for me, but leaving me her camera when she died was one of the best. Sometimes I wondered what she'd think of everything that'd happened the past three years. Some days, I missed her so much it felt like I couldn't breathe. She was all I had in this world until I met Winston. Then I learned how much more I had to lose.

Blowing out a breath, I looked down at the little ball of fluff currently ripping at the faded blanket on the lumpy motel bed, scooping him up into my arms and burying my face in his soft fur while he wiggled to try and get free. A smile crept onto my lips because, for the first time in a year, I wouldn't be alone today. Despite his name, maybe I was the lucky one in this situation. Or maybe we both were.

My beat-up laptop sat on the desk-slash-table, and I pulled out the single chair, sitting down and absently stroking Lucky's fur while I waited for the dark screen to come to life. He nipped at my fingers, and I set him down, watching him bound around the room, his tiny *yips* making me smile.

Just as Lucky tackled the plastic bag with a couple of new toys and his new food dish in it, his tail wagging and making the plastic crinkle with every swipe, my screen powered on, and the bright light distracted me from the adorable scene. For the past six months, I'd been sending out resumes to every record label and management company I could find.

I'd always been interested in music, but I didn't have a single shred of talent. Instead, when I started college, I figured maybe I'd become an agent or something. It wasn't until everything with Winston happened that I decided my best bet was to become a tour manager. I switched up some of my classes in the last year of school so I'd have the degree I needed, but those jobs weren't exactly easy to come by.

Like I said before, settling down into a cozy job in one place just wasn't going to work for me.

Managing a tour and with the constant travel would be perfect if only I could get a job. The problem was everyone wanted experience, but no one was willing to take a risk on someone new. So, for now, every day, I sent out my resumé diligently. I figured the worst that could happen was I heard nothing back, but at some point, just by sheer numbers, someone had to at least call me in for an interview... right?

I sighed, typing out a couple of adjustments to my cover letter and sending out another email. My inbox was woefully empty, but I refused to give up. Photography was fun, but working with music and travel were what I wanted to do. I *needed* this more than I'd ever needed anything.

More than I needed friends or family.

More than I needed a home.

More than I needed money.

It wasn't until a year ago I discovered there was a desperation clinging to me, and the only way to get rid of it was to run and never stop. As long as I kept running, I could hold the broken pieces of me together and cling to the idea of being normal, even if it was just an illusion.

That thing that I needed the most? It was safety.

We all took it for granted until we experienced something that made us realize how precarious it actually was. I'd had the myth shattered for me by someone who claimed to love me, who was the person who was supposed to protect my heart and guard it as if it were precious.

But the true wickedness of his promises had been unmasked. They'd been hidden behind a beautiful facade of sweet nothings and normalcy that hid a monster just below the surface. I shivered, the memories an assault on the carefully constructed armor I laid over myself and did my best to strengthen every day.

My eyes had been opened now, and more than ever, I realized that my life could be whatever I made it. Never again would I fall for darkness masked in charm. I could see past the facade and into the depths of what laid beneath, and for now, I was content to focus on myself instead. Trusting other people was a danger I wasn't willing to risk.

I glanced down at Lucky, where he'd curled up half inside his metal food dish that still rested inside the plastic bag, and I chuckled. He happily snored away, content in a position that in no way could have been comfortable.

Now it wasn't just me, was it? I had the little guy to keep me company, and I couldn't think of a better companion. With a sigh, I started to push the laptop screen closed when a ping caught my attention. I pushed the screen back open, and my mouth fell open with a gasp when I saw an email in my inbox. I clicked into it with shaky fingers and quickly scanned the message, the speed of my heartbeat picking up with every word I read.

Ms. Dawson,

I received your resume and am very interested in speaking with you. As you may or may not know, the band I manage, Shadow Phoenix, is getting ready to kick off a national tour for their latest album. We are running on a short deadline, so I understand if you aren't available, but let me know ASAP if you're interested, and I'll set up a meeting.

Regards,

Montana Blackwood

Holy crap. I sat in front of the screen a little dazed, not even blinking, and letting my mind spin with wonderful possibilities. I hadn't even let myself imagine that I could manage a tour for a band I'd heard of before, but Shadow Phoenix? Practically everyone knew who they were.

It was only the sound of Lucky's paws twitching in his sleep, brushing against the plastic underneath him and making a rustling noise that snapped me out of my stupor. I typed out a quick reply letting her know *yes, of course*, I'd be up for the job and could meet with her anytime. I sort of blacked out when I wrote my reply, but when I looked back at the sent message, I cringed when I read the words *I will literally meet with you anytime, day or night*, but what's done was done. Was I desperate for this job?

Heck, yes.

That didn't mean I wasn't perfect for it. I was a quick learner, and I'd spent the last year-plus preparing for this. I'd researched everything I possibly could, spent countless hours on the internet and YouTube figuring out all sorts of secret tricks and hacks for managing travel and booking venues. If I could convince just one person to give me a chance, I was confident I could handle whatever they threw at me.

I needed to with every fiber of my being. I wanted it even more. I could even be convinced to hand over my Grammy's famous (and top-secret) biscuit recipe for the opportunity, something I'd barely managed to get out of her on her literal death bed.

Before I could even shut my laptop, I had a message back from Montana with a time to hook up on a video call later this evening. I'd have just enough time to do the photo shoot before I had to rush back and jump on with her, but I'd make it work.

My stomach fluttered, and I swallowed hard. My first real chance at freedom was so close I could taste it. The pressure of the moment weighed on me, but more than that, I was excited—so excited I could hardly contain it inside my body. I wanted to jump up and down and stomp my feet and scream and dance and twirl in circle after circle until I collapsed with dizziness. If I felt this way now, how would I feel when I got the job?

Because I *would* get the job. Standing up, I started to gather my camera equipment, making sure I had my fifty-millimeter lens, my silver and gold reflector, a diffuser since it was a bright, sunny day, and a telescopic lens just in case. I packed an extra battery into my bag and checked my data card, making sure I packed an extra one of those, too.

Hopefully, this would be the last photoshoot I'd have to do like this. Photography was my hobby for a reason—I liked taking pictures of the things I found beautiful. Once I started charging for it, it lost its appeal. Taking pictures of high school kids covered in acne, local sports teams, couples, babies... none of it captured me like the beauty of nature.

With any luck, tonight, I'd get the job of my dreams. No, I didn't need luck. I needed will and determination. Something about me had caught the attention of the right person, and I wasn't going to mess that up.

I wasn't going to let her walk away until she gave me that job, either. It was as good as mine.

THREE
GRIFFIN

"How big do you think the bus is, dude?" Maddox stared at my bags dubiously.

"How the hell should I know? It's not like I've ever done this before," I snapped, sinking down on top of one of my suitcases and using my body weight to hold it closed while I fought with the zipper. "If you're going to stand there, you could at least help."

One of my brother's greatest joys in life was talking shit, so I didn't expect anything less of him. I'd learned that early on in our relationship, and I didn't fault him for it. It was just who he was.

"We're tripping over each other constantly on that thing even if it's a double-decker. I'm just busting your balls, though. One of the roadies usually drives a truck hauling a trailer with all of our wardrobe shit in it. You can bring whatever you want, but the more shit you bring, the more you have to keep track of," he warned.

"I can't even imagine what the rest of the guys are packing with their wives and kids. I don't know if one trailer's going to be enough," I mused, debating whether or not I missed anything while I looked around my room at my brother's house.

Yeah, I lived with my brother and his wife. Yes, I had to wear noise-canceling headphones a lot, but it was worth it. His house was gorgeous, our relationship was rock solid, and living here kept me close to all the rest of the guys in the band. Plus, he had plenty of room.

We were a family, and they'd welcomed me with open arms. Even Jericho, though he'd been an asshole at first. I managed to get under his skin, and now I was pretty sure he looked at me like his little brother, too.

There was something about the pain in his eyes that drew me to him and made me want to get closer. That was a thing I did. I collected broken people and made it my mission to fix them. There were so many people in the world who'd grown up with shitty childhoods, parents who didn't love them, who'd abandoned them, or worse. Just look at Maddox. His dad was a real-life demon who hurt my brother so bad, it was a miracle he turned out as well as he did.

I didn't grow up that way. I was lucky. My parents were still married, and they loved me and supported me in anything and everything I wanted to do. True and I were the same in that way. Sometimes I was surprised Maddox didn't hate me for having the childhood he should've had, but for whatever reason, he didn't.

I looked up when Maddox didn't respond to my comment to see a faraway look in his eye that I didn't know what to make of. Instead, I ignored it and filed it away to analyze later. He finally snapped out of whatever was on his mind and glanced at his watch. "We've got half an hour, and I have to load all of Ryan's bags into the car."

"Where is my sister-in-law this morning?" I wondered, unzipping the bag underneath me and pulling out a pair of boots. I tossed them back in my closet before easily zipping it back up.

Maddox got this ghost of a smile that he only ever got when he thought about his wife, and I rolled my eyes. It was sweet, and such an un-Maddox thing to do it almost made me laugh every time. He'd probably try and kick my ass if I did, though, and I didn't want a broken nose or a black eye to start the tour, so I kept that shit inside. "Meeting with Connor's team about tour security. She'll meet us at the bus."

It must've been nice for the two of them to get to work together, and both do what they love. I swore they were made for each other. When I thought about Wynter and compared our relationship to theirs, there was no contest. I didn't know if we could ever get there, either, but I was still pissed at her for her little stunt during the tour promo, so I didn't really want to think about her. I was starting to wonder if the girl I met and really liked all those months ago was ever going to come back.

She sure as hell was nowhere to be found lately.

The zipper on my last bag finally closed all the way, and I stood up, slightly out of breath at the effort and making a mental note to spend more time in the gym. Maddox already insisted I work out with him every day, but I wasn't one of those guys who liked spending hours in the gym. I did it because I had to to keep up with them during rehearsal and at our shows. I was about to put my conditioning to the test on this tour, and I'd been gearing up for months to make sure I was ready.

When I lifted the bag, it was heavier than I expected, and the trek out to Maddox's SUV through his big-ass house took forever. I finally tossed my suitcase in with all of his and Ryan's, turning back to get the rest. Once everything was loaded, the two of us jumped in, and I made sure my seatbelt was buckled.

Something my brother and I had in common? We both were fucking insane behind the wheel, but he was worse than I was. "You picked a good tour to start on," Maddox noted, slamming his foot down on the gas and rocketing us forward.

"Why's that?" My fingers tightened around the handle in the door, stabilizing myself as he swerved around a car going too slow for his taste. I'd have done the same thing.

"It's not international, and it's only got like fifteen stops." He stomped on the brakes when a car stopped abruptly in front of us, and I lurched forward in my seat, the seat belt cutting into my skin a little bit.

"Shit," I hissed, rubbing the spot as he jammed the gas pedal down again. Every time I got into the car with my brother, I was glad I didn't get motion sickness.

"It's a good starter tour like it's got training wheels or some shit for the baby rockstar," he teased, taking his hand off the wheel for a couple of terrifying seconds to ruffle my hair. I side-eyed him hard.

When he noticed, he cracked up, complete with head thrown back and eyes closed—all while speeding down the freeway at probably a hundred miles an hour. "Watch the goddamn road!" I yelled at him, and he just laughed harder before finally—fucking *finally*—staring back out of the windshield with just enough time to slam on the brakes again.

I would definitely have a bruised rib or two by the time we got to the venue to load onto the tour bus. As that thought crossed my mind, Maddox shot across five lanes of traffic in some kind of miraculous witchcraft that didn't end up with us dead in a fiery crash, and we pulled into the venue's parking lot a few minutes later.

"Two days until showtime, brother. You sure you're ready for this?" Maddox looked over at me as he asked the question, but thankfully this time, we were parked. I glanced over his shoulder at the tour bus and the semi-trucks and roadies and crew loading everything up. My heart started to race, but it wasn't fear. It was excitement. I'd never played in front of such a massive crowd before. I learned to play, ironically enough, by watching Shadow Phoenix videos on YouTube.

There was a reason it was a huge fucking deal to take over for Jericho Cole. He was the best drummer in the industry right now. Not going to lie; I was a little bit starstruck when I met my musical hero in the flesh.

In other words, he left huge shoes to fill. I planned on doing my best. "Ready as I'll ever be," I replied, reaching for the door handle. I walked around to the back of the SUV and opened the hatch, starting to unload our luggage. Maddox took one look at me, smirked, and then walked off, presumably to find his wife.

Screw him; his bags could stay in the back of his car for all I cared. I wasn't his slave.

I slung one bag over each shoulder and rolled the biggest one behind me, finally stopping in front of the bus where Zen and True were having a heated discussion about who got which bunk. Their wives were nowhere to be found, but I was sure they were around somewhere. It was chaotic, with everyone scrambling around trying to get everything loaded and ready for us to hit the road in the next couple of hours.

"Hey," I greeted them with a head nod, struggling a little under the weight of my bags. What the hell had I packed in here, concrete blocks? Jesus. "Where should I put my stuff?"

"The one with all your everyday shit, like a couple of outfits, toiletries, phone charger, whatever… that goes in your bunk. Give the rest to the guy by that trailer," Zen explained, pointing in the direction I'd just come, his black painted fingernails catching my attention. That was new. "And you get a bottom bunk, sorry." He didn't sound sorry at all.

From what I could tell, True and Zen were fighting over the top bunks since somehow Maddox had already claimed one, and Jericho, who wasn't even going to play but insisted on touring with us this time for some ungodly reason, had claimed one of the others.

"Aren't there like twelve bunks? Wouldn't that make six on top?" I questioned, trying to remember how many people Maddox said this thing slept.

"Yeah, but between all the spouses and kids, plus crew, it's going to be a tight fit."

I blew out a breath. "Look, I'm not picky. Point me in the direction of my bunk, and I'll put this away." I patted the bag still slung over my shoulder.

"Follow me, kiddo," Zen cut True a look that said they weren't finished with their conversation yet and then climbed up the steps to the bus and up the second set—the bus was two stories—and into the hall of bunks with curtains pulled closed in front of most of them. "Take any of the bottom bunks on this side," he gestured to his right.

I threw back the curtain on the first one and crawled inside, shoving my bag to the back. This was like being at summer camp, only I'd never gone to summer camp, so it was what I imagined it would be like, bunk beds and all. There were a couple of soft pillows and a plush blanket in there, so at least the bedding would be comfortable. I hoped the bed was long enough for my six-two frame, but there wasn't much I could do about it if it weren't.

A couple of the other guys were taller than I was, so if they weren't complaining, I was sure it would be fine for me.

"We may need to get a second bus," Zen muttered as he looked around, his eyes narrowed before shrugging. "This is the first time we've taken all the families along. On our last tour, Kennedy was with us, and Amara was there for part of it, but it wasn't like this with wives and kids for pretty much everyone. It's going to be a shitshow," he concluded, but he said it with a grin on his face that contradicted his words, almost as if he couldn't wait for the chaos to begin, and I laughed.

"Yeah, I imagine it is, but it'll be fine." I stood up and leaned against the top bunk. "My brother abandoned me as soon as we pulled up, the dick, so do you mind showing me around?"

"Anything's better than arguing with True over dibs on the beds," he agreed and then led me around the bus, pointing out all the nooks and crannies and hidden places to maximize space. There were two lounges—one upstairs and one down—and a surprisingly decent sized kitchen with a little island. The bathroom was tiled and had a full shower, toilet, and sink. This bus was nicer than my apartment back in Texas.

When we were done, I followed him outside where their wives had arrived and smoothed the whole bed incident over. Maddox walked by me and shot me a glare as he hauled his bags inside, followed by Ryan, who winked at me as she climbed the stairs. Sometimes I thought she liked it when I gave my brother shit as much as I did. He was fun to mess with.

We stood in a huddle, and while the guys sorted out how they were going to deal with all of the people and stuff they had to bring along, I closed my eyes and tilted my head back, taking a deep breath and enjoying the warmth of the mid-morning sun on my face. Before I knew what was happening, hands slipped over my eyes and yanked my head backward so I had to bend my back just to keep from falling over. "What the hell?"

"Guess who?" someone sing-songed behind me, and my blood ran cold.

"Wynter?" I choked out, yanking her hands off my face and noticing how everyone had gone still and silent around us. The guys were gaping at her, and the girls all wore matching glares. Even Moon, Jericho's wife, who pretty much liked everyone, looked irritated to see my girlfriend. "What are you doing here?" I asked in a monotone voice.

I'd been excited about this tour for a few reasons, but one of them was to get a little distance from Wynter so I could figure out where our relationship was going. I wasn't sure I liked the person she'd become during the course of our relationship.

"I'm here to go on tour with you, silly," she exclaimed, bouncing on her feet a little. I looked behind her to see her assistant, Ross, overloaded with bags and definitely struggling under their weight.

How the hell she even found out what time we were leaving and from where was a mystery because I sure as hell hadn't told her. She had a habit of showing up to most of our promotional stuff, even if I didn't tell her it was happening. Sometimes I wondered if she'd paid off someone on our team to fill her in.

For months, the guys had been telling me that she was using me for my fame, but I refused to believe it. The girl with wide eyes and big dreams I'd started dating still tugged at my heartstrings, and up until now, I refused to believe she could be that manipulative. Now with this stunt, I was starting to question my judgment.

"Griff, band meeting. *Now*," Zen announced, and Wynter rolled her eyes. I ignored her and followed the guys around the back of the bus, leaving Kennedy, Amara, Ryan, and Moon to deal with Wynter.

"What the actual *fuck* is that chick doing here?" Maddox started in. It was no secret my brother didn't like my girlfriend. He was protective of me and liked to ramble on about how she was using me. I usually tuned him out, but I never brought her home because of it.

I shrugged. "I don't know. I didn't invite her or tell her when we were leaving. Truthfully, I was hoping to get a little distance on the road and figure out how I feel about her. She's changed a lot."

"No, shit." Jericho folded his arms across his chest and leaned against the back of the bus. "You know she's just using you. She doesn't even try to hide that shit. You need to dump her." It wasn't a question or a suggestion. That wasn't how Jericho worked. Like Maddox, he saw a problem, and he fixed it. To him, Wynter was a problem that needed to go away. I still wasn't so sure.

"Look," True started, playing with his nose ring, so I knew he was uncomfortable. "We get that you like this girl, but do you see a future with her? Is this relationship going anywhere? Because if it is, we'll respect that and make more of an effort to welcome her." Jericho scoffed, but True ignored him. "But if it's not, she's got to go. None of us can stand her. All the other girls integrated seamlessly into the group. It was effortless. Sorry to say, bud, but no one likes your girlfriend. She told Amara she should get her skin bleached so it wouldn't be, and I quote, *the color of mud*. Amara was upset, and then I wanted to kill Wynter."

Jesus. I didn't know that, and I was pissed off on True's behalf. "I'm sorry she said that. I'll talk to her."

Zen held up his hands. "Just tell her she can't come on tour. There isn't room for her, all her bags, and her assistant. Are all three of you going to sleep in your bunk? There's barely enough room for one person, two is a squeeze, and three is fucking impossible. We don't have any spares."

My stomach flip-flopped worse than when I was in the car with Maddox. "Let me talk to her."

"Fine, but if you don't get rid of her, it's going to be a long-ass tour. You know you deserve better than her, right?" Maddox stepped up beside me and clasped me on the shoulder. "She may be hot, but she's fucking poison inside, and she's going to infect you if you don't open your eyes and see what she's really doing."

I didn't know what to think about everything the guys were saying. It was hard to reconcile their words and issues with the girl I got to know over the last several months. She was different when we were alone together, but even then, she'd become more and more withdrawn. Lately, she only wanted to be affectionate or close to me physically when we were around paparazzi or broadcasting to her social media followers. Something about that didn't sit right with me, either, which was why I wanted space to figure it all out.

I'd always brushed off the guys' opinions of my girlfriend as Wynter making a bad first impression and them holding a grudge, but maybe there was more to it than that. I didn't want to admit that she was using me for my fame or my looks. How shitty would that be? My first ever girlfriend was only with me because of what I had to offer, not because she liked me for who I was. I was afraid to admit that shit to myself because it had the power to wreck me. If all she thought I had to offer was my career, what did that say about who I was as a person?

Those were questions I wasn't ready to dig into and ask myself right now.

So, I promised the guys I'd talk to her and figure it out. I left them behind the bus and walked around to find Wynter snapping at her assistant while holding her phone out in front of her face, seemingly snapping selfies of herself in front of the tour bus. Kennedy shot me a look before leveling her glare on my girlfriend. I sighed heavily, knowing I had to deal with Wynter, and the conversation wasn't going to be fun.

She spotted me in her camera before she actually saw me, and she brightened, leaning back against my chest as I stepped up behind her. "Smile!" she chirped, and I slapped a cocky grin on my face out of habit. Apparently, she'd trained me well.

"We need to talk." I grabbed her elbow lightly and dragged her away from everyone. She spun on me and narrowed her eyes. "Do you know how long it took me to find the perfect angle? Why would you pull me over here and ruin my shot?"

My muscles tensed up. When she got like this, there was nothing to do but let her rant until she got it all out, so I stood there while she huffed and complained about every little thing before she finally stopped talking. "You can't come on the tour with me." There. I just laid it out there straight up. There was no way for her to misinterpret my words.

Immediately her narrowed eyes widened, and her lower lip wobbled. Wynter seemed to be able to flip a switch between her emotions like no one I'd ever met before. "What do you mean? Do you not want to spend the next month with me on this trip?"

My fingers tore through my hair as I thought about how to phrase what I wanted to say without triggering one of her tantrums. "It's not that I don't want you here, but there's no room. There's a reason I didn't invite you along. We don't have space, and even if we did, you haven't exactly made a great impression on the other women."

She rolled her eyes. "Please. They're all boring. Who cares if they like me?"

Anger was starting to simmer in my veins. It was getting harder and harder to remember why I liked spending time with this girl when she acted like this. Having her around was exhausting. "I care, Wynter. They're my family, and you don't even try to get along with them. I'm sorry, but you can't come."

She immediately dropped her attitude, and her eyes welled with tears. Shit. I couldn't handle it when women cried. "I'm going to miss you *so* much, Griff. I don't want to go without seeing you for a month. I'll make an effort toward them, I swear."

She stepped forward tentatively and wrapped her arms around my waist, resting her head on my chest while she sniffled. My resolve weakened, and I wrapped my arms around her, kissing the top of her head. How could I be upset that she didn't want to go a whole month without seeing me? Was I really that upset that she wanted to spend time with me? At least she was making an effort.

"Fine, we'll make it work. But Ross will probably have to sleep on the couch," I relented, knowing I was in for a fight with my brother and the other guys. But if their wives were allowed to come on the road, my girlfriend should also be able to.

She jumped back and clapped her hands, pulling her phone back out and starting a live broadcast. Before I could say another word, she'd already moved away from me and climbed onto the bus with Ross following in her wake. I could hear her chattering to her followers about the Wild Ride tour and how she was coming along and showing off our bus—the one she'd never been shown around and had no idea where she'd be sleeping. Hopefully, she wouldn't complain about the bottom bunk.

The group of Shadow Phoenix wives turned and glared at me as one unit, and a chill ran over me. Those were some formidable women, especially my sister in law. She'd been learning krav maga, and I'd seen her kick Maddox's ass more than one. If she could take him down, she could take me down, too. She wasn't someone I wanted to piss off.

"You've got to be kidding," Amara snapped. "I can't live on a bus with her for an entire month."

"She promised she'd try harder with you guys and make more of an effort to get to know you," I told them, hoping that would be enough to get them to relax a little.

Kennedy just rolled her eyes, and she balanced her son, Nico, on her hip. He watched me with those bright green eyes that were exactly like Zen's, like he knew I was fucked. "I'll believe that when I see it. If she says or does anything mean or hurtful, I'm holding you personally responsible, Griffin."

Moon smiled at me as she passed her son, Benji, back to Jericho, who shook his head in disappointment at me. Moon was the first warm reception I'd gotten from the group where Wynter was concerned. "Maybe being forced into close quarters with all of our crazy will pull that stick out of her ass," she announced cheerfully, and I chuckled.

"Maybe."

Phoenix ran between my legs, and I almost tripped over her little body moving like only toddlers can—unsteady but fast as hell and with no fear whatsoever. True chased her and finally grabbed her, tossing her in the air while she squealed. I couldn't believe the legendary guys from Shadow Phoenix were like this in real life. They weren't at all what I imagined them to be when I grew up idolizing them, but then again, they'd grown up themselves.

Maddox came to stand beside me, watching True with his daughter and his other friends with their wives and kids. "She's coming along, isn't she?" He sounded resigned, and I just nodded.

"She said she'd make an effort, so don't I owe it to her to give her a chance?"

"Fuck, no. You don't owe her shit. She's a horrible person, and she's using you. I don't know why you can't see it, but someday you will, and when you do, I'll be there beside you to help you kick her ass to the curb. As much as I hate to admit it, maybe the torture of living in such close quarters with her will be what finally wakes you the fuck up to the kind of girl Wynter is."

My brother's words stuck with me long after he went back to his wife, and we climbed into the bus. I wasn't sure why he was so insistent that my relationship with Wynter was on borrowed time, but I didn't know what I was hoping would happen during this tour. Did I want to get to know Wynter better and improve our relationship? Or would it be better to end it, face the sting of betrayal and pain, and try to move on?

Only time would tell.

FOUR
MAGNOLIA

"You're going to fit right in," the fiery redhead riding beside me in the car announced as her eyes danced with amusement. "But you can't let those assholes get anything over on you. They'll take advantage. Just set the expectation early that you're not going to take their shit, and you'll be fine."

I laughed a little nervously. I still couldn't believe she'd given me the job. "I'm gonna be fine. Don't you worry about me. I know how to handle rowdy boys."

She smirked at me like she knew a secret I didn't. "Sure, you do." She patted my knee, and I wasn't sure whether to be offended or not. "Be glad they've settled down now. A few years ago, this tour would already be off the rails, and we haven't even left yet."

I snorted because I could only imagine. Also, they'd never had me running their tour before. I was the queen of organization. Lucky yipped from where he curled up on the floor and started gnawing on his leash. His little needle teeth were like razors, and I'd already had to buy him a new one, so I tried to pry it out of his jaw, and he growled at me.

He was so tiny and so fluffy that it only made me giggle, and he stopped his chewing to look up at me with his bright blue eyes and his head tilted to one side. It was a *what the hell's so funny* sort of look, and it only made me laugh all over again. Montana joined me this time, watching it all unfold.

"He's adorable," she laughed, watching as Lucky stood up and tried to attack a loose string on the bottom of my jeans. The car rocking made it nearly impossible, and he flopped over with a huff.

"Oh, we're here," Montana exclaimed, sliding her arm through her gigantic handbag. I looked out the tinted window and saw the two huge buses for the bands, a couple of semi-trucks, and some pickup trucks with trailers attached. There had to be at least fifty people scurrying around trying to get everything set. They were all now my responsibility, and the weight of that sat heavily on my shoulders.

I sat up straighter. I was ready for this. Tightening my grip on Lucky's leash, I reached down and scooped him into my arms, burying my nose in his fur and letting the soft strands soothe my nerves. I mentally went back over all the members of the two bands I'd be responsible for—Shadow Phoenix and their opening act, Tuesday Told a Secret.

Shadow Phoenix I was somewhat familiar with. I didn't know their members by name, but I could sing along to a couple of their songs. Tuesday Told a Secret was brand new, and I didn't know them at all. I was up all night last night going over every detail of the parts of the tour that the previous manager had already arranged and studying the band members so I could greet them by name.

I was terrified of messing this up, but I wouldn't let that stop me. Once upon a time, I let fear keep me from walking out on a situation I should've left a long time before I did, and it almost cost me everything. From that day on, I vowed never to let fear get in my way, and so far, I hadn't. That didn't mean I didn't feel it—I did. It didn't matter, though. This tour would be the first huge step forward in a life that had felt stagnant for way too long.

The red-eye flight from Tennessee—where I'd been staying for the past couple of months—to LA had been long, but my exhaustion took a back seat as I grabbed the door handle and got out of the car, setting Lucky down on the warm pavement. He looked up at me with an offended glint in his eye that he'd have to walk on such a hard surface, but he could just deal with it. I had bags to deal with and not enough arm space.

"I'll introduce you to the band, and then you can set your stuff in your bunk, and we'll go meet all the roadies and crew. Hopefully, the guy before you hired some decent people this time. The last tour was a complete shitshow," Montana recalled as we walked side by side toward the buses. She marched straight up to the front bus in her super tall high heels and climbed the steps like she didn't have one single reservation about it. These were her people, and she belonged.

I just hoped they'd accept me as one of their own, too.

She clapped her hands loudly near the kitchen area while I struggled up the stairs with Lucky, who hadn't figured out how to deal with steps yet. He sat back on his haunches and looked up at me expectantly. I sighed and bent down to pick him up, trying to balance my suitcase, purse, and laptop bag at the same time.

"Boys! Get your asses down here!" she yelled and then propped her hands on her hips. One guy came from the lounge room behind us, the blonde one—True, I think—and he wore an easy smile as he plopped down at the booth surrounding the table. He looked me over curiously, but he looked friendly enough, giving me a small wave.

Four other guys came down the stairs from the second floor. They were all hot. Seriously, that much hotness shouldn't be allowed to exist in such a small space. Three of them were covered in tattoos, and two looked similar, like they were related. They all piled around the table with True, but my gaze lingered on the last one in the room. The cocky smirk on his face as he watched me right back turned my stomach—or maybe that was stupid butterflies—but I couldn't look away.

I'd seen a smirk like that before, and it never led anywhere good. I tried to ignore how ridiculously attractive he was with all of his muscles and tattoos and piercings—yes, he had both sides of his nose pierced, a hoop on one side and a stud on the other, plus when I didn't look away from our little stare down, his tongue ran along his lower lip, and I thought I saw the flash of metal that meant he had a tongue piercing too.

Nope. Nothing good ever came from someone that sexy, and the worst part was he seemed to know exactly the effect he was having on me. I finally managed to wipe the metaphorical drool off my face and tear my eyes off of him.

I straightened my spine while he let out a low chuckle that wrapped around me and made my insides clench up unhelpfully, and then he slid into the booth with all the rest of the guys.

I was extra glad I wore a padded bra today so he wouldn't be able to see that my nipples were painfully hard. I had a feeling giving this guy any indication of how much he affected me wouldn't be in my best interest.

Montana cleared her throat from where she stood beside me, and all five sets of eyes were on her. "This is Magnolia Dawson, the tour manager we discussed." Their stares slid over to me, and a cold sweat broke out across my skin, but I tried to ignore it as my heart pounded away in my chest. I gave them a little wave. "She's the one in charge for the next four weeks, so don't fuck it up. I'm not finding you anyone else."

She flicked her bright green eyes in my direction, and I swallowed hard. I could do this. "It's nice to meet y'all. I've read over the itinerary and familiarized myself with all the stops and what the previous manager set up before leaving. My aim is to get us through this tour successfully and smoothly. If y'all have any special requests or anything comes up, let me know, and I'll do what I can to accommodate you." Lucky squirmed in my arms before licking my face, and I couldn't stop the giggle that escaped me before I straightened back out and lowered him to the floor.

He immediately started whining, of course, but I tried to ignore him for the moment. I also tried to avoid the dark brown eyes watching my every move, but it was impossible. His stare was like a caress on my skin, tempting me to look his way. "I'm sure we'll get to know each other well over the next four weeks, but for now, I'm gonna put away my bags and let this little guy stretch his legs."

"And I want to introduce you to the other band and all the wives. You're going to love them," Montana added, pushing me lightly in the back toward the stairs. I almost tripped over Lucky's leash, and the guy I'd been trying not to look at darted out of his seat and caught my wrist, steadying me.

"Careful." His voice was gravelly and deep, and I tried not to shiver at the heat from the touch of just a couple of his fingers on my skin.

I took a deep breath and untangled my legs, pulling my arm out of his grip. No matter how much I liked how he looked, I would not repeat my past mistakes. More than anything, I knew people weren't always what they seemed on the outside, but I wasn't willing to risk the job I'd been working for a year to get on a stupid crush. "Thanks." My tone was a little cold and snippy, but it was best if I kept things overly professional, if not a little bitchy, just so there was no confusion on where I stood.

Climbing the stairs, Montana followed behind me, and we found an empty bunk in the back of one row on the bottom. I stashed my bag inside, and we turned to go back downstairs when a shrill screech came from what looked like a lounge room in the front of the bus's upper level. "Where is it?" the screech came again, and I realized it wasn't some mythological banshee or something; it was a woman who looked to be having a tantrum.

Montana and I exchanged a look before she rolled her eyes. "Wynter is here," she snickered, and I bit my lip at her Game of Thrones reference. "Trust me, she's worse than anything that show conjured up."

I looked up at the girl with bleached blonde hair and overly tanned skin who was teetering in at least four-inch heels and had on a skintight mini dress. "I didn't have a Wynter on the manifest, did I?" I asked Montana, trying to remember all the names on the list of band members and their guests. That stuff was way more complicated than most people could imagine. There was so much to consider and plan for everyone traveling that it was too late to add any unexpected guests.

Ten minutes into my new job and I was already getting thrown a curveball. Great.

"No, she wasn't. The guys would've given Griffin all sorts of shit if they knew she was coming." Crap. I was going to have to kick her off the bus. We didn't have room. I didn't have any of the travel insurance or accommodations reserved. I hadn't ordered food for her.

"I know I packed it. Let me recheck my bag," a whiny male voice interrupted, and what fresh hell was that? There were *two* unexpected people? No. That just wouldn't work.

I pushed my way into the lounge room. It was decent-sized and could probably fit about six people in it, but it looked like an explosion had gone off, and there were clothes, shoes, makeup, and electronics spread out everywhere. It was like the two of them had made themselves completely at home.

"What are y'all doing?" I asked them, not bothering to introduce myself. The southern woman in me cringed a little at the rudeness of not handling this with grace, but we were leaving in less than an hour, and I didn't have time for this.

The girl, Wynter, stood up and glared at me, putting her hands on her hips. "We're looking for my phone charger. Now run along and fetch me a latte or a new charger or something. Make yourself useful," she ordered, and I bristled.

Lucky was squirming in my arms, and I passed him back to Montana, who stood behind me. She cooed at him before leaning in to whisper, "Oh, hell, no. This bitch needs to be taken down a peg or ten."

My heart beat wildly in my chest because standing up to people and confrontation was basically my biggest fear, but I had to get over it if I was going to run this tour like it deserved. I couldn't let her see my fear. "I'll do no such thing. You're going to pack up your stuff and get off my bus. I wasn't notified you'd be traveling with us, so we don't have room for you or him."

She narrowed her eyes even further, and I took a step back. I flinched, and the triumph that flashed in her eyes made me hate what I'd become even more than I already did. I hated cowering when someone acted aggressively toward me, but I couldn't help it. It was instinctual now. She tossed her blonde hair over her shoulder and smiled at me, though it was more teeth than anything. "Make me," she challenged, and then her smile widened as she looked over my shoulder.

"Besides, Griffin wants me here, don't you, baby?" she purred, and I wanted to dry heave on the spot, but I somehow refrained.

"Sure," he answered easily, and I hated what his voice did to me, especially right now when he was defending this harpy.

Spinning, I turned my glare on him, and he backed up a step. "They can't stay. We don't have the bunks or liability insurance. I don't have passes for them or clearance at any of the venues. I don't have hotel reservations for them. There are a hundred reasons why they need to get off this bus right now." I stared him down while he looked at me thoughtfully, but it was her grating voice that broke our standoff.

"Isn't that, like, your job? Better get to it," she ordered, clapping her hands at me. I saw red, but I really didn't want to spend the entire tour fighting with one of the band members. He said he wanted her along, so I was just going to have to suck it up and make it happen. That didn't mean I had to be happy about it. I snatched Lucky back out of Montana's arms and stormed past Griffin, slamming my shoulder into his as I walked by and ignoring the sparks that shot down my arm and through my body at the close contact.

His spicy, citrus scent invaded my senses as I passed by, but I didn't breathe in deeper and try to commit it to memory. Nope, not at all.

Too bad he had crappy taste in women, and if he was into a woman like Wynter, what did that say about the kind of guy he was? I was so mad about what just happened I was shaking. I lowered Lucky to the ground, and he flopped down on top of my feet and looked up at me with his tongue lolling out. The anger started to dissipate as I bent down and scratched his belly. "What a jerk, huh?"

"I can't believe you're letting that bitch stick around," Montana mused as she climbed out of the bus behind me. "She's going to poison the whole tour, and believe me, the wives already hate her. You don't know what you're signing up for."

I sighed and stood up, facing her. "What am I supposed to do? She was going to fight me, and he-"

"Griffin," she filled in.

"Right, Griffin said he wanted her here. I don't want to be on bad terms with the band on the first day." I threw my hands up in irritation and started stalking off, not really sure where I was going. Montana let me go, and I walked to the far edge of the lot to a little patch of grass to let Lucky do his thing.

"Hey!" I turned around and watched as Griffin jogged up to me. My muscles tensed up, and he must've sensed my unease because he held his hands up in surrender. "I didn't get the chance to introduce myself. I'm Griffin." He held out his hand for me to shake, and I eyed it warily before reluctantly putting my hand in his. His fingers were warm as he closed them around mine. I snatched my hand back as quickly as I could without seeming rude.

I didn't like the tingles moving under my skin at his touch, or maybe I liked them too much. I didn't want to examine it—stupid hot rockstar.

"I know. Montana told me who you are." Lucky looked up and yipped at Griffin before jumping on his legs. He was still tiny, so he only came to mid-shin, but Griffin's whole face lit up before he dropped down and scooped my puppy into his arms, cradling him like a baby while he gave him belly scratches.

What was happening?

Whatever it was, it wasn't good for my vow to keep my distance from the guy because watching him love on my pup was melting my resolve faster than I could build it.

Then I remembered his banshee of a girlfriend, and my willpower was firmly back in place.

"I wanted to apologize for Wynter. I didn't know she was coming along until right before you showed up, or I would've let you know ahead of time. She has a habit of just sort of popping up to surprise me. Can we try just one stop and see how it goes? If she causes problems, I'll ask her to go."

I sighed, meeting his pleading eyes. I'd already given in to the idea that I wasn't going to get rid of her anytime soon, so at least he was willing to work with me. "Fine. But you're going to have to share your hotel rooms with her and her assistant or pay for them out of your own pocket. We don't have the budget to accommodate extra rooms. Oh, and they'll both have to sign waivers since I can't get them on the insurance this late."

"Done." He grinned up at me before standing up and handing Lucky back over. "Thanks for doing this for me, Magnolia. I know it's a pain in the ass for you."

"Yeah, well..." I waved my hand around, and with one last smile, he turned and walked back to the bus. I followed behind at a distance, taking a few last deep breaths and going over a mental checklist of everything I needed to do before we left. I rounded the back of the bus to see Montana accepting a huge bunch of flowers from a delivery guy.

"Oh! There she is," she exclaimed, waving me over. My eyes flicked toward Griffin, who was watching with a scowl on his face. What was that about?

"Here, these came for you," she said before shoving the bouquet in my arms. My blood ran cold, and I was sure my face showed it because her smile dropped. "What?"

I passed her Lucky's leash with shaky hands and searched inside for the card I knew would be there. *Congratulations on your new job, babe.*

My stomach rolled so hard I almost threw up. I frantically searched for a trash can and hurried over, throwing the flowers and card inside. My eyes darted around the area, scanning my surroundings. How had he found me? How had he known I got this job? I hadn't even known until two days ago. The thought was beyond unsettling, and the amount of adrenaline coursing through my veins meant I was a shaky mess.

Montana and Griffin were both watching me with concern. "Everything okay?" she wondered, and I plastered a smile on my face that I was sure in no way looked genuine, but it was the best I could do. Fake it 'til you make it, my grammy always used to say.

"Yep. Now, let's go talk to Tuesday Told a Secret and then meet the wives. Then we can take off," I declared, before taking Lucky back from her and walking toward the other bus. The hairs on the back of my neck were standing up, and a chill ran down my spine. The feeling of being watched made the panic almost overwhelming, but I had a job to do, and I wouldn't let that bastard stop me. He'd already taken enough.

I pushed my shoulders back and blew out a calming breath.

Portland, here we come.

FIVE

GRIFFIN

I hadn't been able to get the image of Magnolia's face out of my mind after she got those flowers. She looked terrified, and I wanted to know why. It was fucking haunting me, and that unsettled me, too. Shouldn't I be more concerned with the tantrum Wynter was throwing?

But I wasn't.

The whole ride to Portland, Magnolia had been holed up in her bunk with the curtain closed. Wynter and Ross had commandeered the biggest lounge for themselves, and all the guys were pissed at me, so I was in my bunk, too.

Their wives hated Wynter and were complaining about her being along and taking up way more than her fair share of room, and whenever Kennedy, Amara, Ryan, and Moon were pissed off at something, the guys moved heaven and earth to fix it. I couldn't really blame them for being pissed off. I was fucking pissed off, too. I didn't want to be dealing with Wynter's bullshit on my first tour.

There was a reason I hadn't invited her along in the first place.

Instead of dealing with any of it, I slipped earbuds in and turned some music up loud enough to drown out everything going on in the bus. I felt weird about obsessing over Magnolia's issues, and I didn't even want to touch my feelings for Wynter. I wanted to sink into oblivion until we got to the hotel and I could hit the gym to deal with my messed up mind.

Shit was really bad if I voluntarily wanted to go to the gym.

I must've dozed off because the bus jolting to a stop woke me up, and I jumped out of my bunk. I glanced down the hall where Magnolia's bunk was, but the curtain was open, and she wasn't inside. I ignored the pang of disappointment and looked toward the front of the bus. Wynter and Ross were still in there, and I ran a hand through my hair, steeling myself to interact with them. There was a voice in the back of my head getting louder by the second that was practically yelling at me that I shouldn't be dreading spending time with my girlfriend.

When we got checked into the hotel, I would have to spend some time sorting out what I wanted out of my relationship. Instead of going into the lounge, I went downstairs where the bus door was open, and from what I could see, everyone else was outside. "Hey," I greeted the guys as I walked up to the big circle they'd formed that included their wives.

I had every eye on me, and all of them looked varying levels of pissed off. I held up my hands in surrender. "Damn, what'd I do?"

"Oh, I don't know, maybe let that fucking demon onto the bus?" Kennedy answered for the group, practically growling at me. Zen's eyes darkened and narrowed even further, and a chill ran over me. That dude was legitimately scary when he wanted to be, and when something made his wife unhappy, he was terrifying. Somehow, I'd managed to irritate *all* of their wives.

I sighed heavily. "What'd she do now?"

"We had to keep the kids in the tiny downstairs kitchen area, and they've been screaming for a couple of hours straight because they're confined. She sent her assistant down twice to tell us we were ruining her live stream, and the third time she came down and yelled at my daughter," Amara explained, and I watched as True's jaw clenched. He was the most level-headed of us all, but Phoenix was his whole world. No wonder he was mad.

Wynter's treatment of them made *me* mad, and they weren't even my wives or kids.

"I'll talk to her," I promised, hoping it did some good. We hadn't even played our first show yet, and I was already way more stressed out than I ever thought I'd be on this tour.

"Bro, why the fuck are you putting up with her shit?" Maddox wondered, moving up beside me and looking at me like he thought he'd get the answer by rooting around in my brain with his stare.

"I've never had a girlfriend before, but I'm pretty sure you don't just ditch them when shit gets hard. She's been stressed out for months trying to get her business going." I heard myself defending Wynter, but I wasn't entirely sure she deserved it.

Jericho scoffed from my other side, and I looked at him, raising my eyebrow. "You have something to add?"

He opened his mouth to say something, but Magnolia picked that moment to join our group, and I was glad for the distraction. I wasn't up for more of their lecturing. They'd all made it crystal clear how they felt about Wynter from the beginning. I forced an easy smile onto my face, one that I didn't feel at all. "What's up, Mags?"

The nickname just slipped out of my mouth, and I froze, wondering how she'd take it, but she let it wash right over her. She looked stressed with a little crease between her eyebrows, and I stopped to really look her over. When we first met, I'd been so upset about how Wynter acted that my priority was trying to fix the damage.

But when I looked at her now, my fingers itched to smooth that crease between her perfectly arched eyebrows. Her sky blue eyes were bright and captivating, and the long, dark lashes that framed them made them stand out almost like they glowed with a navy ring outside the faded to an almost white-blue around her pupil. She had long, dark hair that was almost black, and it fell down her back almost to her waist.

My fingernails dug into my palms to keep from reaching out and wrapping the silky strands around my fist and pulling her head back so I could kiss her. Shit, my dick was getting hard just from looking at this girl. That'd never happened to me before. She hadn't even touched me, barely spared me a look, and here I was sporting wood and hoping she'd pay attention to me like I was a little boy with a crush.

Her sultry voice drew my attention back to what she was saying and away from the fantasies of Magnolia getting acquainted with my cock currently running through my head. "...hotel room assignments."

She passed out keycards and hotel maps to everyone, and when she handed mine over, her soft skin brushed against my fingers, and a shiver ran through my entire body at the contact. Her eyes widened like she felt it, too, and then she schooled her features, but she couldn't hide the peachy blush that crept up her fair skin.

Our eyes were locked together, and I wasn't sure how much time passed, but Wynter's shriek broke the moment, and I looked back to find her hurrying toward me with Ross on her heels. She threw herself into my arms, and I looked over her shoulder, not wanting to lose the moment with the raven-haired beauty with the Southern drawl, but instead, I watched her walk away.

The disappointment twisting my stomach in knots was telling.

"I swear if I had to spend another minute on that bus, I was going to freak out," Wynter whined, a pretty pout pushing out her bottom lip. Wynter was a timeless beauty, the kind that every guy wanted, except now, when I looked at her, I was empty. My cock didn't even bother twitching. He couldn't have been less interested.

Without waiting for my response, she grabbed the keycard out of my hand and let me go, stalking off toward the hotel and yelling at Ross to keep up. I rolled my shoulders and followed in her wake, hoping that once we got inside, I'd be able to talk to her about getting along with everyone on the tour.

That wasn't what happened, though.

When I got to the room, I had to knock because Wynter took the only key and didn't bother waiting for me to show up before shutting the door. I could hear her ranting about something, but through the heavy door, I couldn't figure out what was going on. I knocked again and again, and just as I was about to go downstairs to get a second key from the front desk, Ross swung the door open, glaring at me.

"Don't look at me like that. This is my room," I bit out, glaring right back, and I pushed into the room. My instincts weren't to resort immediately to violence, but Ross always pushed me to the limits of my patience and understanding.

"We're having a crisis, Griffin. You could try being supportive," he snapped right back, and my jaw dropped.

"Are you kidding me? All I've done is be supportive!" I yelled, clenching my fists and taking a few deep breaths, trying to calm myself down. I stilled as his words finally sunk in. "What kind of crisis?"

"I've lost almost two thousand followers this month!" Wynter screeched. Her eyes were wild as she flailed her arms around, her phone in one hand. Her gaze settled on me and her eyes narrowed into a glare. "You."

My eyebrows shot up in surprise. "What about me?"

She stalked toward me and poked her pointy fingernail into the center of my chest. "This is all your fault."

I started to get frustrated with her, but I bit my cheek to hold it in check. "Again, what?"

"You've been keeping me out of all of your promo stuff, didn't invite me on tour with you, wouldn't meet me at the restaurant I wanted with all the paps. This isn't working anymore." She started muttering to herself and stepped away from me with a far off look in her eye.

"You're not making any sense." I was already exhausted by her logic, and I didn't even know what was going on. I ran a hand through my hair and stepped back until I was leaning against the wall.

At my movement, Wynter refocused on me and snapped her finger. Ross materialized at her side. "Pack up our stuff. We're leaving."

"Where are you going?" My voice was void of emotion. I probably should've cared that she was taking off, but I didn't. Not if she was going to act like that.

"It's clear you're no longer useful to me. It was fun when my followers climbed every time I posted a picture with you or got you on my live stream, but it looks like your benefit on my social media accounts has peaked and started to fall." She grabbed her purse from Ross and turned away from me, moving toward the door as he slinked along behind her with all of her luggage.

At the last second, she turned back with a mean smile on her face. "In case I wasn't clear, we're over. Thanks for nothing."

The door closed behind her, and I sank to the bed. Wynter was ambitious, but that was one of the things I liked about her. The cold woman who'd just walked out the door—how had I not seen her for the cunning manipulator underneath the pretty facade?

I'd fought with my brother and my bandmates over her, and for what?

For her to use me and toss me aside when she'd bled me dry and could no longer get any benefit from our relationship?

Fuck.

I was disgusted with myself for falling for her tricks and even more horrified that I'd let her come between my brother and me. How was I going to face any of the guys now? My face burned with embarrassment, and I let my head fall into my hands. I needed alcohol, and I needed it now.

I pushed off of the floor and grabbed the keycard Wynter left on the bed, shoving it into my pocket. It took me all of two minutes to ride the elevator down and find the bar that was in the lobby. I barely noticed my surroundings, focused on where I was going when Jericho stepped in front of me like a shadow from out of nowhere.

"Where are you off to in such a hurry, little brother?" he inquired, tilting his head and studying me with his sharp eyes.

I gestured toward the bar on the other side of the lobby. "I need alcohol."

He must've heard something in my tone because he stepped out of my way without any more questions, but he stayed by my side and walked into the bar with me, taking the stool beside me when I sat down.

We ordered our preferred drinks in silence, and as I tossed back the whiskey in my glass with a wince, Jericho raised his eyebrow at me, and I sighed. "Wynter."

He chuckled darkly. "Ah, the pain in everyone's ass. What'd she do this time?"

I lifted my glass to signal the bartender for a refill. "Oh, nothing. Just dumped me because I was no longer useful to her career."

Jericho tipped back his beer thoughtfully before saying anything. "I wish I could say I was surprised, but she was a fucking nightmare. Thank fuck she's gone. Kennedy threatened to chop off Wynter's hair in her sleep if she didn't start acting like a decent human being, so that was a whole mess waiting to happen."

My second drink burned on its way down less than the first, and I signaled for another. "Just keep them coming," I mumbled when the bartender stopped to pour more of the brown liquor into my glass.

"I hate to say it, but we all told you she had to fucking go. You need to learn to trust us. We've all been through this shit so many times, you wouldn't believe half of the shit women have done to any of us. The four of us have a built-in sensor about people like Wynter, and now you're starting to develop it, too." He sighed and twisted his beer between his fingers.

"I wish I could tell you that it'll be easier for you now, but I swear to Christ women just get more creative with their bullshit. You can't let your guard down."

I scoffed and gulped down my third shot, the warmth spreading through my limbs now and making me feel both relaxed and numb just like I wanted. "If that was true, how'd you all meet your wives?"

"We trusted each other's judgment, and that gut feeling you get when you know something's just fucking *right*. If you really searched yourself, I bet you'd realize you never felt quite right about Wynter."

He let me sit and stew in that little bomb he dropped, and fuck if he wasn't right. I didn't know what to do with that information, so instead, I sipped my whiskey.

"That's what I thought. Look, I need to get upstairs before Moon kills me for leaving her alone with Benji." He stood and tossed a couple of bills on the bar. His son was cute but an absolute terror. I wouldn't want to be left alone with him either. "If you need me, text, and I'll come haul your drunk ass up to your room."

I tipped my glass at him, and he left to go do whatever he did with his family in the evenings. They all had their families, and then there was just me. My thoughts were fuzzy from the alcohol, but I tried to figure out where I'd gone so wrong when it came to my relationship with Wynter. Being around all the couples from the band often left me on nights like this—drinking alone, going out alone, or generally just being alone.

I had a lot of solo time for someone who had people around him all the time, and maybe because of that loneliness, I'd forced myself to stay in a relationship with an awful woman so I wouldn't have to feel so alone.

Damn, I was a mess.

Jericho was right about one thing—I needed to listen to the guys when it came to any future dating I did. Right now, I couldn't trust myself to make those decisions. An image of Magnolia flashed through my mind, but I pushed it away. I was in no place to think of another woman in that way until I figured out not only what I wanted but how I'd gotten things with Wynter so wrong.

I wouldn't let anyone take advantage of me like she had again.

Doubts crept in, though, as I tossed back enough alcohol to make the room spin. Had Wynter ever seen anything in me besides my growing fame? Had she liked anything about me? Or had she just endured our relationship to get whatever she could out of it to elevate herself?

Was there anything redeeming about me? Anything I had to offer someone outside of my career?

Shit, I was drunk, and that train of thought was dangerous and unproductive, and I was pretty sure I was starting to feel sorry for myself when everything was Wynter's fault.

I was fucking awesome, and if she didn't like me, that was on her, not me.

I had no idea how much time had passed since Jericho left, but when my stomach sloshed and the room tilted, I decided to call it a night. I pulled out my wallet and threw my card onto the bar, not waiting for the bartender to come pick it up. I had about two minutes before I was going to pass out or throw up, or maybe both.

Stumbling to the elevator, I texted Jericho, squinting through the double vision and hoping my message made sense. My coordination was shit, and I needed help to get into my room. The elevator dinged, and I wasn't sure how I'd even gotten on it or stayed standing, but when the doors slid open, Jericho was waiting with an amused grin on his face.

We didn't need to exchange words, but he patted me down and found my room key, unlocking the door and stepping aside to hold it open for me. I stumbled inside and face planted onto the bed. He pulled my shoes off, and I heard the water running in the bathroom, but I couldn't keep myself conscious long enough to figure out what he was doing.

I was blissfully dead to the world.

***

The banging could've been coming from my skull or the door; I couldn't tell which. All I knew was I wanted it to end before I hurled. When I pried my gritty eyes open, it became clear the sound wasn't in my head—or at least not *just* in my head—but someone was pounding on the door.

"Open this door right now!" a smooth feminine voice with a twang yelled out, punctuating each word with another slam of her hand into the wood.

With a groan, I pushed myself up off the bed. I was sure I looked horrible, hungover as hell in my rumpled clothes from last night. I shuffled to the door and pulled it open, taking in Magnolia's narrowed eyes and pink-tinged cheeks. She was cute when she was mad.

"What's up, Mags?" I shoved my hands into my pockets and leaned against the door frame, mostly to keep myself from falling over but also to keep from reaching out for her and tucking her disheveled hair behind her ear.

Her eyes narrowed even further, and she scanned me from head to toe, disgust filling her eyes. "Oh, Sugar." She clicked her tongue. "If you think I'm gonna let you screw up this tour for me, you're in for a rude awakening. You missed the meet and greet, and you better get yourself together before the show. You will *not* mess up this tour."

I could practically see the smoke billowing out of her ears, and I bit back a smile. Something about her being riled up made me want to laugh. "Yes, ma'am." My charm could come out when I wanted it to. My mom taught me to be a gentleman, even if I'd lost sight of it a little bit since I moved to LA.

She relaxed a fraction. "Good. You have an hour to shower and eat something before you need to get to the venue. I suggest you be on time."

I nodded at her before closing the door and doing what she said. She'd been so angry, she was practically vibrating, and as I washed away the events of yesterday and the stale liquor I was sure I smelled like, my thoughts drifted back to the raven-haired Southern beauty who'd been so haunted yesterday morning when we left.

Magnolia wore her emotions all over her face, and I doubted she could hide what she was feeling from anyone. I cracked a smile, trying to picture playing poker with her. She'd be terrible at it, but that'd be what made it fun—

especially if I could convince her to play strip poker.

I dried off and scolded myself for my wayward thoughts. Wynter left yesterday, and the last thing I needed on this tour was another complication. I begrudgingly shoved thoughts of Magnolia aside and finished getting ready.

I couldn't help it that my brain wouldn't let me rid myself of my fantasies that easily, and images of Magnolia kept popping up as I went to meet the guys before our show. I couldn't help that I kept searching her out, looking for her long, nearly-black hair or lithe body.

Blowing out a breath, I stepped up to the bus as my eyes flicked over to where Magnolia was walking her puppy, Lucky. Everything in me wanted to go over and join her, flirt and make her like me. It was a compulsion, but this time I wouldn't give in.

Somehow that felt like the biggest challenge I'd had in a while.

SIX
MAGNOLIA

Watching from backstage, I was transfixed as the guys from Shadow Phoenix performed *Vicious* from their latest album. My eyes kept drifting back to Griffin as he played his drums with frantic arms, using his whole body to make his music. It was mesmerizing, and I had to make a serious effort to peel my eyes away.

If I hadn't known that his girlfriend broke up with him last night, I wouldn't have thought anything at all was wrong with him. He wore a happy grin as sweat poured down his chiseled body, and my breath caught before I scolded myself for watching him again. He might be available now, but that didn't mean I was.

I shivered when I thought about the delivery Winston sent yesterday; the flowers meant to remind me that he was watching. He was *always* watching. I thought this time I'd run far enough, stayed under the radar so he wouldn't know where I was, but I was wrong. I felt defeated.

Would there ever come a day where he'd let me go? Where he'd realize that I wasn't his to torment and let me live my life?

I doubted it.

Brushing off the unsettling and frightening direction of my thoughts, I refocused on the band for one more song before I had to rush off and make sure everything was set up for packing up and traveling once the show was over.

Griffin's inked skin was slick with sweat and his muscles rippled underneath all that ink as he threw himself wholly into his music, and this time I decided I'd enjoy watching him for just a minute.

It wouldn't hurt anything, right? At least no one could read my thoughts. Besides, thoughts didn't mean anything had to happen, or I had to act on them.

Sure, keep telling yourself that, Magnolia.

When the song was over, I took a deep breath, throwing my boss mask back on, and walking away from the show. I needed to check in with the equipment guys to make sure they were on track and then food service to check on the post-show meal that needed to be on the bus so the bands could have their downtime before we hit the road for Denver.

It took me about an hour to check in with everyone, but I found myself fitting into the role of tour manager easily. I was good at staying organized, always had been. Holding a whole bunch of plates in the air while they were spinning and keeping them balanced was something I always thought I would excel at, and I was glad my self-reflection had been right. Maybe my impression of the job I was doing would change when something went wrong.

Memories of this morning washed over me as I walked back toward the buses. I'd been irate when Griffin missed the meet and greet this morning. The guys had covered for him smoothly, but people were disappointed. He was the newest member, the one their fans had the most curiosity about, and they'd paid a lot of money to get the chance to meet him, get an autograph, and take a picture.

As I was on my way to tear into him for being such a selfish, inconsiderate jerk, Jericho had pulled me aside and filled me in on what happened. My anger went from a full, rolling boil down to a simmer at his explanation. I was still pissed, but if anyone knew what he was going through—feeling like the person he'd been with wasn't who he thought they were—it was me.

Rounding the corner, the two buses loomed in the distance, and I started to walk faster. The concert should be over now, and I needed to start prepping for the next stop, but more than that, Lucky needed to stretch his legs. He'd been trapped in the bus for the last couple of hours, and puppies weren't great at not ruining everything around them. I cringed as I thought about everything his tiny dagger teeth could have shredded in the time he'd been on the bus by himself.

Out of my peripheral vision, I saw Lucky trotting down the hall with my pillow between his teeth, but outside of that, everything looked like it was okay, and I let out a sigh of relief before looking down at the ball of fluff that had flopped down onto my feet and was gnawing happily on my pillowcase. "That's not yours, you little demon," I scolded, but there was no anger behind it. How could I be mad at that tiny, sweet face?

I bent down and picked Lucky up and pried my pillow out of his mouth. He yipped in protest, but I ignored him as I tossed it back into my bunk. I'd need to remember to change my pillowcase later. "Who's the best boy?" I cooed at him as I ruffled the fur between his ears and carried him down the stairs and outside the bus. The distant murmur of people laughing and shouting, of cars starting told me the show was definitely over. These were my last few minutes of quiet before everyone came back.

With all the people in both bands, their partners and spouses, and the kids, it was rare to get a quiet moment alone, and we'd only been out here two days. I couldn't imagine how I'd feel when the tour came to an end. I set Lucky down, and he looked up at me with what I would swear was an annoyed expression. The night air was cool, and the concrete under his paws had to be chilly. "What?" I asked him, gesturing around me like he'd understand anything about what I was saying or doing. "You need to stretch your legs."

He blinked lazily a couple of times before turning away and sniffing at the air. The scent of grilled meat hit my nose, and my stomach growled. I wondered what catering had put together for dinner tonight. One of the perks of traveling with a band on tour, I was learning, was having delicious meals served up three times a day and snacks always available. I never had to wonder what I was going to make for just myself. It was a nice break from my normal life.

I hoped this would become my normal life, at least for a little while. It was unrealistic to think I could spend the rest of my life on the road touring with bands. I wanted to settle down someday, have kids, and get married.

But until Winston finally let me go, I could never have those things. He'd never let me.

"Did you enjoy the show?" a smooth, deep voice asked from right over my shoulder, and I spun, throwing my fist right at his face. Griffin reacted so fast, he managed to catch my punch instead of letting it smash into his too-perfect face. "Damn, what'd I do to piss you off this time? I was coming to apologize."

I jerked my hand out of the hold he had on it, horrified at myself for reacting that way. I learned a long time ago someone sneaking up on me wasn't a good thing, and now I reacted accordingly. "Hasn't anyone ever taught you not to sneak up on a woman?" I snapped, my heart racing a million miles an hour.

He studied my face carefully before lifting his hands in surrender and taking a step back. "I didn't mean to scare you." He raked his fingers through the damp strands of his wavy brown hair. "I wanted to apologize again for this morning. It was unprofessional of me to not even let you know I wouldn't be able to make it, and it won't happen again."

My shoulders relaxed as I deflated. I hadn't expected him to take my anger seriously. He was a rock star, after all—full of ego and cocky swagger. I was still skeptical of his intentions and if he was showing me the real him. There was no doubt I was attracted to him. He was stunning—muscular but not overly so, skin etched with tattoos down his arms and up his neck, piercings in his nose and tongue, but his features were almost delicate. His nose was straight and perfect, his lips plump and luscious, and his hair wavy and fell artfully even when it was messy. His eyes were deep and hypnotic, and in this light, the deep brown almost looked like a glittering black. Standing next to him made me feel plain and small—something not very many people could do considering I towered over most other women at a supermodel-esque height.

"Thank you for apologizing. I'm sorry, too. I know I came off harsh, probably harsher than called for. This tour is really important to me. I need it to go well." I wasn't sure why, but he made me want to spill everything out, all my fears and plans and truths. The taste of copper filled my mouth as I bit my tongue to keep from speaking.

Griffin stared down at Lucky, who was attempting to climb up a curb and into a grassy area. He couldn't quite get his chubby little legs over the top and kept falling over himself. Griffin chuckled at Lucky's antics and bent down, sweeping him up into his arms and cuddling him for a second before dropping him back into the grass. "There you go, little guy."

Watching him with my puppy made my ovaries want to burst. Was there anything more adorable than a super hot guy with a fluffy puppy? I didn't think so.

"His name's Lucky," I supplied, folding my arms across my chest. A part of me felt like I needed to protect myself from him—not physically, but emotionally. Wanting to bare my soul to this virtual stranger was so far beyond unlike me, it wasn't even funny.

He smirked at me, the side of his lip lifting in an equally tempting and infuriating way. "I know, I heard the other day. What'd he do to earn that label?"

"Got a second chance at life. I rescued him from a cardboard box outside of a grocery store. Someone had left him in it; they didn't even wait around to see who picked him up or *if* he got picked up. But he did, and he'll never know anythin' but bein' completely spoiled." I leveled a challenging glare at him. I was determined, and I wouldn't be dissuaded by critical words, but then he surprised me.

"Good," he nodded. "He deserves nothing but the best." He shoved his hands in his pockets, and we stood in silence for a few minutes, watching Lucky sniff around every blade of grass and flower. It wasn't awkward like I thought it'd be. It was comfortable, which was another surprise.

Everything about Griffin was surprising, and that had me on edge. I didn't like surprises or being caught off guard. I stepped forward and grabbed Lucky, turning toward the buses. "We better get back so we can grab whatever's left of the food, and I can check in with the drivers."

We walked side by side back to the buses, the noise of conversation and children running and playing getting louder and louder the closer we got. The relaxed ease everyone had with each other brought a smile to my face. They all felt safe and secure, and I intended to make sure it stayed that way.

My phone buzzed in my pocket, but I ignored it, setting Lucky down and grabbing a plate. While I waited my turn to dish up, Griffin moved away and joined his friends, and I looked at the head of the security team Shadow Phoenix brought with them, Connor. He nodded at me and went back to watching. Every time I saw him, he was watching everything. I had a feeling nothing was missed by his penetrating gaze.

Having them around meant I could take a deep breath, but it didn't mean I could relax my security standards. I couldn't get complacent. I'd done that before—thinking I was safe, only to be proven wrong. So, so wrong. I wouldn't let that happen again, so I'd make sure to stay vigilant.

It was a good thing I was an expert multi-tasker because I had to fend off Lucky with one hand while shoveling food into my mouth with the other as I balanced on a small cement curb I found to sit on. I only had a couple of minutes to eat before I needed to go make the rounds again. The road crew should have the equipment mostly packed up by now and be working their way through their final checks before we left for Denver. We had a strict schedule to maintain, and I intended to make sure we kept to it.

Lucky's pleading eyes finally cracked my resolve, and I passed him a couple of scraps of my chicken before I stood and tossed my plate in the trash. The first couple stops I made, everyone was right on time with their preparations. It wasn't until I got to one of the final stops—the buses—that I ran into a problem.

The clanging sound of metal on metal slamming together had me gritting my teeth, and I looked down at Lucky, who jumped with every bang. I bent down and picked him up before walking around the front of the bus where the grill was open, and the driver was bent over inside muttering obscenities.

"What's the problem, Eric?" I asked, and he moved back, turning to face me with his jaw clenched and his skin covered in grease.

"Our radiator hose is busted. I noticed the engine running hot when we pulled in, and when I checked it, the hose was a mess. I need to get it replaced, but it won't be done until late tonight or tomorrow." He looked apologetic, but it wasn't his fault. I bit my lip as I considered my options, pulling out my phone.

Solving problems was my thing. I liked the challenge, and this wouldn't hold us back. I couldn't charter a private plane for everyone; it was too expensive. The band had a plane, but it wasn't big enough to hold everyone. I needed to get them on commercial flights and soon. I made a mental checklist—book flights, call a mechanic, get a car service to take them to the hotel. Eric knew the basics, but he was the driver, not the guy who'd crawl up in the engine and fix it. We needed a reliable fix, not just a patch job.

"I'll get someone out here and on it. In the meantime, why don't you rest up? You're going to have to drive the bus overnight and meet us at the venue tomorrow," I instructed, and he nodded, wiping his hands on the rag he pulled out of his back pocket.

"You got it, Magnolia."

I spun on my heel and hurried back to the bus to drop Lucky off. I closed him in my bunk, hoping he'd stay put, and then went back outside. My fingers flew across the screen as I booked tickets for the band and their families. Luckily, the Tuesday Told a Secret crew had their own bus that seemed to be working just fine, so I signaled them it was okay to leave. The semi-trucks filled with equipment and stage crew all took off, leaving just the Shadow Phoenix bus and security behind.

Once the tickets were booked, I went to find Connor. He was standing away from the buses with a couple of his team in a semi-circle, and I interrupted their discussion with my presence. They all turned to look at me, but I focused on the man in charge. "The SP bus is havin' mechanical issues, so I booked airline tickets. They're split up on two flights, two different airlines, but they leave in about an hour and a half. I'm forwardin' you the tickets and the hotel reservations. Y'all should land within fifteen minutes of each other, and there'll be cars waitin' to take you to the hotel."

Connor looked down at his phone as it vibrated with the incoming emails I'd just sent him. "I'm gonna need your help, your team's help, to keep everythin' running smoothly since I can't be in two places at once. I need to stay behind and make sure the bus gets taken care of. I'm gonna take a later flight once Eric gets on the road, and I'll meet y'all at the hotel in the mornin'."

Connor nodded. "I'll take care of it. One of us will text you and let you know when everyone's checked into the hotel."

I nodded my thanks and stepped away, making calls to find a mechanic. It was surprisingly hard to find someone willing to come out at eleven o'clock at night to fix a bus engine, but I managed with Southern charm and a little bit of bribery. It would be an hour before the guy showed up, so in the meantime, I went to find the band.

The parking lot was nearly empty now; just the security team and the band members were left after the rest of the caravan took off. I approached the band members and their families hovering near the bus door. I purposefully avoided Griffin's gaze, but I could feel it sinking into my skin as if he was caressing me, and I hoped my shiver wasn't noticeable.

"We've got a change of plans," I announced, waiting for all of their attention to fall on me. One by one, they stopped talking and turned toward me. I shifted, uncomfortable under the weight of their attention, but this was my job, and I had to suck it up and get it done. "The bus won't be able to leave on time. It's got a malfunctionin' radiator, and a mechanic is on the way, but I need y'all to pack an overnight bag, and then Connor and his security team are gonna take you to the airport. You've got a flight in a little less than an hour to Denver. When the bus is fixed, Eric's gonna drive it overnight, so it'll meet us tomorrow before the show. Do any of y'all have any questions?"

They all shook their heads and started to move away to go pack. I looked down at my phone to make sure everything was in place, and I hadn't forgotten anything. "I've got a question," Griffin said, and I tensed, not wanting to admit how much he affected me and definitely not wanting him to see it.

"What is it?" I tried to sound annoyed, but my voice was a little breathy.

"How are you getting to Denver?"

His question caught me off guard. It wasn't his job to worry about my travel arrangements—it was mine. I wasn't sure why he cared. Instead of giving him the answer, I replied with a question of my own. "Why?"

He ran his long fingers through his hair, fingers that could make such beautiful music. I found myself staring and ripped my eyes off of the motion, dropping them to a point just over his shoulder. "Don't take this the wrong way, okay?" He pleaded with his eyes when I chanced a glance into them.

I folded my arms over my chest and raised an eyebrow but waited for him to continue. I'd heard every pretty promise and flowery word out of my ex, and they'd all been followed by violence and pain. I wasn't promising not to react to anything out of Griffin's mouth. It wasn't like I knew him.

"It makes me uncomfortable to leave you here by yourself, especially since we're taking security with us." He rushed the words out like he was afraid to admit them out loud, or maybe he was afraid of my reaction, and I rolled my eyes.

"I'm a big girl, Sugar. I can manage a mechanic, a bus driver, and gettin' myself to the airport."

He narrowed his eyes, probably not appreciating my nickname for him, and I held back the snort of laughter that wanted to bubble up. Somehow, *sugar* was a fitting nickname for him. He came off as sweet, but I still hadn't figured out if that was an act or not. Sometimes it took a while to dig underneath the mask someone wore.

"Let me rephrase. I'm not leaving you here by yourself, so book me a ticket on your flight." His stare dared me to challenge him, but I wouldn't. Instead, I shrugged.

"Fine, if you want to hang around a dark parking lot bored out of your mind, be my guest." Internally, I was freaking out. One part of me was squealing at the attention of this hot as hades guy who wanted to stay with me just to keep me safe. The other part of me knew better than to trust those feelings or intentions.

Once upon a time, I'd been the kind of girl who took everything at face value and who believed in happy endings and beautiful dreams. Now I knew better.

"I won't be bored," he answered confidently. "I'll be hanging out with you and Lucky."

"And Eric," I added. "Don't forget about Eric."

He laughed, and the sound loosened something in my chest. I didn't like that one bit. I could not let myself soften toward Griffin. I had a job to do and couldn't afford to get distracted. There were so many reasons I needed to keep him at arm's length, but he was making it difficult being so sweet and concerned.

Oh, and hot. So, so hot.

My phone vibrated in my hand, and I glanced down at it. *Winston.* Shit. I tried to put it away, but Griffin was standing too close, and he'd seen the name.

"Who's Winston?" he wondered with a scowl on his face. I didn't want to try and interpret what his expression meant.

I sighed. "My ex-boyfriend." I *really* didn't want to elaborate further. There was too much baggage.

Griffin's whole body relaxed until he looked back at the screen. His jaw clenched as he pulled the phone out of my hand. He did it so quickly I didn't even have time to try and stop him. Whatever Winston's message said, it wouldn't be anything good, and I didn't want Griffin to read it, but I was too tired to stop him.

I studied the beautiful features of his face lit up in the artificial white light from my phone screen as he read. His face was thunderous as he looked back up at me. "Does he live here? In Oregon?"

I shook my head, biting my lip. That urge to spill every last detail of everything Winston had ever done to me—every single night over the past year since I'd gotten away when I was going to sleep with a knife under my pillow and barely sleeping at all because of the fear he was watching me—was back. If I opened my mouth now, it might all come pouring out, and if Griffin really was a good guy, I couldn't burden him with my problems. It wasn't fair.

"Then how the fuck does he know what you're wearing or that you're standing here talking to me? And why is he threatening to—and I quote—*ruin you so only I'll love you*, for talking to me?"

Ugh, I really wished he hadn't read that. He watched me expectantly, and I knew I had to give him something. "Because he follows me and watches me." I grabbed my phone back from him. "And now I have to get a new phone number. Again."

"Fuck, Mags. You were going to just let us all leave knowing your ex is a psycho who watches you? What the hell?" I winced at his loud voice. His frustration with my lack of concern for my own welfare was bleeding through, but he reigned it in when he saw the effect it had on me. I wanted to run away. Every instinct in my body was telling me to do it, but that's what I'd always done, and I didn't want to be that girl anymore. I was stronger than that, even if my heart was racing and my muscles were poised to flee.

"What am I supposed to do?" I whispered, knowing if I spoke any louder, I'd probably start to cry, and that just wouldn't do. "Not live my life because I can't shake my ex? I've done that for too long, and I won't do it anymore."

"Not put yourself in unnecessary danger," he countered, stepping closer and lifting his hand like he wanted to touch me but thinking better of it when I shifted away and letting his hand drop to his side. I was barely holding myself together right now, and I had a feeling if he touched me, I would unravel.

For the first time in years, I wished I wasn't so damaged that I could believe Griffin was the kind of guy who'd hold me when I fell apart, who'd pick me up when I was too weak to do it myself, and who'd protect me from the world when it tried to ruin me.

Instead, I needed to do those things for myself because I couldn't depend on anyone but me.

SEVEN
GRIFFIN

That text from Magnolia's ex still had me quietly fuming. When I read it, I wanted to demand she tell me everything, but one look at her face and her body language, and I backed off. She'd folded in on herself and gotten so pale, she looked like she might pass out. I almost reached out and touched her, my whole body screaming at me to comfort her, but when she'd flinched from my outstretched hand, I'd dropped it.

It was obvious Mags had gone through something terrible—maybe a lot of terrible somethings. I looked down at where she'd fallen asleep on my shoulder as we flew toward Denver. Once we were in the air, it was like all the tension in her body evaporated, and she passed out. The dark circles under her eyes that I hadn't noticed before were another clue about what she'd been through. It didn't take me long to figure out that up here in the air, her ex couldn't be watching, so she finally let her guard down enough to sleep.

My heart clenched because she felt comfortable enough with me to allow herself to sleep. Magnolia was gorgeous—probably the most stunning woman I'd ever seen—but there was more to her than that, and my mind and body were at war over her. My heart wanted me to get to know her better, to dive in with her, but my stupid brain reminded me that I thought Wynter was a good person, too, and she had a lot less baggage than Magnolia seemed to. Could I really afford to get involved with someone who had the kind of baggage she came with?

Did I want to?

A soft sigh escaped her lips, and she adjusted, snuggling further under my chin and against my chest and shoulder, burying her nose in my skin. Her dark hair fell across her face and tickled me, but I didn't move to change a damn thing. Her sweet vanilla and clean laundry scent surrounded me, and I groaned as my cock started to harden. Now was not the time, but I couldn't help it. I hoped she'd stay asleep because if she woke up and looked down, she'd probably think I was a pervert.

After everything that happened with Wynter, I didn't trust myself to make a smart decision with Magnolia and whether or not to pursue her. Obviously, my body was completely on board, and I internally rolled my eyes at my dick's antics. No, I needed to talk to my brother, or maybe even Jericho. They'd tell me what to do with minimal bullshit.

Until then, I'd be her friend. I'd watch out for her the best I could, and I'd do my damndest to keep my hands to myself.

I spent the rest of the flight in my own head, trying to put the pieces I'd managed to collect about Magnolia's life before the tour and what her ex was doing to her together, but I didn't have enough information to do anything with. Based on the way she reacted to yelling and sudden movement, it wasn't hard to figure out she'd had some sort of trauma or abuse in her life.

But she was also feisty, and I'd seen her stand up for herself, so there was a strength and determination about her that surprised me. I'd also seen her collapse in on herself when Wynter came at her, so maybe that strength was a new thing. I didn't know, and somehow I doubted she'd be willing to share with me.

When we landed, she jerked awake, and her eyes darted around frantically before she exhaled and looked over at me with a guarded expression. "Sorry, I must've fallen asleep."

I chuckled, wanting to reach out and brush the hair out of her eyes. I balled my hands into fists to stop from touching her since I wasn't sure she'd be okay with it. "You only drooled on me a little," I teased, and then I laughed at the horrified expression on her face.

"Relax, Mags. I'm kidding."

She glared at me and folded her arms across her chest as the plane taxied to the gate, ignoring me the rest of the way. I had so much I wanted to ask her about, but I held back. If I dug into what was going on with her, I might find myself tangled up in something I hadn't bargained for, and with everything else going on, I wasn't sure that was a smart move. Every protective instinct I had was screaming at me to wrap Magnolia up in my arms and never let anything hurt her again.

But I hadn't been smart with Wynter, and I didn't want to make the same mistakes twice. I scrubbed my hands over my face, noting my usual five o'clock shadow was turning into more of a beard. As soon as we got to the hotel, I was demanding a meeting with my brother no matter what time it was.

By the time we got off the plane and caught a ride to the hotel, I was completely wired. A glance at my phone told me it was two a.m., and while I wanted to keep spending time with Magnolia, maybe follow her up to her hotel room and make sure she was okay, maybe hold her while she slept so I could watch over her, I held myself back.

I didn't trust my decision making, and I had no idea where she was at in terms of the idea of dating or sex. My dick was *fully* on board with making Magnolia ours, but my brain warned me to hold back. Sometimes I really hated my brain.

Standing back from the lobby counter, I pulled out my phone and texted Maddox to meet me in the lobby. It looked like the bar was closed, so we'd have to talk down in the lobby, out in the open. At least the leather sofas looked comfortable where they bracketed a huge fireplace with orange flames crackling inside.

Magnolia handed me my room key. "Do you need me to show you where your room is?" she wondered, adjusting the grip she had on Lucky as he squirmed in her arms and wagged his tail at me. I chuckled and reached out to scratch him between his ears, and he calmed down.

I shook my head. "I'm sure I can find it."

"Okay, then I'm goin' to bed. 'Night."

The last thing I wanted was to say goodnight to her or let her walk up to her room alone, but I had to sort through my shit first. If my hunch was right about Magnolia and what she'd been through, she'd need me to be strong and put together, and I couldn't do that until I figured out exactly what I wanted. It wasn't fair to either of us.

I watched her sexy form as she walked away, unable to take my eyes off her until the elevator doors opened and my brother stormed out with a murderous expression on his face. Magnolia stepped into the elevator Maddox had just left and raised her eyebrow at me. I shot her a grin, and she shook her head with a small smile as the doors closed.

"This better be fucking good, bro," Maddox grumbled. He was *not* a morning person, although to be fair, it was only two a.m.

"I need advice, Mad. I don't trust myself," I confided, walking over to the leather couch and expecting him to follow. He did and flopped onto the sofa across from me. He looked like he'd rolled out of bed and was two seconds away from falling back to sleep as he stretched out on the couch.

He yawned loudly. "Don't trust yourself with what?"

"You know what happened with Wynter," I explained since I'd filled him in on everything earlier today.

"Yeah… and? Maybe my brain's fuzzy as fuck because it's the goddamn middle of the night, but what's your point?" Maddox had moved so he was completely lying down on the couch. All he needed was a blanket, and he'd be set for the night, and I bit back a laugh.

"I like Magnolia," I admitted quietly.

He sat up and stared at me with critical eyes. "Really?"

"Is it that hard to believe? She's gorgeous and determined and feisty but has this quiet confidence that draws me in. Plus, she's sexy as fuck." Couldn't forget that last part and my cock was in complete agreement as it twitched in my pants at the memory of her body pressed up against mine while she slept on the plane.

"So? What has you dragging my ass out of bed with my wife in the middle of the night? Sounds like you know what you want to me," he pointed out.

I stared at the flames dancing and flickering in the fireplace for a while before I answered. "I don't trust myself."

Maddox grunted but didn't say anything, and when I looked over at him, his eyes were closed. "What? I obviously don't make good decisions when it comes to the women I get involved with," I gritted out, still angry with myself over not seeing Wynter for who she really was.

He sighed and sat up. "Magnolia's not Wynter."

"I'm aware, but she comes with her own set of complications." I hated talking about the issues I suspected she was dealing with, especially since I hadn't even talked to her about my suspicions yet. It felt like I was spreading rumors or gossiping or some shit. I didn't like it at all.

"Complications? Like what?" He stood up and walked over to the fire, stretching out his hands in front of the warmth. We were in Denver, and it was cold as hell, but I hadn't really had time to process it. I'd had more important things on my mind.

"Like her ex-boyfriend following her and threatening her, and like I think the relationship might have been abusive. Haven't you noticed how she shrinks into herself when anyone yells nearby or how she flinches when someone moves fast around her?"

He looked back at me incredulously. "Seriously? What kind of cowardly piece of shit would hit a woman?"

My brother had a particularly strong opinion of the situation because of the way his dad had beat our mom for years. Thankfully, she'd gotten out before she had me, so I hadn't had to see it, but Russell Everleigh was the biggest piece of shit I had the displeasure of knowing about.

If anyone would understand my desire to pull Magnolia into my orbit and protect her, Maddox would.

"I don't know, I've never met the guy, and the only reason I know about him is because I happened to see a text on her phone. When I asked, the only thing she said was he was her ex, but the text creeped me the hell out. I got a definite abusive ex vibe from him." I leaned back against the cushions of the couch and put my legs up on the coffee table.

Maddox hummed and absently scratched at his stubble. "Mom was all sorts of fucked up when she walked out on Russell. I'm happy she met Grant and got a chance at a happy life, but do you really want to have to pick up this girl's broken pieces and try to glue them back together? Don't you think you have enough on your plate already?"

I scowled at him, not liking the cold, hard truth he was spewing at me. My gut was shouting at me to ignore him and become Magnolia's hero, but how could I be her hero when my life was so up in the air? I *just* got a chance at my dream job—playing drums for a world-famous band—and hadn't even made it through my first tour. As much as I hated to admit it, Maddox had a point.

It made me feel sick to think about keeping my distance from Magnolia, but it was the smart thing to do. Taking on someone else's problems was dumb.

So why did my stomach feel like it was turning inside out at the thought of staying away from her? "Yeah, I guess," I mumbled, the words tasting like ash on my tongue.

Maddox eyed me and then sighed, his shoulder relaxing as he sat back down across from me. "Look, I know more than anyone all the angles in this situation, but we need you focused right now. You committed to the band, and we've only had one show so far, and you missed the meet and greet." He held up his hand when he saw me about to protest.

"I get why; I'm not giving you shit. I'm just saying we need you focused. It sounds like this thing with Magnolia would be full of distractions, which is the last thing you need. We're depending on you. Focus for the tour and if you're still interested at the end, take your shot."

"Yeah, okay," I conceded, hating it. There was something about Magnolia that drew me to her—a lot of somethings, actually. Standing by and watching her from afar over the next month would be complete hell.

"So, we're good? I can go back to bed?" Maddox watched me until I nodded.

"Yeah, we're good. Thanks for talking me through it."

He stood up and squeezed my shoulder. "What are big brothers for?"

I didn't know how he felt, but I was surprised how quickly he accepted me and his role in my life, and not a day went by that I wasn't grateful my mom had reached out and brought Maddox into our lives. Watching him walk back up to his room to go crawl back in bed with his wife, I'd never felt more alone or more exhausted.

My bones felt heavy under my skin, almost like if I stood up, I might collapse back to the ground under the weight of my exhaustion, but as it was, I was only going to get a couple of hours of sleep, so I needed to get up and get to bed.

When I finally pushed into my hotel room, I didn't even bother turning on the lights. I stripped out of my clothes, fell face down onto the mattress, and was asleep before I could even get under the covers.

An annoying ringing in my dream had me jolting unwillingly into consciousness, and I realized it was the phone on the nightstand. Did people even have corded phones anymore? Apparently, because this one was irritating the shit out of me. "Hello?" I rasped because my voice was still gravelly with sleep. Snapping wasn't really my style. Whoever was on the other end of the line hadn't done anything wrong—yet.

"This is your eight a.m. wakeup call, Mr. Spencer," a cheerful female voice said, and I sighed. I supposed I should've been glad I got to sleep that late, but then a slow smile worked across my face. This had been Magnolia's doing. She probably did it for everyone on tour, but I wanted to pretend for a second she'd done something thoughtful for me so that I wouldn't be late today.

"Thanks," I ended the call, pushing out of bed and heading to the shower. It wasn't until I stepped under the warm spray that I remembered I wasn't supposed to be thinking about Magnolia in any way other than professionally, and my mood soured a lot. I didn't know if I could do this.

How did you keep your distance from someone you felt compelled to spend time with? It almost felt magnetic, my interest in her. When I first met her, I tried not to pay attention to how silky her hair looked or how her hips swayed when she walked because I had a girlfriend. But now that I was free, all bets were off—or at least they had been until my conversation with my brother last night.

But now that I was thinking about how her cheeks flushed a soft pink-peach color when she was excited or how her eyelashes fluttered when she tasted something delicious, I could only imagine how her soft lips would look wrapped around my cock. I groaned, closing my eyes and leaning my forehead against the shower wall, taking my dick in my hand and squeezing it. Imagining sinking into Magnolia's body while I stroked myself was the sweetest kind of torture, and I knew it would only make it harder to stay away, but I couldn't resist.

My abs flexed as I worked my shaft, images of Mags throwing her head back with my name on her lips running through my mind. It didn't take long for me to get off, hot ropes of come swirling down the drain as my body shook with the aftermath of the most intense orgasm I could ever remember having—all with just the idea of burying myself inside the raven-haired beauty.

I couldn't even imagine how good her body would feel for real, if I ever let myself go there, and if she wanted me, too.

I would've thought jerking off to thoughts of Magnolia would have taken the edge off when I saw her, but if anything, I was more wound up than before. Not good. When she breezed into the restaurant and grabbed a bagel, every muscle in my body tensed, and my senses all focused in on her. I swore I could smell her sweet scent from across the room—a heady combination of vanilla and clean laundry dried in the sun. It was the best way I could describe it, and every time I was close to her, I ended up breathing in lungfuls because I couldn't seem to get enough.

True pulling out the chair next to me had me forcing my attention away from Magnolia and over to him. He had his daughter in his lap, and she was grabbing scrambled eggs off his plate with her chubby little hand and shoveling them into her mouth. It was an adorable mess. "Morning," he said cheerfully as he watched Phoenix with a look of total devotion on his face.

"Morning. What's on the agenda today?" I never knew what we were doing from one day to the next or where we were going. I figured they'd tell me when I needed to be somewhere important, and otherwise, I was just along for the ride. I'd show up and do whatever I needed to, and then the rest of the time, I'd try and relax and soak up the experience. At least that'd been the plan until I met Magnolia. Now my energy was going to go to keeping myself away from the girl I couldn't seem to stop thinking about.

My gaze had drifted over to where she was sitting with a group of the equipment guys as she laughed at something one of them said. A flame of irrational jealousy flared up inside me, but I tamped that shit down. I didn't have any right to be possessive of Mags, but like with everything else having to do with her, I couldn't seem to help myself.

"An interview, I think. Something about a local news show." True's voice pulled my attention away from where it'd drifted to Magnolia again.

Once we finished eating, True passed Phoenix off to his wife, and the rest of us met out front and got into an oversized black SUV. We had a matching one in front of us and one behind us, filled with security. It was freaky. Sometimes I forgot that I wasn't exactly living a normal life anymore. The day-to-day still felt like it always had, so it was easy to forget.

The drive through downtown Denver was short, and we were escorted out of the underground parking garage and into the news studio. All of us refused their offer of hair and makeup—get out of here with that shit—and only had to wait a few minutes before they ushered us in front of the cameras. Zen and Maddox sat on the couch, and they had True and me on stools behind it.

The plastic blonde host was perched on the edge of an armchair off to my right. "Okay, we've got two minutes until we're back on the air. The segment will only last about five minutes, so not too bad. Whatever you do, do *not* use profanity in your answers. We're live and can't edit it out," she warned, glaring at us all as if she thought we were the scum of the earth. She hadn't even bothered introducing herself. I glanced over at True, and he rolled his eyes at me, just as annoyed with her as I was.

The difference was he'd been through this shit about a thousand times before. I had not. I planned on staying mostly silent unless asked a direct question, letting the rest of the guys handle this. They had tons of experience, and I figured it'd be a standard interview for them. Someday when I felt more comfortable with how to act or answer so that I didn't end up in a heap of shit over my words, I might dive in.

Today was not that day.

"Welcome back to *Good Morning, Denver!* I'm here with the guys from one of my favorite bands, Shadow Phoenix." I scoffed internally at her fake words. She seemed like she hated us two seconds before the camera started rolling. "They've got a show coming up tonight at the Denver Arena, which we're all very excited about, but first, I wanted to ask you guys a few questions."

The host—I still didn't know her name since she hadn't bothered to give it to us—turned her predatory gaze on me with a glint in her eye I didn't like one bit. I swallowed hard, bracing myself because I could tell something I wasn't going to like was coming.

"Griffin, you were added to the band just before you guys recorded *Vicious*, your latest studio album. It must have been so nice to have the spot open up to you because of who your brother is, huh?" I watched Maddox tense on the sofa in front of me, his body language radiating pure pissed off energy, and my stomach twisted. I always knew there was a possibility people would think I got my spot because of who my brother was. It wasn't a stretch to think that, and her words were tearing open a wound that had only just scabbed over from Wynter.

Did I really have so little to offer the world that people only wanted me because of my connections and what I could do for them? They didn't see *me*. They didn't see my talent, the hard work I'd put in, the years of practicing until my hands bled, of annoying my neighbors with the sound of my drums at all hours of the day and night. Growing up, we'd had to move three times because of neighbor complaints, and my parents never made me feel bad about it once.

But all anyone saw was that my brother was Maddox Everleigh, and because of that, I got my spot. They didn't think I earned it, and I didn't know why, but that bothered me a whole helluva lot.

I became aware that I was taking way too long to answer, and the silence was awkward. The host's evil grin widened as she realized she'd flustered me, but I plastered my cockiest smile on my face and forced back the self-doubt swirling inside. I'd have to sort through that later. Zen slid a couple of inches closer to Maddox and looked like he was ready to hold him back if he decided to lunge for the host.

"It sure was. Hey, it's not like I'm any good at what I do, right? I'm just a body they could throw back behind the drums. You know, pretty much a monkey throwing my sticks around." I grinned even wider as she narrowed her eyes and the smile slipped off her face. I probably should have been more politically correct or whatever, but I couldn't help myself. People underestimating me, and using me were starting to get under my skin, and I needed to stand up for myself at some point.

I was starting to realize the world was a lot different of a place than I thought it was before this past year.

The rest of the interview passed in clipped sentences and thinly-veiled hostility, and before we were even back in the car, Maddox was on the phone with Harrison, our PR guy, demanding he blacklist that host from ever interviewing us again. My brother was crazy protective, and I was happy to know I was included in that now. I'd do the same for him if it ever came down to it. I'd do the same for any of the guys.

My phone vibrated, and I looked down to read the text as the SUV left to take us back to the hotel.

Jericho: What a bitch. You know we don't think you're just a monkey behind that kit, man. If anyone knows how good you are, it's me.

His words relaxed me a little, but shit, everything that happened this week had seriously wreaked havoc on my previous unshakable confidence.

When we got back to the hotel, I holed up in my room, not wanting to talk to anyone or least of all see Magnolia. I didn't know how to act around her, and I wondered if she'd seen the interview—if she thought of me like that host did, as someone who only got to where he was because of who he knew. The hours ticked by slowly, and every minute that passed, my resolve grew stronger to prove to the world that I'd earned my spot and that I wasn't someone who could be used or walked all over. It was time I grew up and realized that I had all the power here to be whoever I wanted to be and to tell anyone I didn't want near me to fuck all the way off.

The show that night had been intense, and the adrenaline still coursed through my veins, making me buzz hours later. We'd eaten a late dinner and then piled on the bus for the long drive to Chicago. Lying in my bunk, I was scrolling through my phone. The bus was quiet outside of the gentle rocking and the sounds of the road.

One earbud was raised as I was about to pop it into my ear to listen to some music so I could hopefully get some sleep when a distressed cry caught my full attention. I pulled back the curtain and listened, hearing it again, almost like a soft wail. I climbed out of my bunk and moved down the aisle, listening.

I stopped outside of Magnolia's bunk, just two down from mine, where the curtain was closed, but it sounded like she was crying or in pain behind it. Indecision warred in my brain for about two seconds until she cried out again, and I said *fuck it* and tore the curtain back.

She was thrashing around, and her face was wet with tears, but she looked to be sleeping. Lucky was huddled at the bottom in the corner, looking at me with pleading eyes as he trembled. "Magnolia," I whispered, not wanting to wake everyone else. I shook her shoulder gently, but she didn't wake, continuing her cries of pain.

I made a decision and slid into her bunk. It was a tight fit with the two of us in here, but not impossible. The curtain stayed open, and I wrapped my arms around her, pulling her close to my body and stroking her hair. "Shhh, you're okay," I soothed her softly. "It's going to be okay."

Her body stilled, and awareness came over her as she blinked up at me but didn't pull away. "Griffin?"

"I'm sorry if I overstepped, but you were crying in your sleep and flailing around. I think you were having a nightmare."

Her cheeks flushed with what looked like embarrassment, and I bit back a grin. This girl was so sexy it almost hurt. "Oh. Well... thanks." She sounded hesitant and unsure as she whispered her gratitude, and I knew I should let her go and go back to my bunk, but I didn't want to.

I never wanted to.

"Okay, well, I guess I should go." I started to loosen my grip on her, and she grabbed a fistful of my t-shirt and pulled me back, burying her face in my chest. Hot tears soaked into my shirt, and I held her tighter.

"Don't go," she mumbled against my chest so quietly I almost didn't hear her. My whole body relaxed at her words. There was nothing in this world I wanted to do more than stay right here and bring Magnolia any comfort I could.

"Don't worry, I've got you," I assured her, and I did.

I *so* fucking did. To hell with waiting; I was done. It didn't matter what my brother thought was the right thing, and it didn't matter that my gut had let me down when it came to Wynter. Magnolia was different. I could feel it.

Right then and there, I decided from now on, Magnolia belonged to me.

EIGHT
MAGNOLIA

The Chicago skyline glittered with city lights outside of my hotel room window. All the lights in my suite were off, and the city below had gone quiet hours ago. Lucky was curled up in the middle of my unused bed as I stared out the window, ignoring my phone buzzing on the table beside me. It'd been doing that for the past three hours, and if I could turn it off, I could get some relief.

Unfortunately, I was responsible for almost a hundred people on the tour, which meant giving everyone access to me twenty-four-seven.

My nerves were on edge as I bit my fingernails down until there was nothing left. I knew Winston, and he wouldn't tolerate me ignoring him. I had no idea how he always managed to get my new phone numbers. It didn't matter how many times I changed it or that I didn't give the number out to anyone. He always managed to find it and usually in only a matter of days.

I jumped a little when the buzzing started up again. If I didn't answer soon, he'd start in with the text messages. It was his pattern, and I knew it well. I wished I could go down the hall and curl up in Griffin's arms like I had last night on the bus. I hadn't felt safe enough to sleep in over a year, outside of the night on the plane and last night on the bus.

Griffin had questionable taste in women, and maybe that was why I was drawn to him. Maybe I liked the idea that he wouldn't outright reject me if he ever knew the truth about my past. What I'd allowed Winston to do to me. I was embarrassed about how weak I was and how much I took before I finally walked away.

If I didn't respect myself, how could I ever expect anyone else to? I sighed, combing my fingers through the tangles of my long hair. Lucky let out a little *yip* in his sleep, and his paws twitched like he was chasing something. A small smile crossed my face as I watched him, one of the few rays of light that had broken through the cracks of my shattered psyche over the past month.

My job was another... and Griffin. I wasn't sure what he was yet, but he made me feel something I hadn't felt in so long, I forgot what it was like.

Hopeful.

It didn't hurt that he was so hot, it almost hurt my eyes to look at him directly—sort of like the sun. I'd always shied away from the bad boy look, assuming that they were all like Winston. Not that Winston looked like a delinquent or anything. He was clean-cut in a senator's son kind of way. You'd never think that lurking below his pastel polo shirts and khaki slacks was a monster who got off on controlling women and causing them pain.

I shivered like I always did when it got late, and my exhausted mind could no longer hold up the barriers that kept the memories at bay. The nights I'd held ice to my swollen eyes to try and ease the pain. The makeup I'd caked onto my skin to cover the bruises when he'd gotten careless and decided to hit me where everyone could see instead of in places my clothes usually covered. The weekends I'd spent in the hospital, including twice being intubated when the swelling on my brain meant I couldn't breathe on my own.

He'd almost killed me more times than I could count, and yet I hadn't left. Somehow, Winston had convinced me I wasn't worth anything, that nobody loved me, and I deserved every scar he left on my body. After my grammy died when I was a teenager, and I was on my own, I had no one until Winston. So, in a way, he was right. He had been all I had.

It wasn't until I woke up in the hospital the last time that a kind nurse had kicked him out of the room and vowed to help me get away. She held me while I cried, and then we made a plan, and I never looked back.

As soon as I was on my feet, I started therapy, and now I could see how brainwashed I'd been. I knew it would take a long time for me to be healthy and actually believe I was worthy of love, but I was getting there.

Being on this tour was a huge step for me in reclaiming my independence, and I refused to let Winston ruin it for me. I'd worked damn hard over the last year to find myself and stand on my own two feet, getting my life back.

I stood up and stretched as my phone screen lit up over and over again. I flipped it over, needing a break for a minute. Crossing the room, I checked the locks for the fifth time. They were still all in place, but it'd become a habit of mine to check and then re-check. I didn't think it was OCD, but more of a self-preservation strategy. If I didn't lock the doors, Winston would get in.

It wasn't a secret where the band was traveling on tour. He would know, and more than likely, he would follow. I hoped he wouldn't find out I'd gotten this job, but those flowers on the first day meant he knew, and he wanted me to know he knew. So, here I was, awake at four a.m., waiting for the sun to rise because I wouldn't be getting any sleep.

Again.

Maybe tonight, on the bus on the way to Philly, I could convince Griffin to sleep in my bunk with me. Was it fair of me to ask that? I didn't know, but he was the first person I'd wanted in longer than I could remember. Instead of recoiling from his touch, my body craved it. I wanted more of him and his spicy citrus scent that reminded me of summer.

Once I was sure the locks were secure, I dragged myself into the bathroom to shower and get ready for the day. It was early enough that I could go down to the hotel gym and get in a workout before I had to head to tonight's venue. Working out was one more way I'd taken control of my life, and the self-defense classes I'd been taking over the last year helped me feel a little less helpless.

My shower was quick and cool. I wanted to wake up, and the cold water did the trick. I tossed my hair up into a messy bun and threw on some leggings and a crop top before I took the elevator down to the gym.

It was early enough that even the early rising businessmen weren't up yet, so I had the place to myself. Thankfully, Winston seemed to have given up on his calls now that I'd been up all night, so I was able to open my streaming music app. I pulled up my workout playlist and slipped my earbuds in, climbing on the treadmill and starting a light jog to warm up.

I was completely focused on my running, having turned up the speed until I was sprinting. Sweat poured down my body, and my legs were screaming at me, but I couldn't stop. Not until I wasn't able to run another step. When my lungs burned with every breath, and my steps faltered, I slammed my hand down on the emergency stop button and bent over, gasping for air.

Someone tapped my shoulder, and I jumped, my already racing heart feeling like it was going to give out from stress. I ripped my headphones out and turned around to find Griffin watching me with concern. I was momentarily distracted by the fact he was shirtless and in grey sweatpants—every girl's kryptonite. His skin was splashed with ink across his entire torso, and his defined muscles glistened with sweat. How had I not noticed he'd come in?

I should definitely have been paying better attention to my surroundings.

"Are you okay?" he asked, taking a step closer while he looked me over as if searching for injuries.

I laughed, and it started out as one of those laughs that aren't funny at all before it morphed into me laughing and crying hysterically at the same time. It was *not* a good look. "Am I okay?" I repeated his question back to him while shaking my head. "Not even a little bit."

My legs were shaking from both the intense workout and the adrenaline, and I sank down to the floor, wrapping my arms around my knees and resting my forehead on top of them while tears streamed down my face. The last thing I wanted Griffin to see was me looking like a hot mess express, yet I couldn't seem to help myself. Every time he was around, I completely lost it. There was no way he could be interested in me. I was a disaster with more baggage than an airplane cargo hold.

I couldn't look at him, but when his arms wrapped around me, I cried even harder. I was all sweaty and gross with tears and probably snot running down my face, and he was so sweet I didn't know how to process everything. With my lack of sleep, my emotions were all over the place. "It's okay, Mags," he repeated the same comforting words he'd whispered to me that night on the bus.

Somehow, when he said them, I believed him.

"You don't know that," I countered in a shaky voice while I tried to calm myself down. Slow deep breaths were the name of the game, and it was one I was good at.

"Tell me what's wrong," he demanded, but it was a soft demand. Not like he was going to really force me or make me tell him if I wasn't ready. More like he was curious and wanted to help me fix whatever the problem was.

I exhaled slowly, debating with myself what to do. He made me want to confess everything about my past and Winston and how he tormented me even now, but there was another side to me that didn't want him to know. It was humiliating, and I didn't want him not to like me. When I lifted my head, my no doubt bloodshot and swollen eyes meeting his open and earnest deep brown gaze, my decision was made.

"My ex-boyfriend, Winston…"

"The one who texted you the other day," he guessed.

I nodded. "He's obsessed with me. We met my freshman year of college. My grammy died two years earlier, and I'd been on my own since then. I did the whole foster care thing for two years, but I had a plan: Go to college and see the world." I smiled wistfully, and Griffin rubbed my back, encouraging me to continue.

"At first, Winston was the perfect boyfriend. He was sweet and attentive, and caring. He went out of his way to do nice things for me or make me feel special and loved. But as time went on, he started making little suggestions about the outfits I'd wear or when or where I could go out with my friends. At first, I thought it was because he loved me and he was trying to keep me safe, but one night he didn't want me to go to an engagement party for one of my friends. I told him I was going anyway, and he hit me." My whole body shuddered as I remembered that night. It was a turning point, but we'd been leading there for a long time.

My therapist had helped me see how much I'd excused or been blind to before that pivotal moment. It was a *lot*.

Griffin cursed softly but didn't stop rubbing my back, so I kept going. "That was only the beginning. At that point, we'd been together for about a year, but he apologized, and things got better for a while. Until they didn't. I don't need to go into all the details, but we were together for over three years, and he put me in the hospital more times than I could count. I almost died more than once, a lot more than once. I finally got out when a nurse helped me, and I've never looked back. Unfortunately, he's never let me go, either."

Griffin was quiet for a long time, his fingers gently tracing up and down my spine before he moved closer, wrapping his legs around me and putting my face between his hands, so I was forced to look into his eyes. "You're the bravest woman I know... well, besides my mom." He gave me a soft smile. "Do you know about my mom?" he asked.

I shook my head. I hadn't exactly had time to stay up to date on gossip over the past few years.

His thumbs stroked my cheeks, wiping away the tears as they fell. "When my mom was still married to Maddox's dad, he used to abuse her like your ex did to you. He almost killed her, too, and she finally had enough and got away. It was a whole thing because she didn't take Mad with her, but that's a story for another day. The point is I've seen first hand how a woman can endure something so horrific and rise from the ashes to become the person they were always meant to be. My mom is unbelievably strong and resilient, and I see the same traits in you. You're going to be just fine, Magnolia. I promise." He pressed a soft kiss to my forehead, and I wanted to break down all over again.

"Someday, I hope I get the chance to meet her. It would be really nice to know someone who's gone through what I have," I voiced my hope, not giving a lot of thought to how he might take it. I wasn't trying to imply I'd meet her as anything other than a friend, even if there was a part of me that hoped for more.

"I think she'd like that," he agreed, before adding, "I know I would." My heart leaped, and my stomach fluttered at his insinuation. Did that mean he was interested in me? I had to have heard him wrong.

He was staring into my eyes again as if searching for something. "Go out with me," he breathed, our faces close together. He said it so quietly, like a secret just between us. Nervousness and excitement battled it out inside me. Griffin had never been anything but sweet and protective, but Winston started that way, too, and look how that'd turned out.

Yet, the story about his mother... He was different, wasn't he?

My therapist would tell me to take a chance—that life was far from over, and I needed to put myself out there again to experience it. The only way to truly free me from the fear was to go through it and come out the other side.

The only way out was through, and that was how I found myself nodding. "Okay."

His eyebrows shot up in surprise. "Okay? Really?"

I nodded again and then laughed when he gripped me in a tight hug and whooped excitedly before jumping up and holding out his hands for me. When I stood, he wrapped me in another hug and kissed my temple before stepping back. "Tomorrow in Philly. After the show, we'll get dinner."

I nibbled on my lip, wondering if I should tell him about Winston's other threat and deciding I needed to. It wouldn't be fair if he didn't know everything he was getting himself into. "There's one more thing you should know before you decide if you want to go on a date with me."

He stopped his backward walk toward the weights. "What?"

"Winston has threatened to kill anyone I go out with, and he's been watching. I don't know where he is specifically, but he's out there right now. It's not fair to put you in danger." My eyes were welling up with tears again, and he dropped the bottle of water he'd picked up before wrapping me back up in a hug.

"Baby, you have no idea the kind of stuff I've dealt with the past year, and the guys we have here with us? On security and in the band? They know how to handle threats like your ex. Trust me, nothing will happen to me. And as long as you're here with me? Nothing's going to happen to you either."

I closed my eyes and leaned against him for a second, hoping that he was right. That little voice in the back of my head told me Winston shouldn't be so easily dismissed, but right now, I was exhausted, and for just a second, I wanted to believe I didn't have to be afraid anymore.

"How much meat can you fit in your mouth?" I snorted through my laugh, trying not to choke as I watched Griffin shove more of his cheesesteak into his face. He grinned at me as his cheeks were puffed out like a chipmunk.

That was what I got for daring him to eat an entire sandwich in one bite. Was a cheesesteak even considered a sandwich? I didn't know. Neither of us had been to Philadelphia before, so we did a little Googling and decided we'd skip the rivalry of Pat's and Geno's and go straight for Sonny's instead. The food was delicious, but the company was better.

Getting to goof off and have a little fun for a change was something I hadn't realized I needed so badly until I was here with Griffin. Maybe it was just Griffin. It was hard to look away from him, and my body heated every time his attention fell on me, which was a lot. I blushed when he stared at me like he wanted to feast on me. His dark gaze was so intense, he had me squirming in my seat by the time we were done eating.

He stood up and stretched, and my eyes fell to the sliver of skin and abs now on display, and I licked my lips, wanting to reach out and touch him. His gaze darted to my mouth and darkened before he shook his head and grabbed my hand. "I hope you're not too full."

I followed him out onto the sidewalk and into a waiting car. "I'm not. Why?"

"There's something I've always wanted to do." His words were cryptic, and his smile was wicked, and I tried to contain the butterflies taking flight in my stomach as we pulled up to a familiar landmark, and I laughed.

"Really?" I turned from my view out the window to look at the childlike excitement on his handsome face.

"I was obsessed with these movies as a kid. We're doing it." He grabbed my hand and practically dragged me out of the car where we stood at the bottom of a tall set of grey, concrete steps that stretched way, way up.

"I doubt Rocky ate his weight in cheesesteak before he ran up these steps," I teased, secretly glad I'd only eaten half my sandwich.

"Well, I did, but I'm still doing it. This counts as our cardio for the day," he added before taking off.

"We already did cardio this mornin', plus you played a show!" I argued while cracking up laughing and chasing after him. I was glad I'd worn flats on our date.

When he got to the top, he threw his arms in the air and hopped from foot to foot just like the character in the movie, and when I got to the top, huffing and puffing, he wrapped me up in his arms and picked me up off the ground, spinning me around. I squealed and held on tight while he peppered my face with kisses.

He finally set me down, but he stared down at me with such an intense look in his eye, I almost had to look away. Griffin leaned in closer, and I knew he was going to kiss me, but he was moving slowly to give me a chance to back out, but I didn't want to. I wanted this—him.

When he realized I wasn't going to pull away, he kissed me like he'd been waiting to do it for years. His lips were soft as he nipped at my lower lip, taking his time and savoring the kiss. His hands wound their way into my hair, and our kissing grew more fevered and all-consuming. His tongue piercing clicked against my teeth, and I could only imagine all the things he could do with the metal stud. I forgot where we were, and I forgot how to breathe, and the only thing I knew was the feel of Griffin's lips on mine, his hands on my body, and his spicy citrus scent wrapping around me.

A shiver ran down my spine, and I pulled him closer, relishing the feel of his hard length pressing against my stomach. His reaction to our kiss only made me hotter, and he groaned when I pressed my body against his erection. I was practically rubbing on him like a cat, and he pulled back, dropping a couple more slow and lazy kisses against my lips before resting his forehead against mine.

"I want you so bad," he confessed, his lips almost touching mine with his whispered words. His confession made my heart race and my nipples tighten. If he opened his eyes, I bet he'd see I was blushing. "But," he continued. "We're in public." He finally opened his eyes and studied my face before smirking. Yep, I was definitely blushing.

"Come on, we've got one more stop to make, and I promise there's less physical exertion." Was it so wrong I hoped there'd be *more* getting physical at the next stop… and hopefully more privacy, too?

When we got back in the car, it hit me. I'd kissed Griffin. Or, he'd kissed me. Either way, it'd been in public where anyone could see. Where *Winston* could see. Crap. If he'd been following us, Griffin would be on his radar for sure.

I hadn't realized I'd been biting my lip until Griffin gently pulled it out from between my teeth and laced out fingers together. "Where'd you go?"

"That kiss…" I didn't want to ruin that perfect moment, but I was starting to freak out about something happening to him.

His face fell. "Do you regret it?"

"What? No!" I reached over and ran my hand along the stubble on his jaw, and he leaned into my touch. "No. I would never regret kissing you. It was just so public. If Winston's followin' me, you're definitely on his radar now."

He relaxed and pulled my hand away from his face, kissing the back of it before holding it in his lap. "Baby, I told you. Everything's going to be okay. I'm sure trust is something that I'm going to have to earn from you, and I'm good with that. You'll see."

I gave him a bit of a wobbly smile as we pulled up to our last stop. "Reading Terminal Market?" I read the sign aloud.

He nodded. "I figured we could walk around and check out the local artisans and stuff." He watched for my reaction, but I was excited. I loved stuff like that—local foods, arts, crafts, and flowers. I was obsessed with flowers, but I'd never told him that. I couldn't wait to get inside and see what they had.

I stepped out, and he followed behind me, wrapping his arm around my waist and dropping a kiss behind my ear that made me shiver. He let out a low chuckle that told me he knew exactly what he was doing before weaving our fingers together and leading me inside.

We walked the entire market, sampling all sorts of foods, and checking out beautiful art. His interpretations were always off the wall and hilarious, and he was great at making me laugh. There was something still innocent and so sweet about Griffin that made him easy to be with and completely contradicted how he looked. He made all my burdens and issues disappear when he was around.

On one of the last stops before we left to go back to the hotel, we stopped at a flower stall, and I turned to him. "Confession time. I'm what you might call a flower enthusiast," I divulged, whispering loudly like it was a big secret. His eyes widened almost comically, and he held his hand up over his mouth.

"No!" He said it with an exaggerated version of my Southern twang and a hand that flew up to his chest that had me giggling, and his expression morphed into an easy smile.

"Like this bouquet here?" I pointed to a bunch of red roses. "It's classically romantic and means love, but it's also boring." I wrinkled my nose, moving on to another group.

"And these?" I pointed to a group of colorful tulips. "Since they're yellow, they symbolize hopefulness."

"How about these?" Griffin asked, pointing to a bouquet of soft pink peonies, and I smiled softly. "Ah, these. Well, these are my favorite. Peonies are for telling someone you love that they're the most beautiful person you've ever seen."

"Oh, well, I'm definitely buying them for you then." He lifted them out of their container, and I blushed furiously. The only time I'd ever gotten flowers was when Winston was trying to apologize for losing his temper at the beginning. By the end, he didn't even try to act sorry for what he'd done. It was why I hated red roses.

Peonies, on the other hand, made me feel all dreamy and squishy inside with stupidly crush-like feelings toward Griffin. He handed me the bouquet after he paid, and I looked down at the soft pink petals and tried not to cry.

"Thank you." My voice was shaky and quiet as I leaned up on my toes and pressed a kiss to his cheek, feeling his rough stubble underneath my lips. I wrapped my arm around his bicep and rested my head on his shoulder as we walked back to the car in comfortable silence, and I tried to commit to memory the most perfect first date I'd ever had.

NINE
GRIFFIN

Leaving Magnolia at her door last night was brutal. We kissed and kissed until we were both breathless, and her lips were swollen and this gorgeous dark pink color. Since that night on the bus, I'd been dying to curl my body around hers and protect her while she slept. The dark circles under her eyes told me she wasn't sleeping, but I wasn't going to force myself on her.

I couldn't be the one to go to her again. She had to ask me, but once she did, that would be it. I wouldn't be going anywhere again. It killed me not to be able to make sure she got a good night's sleep or that her ex wasn't keeping her up with his harassing texts and calls.

What I wasn't so concerned about anymore were the reasons it wasn't smart for me to get involved in her problems. Somehow, all the reasons why I shouldn't didn't matter anymore. After last night—and if I was being honest with myself after the night we curled up in her bunk together—I didn't want to hold back anymore. There was something about Magnolia's wide-eyed innocence and damaged emotions that called to me to show her the world wasn't only filled with cruelty.

It was my new life's mission.

"Earth to Griffin," my brother's snarky voice cut through my Magnolia-centric thoughts.

I shifted my eyes in his direction and raised my eyebrow, lifting my orange juice, and taking a sip. He rolled his eyes, but his expression was amused. "Care to share what you were just thinking about, brother?"

I let a smug grin slip onto my face. "Not even a little bit."

He laughed as he cut into the stack of syrup-drenched pancakes on his plate. "I bet this has nothing to do with the sweet girl with the Southern drawl you're supposed to be keeping your distance from, right?"

Instead of responding, I grabbed a scone off the platter in the middle of the table and took a bite, leaning back against my chair and adopting a mask of indifference. If there was one thing I knew for sure, it was that I didn't want to hear judgment from my brother about how I wasn't listening to his advice.

"Fine, don't answer, but if you're anything like me, it was hopeless from the start to think you could stay away from the girl who finally caught your attention. I almost killed myself trying to keep my distance from Ryan." He got a far-off look in his eye and shuddered before his attention shifted back to me. "I sure as fuck don't want that for you. I had a feeling the other night it was already too late, but logic doesn't always win out in matters of the heart."

I choked on the sip of juice I'd just taken to wash down the dry scone, and Maddox reached over and pounded on my back. When I could breathe again without coughing, I laughed. "Matters of the heart? When the hell did you become a nineteenth-century poet?"

He looked smug as he shoved another bite of pancakes in his mouth. I looked around for Ryan, but she wasn't anywhere in the restaurant. No wonder he was eating like a complete slob. I wrinkled my nose at his antics. "What?" he wondered, taking in the disgust on my face.

"Nothing. I can't believe your wife lets you eat like that."

Maddox laughed. "I don't eat like this in front of her. That's a privilege I save just for you and the guys."

"Charming," I muttered, tossing my napkin onto the table. Not that I didn't love having my brother and the guys around every hour of every day, but I hoped I'd get to spend time with Magnolia before we had to be at soundcheck and the meet and greet this afternoon.

"And where the hell do you think you're going?" Maddox wondered, looking at me with a knowing glint in his eye as I stood up from the table.

"Out."

"Sure. Tell Magnolia I say hi."

I flipped him off as I left the restaurant with his laughter fading as I walked toward the hotel exit, going to do exactly that—find Magnolia. I hadn't seen her since I left her at her door last night, and I was worried about how she felt about our date and the very public makeout session we had now that she had time to think about it. My goal the night before had been to have fun and show her I was done trying to stay away.

Had I hoped the night would end like it did? Hell, yes. But I hadn't expected it. If anything, I figured Magnolia was the kind of girl who was cautious at best, who wanted to take things exceptionally slow, and who didn't trust easily. She'd surprised the shit out of me by not only opening up to me about her interests but also her ex—and letting me kiss her until neither one of us could breathe, and all I wanted to do was strip off her clothes and worship every inch of her body with my tongue.

I really liked that she wasn't predictable, and I had a feeling the more I got to know her, the more she'd keep me on my toes. I couldn't help the grin taking over my face at the thought.

Stepping into the parking lot, it didn't take me long to scan the area and realize Mags wasn't here. I wasn't all that surprised—it was almost ten a.m., and she was probably already at the arena making sure everything was running smoothly for tonight's show. I flagged down one of the security guys and caught a ride with him to the stadium.

If I had a few hours to kill before my to-do list kicked in, I wanted to spend them with Magnolia, even if it meant following her around like a desperate little puppy. When I stopped to think about it, that probably wasn't a great look for me, but I couldn't help it. She sucked me in and made me want to be around her in whatever capacity I could.

Waving my thanks at the tour security guy, I jumped out of the car and immediately spotted Magnolia's long, dark hair in a crowd of roadies carting our instruments into the venue. The stage had apparently already been set up, but I didn't really know. This being my first tour, I'd never given a lot of thought about how everything got to where it needed to be. I just showed up when I was told to and didn't ask questions.

Watching Magnolia take control of the situation and command these grown men to do her bidding shouldn't have been a turn on, but it was. My cock twitched in appreciation as I watched her work, content to stand back for a minute and observe as she spoke into the headset she wore before bending down to scoop Lucky into her arms.

That was my cue to make my presence known. She looked like she was having trouble balancing her job and the tiny puppy, so I'd take him off her hands for a little while. Whatever I could do to make Magnolia's life easier, and possibly get one of her sweet smiles that made my insides feel like they were melting into a puddle of lovesick mush, was exactly what I intended when I decided to come here early just to spend time with her. Or in her presence. Whatever I could get, really.

I stepped up behind her and waited for her to finish what she was saying to the guy in front of her. I recognized him as one of the equipment guys and gave him a head nod in greeting. Magnolia tensed up in front of me, and I stepped a little closer, wanting to reassure her it was just me, but I didn't get the chance before she was dismissing him and turning around to face me.

Her icy blue eyes widened with surprise and then warmed up when she realized it was me. "Griffin. Hey." Her voice came out a little husky and breathless, and my gaze dropped immediately to her soft, pink lips. I wanted to kiss her more than anything, but I didn't know where we stood after last night or how she was feeling. One thing was for sure—I wasn't going to do anything to make Magnolia uncomfortable. I'd rather chew off my own arm, and I was a drummer, so that would really suck.

I reached out and tucked a stray piece of her long, dark hair that had blown into her face behind her ear, letting my finger brush the velvety skin of her cheek, and she shivered under my touch. I grinned, loving her reaction to me, and she bit back a smile. "Hey. I thought I could take this little guy off your hands until soundcheck."

I reached for Lucky, and his tail started thumping against Magnolia's side. She laughed and handed him over as her shoulders relaxed. "Really? That's so sweet of you. I thought I was gonna have to learn to write left-handed."

"Not today. Do you need help with anything else? I'm here for whatever until soundcheck." I watched her expectantly, waiting and watching every tiny reaction and movement in her face, trying to interpret how she felt toward me this morning.

"Nope, I think I've got it." She gave me a smile that turned suddenly shy when we made eye contact, and my grin turned a little wicked as a soft pink blush stained her cheeks.

"Are you sure?" I wondered while running my fingers down her bare arm. I watched as goosebumps popped up in the wake of my touch, and she inhaled sharply before she stepped back and looked around to see if anyone had seen us.

Then her smile turned sad. "I'm sure. Thanks, Sugar." Her nickname for me up until now had always been sugary-sweet but dripping venom in a combination that made my dick hard, but not this time. This time she sounded resigned, and I hated it. She wasn't going to just give in to us; I was going to have to work a little harder for her.

My mom used to tell me that nothing worth having ever came easy, and damn if she wasn't right.

I took Lucky over to a grassy spot under a tree and plopped down, leaning my back against the rough bark where I could let him play in the grass and also watch Magnolia work. I wanted to be near her, sure, but I'd never interfere in her work. Her job was everything to her right now, and I wouldn't distract her from it, even if I wanted to pull her into my arms and kiss the shit out of her.

Besides, I was feeling pretty good about where we stood. We hadn't discussed where things were going with us yet, but she hadn't put up that cold front of hers again after last night, and that had to be progress. Right?

Lucky let out a tiny bark, and I chuckled as he attacked the laces on my boots. Spending time with the little grey ball of fur made something inside me click into place. Being young didn't mean I wasn't looking for more out of my life. I was living one dream now, but it wasn't my only one. Most of the guys in the band grew up in shitty homes or with parents who didn't give a crap about them. But not True and not me.

He and I had many late-night discussions about our families, and we were more similar in our upbringings than any of the other guys. My parents had always been loving and supportive, but more than that, they loved each other just as much as they loved me. Someday, I wanted a family like the one I'd grown up in. It'd taken me venturing out on my own into the world to realize that I didn't want the cold and detached feelings that came along with nightly hookups and having nothing to go home to at the end of the day except your money.

It all seemed so pointless, and after my relationship with Wynter, I was even more sure about wanting to settle down. Some guys needed to mess around before they were ready to stick with one person. I'd quickly discovered I wasn't one of those guys. I had only had the one relationship, and it'd been shitty, but I hadn't lost hope.

More and more, I wanted Magnolia to be the one I ran to when something amazing happened or to lean on when shit went south. For some reason, she made me feel like she was strong enough to hold me up when I couldn't do it myself but soft enough to let me hold her, too. That was something I wanted to explore.

My gaze drifted from where Lucky had curled up on my lap and passed out to where Magnolia was walking into the arena, followed by the audio engineer and Jericho.

At first, I wondered why he wanted to come on this tour and drag Moon and Benji along, too. But he explained he wanted to be sure the tour engineer did everything right, and Moon insisted on sticking around for our opening act, Tuesday Told a Secret. She and the lead singer, Bellamy, had become friends, and she didn't want to leave her alone on a tour with so many guys.

One thing was for sure—Jericho was a certifiable control freak. I was still glad he was on the road with us. He felt like my safety net. If, for some reason, I screwed up, he could step in, and the show would go on. Not that I thought a lot about messing up, but the doubt would creep in from time to time, and one look at Jericho and I'd relax.

When the door slammed against the wall where Jericho pulled it too hard, Magnolia jumped, and I could see her skin drain of color all the way from across the lot. I raked my hand through my hair as I kept watching her try to catch her breath as her gaze darted around the lot full of people who hadn't noticed anything was wrong with her. But I noticed.

She explained what happened with her ex, but she was really fucking rattled, and I hated it. I wanted to stalk across the parking lot and pull her into my arms and whisk her away someplace safe where the world couldn't touch her, and I had to clench my hands into fists and push my back harder into the scratchy bark behind me until it hurt to keep from jumping up and doing just that.

Somehow I didn't think she'd appreciate my protective display right now.

In an effort to keep myself grounded, I slid down further under the tree and picked Lucky up, setting him on my chest and petting his soft fur while I closed my eyes. The wind was blowing lightly, and between the perfect temperature, and Lucky's steady breathing, the tension slowly unfurled from my body, and I relaxed.

I didn't exactly fall asleep, but I lost track of time under that tree, daydreaming about the future and possibilities I wasn't sure I could ever have. It wasn't until Lucky's tiny body was lifted off of mine before my eyes snapped open, and I found myself staring into Magnolia's striking eyes. The light blue in the middle faded to navy around the edges, and I wanted to dive into them and never resurface.

She blinked a few times and then poked me in the side. "Time to get up, Sugar. Y'all have sound check in five minutes."

I scrubbed my hands over my face and prickly jaw before sitting fully up and stretching my arms overhead. My neck muscles were screaming at me for spending so much time slumped over next to a tree, but I was refreshed. I caught Magnolia's interested perusal of the exposed sliver of skin when the hem of my shirt lifted with my stretch, and I bit back my grin as she averted her eyes.

"Thanks for the wake-up, Mags." I pushed off the ground and stood up, dusting off my jeans.

"No problem. I appreciate you taking this little monster off my hands for a couple of hours," she said affectionately as Lucky gnawed on one of her fingers, and she giggled. The sound of her being happy ignited something inside of me, something that wanted to make her laugh like that every day. If anyone deserved to be happy, it was Magnolia.

"Anytime." I shoved my hands in my pockets, needing to touch her but not trusting myself right now with all the feelings rushing through my body. "I guess

I should go," I finally said, not moving from my spot. Walking away from her was always hard.

"I'll see you after the show." I tried not to get my hopes up at the promise in her voice. I wasn't entirely sure I wasn't projecting my own desires onto her, so instead, I nodded and took off for the arena. It was time to shut down everything else in my brain except the music.

The responsibility of entertaining thousands of people who forked over their hard-earned money to come see you was a heavy one, but one I took seriously. Thoughts of anything, but my job were pushed aside as I stepped into the building.

My eyes burned as sweat dripped down from my hair, and I tried to wipe it away, but the skin of my arm was just as slick. "Shit, someone throw me a towel," I demanded as I stepped off the stage, and soft cotton hit me in the face. I was quickly learning performing on stage for ninety minutes was the best workout I would probably ever have. I'd never been so completely drenched with sweat before in my life.

But it was a total fucking rush. There was nothing quite like the cheering crowd to pump my adrenaline so high, I felt like I could fly. I could see why the other guys wanted to keep playing even after they got married and had kids. This was only my third show, and I was already fucking addicted.

I dried off my face and neck the best I could before tossing the towel into a trash can and following Maddox's retreating back into our dressing room. Energy was bouncing around inside me, and I had no idea what to do to get rid of it. I figured I'd be exhausted from performing, but I wasn't. If anything, I was even more wound up.

"Let's go out," I suggested to the guys as they sat around shooting the shit and drinking their cocktail, or beer in Jericho's case, of choice.

The four of them all stopped what they were doing and turned to me at once. It was like a damn family of owls slow blinking their giant eyes at me at once, and I lifted my chin, not wanting to shrink back under the weight of their attention, but then Zen burst into laughter, and the rest of the guys followed him until they were all cracking up.

Assholes.

"What's so damn funny?" I demanded, scowling at them all as a group.

"Dude, it's midnight. You think my wife's going to want to get out of bed and leave our three-year-old to come out dancing?" True scoffed. "And who'd watch Phoenix? Magnolia?"

I shot an unimpressed glare in his direction at his suggestion. If I was going dancing, Mags was definitely coming, too. I had exactly zero interest in letting some random girl—or girls—from a club put their hands anywhere near me.

"Same goes for the rest of us. Sucks for you, kiddo, but we're all done with the bar hopping after a show shit," Zen answered more diplomatically than the rest, but he was still catching his breath from the fit of laughter at my suggestion, and so I didn't spare him the glare I'd just given True.

I groaned in frustration. "What am I supposed to do with all of this then?" I gestured to myself. "I feel like I'm not going to be able to sleep for days."

"Well, you could find a random groupie and fuck it out of your system," my brother suggested, an evil smirk tilting his lips up.

Folding my arms across my chest, I gave him my most unimpressed look, and he chuckled. He knew exactly what he was doing, the bastard. Finally, I threw my hands up. "I'm going back to the bus. I need a shower and food."

Leaving the assholes behind, I beelined it for the tour bus. That shit was crowded at the best of times, but if I could get there before all the families got back from the hotel for the drive to wherever we were headed next, I could hopefully squeeze in a quick shower.

I got lucky and managed to shower and get dressed before anyone else ventured onto the bus, so when I stepped out into the crisp night air, I closed my eyes and just let go. Breathing in and out, relaxing my shoulders, and listening to the sounds of the city. It wasn't until a soft hand wrapped around my bicep that I opened my eyes and looked down to find Magnolia staring up at me with a soft smile on her face.

I wanted to imprint that look into my memory forever, just one of a thousand I hoped to collect that showed all the different sides of Magnolia. This girl was seriously doing a number on me.

"Hey, beautiful." I smiled right back, and her grin widened. "Have dinner with me before we have to go?"

She bit her lip and looked away while she considered my offer. "I can't leave this area, but there's a food truck out front. Want to walk over there with this little guy and me?" She held up Lucky in her other arm, the one that wasn't still touching me and causing heat to soar through my veins straight to my dick.

The puppy perked up when he saw me and started squirming in her arms to try and get to me. I laughed and ruffled his ears before she set him on the ground and handed over his leash. "I'd love to."

We walked a little way across the emptying parking lot before either of us spoke up, and it was me that broke the silence. "Where are we headed next?"

"East Rutherford, New Jersey," she responded, and I noted she still hadn't let go of my arm. If I had it my way, she'd never let go. "We leave in a couple of hours."

I looked down at her, and her eyes were clouded, and a wrinkle had formed between her eyebrows. "Where'd you go, Mags?"

She blinked a couple of times before shaking her head slightly. "Sorry. I... am not looking forward to sleeping on the bus."

Last time we'd had an overnight on the bus, she had a nightmare, and I ended up in her bunk with her. I hated that she'd had a nightmare, but I loved that she let me hold her. "Want me to sleep in your bunk with you?" I offered, and I didn't even hide the hope from my eyes.

She looked at me warily before her shoulders slumped in relief. "Could you? Is it too much?"

"Hell, no. I was hoping you'd ask me, but you know what this means."

She stopped walking and looked up at me. "What does it mean?"

"There's no way you're getting rid of me now." I grinned at her and tugged her forward toward the food truck, which was only a few feet away.

"I don't think I want to," she mumbled, and I pretended I didn't hear her even as my heart jackhammered in my chest, and a slow smile stretched across my face.

After a surprisingly delicious meal eaten sitting on a curb, I took Lucky back to the bus while Magnolia finished checking off everything that needed to be done before we could leave. I set the puppy down on my bunk while I changed into a pair of grey sweatpants and a white t-shirt. I normally slept in just my underwear, but I didn't think Magnolia would appreciate me hopping into her bunk in only a pair of tight boxer briefs, so sweats and a t-shirt it was.

Lucky watched me knowingly while he rolled around on his back, his tongue lolling out of his mouth, and I chuckled at his antics. "You're getting hair all over my bed," I scolded, but I really didn't care. He was too damn cute for his own good, and sometimes when he looked at me, it felt like he knew what I was thinking.

Once I was done, I grabbed my phone and pulled the curtain closed on my bunk after scooping Lucky up into my arms and moved down the hallway to Magnolia's bunk. I pulled the curtain aside and slipped inside against the back wall, dropping Lucky near my feet. He curled up and settled in, and I took out my phone and opened Netflix. I still had probably another hour before Magnolia climbed onboard, and everyone else had already gone to bed.

Despite my earlier energy rush, I was definitely ready to wind down now, so I turned on an episode of *Stranger Things* even though I'd seen it probably ten times and zoned out to it until Magnolia pulling back the curtain to climb inside made me jump. "Hope you don't mind me hanging out in here waiting for you," I whispered, not wanting to wake anyone up. She shook her head and smiled tiredly at me.

"I don't mind. I'm going to change. I'll be right back." She got up and grabbed some clothes from the storage space under the bunk, and I rolled over onto my back, staring at the ceiling. What were the chances that Magnolia liked to sleep in oversized shirts and ratty flannel pants?

My hopes of that were dashed when she came back looking like a fucking wet dream in tiny sleep shorts and a tank top that left *nothing* to the imagination.

I could not only see a sliver of her flat stomach, but her hard nipples, too, and I groaned, ripping my eyes away. "Jesus."

"What?" she whispered, looking down at herself.

I ignored my cock, which was suddenly very much awake and wanting to play. "Nothing. Come here," I demanded, holding open my arms but trying not to look at her as she climbed into bed with me and settled her back against my chest.

Shit, my hard-on was definitely noticeable against her ass as she wiggled against me and settled in, and it took everything in me not to push my hips forward and show her the extent of the effect she had on my body. Instead, I took a shaky breath and wrapped my arm around her waist with the other one under her head. "Is this okay?" she whispered again, and her vanilla scent filled the bunk, and every sense I had was filled with Magnolia.

It was overwhelming in the best way, and I let go, surrendering to the inevitable. This girl had the ability to destroy me completely, and I'd happily let her if she let me hold her like this every night. "Better than okay, Mags. Now go to sleep." Even to my own ears, my whisper sounded deeper and more gravelly than usual.

It was going to be a long damn night of the best kind of torture I'd ever experienced. I only hoped she'd let me do it again and again.

TEN
MAGNOLIA

My back was warm, and something hard was poking me in the butt. It wasn't until I cracked an eye open, I realized I was still in my bunk with Griffin, and the something hard was his huge erection. And by the feel of it, he didn't have anything to be embarrassed about. His arms tightened around my waist as I wiggled my hips almost involuntarily.

There was something about being close to him that made me want to throw my inhibitions out the window and push his buttons to see what he'd do. If I was honest with myself—and I was trying really hard not to be—I wanted him more than I'd ever wanted anyone. I hadn't even known wanting someone so much was possible until I met Griffin.

Now here I was with his body wrapped around mine in my bed where it was impossible to resist the urge for *more*. When I shifted my hips again, his palm stretched out across my stomach where his fingertips dug lightly into my skin. "Mags," he warned, his voice rough from sleep.

My reasons for not wanting to get involved with Griffin were still there, but they'd managed to take a backseat to the spell he was weaving on my body by his mere presence. Besides, it wasn't like Winston could see what was going on in the bunk on the tour bus while we were driving, was it?

For the moment, I was safe and whatever I decided to do about my self-proclaimed crush on Griffin was free from prying eyes. I wanted to take full advantage of such a rare occasion, and Griffin's warning only spurred me on.

This time, I didn't just shift my hips; I rolled my body against his hard length, and the control he'd been holding onto snapped. One of his hands trailed slowly downward while the other went up until he held a handful of my breast in his large palm, and his thumb brushed across my nipple. I moaned softly, and he bit my earlobe before whispering, "Careful, or someone might hear you."

His voice was full of wicked promises, and I arched my back to try and push his hand lower. His fingers dragged along the skin just above the waistband of my sleep shorts before he slipped them inside.

"*Jesus.* You aren't wearing panties?" he groaned as his hand slid further into my shorts and his fingers circled my clit without ever touching me where I needed him to. Griffin's warm breath teased the sensitive skin of my neck before his lips and tongue were tasting every bit of me he could.

My hand reached back until my fingers tangled in his hair, trying to pull him closer while I tried not to cry out as his finger slipped inside me. "So damn tight," he grunted before pulling his finger out and pushing it back in. My eyes rolled back, and a needy whimper escaped my lips as he added a second finger.

Griffin's fingers were rough and calloused from his drumsticks, but he knew how to use them, playing my body like an instrument he was trying to master. His thumb found my clit, and with just the right amount of pressure, I was coming undone on his hand. When I'd come down enough to be able to think, he captured my lips in a heated kiss that had my toes curling. "You're so goddamn sexy when you come," he whispered against my ear, sucking his fingers into his mouth and licking them clean as my cheeks heated up under the intensity of his dark stare.

Rolling onto my back, his thumb brushed across my nipple again, and when I licked my lips, his gaze dropped to my mouth, and he groaned in frustration. "I'm trying to be good, Mags. I really am. But you're making me so fucking hard, I might actually go insane if I don't get inside your perfect body and soon. Today's not that day, though. When we fuck for the first time, it's not going to be in a tiny bunk on the tour bus. I want room to worship every delicious inch of your body like you deserve."

When Griffin laid it all out like he had, that was exactly what I wanted, too. Our eyes locked, and he tore himself away, reaching behind him for my phone and handing it to me. He confiscated it when I crawled into bed, deciding he would deal with Winston's neverending texts and phone calls overnight so I could sleep. Yet another reason why I was having a hard time remembering why I should be keeping my distance from him.

"You figure out how much longer until we're at the stadium; I'll go grab coffee." He kissed my forehead and crawled over me to get out of the bunk, but not before he noticed my scrunched up face. "What?"

"I don't drink coffee. It's too bitter."

He chuckled softly. "Okay, Mags. What do you drink?"

"Chai tea with milk and sugar." I'd stashed an entire box of my favorite kind in the kitchen as soon as we'd boarded the bus for Portland.

"You got it."

I scrolled through my phone while he left, responding to a couple of emails and texts from the crew before noticing that there weren't any missed calls or messages from Winston to deal with. Either he'd given up—yeah, right—or Griffin had dealt with him. Whether that meant blocking him or deleting the evidence, I wasn't sure, but it was a relief to not have to start the day with the reminder that my ex-boyfriend was hunting me like his favorite prey and not in the fun, sexy way.

More like in a he'll-murder-me-if-he-catches-me way. A shiver worked its way through my whole body at the thought of that, and I checked the itinerary before putting my phone away. I didn't want to tempt fate by staring at it too long this morning.

By the time Griffin got back, Lucky had moved up from the corner he'd claimed at the bottom of my bunk into the warm spot Griffin had been sleeping in, and I had to balance the two steamy mugs he'd brought back with him so he could pick up my puppy and settle back in.

Lucky seemed content to curl up between us, and Griffin held out his arm until I rested my head on his chest, and I handed back over his cup of caffeine. "Alright, Sugar," I started after sipping my perfectly made chai, "we've got an hour until East Rutherford. What do you want to do?"

He let out a low growl that had every bit of me clenching up with desire, but he pulled out his phone. "We're going to binge something on Netflix, minus the chill." He sounded about as happy about that as I was.

I smiled over the rim of my mug as he scrolled through the shows. At least he was just as affected as me. "You ever watch *Stranger Things*, Mags?"

I shook my head, and he grinned in a way that lit up his whole face and made my breath catch in my throat. "Well, then we better start from the beginning."

Staccato beats reverberated through the cavernous arena, and with the way the space was cast into complete darkness, every sense was on high alert as Griffin struck his drum to start the show. I couldn't see him, but I could still picture exactly how his long fingers were wrapped around the rough wood of his sticks and the way every muscle in his body rippled and flowed as if he wasn't quite real with the way he created the beat that reminded me of a headboard banging against a wall.

It was sensual, this song. Pure sex and everyone in the crowd—me included—was turned on by the end. I wasn't all that sexually adventurous or open about it. In fact, my limited experience with sex meant that even talking about it made me blush furiously, but there was something about the way this particular beat pounded through the floor and echoed up my body, vibrating it in just the right spots that had me breathing like I'd run a marathon by the time it was over.

And when the lights came up, and Zen ripped the microphone out of the stand before sauntering over to True, I barely noticed because I couldn't stop watching Griffin, who was watching me right back. "He's good, right?" someone yelled near my ear, and I jumped while Zen's wife, Kennedy, laughed. "Sorry if I scared you."

My heart was pounding, but I gave her a tight smile. I was not a fan of people surprising me, not after Winston, but Kennedy wasn't a threat, and I started to calm down. "Don't worry about it."

I looked down where she had her son, Nico, on her hip, and he was completely fixated on his dad on the stage. His giant ear protection headphones were almost as big as his head, and I laughed a little at the sight.

Kennedy stayed beside me for the rest of the show, where we danced and sang along next to the stage. I tried not to let Griffin's penetrating stare affect me, but by the time the concert was over, my legs were shaky, and my panties were drenched. There was just something about watching his stage presence that made me want to climb him like a tree.

Kennedy swept me up in a side hug before she left to go backstage, and I couldn't help feeling like maybe we could be friends. I wasn't sure I'd ever had a female friend before; even when I was in school, I mostly kept to myself. It was nice to think maybe I could have that with Kennedy and some of the other wives. They seemed like a welcoming and friendly group, but I was scared to let myself hope and let my guard down.

I grabbed my tablet from where I'd left it when I decided to take a few minutes to enjoy the show and scrolled through the list of stuff I needed to check on and get done before we could leave for Atlanta tomorrow afternoon. Thoughts of how hot Griffin was on stage were going to have to be pushed to the back of my mind until later tonight when I'd hopefully be able to convince him to sleep in my bunk again.

It wasn't the most comfortable, and with two of us, there was almost no room, but as long as Griffin was there with me, it felt cozy, and I could actually relax. Being a burden wasn't exactly something I strived for, so I was hesitant to lean on Griffin too much. Still, he seemed to want to spend time with me, and I sure as heck slept better than I had in years in his arms last night.

If I could do a repeat every night, I would. Was that asking too much of him, though?

I didn't know, and I couldn't worry about it right now. Now I needed to make sure all the instruments and earpieces were returned and accounted for, the stage crew was starting breakdowns, and foodservice had dinner ready for the guys and the crew.

It was a couple of hours later when I realized I hadn't taken Lucky out in way too long, so I rushed back to the bus only to find my little furball was nowhere to be found. I checked in with Amara and Ryan, but neither one had seen him. I was starting to get concerned when I spotted him on a grassy area with Griffin holding the end of his leash.

I made my way across the parking lot, trying not to stare at how hot the freshly-showered rock star in front of me looked in his ripped jeans and a tight, white t-shirt. His wavy brown hair was still damp, and the urge to reach up and run my fingers through it was strong. His smile knocked the worry and irritation of a few minutes ago straight out of me, and I found myself smiling back. "I thought Lucky could stretch his legs before another long night on the bus," he explained, looking down at my puppy with eyes full of affection.

I was learning that was how Griffin was, though. He was generous and sweet and thoughtful. Lucky wasn't his responsibility, but here he was, making sure he was taken care of. It was a lot like how he was treating me, and not at all what I expected from someone famous. Shouldn't he be a spoiled, entitled, egomaniac?

"That was really thoughtful of you, Sugar. I know Lucky loves you."

"At least someone around here does," he teased, his lips tilting up in a heart-stopping smile.

"Oh, I'm sure your brother loves you," I tossed back, and he laughed, the sound rich and full and warming me all the way down to my toes.

He stepped closer to me and leaned down so our noses were practically touching, his lips hovering just over mine. "I think your body loves me, too."

It was a struggle not to close the minuscule space between us, but any thoughts of professionalism or Winston were quickly fleeing my brain. "Oh?" I tried for indifference, and I failed miserably when my voice came out shaky, and he smiled like he knew exactly what he was doing to me.

Griffin ran his nose down mine before he kissed me. Kissing him was like being swept up in a storm, like lightning was crackling throughout my entire body, and I wrapped his shirt in my fist and tried to pull him closer. I was lost in him, in the feel of his hard body pressed up against mine, and his spicy citrus scent filling my lungs until all I was breathing in was Griffin. He pulled away and kissed me one more time before grinning. "See?" He asked it as if he'd just proven some great point, and maybe he had.

My cheeks heated, and I bit my lip, looking down at Lucky and trying to catch my breath, but Griffin wasn't letting me escape his intensity tonight. He pulled my lip from between my teeth with the pad of his thumb, and I looked up into his dark eyes. They were practically glittering as he watched me. "Only I get to bite this lip," he decided before he nipped at it, and goosebumps broke out along every inch of my skin in response.

A wicked smile crossed his lips before he looked at the bus and then back at me. "And you can't kiss me like that again until we're in a hotel room. I made a promise to myself I wouldn't make you mine in a bunk on a bus, and you're too damn tempting when you wrap yourself around me like the only thing you want is me inside you."

I stood there speechless, my cheeks burning, not sure what to even say back to that. No one had talked to me like Griffin did. I'd never known anyone to be so blunt about their feelings, so open and upfront with what they wanted. It was a huge turn on, and I found myself liking it more than maybe I should.

Or maybe I'd been punished and dragged down long enough by my past, and it was okay to want something again. Maybe Griffin wasn't Winston, and I should give him a shot until he proved me wrong. It was so hard, though, to trust because where Winston had hit me with a wrecking ball and destroyed everything about myself I used to love, I had a feeling if I let Griffin in, if things went the way they had with Winston, I would never recover.

At what point was it okay to take a chance on something that had the potential to be life-changing? I was still figuring it out, but one thing I knew for sure was I found myself wanting to spend all my free time—and all of my not-free time, too, if I was honest with myself—with Griffin.

"Don't hurt yourself," Griffin said, following lazily behind Lucky, who was intent on sniffing every single thing in the area and peeing on at least half.

"Huh?"

He chuckled. "Thinking so hard. You looked like you were going to give yourself a headache."

I cracked a smile at the way he always seemed to be able to pull me out of my heavy thoughts. "No headaches here, but I'm exhausted." I waited to see if he'd invite himself to sleep with me, and he didn't disappoint.

"I don't see how this little guy could possibly have any more urine in his body, so it seems like a good time to go to bed. You know you're stuck with me from now on, right?"

A smile crept onto my face as I nodded slowly at him.

"Good." He tossed his arm over my shoulders and pulled me into his body as we walked back toward the bus with Lucky scampering ahead and yipping happily at nothing at all. Griffin kissed my temple and breathed me in without any shame or trying to hide it. "You smell so damn good, Mags. I can't get enough."

I didn't know what to say to that, so I said nothing. Instead, I leaned into him and relaxed into his body until I had no choice but to pull away because we had to step onto the bus single file.

It wasn't until I ran into his back once we were inside the bus that I noticed his body had become tense as he shielded me from the kitchen space. "Did you order takeout?" he asked, and I leaned around him to see a bag of food with a photo attached.

"No, what is that?" I wasn't sure I wanted the answer.

"Don't know." He moved forward and plucked the picture up, studying it before I watched his jaw clench as he picked up the bag and threw it and the picture away. He spun and grabbed my hand, pulling me up the narrow stairs to the top of the bus where our bunks were, leading me over to my bunk.

"What are you doing?"

"Taking you to bed." The words should've had my thighs clenching together, but instead, my heart was beating erratically in my chest because whatever he'd seen in the kitchen had completely thrown his mood off.

Instead of questioning him, I watched as he stripped off his clothes until he was in only a tight black pair of boxer briefs that didn't leave much to the imagination and then climbed into my bunk without one single comment on my obvious ogling. He reached out and grabbed Lucky, pulling him inside and getting him settled while I changed into some boy shorts and a tank top before climbing inside, too, and pulling the curtain closed behind me.

"I want to talk to Connor about Winston," Griffin finally broke the silence by saying, and I tensed.

"Why? What was in the kitchen?" I asked gently, keeping my voice almost a whisper. Everyone else was asleep, and not only that, but I didn't want to make Griffin think I couldn't handle whatever it was he'd seen. I'd been dealing with Winston's messed up antics for a long time by myself—whatever he did at this point wasn't going to be new or shocking.

The only difference now was that I'd gotten close to Griffin, and I didn't know how Winston would react. He'd made threats in the past when the prospect of me being with anyone else had been vague since I had no interest in that. Now it was a matter of waiting to see what he'd do. He'd been ruthless toward me in the past, but he had to have limits to the actions he'd take, right?

It wasn't like he wanted to end up in prison or hurt anyone except me. No, he saved his evil bullshit just for me. Wasn't that sweet of him? I snorted at my internal sarcasm, and Griffin eyed me but didn't ask.

He must've decided I could handle whatever it was, even if it sounded like every whispered word was being torn out of his mouth involuntarily. "A picture of the two of us in Philly." His jaw clenched, and my heart sped up to heart attack-inducing levels.

"I really hoped that since he'd been quiet outside of phone calls for a few days that he would've laid off following me." I twisted my fingers together, trying to distract myself from the fear dousing every nook and cranny of my entire being, but Griffin pried my hands apart and laced his fingers with mine instead.

"Has it been like this since you left him?" he questioned softly, using his other hand to play with the ends of my hair, and I relaxed into him, at least as much as I could while also in a panic.

I nodded. "There have been periods of time—usually when I move to a new place or get a new phone number—where I have a few days or a few weeks of peace, and I think he's finally given up and moved on. Once, I got a whole month Winston-free." A small smile broke free at the memory before it quickly slipped off my face.

"This is why we have private security, Mags. Connor can help."

This time I shook my head. "I don't want to drag your guys into my mess. Winston's mostly harmless. He just likes to remind me that I can't escape him, but after I left, he's never gotten close enough to hurt me again."

It was already unfair of me to get involved with Griffin when Winston was out there making threats, but I couldn't seem to stay away from him no matter how hard I tried. I was exhausted from trying to keep my distance, and with everything else going on, I didn't have the strength to keep it up anymore.

But mostly?

Mostly, I didn't want to.

I liked Griffin. He made me feel safe and beautiful and strong—all things I thought I lost under Winston's oppressive thumb. It wasn't fair of me to want him, but this one time, I was going to be selfish if he'd let me. I glanced up at his silhouette in the dark bunk, the only light coming from around the edge of the curtain.

As if he could read the thoughts running through my mind, his gravelly voice cut through the low hum of the road running underneath the bus's tires. "You know I'm not going anywhere, right? No matter what your ex throws our way, I'm not giving up on you, Magnolia Dawson. Not for anything."

Tears pricked at my eyes, and I blinked them away, but not before one fell down my cheek and dripped onto Griffin's chest where I'd moved to rest my head. I didn't know what to say back, so I let my actions say what I didn't know how to express—all the gratitude and caring I felt toward this man who didn't need to stand by my side but was doing it anyway. I curled against his body, pressing my lips to the spot on his chest just above his heart before his arms tightened around me, and I closed my eyes, drifting off to sleep in the safety of Griffin's arms and with the promise in his words settling something deep inside myself I hadn't even known I needed.

ELEVEN
MAGNOLIA

"If I have to spend another minute on this goddamn bus, I'm going to lose my fucking mind." Maddox was stalking back and forth down the hall from the lounge room to the bathroom at the back, past all the bunks and back again. He'd been at it for about twenty minutes with no sign of stopping, and Griffin laughed at his brother while his thumb rubbed circles into the exposed skin of my shoulder, making me shiver.

He smirked at me like he knew exactly the response my body had to his touch before he looked back up at his brother. "Dude, we only have about an hour until Atlanta. Calm the hell down. Have a drink or something."

Maddox glared at his brother before stomping down the stairs to where the rest of the guys were taking turns entertaining the kids with video games they were definitely too young for. The thirteen-hour bus ride from New Jersey to Atlanta had us all going a little stir crazy, and if it hadn't been for the stop we made for gas a few hours ago, I'd have been worried for poor Lucky.

A tour bus was not an ideal place for a growing puppy to be.

His fluffy body careened into my feet as the bus changing lanes made him lose his balance where he was gnawing on a rope toy Griffin bought him before we left New Jersey. Warmth radiated through my chest at his thoughtfulness. Lucky wasn't his responsibility, yet Griffin acted like he was just as much his dog as he was mine, and something about that made me want to burrow myself in his arms and never come up for air.

"Whoa, buddy," Griffin chuckled, reaching down and picking Lucky up, cradling him under one strong arm before grabbing the rope hanging out of his mouth and tugging on it until Lucky growled.

I sighed, feeling completely content at the moment but knowing it was almost up. When we were moving—on the bus or in the air—was the only time I truly felt I could relax. No matter how hard he tried, Winston couldn't travel and keep his eyes on me at the same time, not unless he suddenly developed the ability to be in two places at once.

At the sound of my breath leaving my body, Griffin looked over at me with an eyebrow raised. "I guess I should go let everyone know the game plan for the rest of the day tomorrow." I pulled the iPad from the seat next to me into my lap, powering it on.

"I'll come with you," Griffin offered, standing up with Lucky still cradled between his arm and his body, the black lines of his tattoos peeking out under Lucky's wispy grey fur. I followed him down the stairs to the bottom level, where everyone was crowded between the U-shaped couch at the front of the bus behind the driver and the booth in the kitchen. It was pretty much mayhem between all the guys in the band, their wives, and their kids.

I clapped my hands a few times to get everyone's attention, and when all eyes turned to me, I felt my cheeks heat but pushed on anyway. "Since we're almost in Atlanta, I wanted to talk to y'all about how the next couple of days are gonna go." I paused, making sure I still had everyone's attention before carrying on.

"I'll be checkin' everyone into hotel rooms for the night, and you'll have the afternoon and tonight off. Tomorrow, y'all won't have anythin' on your schedules until soundcheck at three. There's a fan meet and greet at four, and then you'll have the rest of the evenin' free until showtime." I glanced down at the tablet in my arms to make sure I hadn't left anything out.

"Oh, after the meet and greet, Harrison set up an hour of interviews with local press. The fan meet and press tour will take place in the same room, so you guys can just hang out while everyone comes to you," I added.

"It's been years since we were in Atlanta. What are we doing tomorrow?"

True wondered, looking at Zen on his left, who turned and looked at Maddox.

Maddox shrugged, but Griffin spoke up. "I've got an idea, but it's a surprise. Let's meet in the hotel lobby at ten."

"Whatever you're planning better be kid-friendly, Griffin," Kennedy warned, leveling a glare on him that would have me quaking in my size eight designer heels—a definite weakness of mine and one that always made me feel more powerful when I had them on. Having to leave my collection behind when I'd walked away from Winston sucked, but I was slowly building it back up. Or at least I had been until I could only pack a couple of bags to fit on this bus.

It'd been worth it, though, even if I only had this one pair with me.

He held up his hands in surrender and looked around at the kids of Shadow Phoenix with that softness in his eyes that made me melt every time I saw it. "It will be, promise."

Kennedy nodded, appeased, and went back to trying to wrangle Nico away from the controller he was wielding like a weapon at Phoenix, True's daughter. Benji, Jericho's son, wiggled on his mom's lap like he wanted in on that action, and I bit my lip to stifle the laugh that wanted to burst free. There was never a dull day managing this tour, but the kind of chaos these families caused was the best kind—the kind that made you laugh and your heart feel light and full.

Lucky wriggled his entire body and started making a high pitched whining noise as he tried to free himself from Griffin so he could go play with the kids. His little blue eyes glinted as he watched them, and that spelled trouble, but probably adorable trouble that I'd want to take a thousand pictures of. Griffin laughed and set him down, and before his little paws even hit the ground, he was bounding over to Phoenix, tail wagging furiously.

The giggles of the kids mixed with Lucky's high-pitched yips of delight, and I could've sworn my heart was about to explode with adorable overload. I was right—I'd need a million pictures of this moment because the cuteness was almost overwhelming.

Griffin plucked my phone out of my back pocket and took a couple of pictures while he chuckled at Lucky's antics. My puppy was climbing over Phoenix to get to Nico, who shrieked and climbed over his mom's lap and buried his face in his dad's chest.

Zen laughed, and he and Kennedy exchanged a look—you know, one of those *looks* that couples have where they're talking to each other without having to say a word. I had a feeling Nico had a puppy in his future.

The bus stopped moving, and I looked out the little window over the tiny kitchen sink. We'd come to a stop in the back lot of the arena, and I grabbed Lucky from where he was licking Nico's entire face with enthusiastic strokes of his tongue. His tail thumped against my side as I carried him outside, and Griffin followed me out. I closed my eyes and let the sun hit my face, and Griffin moved up behind me so close that I could feel the heat of his body against my back, just as warm as the sun on my face.

"You're not going to need your own room tonight," he whispered in my ear, his voice like a soft caress that had me practically liquifying into a pool of lust. The promise in his quiet voice wasn't lost on me, and my nipples tightened in response. "Or ever again," he added. My heart flip-flopped in my chest, feeling like it was stopping and starting again at his words.

Did he really mean that? I turned as he wrapped his arms around my waist and searched his eyes for any sign of hesitation or trickery, but there was none. Griffin was an open book, and he wore his heart on his sleeve, something I was learning about him as time went on, and we got to know each other better. Somehow, the world hadn't beaten the kindness out of him yet—the hope and belief that love could triumph over anything and all a person needed was someone in their corner still burned bright deep inside of Griffin Spencer.

"I won't?" I managed to squeak out because if it hadn't come out a squeak, his nearness would've probably made me whimper or moan, and that would've been embarrassing as hell.

He shook his head before leaning down and hovering his very kissable lips right over mine so they were barely brushing against my mouth with every word. "I told you before, but I'll say it as many times as it takes to sink in. You're stuck with me now, and I'm not going anywhere."

If those words would've come from anyone else, I'd have probably gotten angry and told them exactly where they could stick their misogynistic bull crap. But from Griffin? I wanted to believe I could lean on him, and I desperately wanted to trust someone again. Why not this tempting as sin rocker with a heart as pure as freshly fallen snow?

Griffin's deep chuckle vibrated through my entire body as he placed a soft kiss on my lips and pulled back. "Now go do your job, Miss Dawson, and I'll see you tonight." He let me go and walked backward, his smile wide and his eyes lit up with mischief as he continued moving backward toward the bus without taking his eyes off me until he finally had to turn to climb the stairs back up inside.

Once I was able to shake off how flustered Griffin made me, I got everyone settled in and the crews moving like the well-oiled machines they'd become. The hours flew by, and before I knew it, the sun had set, and the stars were out in full effect. I was exhausted as I dragged myself up to the hotel room Griffin and I were sharing.

When he'd collected the room key, he'd also commandeered Lucky and left me with a heated kiss that had my panties soaking and a promise for naughty things to come later tonight.

I couldn't wait, and now that it was later, every step toward the room made my heart beat a little faster until, when I stood outside the door, it felt like I'd just ridden a roller coaster. My hand shook a little as I shoved the keycard into the slot and waited for the light to turn green. One last deep breath, and I pushed inside the room.

It was bigger than I expected, and the lights were low. Staying with Griffin meant I got the chance to experience what staying in a suite was like—something I'd never been able to do on my own up to this point. The soft orange glow of the lit fireplace danced across the wall in a mesmerizing pattern. I stepped inside and set my tablet on the desk, kicking my shoes off and dropping my bag. I hadn't seen Griffin yet, but there was more than one room, and he could be anywhere.

"Griffin?" I called out as I wandered toward the small galley kitchen separated from the living space by an island.

"In here." His voice sounded muffled and like it was coming from what I assumed was the bedroom, so I pushed through the door and quickly scanned the room. The bed was still made, and it looked untouched, but the light was on in the bathroom, and the door was cracked open. I pushed the door the rest of the way open and stepped into a scene that had me giggling in seconds. Griffin was trying to wrangle Lucky in the bathtub, and there were water and bubbles absolutely everywhere.

Griffin's shirt was soaked and clung to every dip and bulge of his muscular chest and well-defined six-pack like a second skin, and Lucky stopped his thrashing long enough to look at me with wild, desperate eyes that were practically begging me to save him from this torture. I was laughing so hard I couldn't breathe, and tears were running down my face. Griffin kept his grip on Lucky and looked at me helplessly. "Are you going to stand there laughing at us all night, or are you going to help me?"

I snorted but stripped off my sweater and moved over to the side of the tub next to him. His scent wrapped around me, and I couldn't help the inhale I took, filling my lungs up with Griffin. "What happened?"

"I found a dog park down the road, so we went for a walk, but apparently something died in there, and this little brat decided to roll around in it. He smelled so bad I gagged riding the elevator with him, so I thought I'd clean him up before you got back. It turns out Lucky isn't a fan of baths."

I bit my lip to keep from laughing, but my eyes started to water from the effort. I reached for the cup he'd brought into the tub and filled it with warm water. "You hold him; I'll rinse."

With the use of both of his hands, Griffin was able to get a much better hold on Lucky while I washed the soap out of his fur. I grabbed one of the oversized fluffy white towels from the rack and dried Lucky off until he looked like a damp poofball. I lifted him out of the tub and then wrapped him up in the towel and set him on the bathmat before standing up where I took in the soaked mess that was Griffin.

"I wanted tonight to be romantic, and instead, you got to walk into this." He gestured to himself and Lucky, who was now cleaner but still completely soaked and with a wild look in his eye that I didn't think meant anything good.

Sliding my hands up his impressive chest and higher still, I brushed some stray bubbles that had been left behind on his cheek away before I pulled his mouth down to mine and kissed him. "Oh, I dunno. Tight, wet t-shirts are a good look for you. Besides, you don't think taking care of my dog is romantic?"

His lips curved into a smile against mine. "Is that all it takes to get you to fall for me?"

"I'd say you're off to a good start," I admitted, letting him kiss me again and ignoring Lucky as he wiggled free from the towel he'd been wrapped in and tore out of the bathroom like hellhounds were chasing him.

Laughter bubbled up from Griffin's chest, and I echoed it as we turned and watched him run around the room. When Griffin leveled his attention back on me, the darkness in his eyes had my breath catching in my throat. His pupils were almost entirely black, and his eyes were hooded with so much desire, it was like a tangible force in the space between us that had goosebumps breaking out along my entire body.

"Come here," he ordered, and there was no way I could deny him. My feet moved forward, closing the small distance between us as he wrapped me up in his arms again. His chest pressed against mine, and I let out a half-whimper, half-moan as he kissed me again. This kiss wasn't like any of the others. This one was worshipful and deep, slow and tantalizing in a way that promised he'd show me exactly how talented that pierced tongue of his was.

I could feel every bit of his hard body as it pressed against mine, and my knees started to buckle, but he caught me in his firm grip and held me up while nipping and kissing a line down my jaw and neck. He bent down and grabbed my thigh, urging me to wrap it around his waist, and I complied first with my left leg, then with my right until my core was settled right over his hard length, and he was holding me up in his strong hands.

There was something about Griffin that set me aflame—something that had my insides quivering and my panties drenched. He was irresistible, someone I couldn't get close enough to, and that scared me. But right now?

Now, I'd push my fears aside and enjoy the pleasure I knew he'd bring to my body. His long fingers dug into my hips and pulled me closer as he walked us into the bedroom and dropped me onto the bed. I watched hungrily as he stripped off his soaked shirt and tossed it aside. "If you keep looking at me like that, this isn't going to last very long," he scolded, and I licked my lips in response.

His answering growl made my core clench in anticipation. I'd only ever been with Winston, and I didn't think he'd ever actually given me an orgasm when we had sex. Since he was all I had to go off of experience-wise, Griffin had practically blown my mind with just his fingers the other night in my bunk.

What would he do with an entire hotel room and the whole night stretching out in front of us? I could hardly wait to find out.

With agonizingly slow movements, he flicked open the button on his jeans and pulled the zipper down, showing off the amazing V where his defined abs ran into his boxers, and I was holding my breath, waiting for him to reveal the rest of himself to me. Instead, he crawled up my body and kissed me like he couldn't take another second without tasting me. His kisses were possessive and deep, the little metal ball in his tongue massaging against my own and making me squirm.

His bare, sculpted chest pressed down against me, and suddenly I hated the layers of fabric between us and reached down to pull my shirt off. Griffin ripped his lips away from mine just long enough for me to tug the shirt over my head and toss it away.

Before it was even out of my hand, his lips were back on mine, consuming me and making me dizzy with fevered kisses. He groaned as he grabbed a handful of my hair and deepened the kiss before tilting my head to the side. He trailed a scorching path with his lips down my jaw and neck to the top of my breasts. My entire body was pulsing like Griffin was creating a beat with his drums, only this time he used his touch to play my body as his instrument.

I gasped as he pulled me upright, unhooking my bra with swift fingers before laying me back down gently and yanking the piece of lingerie off my body as if it had personally offended him. The cool air had my nipples tightening, and when his thumb brushed across one, I arched my back involuntarily up into his hard chest. The man was built like my wet dream come to life, all toned and tattooed. I could've drooled over his abs alone for at least a couple of weeks without blinking.

I wanted Griffin so dang bad it was actually painful, and I wrapped my legs around his waist, trying to pull him closer. He was so hard, and I let out a whimper when he pushed his length against my core. "Shit, baby. You're killing me with those little sounds you keep making."

He rocked against me a few times before moving down my body, his tongue painting a lazy path down my flat stomach and around my belly button before he stopped and nipped at the sensitive skin over my hip. I squirmed underneath him, a mixture of pleasure and pain blossoming across my skin where his teeth no doubt left small imprints I'd be able to see later.

A dark chuckle rumbled through him as he moved lower, pulling my jeans and panties off in one smooth tug, so I laid bare beneath him. "Jesus, Mags. You're breathtaking." I watched as his heated gaze got even darker as he sat back and drank me in. I'd never been all that comfortable in my body—Winston always pointed out my flaws as if I didn't already know they were there. This was so much different.

Griffin looked at me like he'd never seen anything more beautiful, and I was practically panting at the raw lust burning under the surface. "I need to taste you."

His words had me tensing up. No one had ever gone down on me before—Winston always told me it grossed him out, which, of course, made me think *I* must be gross. God, I hated how much that man had messed with my self-esteem.

Griffin watched me carefully as I slowly relaxed, coming to a decision. "Okay." I gave him a small smile, and his answering one lit up his whole face like I'd just made his year.

He didn't even hesitate, and when the first lick of his tongue slid up my center and circled my clit, the tiny metal piercing in his tongue flicking against my sensitive flesh, I swore I almost shot off the bed. He chuckled and moved one of his hands up to my stomach to hold me down while he continued licking and sucking at my clit. The sensation was like nothing I'd ever felt before, and it was so intense that I tried to close my legs to get some relief.

Griffin pressed one finger inside me while I writhed underneath him, and I gasped at the feeling. It'd been a *long* time since I'd been with Winston, and I hadn't felt up to taking matters into my own hands over the years. So Griffin's thick finger was a foreign but more than welcome feeling inside of me, and my heart rate kicked up as excitement hit me at what was to come.

He suddenly stopped, pulling his mouth away and his finger out of me, and I whimpered at the loss. I was *so* close to coming that I felt achy and needy and a little bit pissed off. He must've seen the look on my face because he laughed and leaned up to kiss the tip of my nose. "The first time you're going to come tonight, it's going to be on my cock."

The naughty words coming out of his mouth made me shiver. I couldn't *wait*.

He stripped off his jeans and boxers, and I watched transfixed as he climbed back on the bed with his long, thick cock pointing right at me. I bit back a giggle, and he looked at me with amusement as he tore open a condom and slid it on his impressive length. "You think my dick is funny, Mags?"

I shook my head. "Sorry, I sometimes laugh when I get nervous."

He leaned over me, pressing his weight deliciously over top of me as he dropped a sweet kiss to my lips and shifted his hips so his hard cock was pressed against my thigh. "Don't be nervous. We'll go as slow as you need." Only I didn't want to go slow, so I wrapped my legs around him and pulled him close until the tip of his hardness pushed against my entrance.

When he finally slid inside me, it was like magic. It felt like coming home, and when he started to move, I lost the ability to form coherent thoughts. All I could do was cling to him and cry out as he played my body like the most precious instrument he'd ever gotten his hands on.

My core clenched as he pushed even deeper inside me, and the pleasure began to build with the need for release. I nearly lost it when his fingers moved between us, and he started to circle my clit at the same time he rolled his hips in a way that made my eyes roll back. "You're squeezing my dick so fucking hard, Mags," Griffin growled, his voice sounded almost pained.

My whole body trembled as I was overwhelmed by pleasure, by Griffin surrounding me and inside of me. A single tear rolled down my cheek as my whole body exploded with pleasure, and I cried out his name, digging my nails into his back to anchor myself because it felt like my body was splintering apart, and there was nothing left but euphoria and satisfaction. I'd only started floating back down into my sated body when he slammed into me a couple more times and found his release.

Griffin collapsed on top of me as we both caught our breath, and I ran my fingers through his hair, lightly running my nails across his scalp. "Holy shit, Mags. That was…" He never finished his sentence, and I didn't want to let him go, so I didn't. Instead, my eyelids fluttered closed, and I breathed him in, content to drift off more relaxed and safer than I'd maybe ever been in my entire life. Just before I fell asleep, so quiet I wasn't sure if he'd actually said it, I heard Griffin mumble, "Now, you're mine."

TWELVE
GRIFFIN

Magnolia coming apart on my dick was all I could think about this morning—that and the fact I told her she was mine. It was a thought that swept through my mind at least fifty times a day, but one I hadn't expressed out loud because her ex was a psycho, and she might think I was like him if she knew how obsessed with her I was.

It was a healthy obsession, though… At least I thought it was. There was such a thing, right? It didn't matter. Magnolia had given in, I'd claimed her, and now all I wanted to do was make her happy and show her that there was a lot more to life than being on the run and constant stress and anxiety. I wanted to show her she could trust me to keep her safe, and that meant letting her guard down and having fun every once in a while.

I sure as hell wasn't afraid of her ex, Winston. He was an aggressive motherfucker; I'd give him that. The nights I took her phone from her so she could sleep, he called relentlessly. I'd blocked his number, but he always had a new one within a couple of hours, and the calls would start up again. I didn't want to let him taint what we started last night. I'd rather focus on the surprise for Magnolia I arranged yesterday.

My phone lit up on the bedside table next to me, and I glanced at it before sliding as quietly as I could out of bed. Magnolia never got enough sleep, and for once, she'd slept through the entire night. I tried not to smirk at my part in that since I'd given her countless orgasms until she'd passed out from exhaustion.

It was a tough job, but somebody had to do it.

I had last-minute details to work out for today anyway, so I wanted to let her sleep in. I pulled my jeans on and picked up my wrinkled t-shirt from the floor at the end of the bed before stepping out of the room and closing the bedroom door. I looked down at my phone.

Montana: Meet me in the lobby in five.

My lips curved up into a smile. Montana had come through for me. I found Lucky's leash and clipped it onto his collar as he blinked at me sleepily. I figured if I was heading to the lobby, I could deal with taking him out, too.

Once I slipped my wallet and the room key into my back pocket, I put my phone into the other pocket and stepped into my shoes. Thirty seconds later, I was in the elevator descending to meet up with the band's manager. Lucky licked the side of my face, and I couldn't help but laugh. His fur was sticking up all over the place from his bath last night, and he looked wrecked. It was hard not to crack up at him.

The doors slid open as we reached the lobby, and it took me all of two seconds to spot the fiery red hair of Montana Blackwood, one of the scariest women I'd ever met. From what I could tell, she was a damn good manager but not someone you wanted to piss off. Luckily, I'd stayed on her good side, which brought us to now, where she'd jumped on the Shadow Phoenix jet and flown across the country all so she could do me a favor.

"Baby Everleigh," she greeted me, her eyebrow raised as she appraised my less-than-put-together appearance. She sipped at her to-go coffee cup but didn't say anything else.

"My last name's Spencer," I corrected for maybe the hundredth time, but she didn't seem to care.

"Semantics," she dismissed, waving her hand. "Now, you've got me for the day. Tell me what I'm doing."

I explained my plan to her, and the more I talked, the bigger the smile was that took over her face. "You really like this girl, Griff." It wasn't a question.

I nodded as if she had stated the damn obvious because she had. "And?"

She shrugged. "Nothing. I'm just happy to see that harpy Wynter didn't do any permanent damage to you."

I waited for the urge to kick my own ass that I normally got when Wynter was mentioned, but it was completely gone. Huh. "Doesn't seem like it."

"Good." She glanced down at her phone. "Okay, I better get going if I'm going to get everything done. Harrison flew in with me, so I'm going to make him help." She had an evil gleam in her eye, and suddenly I felt a little bit bad for our publicist. Then I remembered he's generally a dick, and I cheered right up.

"I owe you one."

"You owe me like ten, kiddo. Byeeee." She dragged the last word out as she spun on her heel and sashayed off across the lobby, her fingers already flying across her phone.

Lucky squirmed in my arms, and I set him down, his little body not wasting any time before he was bounding toward the door and trying to tug me along with him. Unfortunately for him, he wasn't big enough to be able to do anything more than fall back on his ass and stare up at me with his floppy ears while he whined. It was pathetic.

Pathetic and adorable.

"Okay, let's go." He jumped up and took off again, this time not stopping until we were outside. I distantly thought about the fact he needed to be trained or go to obedience classes or some shit, but that was a problem for after the tour.

I shielded my eyes, blinking against the bright sun. I should've brought sunglasses out with me, but I hadn't been thinking about anything but getting to Montana. I pulled my phone out of my pocket while Lucky sniffed around and shot a group text off.

Griffin: I'm taking Mags out today. You guys want to join?

Zen: Is it family-friendly?

I rolled my eyes. Like I'd invite any of them along to something that wasn't safe for kids.

Griffin: Thought we'd hit up a swinger's club, and then there's this illegal fight club I heard about.

True: Dude.

Griffin: Chill. We're going to the botanical garden. I was thinking picnic. Plus, I told Kennedy yesterday it was family-friendly already.

Zen: I had to check. Kennedy says we're in. Nico needs to stretch his damn legs. He's like a tiny terror locked in this room.

True: We're in, too. Phoenix literally climbed the wall last night.

Zen: I'm gonna need pictures.

True: I've got video.

Griffin: GUYS. Focus.

Maddox: It's early af. Why are you all blowing up my phone?

True: Says the guy who wants to knock up his wife. Just wait.

Zen: Hahahaha

Maddox: Fuck off. We'll be there, Griff.

Jericho: The gardens sound chill. I'm in. Benji could use a new place to destroy.

Today was important to me for more than one reason. Sure, I wanted to give Magnolia a break and show her we could be good in a setting away from the tour, but I also needed to see how she fit in away from all the chaos with my extended family. In a professional setting, they got along fine, but in a personal one? Guess I'd find out today.

Walking back into the hotel, I shot off one more text.

Griffin: **The guys, wives, me, and Mags are going out today. We'll probably need you.**

Connor: **I'll handle it.**

A little twinge of guilt shot through me because I hadn't talked to Connor about Winston. Magnolia asked me not to, so I'd kept it to myself. I needed to talk to her about it again, even if it meant Connor didn't do anything or handle him. He still needed to know because keeping everyone on this tour safe was his job. Keeping something like a dangerous ex-boyfriend from him felt like asking for trouble.

That was a problem for a different day because right now, I had a gorgeous woman sleeping naked in my bed, and hopefully enough time before we had to leave to order room service and hopefully sink back into her body before we had to leave.

"Aren't you going to tell me what we're doing?" Magnolia sat on the side of the bed dripping wet with only a small towel wrapped around her body, and she flashed me a knowing smirk when she caught me staring at a droplet of water running down between her fantastic breasts. It didn't matter that I'd been buried as deep inside of her as I could get less than ten minutes ago. When it came to her, there was no such thing as enough.

"What?"

She giggled, and the sound made me want to wrap her up in bubble wrap and never let anything hurt her again. "What are you planning for today?"

"Nope. You're not getting it out of me."

Her laughter turned into a scowl, but her eyes were still bright and dancing with amusement, and she let the towel drop and stood up, completely naked, walking slowly across the room to where I was leaning against the dresser.

I was in so much fucking trouble with this girl.

"What are you doing?" My voice sounded huskier than usual, and I tried to clear my throat, but I had a feeling it wouldn't help.

She stepped right into my space and ran her fingertip down between my pecs, all the way down my abs, until she slipped it inside the waistband of my jeans. "Shit," I grit out, trying to remember what she'd even asked me or, hell, what my own name was.

Shaking my head, I grabbed her wrist and placed a kiss on her palm before gently pushing her away. "You. Get dressed. Now."

She stuck her lower lip out just a little bit in a pout that tested every ounce of my willpower. Why the hell was I trying to be all cute and shit and keep what we were doing today a secret?

I stalked out of the room, calling over my shoulder, "We're leaving in ten minutes."

My cock had never been harder, but I still managed to walk away, which I patted myself on the back for. Leaving a wet, naked Magnolia in the bedroom without doing anything about how turned on I was had been practically impossible.

A few minutes later, she stepped out of the room dressed in a sundress with her nearly-black hair braided and tossed over one shoulder. She looked like the epitome of southern sweetness, and now that I knew just how sweet she tasted, it was going to be hard as hell to not have my hands and mouth on her all the time. I couldn't remember why I thought it was such a good idea to include my brother and the other guys in my plans for today when I was faced with having to keep my PDA mostly PG.

That was fine. Magnolia deserved to be treated like the gorgeous, smart, compassionate, and strong woman she was. Keeping her locked in my bedroom all the time might make her think I only wanted her for one thing, but I wanted her for *everything*. She just didn't know it yet.

"You look beautiful," I murmured against her temple as I pulled her into my arms and breathed her in. How could I have missed her when I was out of the room for five minutes?

She rested her hand on my chest and leaned into my touch with a contented sigh, and I reluctantly stepped back, capturing her hand and lacing our fingers together. "Ready to go?"

She bit her lip, and her forehead wrinkled a little as her gaze got a little far off, but then she shook off whatever reservations she might've had and grinned up at me. "Yep, ready."

I attached Lucky's leash and led us all out of the room and down to the lobby where everyone was meeting. Connor was dealing with security and transportation, so all we had to do was show up. Oh, and grab the picnic lunch I'd requested the hotel pack for us from the front desk.

When we got down to the lobby, we hadn't moved two steps off the elevator before Phoenix and Nico were crashing into us, getting tangled in Lucky's leash in an attempt to play with him. Magnolia surprised the shit out of me when, instead of getting annoyed with the kids like Wynter would've done, she dropped to the floor beside them and reached up to take Lucky's leash off my wrist.

She gave Phoenix, the oldest of the three, a serious look. "I have a very, very important job for you. Do you think you're up to it?"

Phoenix's eyes got almost comically wide, and she nodded. Magnolia held out the loop for Lucky's leash. "I've got to help your uncle Griffin carry everything to the car, so I need you to keep a hold on Lucky for me. Be extra careful not to let him go, okay?"

She nodded again, a smile breaking out across her whole face as she slipped the leash loop around her wrist, and Magnolia showed her how to hold it securely. Phoenix jumped up from where she'd been sitting on the ground and ran off with Lucky and Nico right on her heels. Benji squirmed in Moon's arms as he watched.

"You're good with kids," I observed, tucking that info away for later.

"Growing up, I always wished I had a big family, you know? It was always Grammy and me, and it got lonely. Plus, kids have this light and innocence around them that's infectious. Just look," she gestured toward where Nico was wrapped up on the ground, tangled in Lucky's leash with the puppy on his chest licking his face. All three kids were giggling, and something in my chest cracked open, watching them.

Seeing all the guys watching their wives and kids with looks of contentment and satisfaction in their eyes made a lot more sense all of a sudden. I probably should've been freaked out considering I was only twenty-three, but I wasn't. Maybe it was because I was close to my parents and even my brother, but I wasn't like most guys. Settling down never scared me. I never wanted to be the kind of guy that messed around with tons of women. It always seemed shallow and unfulfilling, and after sharing what I had with Magnolia last night?

Why would I ever want something meaningless and casual?

"They're pretty damn cute," I admitted, holding out my hand to help Magnolia up off the floor. "But you're cuter," I murmured against her forehead before kissing her. After last night, I couldn't seem to keep my damn hands off her. She looked up at me with a smile that said she didn't mind one bit.

"Sorry to break up your moment," Kennedy stepped up next to Magnolia. "But everyone's restless, and we don't have a huge window before nap time. So, how about I take your girlfriend here so us girls can get to know each other better, and you ride with the guys."

Magnolia's looked at me with wide eyes as Kennedy pulled her out of my arms. All I could do was shake my head and watch them go. I had no interest in correcting Kennedy. In my mind, Magnolia *was* my girlfriend, even if we hadn't talked about it yet.

When Kennedy got something in her head, there was no stopping her. Zen shot me a knowing look as he wrangled his son and followed the girls outside. My brother fell into step beside me as we walked up to the front desk, and everyone else went out to the front drive.

"Family day with Magnolia, bro? You went from zero to sixty real fucking fast." His tone was teasing, but he eyed me with concern. I clapped him on his shoulder.

"Don't worry, Mad. I know what I want, and I know what I'm doing." I hefted the huge picnic basket the concierge handed over up into my arms, and Maddox grabbed the second one.

"If you say so," he muttered, but it didn't matter what he thought. He'd support me either way, and the rest of the guys would, too. That was just how we worked, and I learned that really quickly after I followed Maddox back to LA from Texas.

He let it drop after that as we loaded everyone into the cars and made the short drive to the botanical gardens. We rode in different cars, so I didn't get to see her expression until she got out of the car, but the look of wonder on her face had been worth all the work of arranging this date. She gravitated toward me without even looking, and she wrapped her arms around my waist and buried her face in my chest. "This place is amazing. Thank you."

I could already feel myself falling hard for this girl. Making her happy? That was right up there with my favorite things to do, right alongside making her come. Both were new additions to the list, but I had a feeling they'd be sticking around.

"C'mon, there's so much to see." I grabbed her hand and reached back to pick up the picnic basket. "How do you feel about orchids?"

As a group, we walked through the shrubbery sculptures of Alice in Wonderland, a bunch of fountains, and my personal favorite—tons and tons of flowers. I wasn't into flowers; that wasn't why they were my favorite. It was all Mags, and her reaction to every single new bloom we came across, lighting up like each one was the best thing she'd ever seen. How could I not get caught up in that?

The kids had plenty of room to run and explore, and by the time we found a good spot to sit and eat, everyone was starving and happily worn out. We ate in mostly silence—as much as there could be with little kids around—before Magnolia spoke up.

"You guys are already such an established group. I've gotta admit it's a bit intimidating to try and get to know you all. How about we play a game? Alcohol optional," Magnolia suggested and leaned into my body. I was surprised at her bravery, putting herself out there with my friends and family. I figured based on her past, she'd be a lot more shy and hesitant.

"I love it," Kennedy clapped her hands, and Amara laughed.

"We're definitely in. What'd you have in mind?" Amara asked while Ryan leaned back and reached into the cooler she'd brought along.

"Truth or dare?" Magnolia suggested, and Ryan and Maddox exchanged a dark look before my brother shook his head, but his eyes glinted, and I knew that look. That look meant he'd done something he was probably proud of, but the rest of the group might give him shit for.

"The last time we played truth or dare... Nevermind. Next idea?" Ryan shifted her eyes away, and I saw the moment Kennedy decided to let it go... for now. I had no doubt she'd be dragging that info out of my sister-in-law before we even got back to the hotel. I glanced at my brother, and he grinned at me over the top of his beer. If he was grinning, it couldn't be that bad, right?

"How about each person gets to ask a question of someone else. If they answer, they get to ask the next question. If they don't, they have to drink." I raised my eyebrow at my brother, daring him to say no. I knew exactly what I was going to be asking him.

"Sounds simple enough. I bet we get through one round before the kids have had enough, and we have to leave," True added, and Amara laughed as he wrapped his arm around her.

"I bet we don't even make it through one round," she countered, and one of the kids shrieking pierced the air, making everyone laugh.

"Okay, then we better start. I'll go first," I pointed my beer bottle at Maddox.

"What happened the last time you played truth or dare?"

Ryan rolled her eyes, and Maddox's lips curled up into a wicked smile. "Quinn and I kissed."

Ryan scoffed. "More like made out." I noticed her freckled cheeks turned a little pink like the image was replaying in her mind, and she liked what she was seeing.

"Who's Quinn?" Magnolia asked, and my brother looked away from his wife, where it looked like they were having some kind of silent communication.

"Ryan's best friend. You'll probably meet him at some point; he works with Kennedy's brother, Grayson."

"Oh. Wait. He?" Magnolia's forehead got this adorable wrinkle between her eyes.

Ryan laughed. "Yeah, he's my gay bestie… or, at least, I thought so. Now, I think he's exploring his options. Anyway, Maddox surprised the hell out of me that day."

"I bet." Magnolia laughed, and her body relaxed against mine, so I didn't think she was being judgmental or anything, which made my shoulders relax.

"My turn," Maddox announced, scanning everyone sitting in our little circle on the grass. His eyes landed on Jericho's wife, Moon, and lit up. "Moon," he started, and Jericho shot him a death glare that only made my brother smile wider. "What kind of crazy shit do you have planned for the girls this tour?"

She laughed, and I could've sworn Jericho growled. Moon's wild streak was pretty legendary in the group. She glanced up at her husband and then slowly sipped her drink, never breaking eye contact. "Guess you'll have to wait and see."

I thought Jericho might snap, but instead, he smiled, looking smug as hell. "She knows what'll happen if she tries to pull shit like she did in Vegas again."

"Vegas?" Moon asked, stretching her legs out in front of her. Damn, they were long.

Moon laughed. "I kinda sorta had us all play strippers for the night."

"Our wedding night," Jericho added.

Moon patted Jericho on the middle of his chest. "This guy got all possessive. It was hot, not gonna lie."

The other girls laughed knowingly, but Magnolia choked on her drink. She probably wasn't used to people being so open about their sex lives, but she would have to get used to it with this group. I sure as hell had to when I moved in with my brother and Ryan. I still cringed when I thought about some of the shit I'd walked in on.

Phoenix ran up to True with Lucky's leash still wrapped around her little hand with tears streaming down her face. "What happened, Little P?" He pulled her onto his lap and handed Lucky's leash over to Amara, who was brushing their daughter's hair out of her face and wiping away her tears. They huddled around her protectively, and I had a feeling our relaxed picnic was about to come to an early end.

Nico walked sheepishly up to his parents and sat down quietly, which wasn't at all like him. He was a hellion at the best of times, so if I had to guess, I'd say he was the cause of Phoenix's tears. My brother and I exchanged a look, and I started packing up the remnants of our lunch. "And that concludes our little game. We only have about an hour until soundcheck anyway. Ready to go back?" I asked Magnolia, and she smiled up at me.

"I'm ready, but you might have to make it up to me in orgasms." Her grin turned wicked, and I groaned, already starting to get hard. My innocent girl might not be so innocent after all, and I couldn't fucking wait to explore just how naughty she could be.

THIRTEEN
GRIFFIN

"Goddamn, that bus ride was long as fuck," Maddox complained as he jogged on the treadmill next to me. Last night's show had ended late, and we drove overnight to Miami. It made us all restless being locked in such a confining space together, so we hit the gym together to burn off our excess energy whenever we got the chance.

"At least you slept through it, asshole. Nico was up half the night," Zen grumbled from across the room where he and True were taking turns spotting each other as they lifted.

I increased the speed of the treadmill, so I was full-on running. The door opened, and Jericho walked in like a damn shadow, silently setting down his bottle of water and getting on the treadmill beside me. I tilted my chin at him in greeting, and his dark eyes slid from me over to my brother, who flipped him off while he ran. Jericho rolled his eyes and started his machine.

"I hear the girls are going out today. Our wives let loose on Miami with Moon at the fucking helm. Can't imagine anything's going to go wrong there," Maddox drawled, probably trying to get a rise out of any one of the guys. He could be an antagonistic fuck when he wanted to.

"At least you don't have to worry about what Magnolia's doing today, huh?" True smirked, but I wasn't taking the bait. I *was* glad I didn't have to worry about her today since she was back at work.

"Yep," I said in between breaths, popping the *p* like an asshole.

"What's the deal with you two? Maddox told us you were keeping your distance." Zen switched places with True, laying down on the bench and gripping the weighted bar.

I eyed my brother, who didn't even bother trying to look sorry he'd blabbed our private conversation around the group. "The deal is I want her, so I'm making her mine."

Three of the guys laughed, and even Jericho let out a low chuckle. I scowled at them all as I slapped the *stop* button and got off the treadmill. "What's so damn funny?"

"It's just that simple, huh?" True helped Zen put the bar back in the holder, but his eyes were focused on me and amused like this was the funniest shit to him.

"Pretty much," I confirmed, moving over to the pull-up bar.

"What if I told you Harrison sent me something this morning about Wynter having a new boyfriend?" Zen joined in with the teasing, and I scoffed.

"Good for her." My arms and back burned as I lifted my body weight above the bar over and over until I couldn't do it anymore.

"I see you got the possessive asshole gene, too," Maddox nodded at me approvingly. "All that shit about *making her mine*. You sound like me."

"Yeah, well…" I didn't really know what to say to that. Instead, I let the words hang out there unfinished while I continued my workout.

"So, why'd you hesitate?" Jericho startled the crap out of me as his words came from way closer than I thought he'd be—right on my other side, leaning lazily against the rack I was using for my pull-ups.

I was torn. It wasn't like I kept anything from the guys before, not really. At the same time, Magnolia's past wasn't mine to share. How much did I tell them? I took a sip of my bottle of water while I figured out how to explain. "Magnolia has some messed up shit in her life, and it's not all in the past yet. In case you haven't noticed, this is my first tour, so I wasn't sure if it was smart to get involved, even if I wanted to. I couldn't stay away, though, so here I am, making it work."

True laughed across the room where he was wiping the sweat off his face with a towel. "I think we can all relate to not being able to stay away at one point. What kind of *messed up shit* are we talking about exactly?"

The weight of all their eyes on me made me uncomfortable, and I was sure as hell not that guy. I'd never had to wonder what I could or couldn't share of someone else's life, and the responsibility of that wasn't lost on me. Most of all, I didn't want to let Magnolia down.

Sighing, I moved over to sit down on the weight bench, and the rest of the guys had stopped their workouts and were standing in a half-circle around the room. "She hasn't told me everything," I warned because I still didn't have the full story. "And what I say in this room goes no further. You don't tell your wives. You don't talk to each other about it outside of now."

"We don't tell our wives everything, kiddo," Zen argued, and I narrowed my eyes but said nothing.

"Okay, fine, we do. But this is different. We won't say shit."

I looked at the other three, and they nodded their agreement. "She has an ex-boyfriend who's completely fucked in the head. She hasn't outright said it, but I'd be willing to bet everything I own that he hit her. Now he's harassing her. He calls and texts relentlessly no matter how many times she, or I, block him or change her number. He sends her flowers with passive-aggressive messages letting her know he knows where she is or what she's doing. The other night, there was takeout food he'd sent waiting on our bus after the show with a picture of us on our date in Philly, so I know he's watching."

"Damn." That was Maddox, and he pushed off the wall and walked toward me, sitting on the bench next to me. "That's heavy shit. We've all dealt with stalkers before, but never a guy or an ex. Have you talked to Connor?"

I shook my head. "I offered to, but Magnolia asked me not to. The whole reason she wanted to get into managing tours was so she could be on the road, and hopefully, he wouldn't be able to find her. Obviously, her plan failed because he seems to be fucking everywhere, but she's still so damn professional. She doesn't want to take away from our security and put the attention on herself."

"That's bullshit," Jericho practically growled. "First of all, that's what Connor's team is for and why we pay them. Second, you keeping this from them is putting everyone in even more danger. Man the fuck up and make the hard decisions, Griff. When all that shit went down with Moon, the first thing I did was call in Connor. I wasn't willing to risk her, and I can't even fucking believe you'd gamble with your girl's safety like that."

I stood and raked my hand through my hair. "What the hell am I supposed to do, Jericho? She specifically asked me not to. It's not like I've known her that long, and I didn't want to go against her wishes. I figured if things escalated beyond what they are now, I'd bring it up again."

True eyed me warily. "Look, I know it might seem messed up to go behind her back, but we have to do whatever's necessary to keep our loved ones safe. This life, it's not for everyone, and it's not normal. Because of that, we have to make hard choices." A dark cloud passed over his eyes for a few seconds before he shook it off and refocused on tracking my movements since I was now pacing back and forth. "All I'm saying is she might get pissed at you in the short term, but isn't that better than her hurt or worse?"

"We've all been where you are, man," Zen added. "Like True said, this life isn't normal. My stalker tried to kill Kennedy, True had to handle a couple of guys who wouldn't take no for an answer from Amara, and you were there for your brother's and Jericho's clusterfucks with their wives. My point is, part of being in this band is the music, but the other piece is being a part of this family. We take care of our own, and we don't let people hurt the ones we love."

"I don't know if-"

Maddox laughed. "No pressure, bro. If you're not there yet, it's cool. Zen just means we don't let anyone fuck with the people we bring into the fold. You like Magnolia, so she's one of us until you say she's not."

I relaxed and then bristled at his words. I didn't want Magnolia ever not to be a part of the little makeshift family I now found myself a part of. That told me all I needed to know about how I felt about her, even if I wasn't ready to think about the "L" word.

"You need to fucking tell Connor," Jericho ordered, glowering at me. "If Magnolia's ex puts our families in danger, that's going to be on you, and trust me when I tell you, you sure as fuck don't want to be on my bad side."

Swallowing hard, I nodded once. Jericho was one helluva scary dude, and there was no way I wanted him pissed at me for endangering his wife or son. I wasn't exactly sure how far he'd go to avenge whatever wrong he thought had happened, but I didn't want to find out. "Yeah, you're right." And he was. I hadn't thought about the danger I might be putting everyone else in by keeping Magnolia's secrets. "I'll talk to her after the show tonight, and then I'll go to Connor. I don't want to blindside her by going behind her back."

Jericho nodded at me, but his jaw ticked, and he still looked pissed. He walked over to the heavy bag hanging in the corner and started hitting it with bare knuckles. I looked away, re-focusing on the rest of the guys. None of them looked concerned about Jericho's dark mood, and in fact, they were already teasing each other and going back to their workouts as if the conversation we just had hadn't happened at all.

Unfortunately for me, I couldn't let it go so easily because I knew after the show tonight, I was going to have to tell Magnolia I couldn't keep her secret anymore.

"Can someone get another mic on Griffin? The one we've got now is garbled," the audio engineer's voice crackled over the system he was using to communicate with us. An assistant hurried over and swapped out the offending microphone in front of my kit.

I looked down at the setlist for the show, making sure I knew the changes we'd made for tonight. The guys always liked to play around with the song arrangement as much as possible for every show, so it kept things interesting. Convinced I wasn't going to memorize it any more than I already had before tonight, I set it down and scanned the mostly empty arena for Magnolia.

I hadn't seen much of her today, between the gym with the guys this morning and her being busy making sure everything on the tour kept running smoothly. This was my first tour, but even I could see she had a talent for organizing and keeping everyone on track, and I was proud as hell.

As soon as she stepped into the area, my attention honed in on her like a damn heat-seeking missile. Everything else faded into the background as I watched the tense set of her shoulders as she checked in with the equipment manager and the crease form between her eyebrows as she checked her phone. She nibbled on her plump bottom lip, and I couldn't help but wonder what had her so on edge.

When I left her this morning, she was still half asleep but with a lazy smile on her face, completely relaxed after two orgasms. The memory had my dick hardening and my lips curving up into a smile. Even tense as hell, her body moved like a dream, and I was completely captivated by her.

I blinked as my brother snapped his fingers in front of my face. "Snap the fuck out of it, Griff. We'd like to get out of here, so we get a break before the meet and greet." Maddox shot me one last irritated look before going back to his spot on the stage.

We ran through a couple more songs, waiting as the engineer adjusted the sound levels until he was happy with them, with Jericho glaring at him over his shoulder. By the time we were done, and I handed my sticks and earpieces over to the equipment manager, Lucas, I was starving and only had about forty-five minutes until the fan meet and greet.

Plus, I wanted to see if I could corner Mags in a hallway or closet somewhere and kiss the shit out of her until she forgot about whatever it was that had her on edge. I jogged down the stairs on the side of the stage and turned toward the food services tent.

One great thing about being in the band—and there were many—was how I never had to wonder what I was going to eat. There was always a ton of healthy and delicious food whenever I was hungry. I smiled gratefully at the guy in the chef's jacket manning the grill behind the white tent. He was the reason I was able to pile my plate with grilled chicken and pasta and salad, and I was determined never to turn into one of those ungrateful assholes who took everything for granted.

No, I knew how lucky I was, and I didn't plan on ever forgetting it.

I'd just found a spot next to a couple of palm trees and taken my first bite when Magnolia sat down beside me. I didn't even have to look up to know she was there—my whole body was so tuned in to her, my heart rate picked up, and it was like I could feel the heat of her on my skin even though it had to be at least ninety degrees outside, even in the shade.

She reached over and plucked a tomato off my plate and popped it into her mouth before leaning against me. "Today sucks."

I chuckled. "It can't be all bad considering how it started." I winked at her when she blushed, that soft pink color splashing across her cheeks.

"You're sayin' an orgasm-"

"*Two* orgasms," I corrected with a dirty grin that I hoped promised everything running through my head right now.

She rolled her eyes. "Two orgasms should be enough to counteract bein' down two chefs, the equipment guys accidentally ruinin' all the strings on True's favorite guitar, and this?" She held out her phone and showed me the ridiculous amount of texts and calls she'd gotten from Winston today. The dude needed serious psychological help.

I grabbed the phone out of her hand and blocked his number. Again. It wouldn't do any good, but maybe she'd get a few minutes of a break from his harassment. "Isn't it weird for him to call so much during the day?"

She nodded. "Yep. He usually sticks to makin' sure I don't sleep. Maybe since he knows I've been spendin' the night with you, he thought he'd change it up. Who knows what's goin' through his deranged mind?"

Listening to Magnolia speak in her heavy drawl made goosebumps run across my skin, and my cock spring to life. If she could do that with just her words, I stood absolutely no hope of getting out of this thing unscathed, not that I wanted to.

"Speaking of Winston, we need to talk about what we're going to do about him, but I don't have time now." I reluctantly looked down at her phone in my hand and noted I had fifteen minutes until the meet and greet, and I still needed to change. "Go for a walk with me after the show."

She eyed me suspiciously, and her next words were syrupy-sweet and dripped with venom at the same time. "You're not breakin' up with me, are you, Sugar?"

Maybe I should've been concerned about how attached to me she was, but I wasn't even a little bit bothered. In fact, I was fucking ecstatic, and my inner caveman was definitely pounding his chest. "Breaking up? Does that mean you think we're together?"

Her cheeks flushed even darker pink, and I dropped her phone in her lap, reaching out and trapping her face between my palms so I could look straight into her icy blue eyes. "Are you my girlfriend, Mags? Because I sure as hell want to be your boyfriend."

She blinked a couple of times. "Are you sure? I don't know if you've noticed, but I'm kinda a mess, and you're…" She gestured to me.

My lips tilted up, and I bit my cheek to keep from laughing. Somehow I didn't think she'd appreciate that. "I'm what?"

Her shoulders slumped, and she heaved out a resigned sigh. "You're so hot; you're like a walking billboard for sin. The perfect tattooed, muscled, pierced bad boy that every girl's mama warns them away from, and for some unknown reason, you're interested in me when you could have anyone."

I laughed at her assessment of me—hard. She was scowling when I finally caught my breath. "Bad boy?"

"Not how you act, how you look."

"Baby, I'm the farthest thing from a bad boy."

She wrapped her delicate fingers around my wrists, where I still held her face between my palms, her peachy skin a stark contrast from all the black ink etched into mine. We were practically nose to nose now. "I know," she admitted, and it was so quiet I almost didn't hear her, but then I closed the distance between us, and we were kissing. My plate fell off my lap and onto the ground as she swung her leg over my lap until she was straddling me.

I let go of her face, moved my hands down to her hips, and pulled her closer, so she was grinding right over my dick. It took all of two seconds before I was so hard it hurt, and I wanted to reach between us and free myself, so I could push right up into her pussy—the one I knew would already be soaking wet for me and fit like she was made for me.

After a few more heated kisses—and more than a little grinding against her while she made all kinds of moans that drove me fucking nuts—I pulled back, never hating my life more than in that moment. "Baby."

"Hmm?"

"I have to go get ready for the meet and greet. I've only got a couple of minutes."

She whimpered, and if it hadn't been for the fact me skipping would hurt both of our careers, I'd have done it in a second. I couldn't let the guys or Magnolia down, so I gently helped her off my lap before I stood up and adjusted myself because I was hard as fuck, and it didn't show any signs of going down anytime soon. "See you after the show?"

She nodded, looking a little dazed and *mission accomplished* because she wasn't worried about any of the shit that'd been weighing her down when she first found me.

It took me about three minutes to get on the bus, change, and walk back into the arena, moving down a couple of halls and following signs pointing to the back entrance for the meet and greet room. I pushed in the heavy metal door and noticed the other three guys were already inside.

"Look who decided to grace us with his presence," Maddox drawled, and I flipped him off as I sat down on the leather couch next to him. These things were always arranged differently at each venue, but usually, there were a couple of couches for us to hang out on between groups of people. There was a table off to one side and a backdrop with our logo for photo ops beside that. Every time they let a new group in, they waited in a roped-off area before moving through the table, and then we posed for pictures last.

I wouldn't say the other guys were bored with this per se. It was more that they were wary. Most of them had had bad fan experiences at some point, so getting up close and personal with the fans now made them cautious. All of this was new to me, though, and I thought it kicked ass having people talk about how much they enjoyed your music or watching you play.

I never would've thought this would be my life, people getting excited over meeting me. It was fucking weird. I still felt like the same guy I'd always been.

Jericho eyed me. "You talk to Connor yet?"

"Not until after the show tonight."

He nodded, seemingly satisfied with my answer even if he didn't like it. I knew he preferred me to tell Connor immediately, but I wouldn't do that to Magnolia. Not without talking to her first.

Zen clapped his hands together once. "We all ready?"

All of us nodded and mumbled our agreement before going to sit behind the long table. Through the doors to my right, excited chatter carried through, and their energy was contagious. Normally Magnolia would be here with us, making sure everything ran smoothly, but she was stuck dealing with the instrument issue to make sure True had his guitar tonight, so it was just us, the photographers, and security.

We waited for the tour photographers to finish setting up before Zen looked over at where Connor stood beside the doors and gave him a nod. When the doors opened, a group of about fifteen people flooded inside. We'd have four of these groups during the hour we were in here, but I liked that they broke it up to make it feel more intimate. Plus, it wasn't as overwhelming for all of us, having that many people in our faces.

There were a lot of hushed whispers, excited squealing, and grabby hands as we moved through the first two groups. I sat back down in my spot at the long table and played with the silver Sharpie pen in my hand, rolling it between my fingers like I did my sticks. I wondered what Magnolia was doing and if she was feeling any better after our impromptu makeout session.

I was distracted as group three moved into the room, and I smiled and signed my name almost on autopilot while my mind played out all kinds of Magnolia-related fantasies I wanted to re-enact later tonight on the bus. The bunk was small, but we could make it work.

A figure stopped in front of me, and I signed the poster that every person who bought one of these passes got for their trouble and handed it over since I was the last in line. Whoever was in front of me didn't bother taking it out of my hand, so I looked up and recoiled at the amount of hate and anger simmering in the man's stormy blue eyes. "I think I've proven how easy it is to get past your pathetic security," he sneered, leaning his hands onto the table and moving into my personal space.

The other guys were paying attention now, and out of the corner of my eye, I saw Zen motion for Connor and Indy, who were standing by the door. "Good job, man. Here's your poster," I tried again, not sure what the hell his deal was but fighting the impulse to tell him to back the hell up out of my face.

"I don't want your fucking poster. I want you to stay the fuck away from my girlfriend."

My eyebrows shot up. "Winston?"

An evil smile formed on his face as he leaned back and folded his arms across his chest. "I see Magnolia can't stop talking about me. I was giving her space to find herself or whatever the fuck women do, but it's time she comes home. You leave her the fuck alone, or next time I won't be so nice."

I stood up, and Maddox and Jericho flanked me at each shoulder. I was most definitely not a fighter by nature, but I had a couple of inches and at least twenty pounds on this guy. His disheveled brown hair looked like he'd been running his hands through it and his clothes were wrinkled. "Magnolia wants nothing to do with you. I thought all the times she blocked your number or told you to go away would've been enough of a hint."

His eyes narrowed and darkened, the storm inside them growing more violent. "You don't know what the hell you're talking about. This is your last warning. Stay the fuck away." There was something in his voice that gave me pause. I knew he was psychotic, but this was next level.

Connor and Indy moved to either side of Winston and gripped his arms, hauling him out of the room. Jericho gave me an *I told you so* look before he sat back in his chair to finish signing posters. I bet he regretted joining us on this autograph session since he didn't have to do these anymore, but I was glad he was here. I didn't know how he could just go back to business as usual, though. The adrenaline coursing through my body made me shaky and anxious.

What if Winston had gotten to Magnolia before he'd found me? I had to find her and talk to her about all of this before she heard it from someone else, and then I sure as hell needed to have a hard conversation with her about bringing Connor in. My brother clapped me on the shoulder. I could fight, but I wasn't a fighter. Maddox was something else entirely and had Winston made one move to get closer to me, I had no doubt Maddox and Jericho would've made him wish he hadn't.

"Go find Magnolia, bro. We'll finish this," Maddox told me as I was already around the table and on my way out the door. More than my next breath, I needed to know Magnolia was okay.

FOURTEEN
MAGNOLIA

W inston. Was. Here.

My body still shook, and it'd been an hour since the police had come and taken him away. I couldn't even think straight because the thought that Winston had managed to get into a situation where he was face-to-face with Griffin—at my job, no less—was worse than I even thought he was capable of.

I really shouldn't be surprised.

"He's not going to be able to get to you anymore," Griffin promised, kissing my temple as I leaned against him. He managed to get me on the bus somehow, even though I didn't remember how. A blanket was wrapped around my shoulders, and I pulled it tighter, trying to fend off the sudden chill despite the heat and humidity outside.

"You don't know him," I argued, clenching my teeth together to stop them from chattering. Maybe I was in some weird form of shock. My whole system felt edgy. What stunned me more than anything was the terror in Griffin's eyes when he found me putting out a fire with the venue manager. Griffin was so pale he looked sick, and his eyes had been wild as he ran over and interrupted my conversation to pull me into his arms, not even caring who saw. I hadn't realized he cared about me so much until that moment.

"I know Connor handed him over to the police, and I know he's not getting out of jail tonight. You can count on him not being anywhere near you, at least for a little while." He sat back and gently tilted my chin until I was looking up at him. "You told me you didn't want to talk to Connor about your ex, but I think we're past the point of keeping it from him, Mags. Winston was here today. He got behind our security because they didn't know to keep him out. What if someone had gotten in his way? Or if he'd just decided he wanted to hurt someone as a message? What if it was Kennedy or one of the other girls? It's not fair to keep it to yourself anymore, Mags."

His words were firm, but his tone was soft. He understood he was asking a lot to share my story with someone I didn't trust, let alone know. But he made a good point. I couldn't endanger anyone on this tour because it made me uncomfortable to talk about my time with Winston.

"You're right." I slumped against him, my body weary and exhausted after everything today. If I was honest with myself, it wasn't just today. This had been going on for years, and I was *so* tired. I didn't even think tired was the right word. It was more bone-deep than that, soul-deep maybe.

If I slept an entire month, I didn't know if I would feel rested. "I'll talk to him."

"Are you up for it now? I can run downstairs and get him."

I shook my head. "After the show. You have to get ready. We've all got jobs to do, and you're not lettin' all those fans down on my watch. The Winston problem isn't goin' anywhere, especially not with him in jail for tonight." I didn't tell him that this was far from the first time Winston had been locked up overnight because the neighbors or someone witnessing his abuse had called the police. It never stuck because I couldn't press charges. If I did, he would've killed me.

This time I felt stronger with Griffin by my side and the blossoming friendships I'd started to form with the band and their wives. They were accepting of me, wanting to get to know me and bring me into the fold. Maybe, when the time came, I'd feel brave enough to stand up to Winston once and for all, but that was something to worry about later. Now the show needed to go on.

"Go, Sugar. I'll be fine," I told Griffin with a small smile. It was all I could manage right now, but I was starting to feel better and shake off my anxiety. The list of everything I needed to check in the next hour before the concert started to run through my head and distract me from any thoughts of Winston. It was exactly what I needed to be able to compartmentalize what happened and move on.

Griffin eyed me before leaning down to kiss me gently. "You better be. Fuck, Mags. I almost had a damn heart attack when I realized who he was, and I didn't even care that he was threatening me. He can't do shit to me, but the fact he would even do that in the first place…" He raked his hand through his hair, and I looked up at him—at his dark eyelashes framing even darker eyes and the light reflecting off the hoop in one side of his nose and the stud in the other—and a peace settled over me, not to mention the spark that ignited in my core.

He was hotter than a freshly baked biscuit and made my mouth water twice as much. I squirmed a little because now was *really* not the time to be getting all worked up over how delicious my boyfriend—that's right, *boyfriend*—was. I couldn't help myself, though, and he caught the movement out of the corner of his eye and smirked at me like he knew exactly what my problem was. He leaned over and whispered in my ear, his warm breath making shivers cascade down my spine. "It looks like you need a little stress relief." It was practically a purr and a promise all wrapped up in one yummy package, but neither one of us had time.

I pressed my palm against his chest and pushed just enough to create a couple of inches of space between us so I could try and think clearly. His fingers dancing their way up my inner thigh were not helping matters, and I groaned. "After I watch you on stage tonight. Right now, we don't have time."

His eyes glinted mischievously. "Does watching me on stage make you wet for me?" His wandering fingers had made their way up my shorts and brushed along my slit until he circled my clit once, and I whimpered.

"You know it does."

He groaned and pulled his fingers back. "Shit, I'm going to be fucking hard for the entire show. At least I get to sit behind the drums." He stood up and adjusted himself, and I didn't even try to hide the fact I watched every second of this show, the private one just for me. I licked my lips, and he practically growled before bending down to kiss me, nipping my bottom lip once before pulling back.

"You're going to kill me, Mags." He turned to leave but looked back after a couple of steps. "You want to walk back with me? Or do you need a minute?" His smile was downright devious, and I couldn't help but laugh as I stood up and straightened my clothes, running a hand through my hair. He watched me like a starving man eyed his next meal, and inner me might've preened a little under his attention.

I reached my hand forward, and he wove our fingers together. It was incredible how he could shake me out of such a bad mood and actually have me laughing and smiling again. I'd never had anyone in my life that could do that, and I was left feeling lighter than I had in a while. I still felt like I could sleep for a month, but there was a new part of me that thought maybe there was a light at the end of the tunnel, and maybe there was hope I could have a normal—maybe even good—life moving forward. At least there was a chance.

The walk into the arena wasn't long, and we parted ways at the dressing room where the rest of the guys were with a kiss that made my toes curl and my knees weak and every other cliched thing you've ever heard about kisses that completely rock your world. The cheers we got from the rest of the guys had me pulling away with burning cheeks, but it was totally worth it.

The next hour went by in a flash, and when I finally had a chance to take a deep breath, Tuesday Told a Secret was taking the stage. Everything was running smoothly backstage; the instruments were ready, the stage and lighting crews were in place, and nothing had come up, so I could just watch for a little while. I hadn't had a chance to watch the tour's opening act much, and they had their own manager, so outside of the logistics, I didn't spend much time with them either.

Even I had to admit, though, that Bellamy Frost's—the lead singer and the only female in a band full of guys—voice and stage presence were something special. I didn't know much about how things worked behind the scenes in managing a band, but I had a feeling Jericho was lucky to find them in a tiny dive bar before anyone else knew how good they were.

"She's good." I looked up as Ryan took her spot next to me. I hadn't spent much time with Maddox's wife because she, like me, wasn't just along for the ride. She had a job to do, and as far as I could tell, she did it well.

I nodded my agreement, and she turned to face me. "I know you don't know me very well, but Griffin's family and I like to think I have good instincts. I like you, and I'm sorry for what happened earlier today. I don't know many details, but I do know it involves your ex-boyfriend. I wanted to offer to be the one you talk to if you want. Connor's good, but he's also a guy." She rolled her eyes. "He's not exactly the picture of sensitivity."

I turned back to the music to give myself a second to think about what she was offering. Ryan didn't have to do this for me. She didn't know me, not really. But she was here willing to sit with me through something that was going to be extremely difficult for me to relive as the words poured out of me while I filled them in on Winston and what he'd done to me. Suddenly the idea of having to share all of that with Connor, or any of the men on his team, seemed daunting, and my throat tightened at the thought.

"Can you meet me on the bus an hour after the show?" By then, any problems the crew might have would've presented themselves, and I should be able to get free. I gnawed on my lower lip as I waited for her response, but she didn't make me wait long.

"I'd be happy to." Her eyes shone as she reached down and squeezed my hand briefly, and her acceptance made my whole body feel warm and a little tingly. I wondered if this was what it was like to make friends since I'd never really had any. "Do you want it to be just us, or will Griff be there, too?"

I laughed. "I don't think he'd stay away even if I tried to force him."

Ryan grinned at me knowingly. "Maddox is the same way. I'm lucky he lets me do anything alone at all."

"You don't look like that bothers you," I noted, still smiling like the lovesick fool I totally was.

She shook her head, and her dark brown wavy hair got a little more wild than usual. "Call me crazy, but something about that possessiveness does it for me." She got a far-off dreamy look in her eye that I was sure I'd had a time or two when I was thinking about Griffin. It was weird to see what it looked like outside of my own brain, though.

"I don't think you're crazy. I think it's hot when Griffin gets all protective. I don't have a lot of experience havin' anyone watch out for me." The energy around us sobered, and we were quiet while we watched the band finish up.

"You may not have had a lot of that before, but you're a part of us now, and that comes with a whole lot of people who care about you and want to keep you safe and make you happy. You'll see." She smiled at me and turned back toward the stage. "I better go finish my perimeter check before they take the stage, but if you need me, I'll be watching from over there," she pointed to a place just off stage on the other side in the shadows. I imagined it would be a good place to scan the crowd and also keep an eye on the guys at the same time.

"Thanks, Ryan."

"Don't thank me, just be good to Griff."

I smiled wide as the man in question took the stage and immediately searched me out, even in the dark, and my breath caught when our eyes locked. "Considerin' I don't deserve him, I don't think you have anythin' to worry about."

"We need to work on your self-confidence, girl." She winked at me. "Gotta go. I'll see you after."

I tore my eyes from Griffin to watch her melt into the shadows before the show started. "Buckle up, Miami," Zen's gravelly voice purred over the speakers, echoing around the still-dark arena. "You're in for one hell of a wild ride."

A steady drumbeat started under his words as Griffin joined in, followed by a lazy strumming of True's guitar, and finally, Maddox added a baseline underneath everything. It sounded like they're just messing around as they got the crowd ready for the show, and I had to admit it was captivating how they owned the audience like they did.

I only got to stay for part of the first song before I got pulled away with a catering issue, but watching Griffin's muscles bunch and tense underneath his inked skin as he ruled from his throne behind the drums was exactly the mental break I needed from the day. As I turned to head toward the craft services tent, my shoulders slumped, and exhaustion barreled through my body. I'd never been more grateful Amara had volunteered to keep Lucky for me after everything went down with Winston today. I hadn't even had the mental capacity to do my job and think about how my puppy was faring.

The ninety-minute show flew by, and once I was sure we had a working grill so the tour crew could actually eat dinner tonight, I quickly ran through my post-show to-do list. We were headed to Nashville tonight, and everything looked to be on track.

I was already so tired I could barely keep my eyes open, swaying a little on my feet as I made my way to the bus. It wasn't fair for me to keep my history with Winston to myself anymore. I didn't have the mental energy to hold up the walls that kept everyone out, and for once, I didn't want to. Maybe if I aired it all out, it'd be like letting the wind carry it off where it couldn't affect me anymore. I wasn't naive enough to think that talking about it once would be enough to heal completely, but the possibility was there that it could be a start.

Trudging up the steps of the bus, I flashed a weak smile at Kennedy and Amara, who were sitting in the booth in the kitchen with their kids between them and Lucky curled up on Kennedy's lap. "Thanks for watching him tonight." I sat down beside Kennedy, and she looked at me with sympathy in her gaze. Normally I hated it when people looked at me with pity, but that wasn't what this was. It was more caring than that and less like she felt sorry for me and more like she'd been through some stuff, too, and knew what it was like.

"My pleasure. Zen's already basically given in to the inevitable. We took one look at Nico with this fluffy guy, and I knew we were getting a dog when we got home." She reached down and stroked the fur on Lucky's head as he slept.

Amara laughed softly. "True, too. You know how he is with Phoenix. She shows the slightest interest in something, and he's all over it. I wouldn't be surprised if we walk through the front door and a puppy is waiting for us."

Someone coming up the stairs interrupted us, and we all looked toward the doorway. Ryan stepped inside and gave us all a little wave before coming over to sink down across from me beside Amara. "You guys didn't want to see the show tonight?" Ryan asked.

Kennedy shook her head. "The kids didn't seem up for it, and we told Magnolia we'd keep an eye on Lucky for her. Moon went and took Benji. She should be back any minute."

Ryan turned her attention to me. "You want to go start talking now? No offense, but you look like shit."

I smirked. "I didn't know we were close enough to say stuff like that to each other yet."

All three of the girls chuckled. "Babe, with us, you're either in, or you're out. There's no halfway. Wynter… she was way the fuck *out*." Kennedy wrinkled her nose at the memory of Griffin's ex. I had to agree with her—the little time I'd spent with Wynter was more than enough, and these girls had been subjected to her for months.

"If I ever turn into a hag like that, I give you my full permission to kick my ass," I laughed with them. It felt good to spend time with other women like this. It was something I'd always wanted, but I'd never quite managed to figure out how to get it.

"We'd never let you turn into anything resembling that she-demon," Amara promised, lifting her can of sparkling water up and taking a sip.

"Are you two going to the upstairs lounge?" Kennedy wondered. "Want me to keep Lucky?"

I pushed out a heavy breath. "Yes, please. We need to talk about today and, well, Ryan offered to be the one to hear it all and relay it to Connor." I shot her a grateful look. "We can go up, but I don't want to start until Griffin gets here; that way, I don't have to go through it twice."

Ryan nodded at me, and we stood up to move upstairs, but I turned back. "I'd like you guys to know, too, but I've never opened up about this before, and the thought of an audience is overwhelming."

"Don't even worry about it. Your taint-sucker of an ex doesn't get to make you uncomfortable anymore," Kennedy said, and I could've hugged her, colorful language choices and all. I snorted from laughing so hard at her words. I'd have to remember her choice name for him when I talked about the things he'd done to me.

I looked over at Ryan. "I'm good with you fillin' everyone in after I tell you, everyone in security and on this bus only. I don't need the whole world to know, but trust has to start somewhere, and if Griffin trusts you all, I'm choosin' to trust you, too." I didn't know if they understood how huge a deal trust was for me, but I couldn't spend my whole life paranoid and uncertain. That wasn't the kind of life I wanted to live.

"Let's get this over with," I sighed, and we walked up the stairs, each step feeling like I was walking to my execution. In a way, I was. I was about to shed the old me by confessing every depraved and damaging thing Winston had ever done to me, and in doing so, I would hopefully emerge stronger for it and ready to really embrace what this opportunity and new life, and new relationship, had to offer.

Instead of turning left to the bunks, we went right and into the lounge at the front of the bus. There was a huge U-shaped bench made of super comfy cushions with lots of throw pillows scattered across it. There was also a flat-screen TV hung on the back wall so you could see it from almost every spot. I sat and pulled a throw pillow into my lap, wrapping my arms around it and hugging it to my body. It was only a pillow, but somehow it felt like armor.

Ryan had taken the seat across from me and reached into the small fridge that was built into the underside of the bench. "Water?" she offered, holding out a cold bottle she'd pulled out for me.

"Thanks." I took it and unscrewed the cap, taking a sip to try and clear the lump that'd formed.

"We can do this tomorrow if you want. I know it's been a long day." She was watching me with concern, but I shook my head.

"No, this needs to happen now. I've put it off long enough, and waitin' until tomorrow isn't gonna make it any easier."

The rowdy sounds of people boarding the bus carried up the stairs. Before I could really register what was happening, Griffin's built form moved into the hallway at the top of the stairs, and I watched as he moved toward me like an animal waiting to pounce on its prey. A shiver worked its way through my body at the thought, and a smirk crept onto his face.

"Hey, Mags." He leaned down and kissed me before dropping onto the bench beside me, his arm draped across my shoulders. He smelled like he'd just gotten out of the shower, and when I looked over at him, his dark hair was still damp.

Griffin finally turned his attention to Ryan, and his eyebrows rose in surprise. "Where's Connor?"

"Hey, asshole. You don't think I'm capable of talking to your girlfriend about this?" Ryan gave shit back to Griffin just as good as he did to her, and I bit back a smile.

"Did I say that? I was just curious. It sounds like my brother's been slacking in the orgasms department because someone's cranky as hell. No need to jump down my throat, Ry. I'll talk to Maddox and get you fixed right up."

I watched as Ryan's eyes narrowed, but there wasn't any real heat behind them. I suspected this was a normal interaction for the two of them, but I needed to get my story out so I could go to bed and pass out. As much fun as watching them was, I was almost deliriously tired. "Can you two finish your sparrin' match later? I'd really like to get this out and go to bed."

Griffin immediately turned his attention back to me. "Sorry, Mags." He looked decidedly sheepish, and it was cute as all get out.

I waved my hand, and he caught it and wrapped it in his much bigger one. "I'd love to see you two battle another time, but I don't have the energy. Okay, so let me just dive in because there's no easy place to start and no right words that are goin' to make this story okay." I took another sip of my water and noted my hand shaking, but I was starting to get a sort of numb detachment as I moved the memories I'd locked away so that I could function on a daily basis into the forefront of my mind.

"I met Winston when I was a freshman in college. Y'all have to understand, I grew up in a tiny town in Georgia where everybody knew each other, my graduatin' class had less than fifty people in it, and I was an outcast because I was the 'orphan girl' and raised by my grammy." I breathed out shakily while I tried to gather myself for the rest.

"Throughout high school, I didn't have friends. I'd come home from school and work in the garden with Gram or bake or crochet. We did all sorts of old lady stuff together, but friends my own age were never an option for me. Y'all can imagine that if makin' friends was that impossible, boyfriends were nothin' more than a stupid pipe dream."

Griffin rubbed his thumb soothingly along the back of my hand, and subtly shifted his body closer to mine. Warmth radiated off him, and I settled under his arm as he tucked me into his side. "After Gram died, I had to get out of there, so I worked my butt off and got into the University of Georgia. It wasn't too far from home, but it was my first chance to see some of the world and be whoever I wanted. It was with my brand-spankin' new outlook on life that Winston found me durin' freshman orientation."

I took another sip of my water, and both of them waited for me to continue. So far, the story was bland, and I knew that, but I had to work up to the bad stuff.

"He made me laugh and paid attention to me. He made me feel special, and sort of took me under his wing. He showed me all the best places on campus to hang out, study, and blow off steam. Winston was always there, and before I knew what'd happened, he was this huge part of my life."

"During the summer between freshman and sophomore years, he asked me to move in with him. I didn't have anywhere to go home to in between, and I loved him and all the attention he gave me, so I agreed. Everything up until that point was completely normal between us." I gripped the pillow in my lap tighter, knowing where the story was going.

"Even that first year of us livin' together was mostly good. I got a job to help with the rent, even though Winston insisted I didn't need to, and we fought about that, but it wasn't anythin' more than small disagreements here and there. I started to meet people in my classes and through work that I wanted to be friends with, but every time they'd ask me to go somewhere, Winston would suggest we do somethin' else. He'd talk badly about them and insist they weren't good people. When that finally stopped workin' on me goin' into junior year, that was when the guilt trips started."

"You're doing really well, Magnolia," Ryan praised, leaning forward so her forearms rested on her knees. "Take as much time as you need."

I nodded my thanks at her and closed my eyes, taking a couple of deep breaths before opening them again. "The first time he hit me, it was because he was convinced I cheated on him when I had to work late one night, and my phone died so I couldn't call him to let him know." My eyes started to sting, and I blinked to try and keep the tears at bay. It was a futile effort, and I knew this story would end in my tears, which was why I kept it locked away, but it needed to come out now.

"When I got home from work, he slapped me across the face. I was shocked because that wasn't the Winston I knew—the one I fell in love with. I made excuses, and for the next couple of weeks, he was overly sweet. He'd bring me flowers or write me sweet notes or go out of his way to walk me to class when he didn't have to. I convinced myself that whatever happened that night was a fluke because Winston would *never* hurt me." I laughed, but it was bitter and not at all funny.

"Fuck, I already want to kill him," Griffin seethed next to me, and Ryan shot him a look. I rubbed comforting circles into the denim material covering his thigh. This was probably going to be really hard for him to hear.

"It wasn't until he hit me again that the fear really sank in. The second time he hit me, we were out at dinner, and a waiter flirted with me. Winston gripped my wrist so hard when we were leavin', he fractured a bone, and I had bruises for a week. He, again, accused me of cheatin' with the waiter I'd never seen before that night and haven't seen since." Recounting it all out loud just reminded me how stupid I'd been to fall for his crap.

"At the time the threats started, Winston was all I had. He'd convinced me to quit my job to focus on school, but then he started guiltin' me about school and how he would always take care of me, and it was a waste of my time. I don't know how many times I had to cover bruises and scratches and broken bones over my junior and part of my senior year of college because he wanted me to stay home, and I refused."

Griffin cursed, and even Ryan had a vengeful twinkle in her eye. "Trust me; I know what you're thinkin'. When it was happenin', it was hard to see my way out. It wasn't that I didn't want to leave, but more that I didn't know how. I was still in school. I didn't have a job and couldn't afford to live on my own, but Winston would never have let me get one to earn enough money to save up to leave. And even if I could, he was the only real friend I'd ever had."

"Baby, he was *not* your friend." Griffin's voice was hard, but the strokes of his fingers in my hair were soft, and I took comfort in the feel of his touch.

"I know that now, but even you've had a little experience with something like that. When you were with Wynter, did you see how horrible she was at the time?"

He winced, and Ryan chuckled. "She's got you by the balls there, Griff."

"Yeah, yeah. So, how did you eventually get out?" Griffin wondered.

"I wasn't sure I'd ever be able to, and even if I could, Winston promised me over and over again that he'd never let me go. He told me he'd hunt me to the ends of the earth and drag me back, that I'd never be able to escape him." I shivered, and Ryan reached behind her and tossed me a fluffy throw blanket that I quickly wrapped around Griffin and me.

"There was an awards reception one night. I'd been recognized for academic achievement, and Winston wouldn't let me go, so I snuck out anyway. I got lucky that night because he didn't show up at the actual event but waited until I got home, but when I walked in the door, he slammed his fist into my face and didn't stop until I was unconscious. When I woke up, I was in the hospital, and the only reason I ended up there was because a neighbor heard Winston screamin' at me and called the police. Of course, he was gone by the time they showed up, but they found me bleedin' on the floor and took me in."

Flashes of that night played before my eyes, and my stomach revolted, the water I'd been sipping sloshing uncomfortably like it wanted to come back up. I breathed through my nose, trying to ride out the urge to throw up.

"Christ, Mags," Griffin bit out, tightening his hold on me. "I wish I would've at least gotten a couple of punches in this morning."

"Yeah, if we ever see him again, there's going to be a line," Ryan agreed, and I smiled wearily, glad to have people in my corner.

"Both my orbital bones were fractured, my nose was broken, my collarbone was broken, I had three cracked ribs on my left side, and my wrist was broken. I was also bleedin' internally from all the kickin' he'd done to my stomach. I had a concussion so bad, I couldn't remember my own name for a while there, and of everything, that was the scariest part." The memory still haunted me. Not knowing who I was or what I was doing in the hospital and not having anyone there with me who could answer those questions had been terrifying.

"One of the nurses who cared for me, she was so sweet, and she took one look at me and knew exactly what happened without me havin' to say a word. She was the one who helped me get away. She helped me get a job, find a women's shelter to stay in, and get out of the city. She told me LA was where dreams were made and stuck me on a bus where one of her cousins picked me up and took me in. I've been on the run ever since. It took a long time for my physical injuries to heal, but I'm still not okay with everythin' that happened. I have nightmares," I cast a glance up at Griffin, and his clenched jaw told me he was reacting exactly how I thought he would.

"I don't trust easily, either. All I've ever wanted was to have people who love me and who I can love in return. I don't feel like my dreams are that big, but somehow they've always felt out of reach like it's my destiny to be alone."

"Hey. I can promise you that being alone isn't what you're destined for. You've got me now, and I don't know if you noticed, but I kinda have a huge family that's a package deal. Plus, you haven't met my mom yet, but she's been through something really similar, and I already know she's going to love you." Griffin pulled me up into his lap and nuzzled his face into my neck like he needed to be close to me just as much as I needed to be close to him.

"Griff's right. I like you, Magnolia, and I know the other girls do, too. You're one of us now, and even if you piss us off or we piss you off, you won't get rid of us," Ryan made her passionate vow before her tone softened. "Thank you for letting me hear your story and get to know you better. It helps that we know what Winston's capable of and what he's done before. I promise he won't touch you again."

For some reason, when Ryan said it, I believed her. I could only hope she was right.

FIFTEEN
GRIFFIN

I'd never actually wanted to murder someone before. I left those feelings up to Maddox and Jericho, where they belonged. Yet, ever since Magnolia told me in detail about everything Winston had done to break her body and spirit, I couldn't stop picturing all the ways I wanted to rip him limb from limb.

I wasn't even a violent guy by nature, but fuck if Magnolia didn't deserve a protector—someone who actually cared about her and wanted to make her happy. Determination set in as I made myself a promise that I would be that for her no matter what happened between us. When she confessed that she thought she'd always be alone, it almost broke me, but then I looked down into her bright blue eyes, and I realized how strong she was, and she made me want to be stronger.

Now she was curled up against my side with an old episode of her favorite show playing in the background, but she was snoring softly. The heat of her body calmed me down enough that I wasn't on the verge of jumping in a car and hauling my ass over to the police station to give Winston a little bit of what he deserved for hurting Magnolia, but I was more dedicated than ever to making sure she knew what it felt like to be happy and safe starting with tomorrow.

The moon was high in the sky when I peeked out the window as the bus pulled out of the arena parking lot and took off on the next leg of our journey. Tomorrow afternoon we'd be in Nashville—a place I'd always wanted to see—

and I planned to spend all of the downtime I could get my hands on showing Magnolia the way she deserved to be treated by her boyfriend.

Once a plan started to form in my mind, I was able to push aside all the bullshit of the day and focus on what came next, and with thoughts of Magnolia's sweet smile, I drifted off to sleep with her cradled in my arms, knowing nothing would hurt her as long as I was breathing.

"Wow. I had no idea anything like this even existed in the US," Magnolia marveled, shielding her eyes to take in the massive Greek structure in front of us. I'd been dragging her to every landmark I could find on Google that was worth seeing because more than anything, I wanted her to be able to experience life outside of her small town and the few experiences she had with that douchebag Winston.

Most of all, I wanted her to experience those things with me. I wasn't like my brother and the other guys. I hadn't already been around the world and seen all it had to offer. Everything was as new to me as it was to Magnolia, and the idea of being able to go through all of these adventures with her was more than I could've asked for coming into this tour.

The way her eyes lit up at every new place we went, or food she tasted, or even as she watched out the bus window when we pulled into a new city was captivating and addictive. Every single time I felt like that moment in the *Grinch* where his chest grew three sizes. My heart felt like it would burst out of my chest, but where that should've been painful, it wasn't. It was something I wanted more of, and that warmth that spread throughout my chest whenever Magnolia was around had me craving her more and more.

"Same. I thought we'd have to jump on a plane to Rome, but I hear this is the next best thing." I wrapped my arms around her waist as we looked up at the massive Parthenon that'd randomly been built in Tennessee. Even though it should've been out of place, somehow it fit. "Walk with me before we go inside."

I reluctantly let go of my hold on Magnolia and took her hand instead. Since yesterday, she'd been even more affectionate with me, sinking into my touch and leaning on me more and more. It was a relief because I hadn't known how she'd react after what happened with Winston and then telling us her story, but it almost seemed like a huge weight had lifted off her shoulders. She was more carefree today than I'd ever seen her and the circles under her eyes were non-existent.

I wanted to see more of this Magnolia—the one who was starting to let herself relax and heal. She was coming alive, and I was the lucky bastard that got to go along for the ride.

She pointed out different flowers as we walked around the grounds, and I finally tugged her to a stop when we got back around to the front of the impressive structure. "Want to go inside?"

Her cheeks were flushed, and her eyes were bright, and I couldn't help myself, leaning down to steal a kiss. She laughed and grasped my face, pulling me closer to deepen the kiss when I tried to pull back. I groaned and wrapped her in my arms, moving closer so our bodies were flush together and every soft curve that was Magnolia pressed into me. I couldn't have stopped myself from getting hard even if I wanted to.

And shit, that was the last thing I wanted.

This more affectionate Magnolia, though? Her, I could get used to.

My whole body practically vibrated with the need to be inside her, something I was trying to be a gentleman about and not push her too much, but once I'd had a taste and I knew how perfect she felt wrapped around me, I thought about it almost constantly. She pulled back from our kiss and gave me a look that would make men drop to their knees in devotion to this woman.

I didn't understand how someone could sweep in and have such an effect on me, but here I was, and damn if I didn't like it maybe a little too much. This tour wasn't going at all how I expected it to, but wasn't that how life was sometimes? It had a way of throwing shit at you before you were ready, and suddenly, you'd realize it didn't matter because whatever you had to do to make it work was worth it.

That was Magnolia to me. I hadn't known she was coming and hadn't been looking for her, not really. Now that she was here, I didn't want her going anywhere and would do whatever I had to to keep her.

"Baby, as much as I want to finish what you just started, I don't think this is the best place. We've got two nights in a hotel here, and I plan to take full advantage," I promised, a wicked grin on my face as her eyes darkened. "How about we go look at some art?"

"Yay. Art," Magnolia said sarcastically, and I laughed, pulling her behind me up the steps into the giant concrete replica, determined to make the most of our time in Nashville and see something outside of the walls of our hotel room. I had a feeling once we ended up there, we wouldn't be going back out unless we absolutely had to.

Magnolia raised her eyebrow at me, and I laughed. "What? You know I'm from Texas."

"Yeah, but you don't strike me as the kind of guy who listens to a whole lot of country music," she noted, letting her striking blue gaze run over all my tattoos and piercings and my body heated under her scrutiny. Again.

I'd been buzzing with the need to feel Magnolia wrapped around my dick all damn day, every brush of her skin against mine driving me out of my damn skull. I felt like I was losing my goddamn mind, and my body was on the verge of overriding logical thought, throwing her over my shoulder and rushing back to the hotel to spend the next however many hours we had left showing her exactly what kind of effect she had on me.

"Well, ma'am, give me any country song from the nineties, and I could probably sing along," I drawled, letting the twang I'd worked hard to bury pop out in an exaggerated way, and she giggled. It was a sound I hadn't heard from her yet, but one that had everything inside me lighting up.

Instead of continuing our banter, she turned on the stage and looked out into the empty auditorium, breathing in deeply. "Just think about all the people who've stood on this stage in the last ninety-five years," she mused. "The music that's been played and all the people in the audience who had a chance to come out and see the show, no matter what was goin' on in their lives. They all came together to enjoy somethin' special. It's really incredible when you think about it."

I stepped up beside her and looked out into the rows of empty seats. The Grand Ole Opry was a place of musical legend, and just like Magnolia, I never thought I'd be standing on this stage. This was one of those places on every musician's bucket list—no matter how famous or not famous you were. "What show do you wish you could've seen?"

Without hesitation, she answered, "When Garth Brooks played here in nineteen-ninety, I would've given anythin' to see it. It was before I was born, but my Grammy had this VHS tape of the show that she watched a lot when I was little. If I would've been alive, I'd have liked to take my Grammy to see it." I couldn't help but watch Magnolia as she described a memory from her childhood. She didn't share them very often, and the wistful look on her face and the soft smile she wore sucked the air from my lungs.

She was so goddamn beautiful that sometimes it hurt to look at her.

"I'm sure she's looking down at you now, impressed that you're standing on this stage," I told her, putting my arm across her shoulders and pulling her into my side. I spun us, so we looked up at the wooden barn backdrop that was part of the original shows that used to happen here every week. "Look at this place."

"It's so much bigger in person," Magnolia noted, a hint of awe in her voice as she took in our surroundings.

I chuckled. "That's what all the girls say."

She glared up at me and hit me in the stomach with the back of her hand. "I don't want to hear about *all the girls*, Griffin Spencer."

My smile only got wider. "Why, Magnolia, are you jealous?"

She huffed and turned away, looking back up at the barn, and I reached around and turned her face back to me. "You are, aren't you?" Her jealousy set my insides on fire, knowing she was possessive of me like I was of her. Confirmation that she wanted me the same way I wanted her made my heart clench and my dick hard.

I moved around her and stepped up, so we stood toe-to-toe and nose-to-nose. "What are you doing to me, Mags?" I whispered, staring into her eyes where she looked back at me with so much intensity, it made my knees weak.

"I could ask you the same thing, Sugar," she whispered back, and all I could do was kiss her. The kiss was sweet and languid like we had all the time in the world to explore each other and communicate everything we were feeling without ever having to use our words. It went on forever, but every whimper and moan out of Magnolia's mouth had the tempo increasing and the heat level rising until I had to tear myself away from her yet again. It was becoming a real problem how out of control she made me feel when we were in public.

A problem I was going to need a bedroom and countless hours to solve.

My thoughts were firmly in the *I need to get between Magnolia legs now* category when her phone buzzing broke me out of the recurring fantasies playing in my head. She looked down at the screen, and her forehead wrinkled.

"Who is it?" I wondered, watching her carefully.

"I don't recognize the number." The phone kept buzzing in her hand as we both watched the number flash on the screen. "I have to answer. It could be someone on the crew."

She sighed and swiped, lifting the phone to her ear. "Hello?"

I kept my eyes trained on her but walked around the stage trying to give her a little bit of privacy, even if it was a joke. This place was built to make sound carry.

Her whole body tensed up, and I gave up the illusion of keeping my distance, quickly eating up the small space between us in case she needed me. "He did? What does that mean?"

A few seconds passed while whoever was on the other line spoke, and then Magnolia said her goodbyes and hung up. Her whole demeanor had shifted during that call, and I had to wonder what happened. She'd been easygoing and relaxed today, but that was all gone now. What was left behind was the same stressed out and tense Magnolia she'd started the tour as.

"What happened, Mags?" I rubbed her upper arms, trying to get her to shake out of her discomfort, but it was like she didn't even realize I was touching her. Her body was extremely responsive to me at all times, so for her to not even react had alarm bells blaring in my head.

"That was Detective Ayers," she started, and my hands froze on her arms for a second before I shook off my unease at the mention of the detective who was in charge of Winston's case, and resumed rubbing her soft skin. I stayed silent, waiting for her to continue.

"Winston posted bail and is out of jail." Her breath wooshed out of her, and she practically collapsed in on herself, like the words took all her strength with them when they left her lips.

"Christ," I bit out, holding Magnolia against me while I fished my phone out of my pocket and sent a text to Ryan to let her know. "We left him in Miami, and he's only out on bail. He can't leave the state."

Magnolia looked up at me dubiously. "C'mon, Sugar. You know that's never stopped him before. It's only a matter of time before he finds me." As her words finished, her phone started vibrating with an unknown caller, and all I wanted to do was take it out of her hand and stomp on it until only tiny shards of glass and metal were left. The frustration in the air between us was palpable. I could practically smell it.

"You want to go back to the hotel?" I hated having to cut our date short, but with Winston out of jail and a wildcard, I wasn't willing to risk Magnolia. Connor and his team would have the hotel on lockdown, so once we were inside, she'd be safe.

She nodded woodenly, and I was glad we took a couple of selfies when we first stepped on stage because I wanted those to be the memory of today and not whatever was happening right now. Fucking Winston had to ruin yet another experience for Magnolia, and I hated him that much more for it, something I hadn't even known was possible.

"Detective Ayers also told me I should get an emergency restraining order. We left Miami so fast I didn't have a chance to do it then, but we have an extra day here. Do you think you could help me with that?" she asked me, looking at me with lost eyes that sucked me in and made me want to promise her I'd do anything she asked, no matter how difficult.

"We'll take care of it today," I promised as we made our way out of the landmark that I wasn't even paying attention to anymore. It was crazy how fast Winston had screwed up the whole day. It was like that was what he was put on this earth to do—fuck everything up and cause pain. He had a damn knack for it, like a sixth sense.

Magnolia was quiet on the ride back to the hotel, and I could see the gears in her head turning, but I didn't think there was anything I could say to make her feel better about the situation. We had to let time pass and let the justice system do its job.

"I think I need to quit the tour," she finally said when we were almost back to the hotel.

"What? Why?" I couldn't hide the shock in my voice. The last thing I wanted Magnolia to do was to quit. Not only was she great at her job, but she seemed happy doing it, and now that she was here with us—with me—I couldn't imagine doing it without her.

She looked up at me, and the defeat in her eyes was like a punch in the face. I sucked in a breath but let her say whatever she needed to, knowing there was no way in hell I'd let her give up on this. "He's always gonna find me, and he's always gonna be there waitin' in the shadows. I'm puttin' everyone in danger by stayin' here, and I can't do that. It's not fair to anyone, but even worse, there are kids involved, Griffin."

Her using my name instead of calling me Sugar let me know she was serious, and I realized how her sarcastic nickname for me had transformed into something between just the two of us, and I loved that.

"It would be for the best if I disappeared and found somethin' to do that kept me completely off the radar so Winston can't find me or put anyone else in danger." She nibbled on her lip, and her body language was completely opposite of the lively girl I'd been working to pull out of her shell just earlier today. She'd been like a new bloom emerging from a seed, and now she was wilting before my eyes.

Now that she was finished, it was my turn. I waited until she turned her attention to me. "You're not quitting, Mags. You said it yourself—Winston always finds you. He's not going to stop unless we make him, and you're safest here with me. We have security, and sure, he may know where we are or where we're going to be next, but that doesn't mean he'll be able to get to you now that everything's out in the open. Hasn't he taken enough from you? Don't let him take this, too. Be here with me. Stay," I begged, grabbing her hand and holding it against my chest just over my heart where it was beating frantically while I waited for her answer.

I couldn't let her go. It wasn't a matter of wanting to. I *couldn't*.

The thought of watching her walk away made my chest feel like it was splintering open. What would it feel like if she actually left? I didn't want to find out.

"I don't want to go," she whispered like she was confessing a secret, and my heart broke a little for the pain in her voice, for everything she'd lost and been forced to endure.

"I know you don't, so stay," I pleaded.

"I'll think about it."

"If you go, I'm going with you." I hadn't thought it through, but when the words came out, they felt right.

She was shaking her head before I'd even finished, her eyes wide. "You can't."

I shrugged, still holding onto her hand. "You can't either, so if you go, I go."

"I won't let you."

I smirked. "Right back atcha, baby."

Magnolia huffed, and my smirk fell. I reached out and turned her, so she was looking at me again. "I know you're not used to relying on people because you've never really had anyone you could count on."

"Besides my gram."

"Exactly, but now you have people in your corner. You're not alone anymore, and you don't have to run. We'll get the restraining order, and then we'll go from there. Okay?"

She watched me, her gaze darting between my eyes as if she was looking for a sign that I wasn't telling her the truth or that I was bullshitting her in some way, but she wouldn't find anything but sincerity and a whole hell of a lot of pleading there. Finally, she nodded as her eyes glittered with unshed tears. "Thank you."

"You don't have to thank me, Mags. I'm going to spend forever proving to you that I'm on your side," I promised, reaching up to brush away a tear that was falling down her cheek.

We pulled up to the front of the hotel, the lights at the entrance blazing against the night that'd fallen on our way back. We should be going to a fancy dinner right now, but instead, we were here, escaping the potential danger that her ex posed. Irritation poked at me, but I pushed it down. It wouldn't be long before Winston was out of her life for good. I had to hope all it would take was the restraining order, but the dude didn't seem like he'd be content just to give up. I wasn't sure what it would take to get him to move on, but I wasn't opposed to seeing him rot in jail for eternity.

I thanked the driver and stepped out of the car, holding the door open for Magnolia, and as soon as she stepped onto the drive in front of the hotel, she glanced around the parking lot. It seemed to be a habit of hers, always being aware of her surroundings. I noticed it when we were in Philly and again in Atlanta. Today she seemed to have relaxed her vigilance, and I hated that she felt like she had to fall back into her old habits.

I watched as her whole body stiffened, every muscle tensing as our ride drove away and we were left exposed. "What? What's wrong?"

Her gaze was locked on something across the parking lot, and I squinted to see. "I think Winston's out there."

I reached out and pulled her back behind my body on instinct, needing to shield her from whatever danger he posed. How the fuck had he gotten here so quickly? Detective Ayers was about to get one hell of a phone call from me for not giving Magnolia more notice. "Where?"

She spoke quietly as she leaned into me, discreetly pointing at a street lamp on the far side of the lot. "There. The figure under the streetlight watching us. He's just standing there." Her body trembled as she leaned into me.

"Shit," I cursed, grabbing my phone out of my pocket and texting Connor and Ryan. "Let's go inside and try to ignore him. They'll take care of it, but we're getting you that restraining order tonight. As soon as he's gone, we're going to the police." I turned and rested my hand on her lower back, ushering her inside the hotel lobby with my back to whoever was out there watching. I hoped it wasn't Winston, but it seemed like he wasn't going to give up.

"Winston's going to get what's coming to him," I assured her, leading her to the elevator. I could only hope that the justice system didn't let us down because while we could deal with Winston's bullshit on our own, I had a feeling

Magnolia wouldn't be open to the way the guys would step in and take him down.

Magnolia was too good and too pure for the darkness we could unleash on him, but make no mistake about it—I'd do whatever the hell I had to do to protect her from him, even if it meant getting my hands dirty.

SIXTEEN
MAGNOLIA

The judge signed off on the restraining order immediately, and the piece of paper folded up in my purse gave me back just a little bit of my power. I wished I'd done this sooner, but I hadn't felt brave enough to bring up everything Winston did in the past to the police. He'd always threatened that if I did, he'd kill me, so I kept it to myself.

I hadn't even been able to confess what was going on to the nurse at the hospital on my last night with Winston. She'd been the one to take one look at me and figure it out, telling me what she thought was going on, and all I'd been able to do was nod and cry.

The sun poured in through windows that made up almost an entire wall in our hotel room, and I got out of bed, leaving Griffin sprawled out and tangled in the sheets, all his delicious ink on display. I shook my head, still in disbelief that he wanted me. *Me.* When he could have anyone. I'd seen his last girlfriend, and I couldn't be further from everything she was. I wasn't polished, and I wasn't all that ambitious.

The only things I wanted out of this life were a place to call home and people to love. For now, I was here, doing what I had to do to survive and keep going, and along the way, somehow, I'd managed to carve out a little bit of what I wanted most.

I pulled on Griffin's discarded t-shirt, smiling as his scent surrounded me. Lucky perked up from his pillow on the floor at the end of the bed, but he just watched me go. He'd claimed Griffin as his, and whenever he was around, Lucky didn't like to leave his side even to come to me or play with the kids.

I couldn't really blame my puppy. I felt the same way about the guy. I moved into the kitchen and dropped a coffee pod into the single-serve machine, waiting for it to brew. My phone was on the counter, and I picked it up, finding I'd been included in a group message with all the girls, and my heart sped up. I was actually making friends, and I was pretty dang excited about it.

Kennedy: Brunch and Mimosas at ten in the lobby. You all better be there. I NEED girl time without kids or husbands. This is not optional.

Amara: True already planned on hitting up a local park this morning with Phoenix. I'm in.

Moon: Benji was up all night screaming. Jericho's going to hate me lol

Kennedy: He'll be fine, or I'll threaten to expose his secrets.

Ryan: We all know about his anime porn thing.

I bit my lip, deciding to jump in and hoping they took it okay.

Magnolia: I didn't know, but thanks for the info

Amara: Hahahaha

Moon: He's going to kill you, Ken, and I've been told it's called hentai...

Montana: Someone better video me in, or I'm going to be pissed, and thanks to you degenerates, I now know way more about Jericho's jerking off habits than I ever wanted to.

Ryan: We've got you, girl lmao

Magnolia: See you guys at 10. Thanks for including me.

I set my phone down after checking the time. It was eight-thirty, so I didn't have to hurry. My muscles ached from the stress of yesterday, getting that call, seeing who I assumed was Winston watching from afar, and then having to recount my entire story—again, for the second time this week—to the police. Waiting to hear what the judge would do was nerve-wracking, and all that tension made my body hurt.

With Griffin still asleep, I decided I wanted to finish my coffee in the bath, so I moved into the bathroom and filled the tub with hot water, using the expensive bubble bath and oils the hotel provided. The bathroom smelled like lavender and vanilla, and I sank into the soothing water, leaning my head back and closing my eyes.

The tension was melting out of me as I soaked, but the door creaking open had my eyes flicking open to see a sexy sleep-rumpled Griffin shuffling into the bathroom. "Morning, sleepyhead," I chimed, eyeing him up and down as he started pulling off his clothes. I planned on enjoying every second of the impromptu sexy show he was putting on. "What are you doing?"

He didn't answer but motioned for me to move forward, so I did, and he slid into the water behind me, pulling my back against his hard chest and starting to massage my shoulders. "You're my every fantasy come to life, Magnolia," he purred against my ear, his warm breath brushing my skin and making heat spiral straight to my core as his hands worked the knots from my muscles.

I closed my eyes and leaned back into him with a moan as the steamy water lapped at my skin with the movements of his hands, teasing my hardening nipples as soft bubbles piled up around us.

Griffin's lips found my neck and pressed gentle kisses along the curve of my damp skin, nipping and licking a path down to my shoulder. His hands slid from my shoulders around to the front of my body, where he palmed my breasts before lightly stroking my nipple with the pad of his thumb. I arched against him, gasping as his hard-on pressed against my lower back.

"Feel that?" he murmured against my neck where he was continuing to turn me on with his sinful mouth. As if to show what he meant, he pushed his hips forward, and his hardness slid along my skin, making me whimper with need. "That's what you do to me."

One of his hands drifted down my body, his fingers lightly skimming along the skin of my stomach until they settled between my legs. I opened wide for him, desperate for his touch, for his talented fingers to work their magic on my body.

I leaned back and kissed him, tasting how much he wanted me on his lips, using my fingers to tangle in his hair and pull him closer to me. It was a taste I was sure I'd never get tired of.

He didn't hesitate to make me squirm as he stroked along my slit, pushing one finger slowly inside and pulling it back out in an agonizing rhythm that teased me because it would never be enough. I tried to push closer, to match his rhythm with my hips, so I was riding his fingers, but he banded his arm around my waist and held me still so I was completely at his mercy.

"I can feel how much you want me," Griffin growled quietly in my ear as his fingers played. "Your sweet little pussy is greedy, isn't it? You want to feel my dick right here, don't you?" His voice was deep and husky as dirty words poured out of him like I'd never heard before. He slid his finger all the way out of me and picked me up by my waist, spinning me until I straddled his hips. Water sloshed over the side of the tub onto the floor, but I'd never cared about anything less.

When his fingers found my hips and dug in just enough, I threw my head back and lowered myself down so his length brushed against all the slickness gathered between my legs. It didn't matter that we were in the bath—I was wet enough that the water couldn't wash it away. My hips rocked almost involuntarily, an intense need screaming throughout my body to get *closer* a constant taunt.

Finally, when I didn't think I could take any more teasing, Griffin shifted his hips underneath me and impaled me in one swift thrust. I gasped at the exquisite feeling of being completely filled up by the most beautiful man I've ever seen; his eyes focused only on me as he murmured sexy promises he was seconds away from delivering on.

Those talented fingers of his tweaked my nipples as he rocked into me, and I came undone, my whole body clenching around him so tightly he cursed and picked up his pace through my orgasm, making more waves crash over the side of the tub and onto the floor. "You're so fucking sexy when you come," he declared, his raspy voice full of wonder and his eyes dark and wicked.

Like he'd suddenly become possessed, he stood with me still wrapped around him and stepped out of the tub, water splashing everywhere, carrying me to the nearest wall and pressing me back into it as he thrust himself in and out of me. The pleasure was overwhelming, and it didn't take long before I was climbing higher again, the feeling so intense it was almost painful.

Discovering I liked a little pain mixed in with my pleasure only had me whimpering and begging for more. The soft sighs escaping my parted lips and my head tilted back against the wall were a testament to how much Griffin was making me *feel*.

"Come with me," he ordered, but it sounded more like a plea as he took what he needed from my body at the same time I willingly gave it. His words threw us both over the edge into oblivion, and if I'd thought my first orgasm was intense, it had nothing on this one. My vision blackened around the edges, and my heart pounded in my chest as wave after wave of satisfaction rolled through me.

"Holy hell," I breathed, bringing my head forward to rest it on his shoulder while I tried to catch my breath. His arms shook as he held me between his body and the wall; his softening cock still twitching inside me.

"You can say that again," he drawled, his lips curling up into a grin that was equal parts cocky and satisfied. I dropped down to my feet, missing how perfectly our bodies fit together, but without his heat, I realized how cool the air in the room really was against my dripping wet skin.

I shivered, and Griffin wrapped me in a fluffy white towel, the cocky grin now replaced with a soft smile as he looked at me with what I could best describe as reverence. I was sure his expression was mirrored in me because I was starting to believe my luck had turned around about the same time Lucky's had.

How could this man want me? With all of my baggage and issues and fears and insecurities, he didn't seem to care. If anything, it drew him closer like he had some compulsion—a need or obsession, maybe—to heal the parts of me that were broken. He mentioned his mom had gone through something similar, so maybe he saw her in me.

It didn't really matter. For whatever reason, he was here with me, standing by my side and propping me up when I needed him to, and that ice around my heart had fully melted into a puddle because of it.

I'd never been more scared at the realization that I'd let him in and let myself be vulnerable, and I was dangerously close to letting the L-word escape my lips, but I bit it back. I wasn't ready yet. I might be terrified, but I was also relieved and excited. The part of me I thought Winston had ruined forever Griffin had mended back together, and like kintsugi—golden veins sealing beautiful shards of china back together after they'd shattered—I liked the version of me I was becoming as I healed.

That was the effect he had on me, and when the doubts inevitably started to creep back in, I hoped he'd be by my side to remind me not to give into them. In the meantime, I bit my lip to keep from letting the post-orgasmic haze I was in spill every love-filled thought out of my mouth and instead went to get ready. I had a brunch with the group of girls I was starting to consider friends, and the idea of that had me smiling wider than ever.

"Ugh, I'm so fucking jealous of you bitches," Montana complained. "I'm chained to this damn desk, and you get to be out there living it up."

Amara snickered, and Kennedy looked smug as hell. I wasn't sure what to say, but Moon chimed in. "Stop whining, lady! You know you could hop on the jet and be here in like four hours if you wanted to. You've got a tablet and the internet. It's not exactly the stone ages out here, so get your cute butt on the plane."

She rolled her eyes and leaned back in her desk chair. "I would if I could in a heartbeat, but the tour has been an incredible success. Even more than the guys hoped, which means prepare yourselves, ladies. The vultures are about to descend."

I didn't know what the heck she was talking about, but looking around the table, the tension had definitely gone up.

Ryan pulled out her phone and started texting, but Kennedy looked resigned, and Montana sighed. "Maybe you'll get lucky, and they'll want fresh meat. Bellamy's got that whole fresh-faced at eighteen thing going for her, and her voice is killer."

"Maybe," Amara agreed, and Moon picked up her mimosa and sipped it. She looked the least bothered about whatever was happening, so I scooted a little closer to where she sat on my right, tuning out Montana.

"What's goin' on?" I asked her quietly, not wanting to interrupt the conversation happening across the table.

She tossed her gorgeous, multi-colored mermaid hair over her shoulder—at least that's what it reminded me of, a mermaid—and smiled at me. Her eyes were so warm, I couldn't help but smile back. "Something you're going to have to learn to accept as an unfortunate side effect of dating a famous musician."

I must've had a blank expression on my face, and she laughed, taking pity on me. "Paparazzi, Magnolia."

I shivered. I'd been so wrapped up in my job and all the crap with Winston, I hadn't given any thought to what it meant to be dating someone famous. Griffin seemed like a normal guy to me, so it was easy to forget that this was his life, and if I was with him, it was about to become mine, too.

"Oh." I wasn't really sure what to say to that. At this point, I wasn't sure anything would make me walk away from Griffin other than him being abusive or cheating on me. Anything else I hoped we could work through together. I'd worked way too damn hard to have anything less than high expectations out of a partner. I was learning my worth, and I deserved to be treated well.

Being followed by reporters wasn't even on my list of the worst things you could experience in life. I was sure I'd be fine dealing with whatever happened. Not only that, but it wasn't like I had family out there to embarrass with whatever fake nonsense tabloids made up about me or my relationship with Griffin. I wasn't all that concerned.

Moon patted my knee and smiled at me. "It's really not that bad, especially with security. I think at the beginning, before I was around, it was worse for Kennedy because none of the guys had ever really had girlfriends before, and they didn't know how to handle it. Now they're like a well-oiled machine. Plus, you've got us to keep you grounded. Us new girls have to stick together, right?" She winked at me, and I relaxed even more.

Girl time was something I knew I needed, but I guess I never knew how much until right now as some part of me that'd been missing clicked into place. "Right," I agreed, picking a piece off the croissant on my plate and nibbling on it while I took everything in.

I smiled as I watched all their interactions, and when they made sure to include me in their jokes and stories, I couldn't help but feel embraced by these women. My life seemed to be turning around, and I was completely here for it. For the first time ever, I could breathe, and I could hope.

If Winston stayed away, it wouldn't take much for life to be perfect.

A loud crash from outside the room where the guys were currently working their way through the Nashville fan meet and greet had me lifting my head from the tablet I was busy making notes on. When it happened again, I stood up and hurried over to the door. The last fan from the second-to-last group had left the room a couple of minutes ago, and the guys were on their break.

Glancing around the room, Griffin and his brother were both missing, and my heart rate ratcheted up. If Winston came back and managed to get past security again, he could've gotten to Griffin, and then what would I do?

Connor stood by the door, and he didn't look all that concerned, so I exhaled slowly, trying to calm the quickly rising storm of anxiety surging through me. Security was here to keep the band safe, but it was my job to deal with whatever uncomfortable situations might come up between personnel or fans, so I pulled on my big girl panties and sucked in a deep breath before pushing the doors open.

What I saw stopped me in my tracks.

My whole body froze up as I shattered.

Devastation rocketed through me as I watched Griffin kiss his ex-girlfriend, the one he said was nothing but a mistake. She was plastered up against him, and I looked away as fast as I could, but the image was burned into my brain.

Was that what I was? A mistake?

When they broke the kiss, his eyes immediately found mine and widened. "Mags-"

I held up my shaking hand. "No."

There was nothing else to say, was there? How could he explain this away? And where had Wynter come from?

The triumphant smile she wore as she turned to look at me twisted her features into something vile and sinister, all that disgust aimed right at me. "Didn't you hear? Griff and I are back together." The gleeful tone in her voice was like a thousand knives shredding the little control I'd managed to hold on to, and I stepped backward, slowly at first and then faster, spinning and taking off at a run.

I had to get away before the tears started to fall because I'd never let them see me cry. I'd been right all along. It had all been an illusion, and my stupid, overly-trusting heart had lapped up Griffin's attention like a starved animal. How pathetic must I look to him to have given in so easily? My cheeks burned with humiliation, and my eyes stung with the effort to hold back my tears.

Getting as far away from the two of them as quickly as I could became my only priority. It was only a matter of time before I couldn't hold the tsunami at bay any longer, but before that happened, I needed distance and privacy, two things that weren't easy to find when you were in a small space with a lot of people.

The first hot tear streaked down my cheek, and I wiped it away angrily, keeping up my quick pace as I zig-zagged down halls, not paying any attention to where I was going.

Distance. Distance. Distance.

It was like a chant, a mantra I clung to as I rounded a corner and found a dead end. I reached the end of my control at the same time like a tether snapping, and I fell against the wall and sunk to the floor, resting my head on my knees and curling my arms around myself as I let the tears flow freely. I couldn't fight them off even if I tried.

How could I have been so stupid? Again?

Sadness blanketed me as I gave in to the familiar self-loathing that was almost comfortable at this point. It was a place I knew well and retreated to all the time with Winston. I never thought I'd find myself back in this dark place with Griffin.

People depended on me now, and no matter what, I could only give myself a few minutes to give in to the despair because even if he'd taken my heart and burned it until all that remained was a pile of ash, I wouldn't let him take my pride or my dignity.

And I sure as hell wouldn't let him ruin my career.

I was done with it all. Done with men. Done with thinking I could depend on anyone but myself.

Done.

SEVENTEEN
GRIFFIN

"What the *actual* fuck do you think you're doing?" I snapped, not trying to keep my voice down at all for Magnolia's sake because she'd taken one look at Wynter throwing herself at me and bolted. The look in her eye… *fuck.* If I thought she'd been broken before, it was nothing compared to the moment before she'd turned and run away from me.

My heart cracked inside my chest, stumbling over itself at the reality of what just happened. I worked so goddamn hard to earn Magnolia's trust, and Wynter—fucking *Wynter*—decided to show back up here uninvited and unannounced to try and insert herself back in my life.

No fucking thank you.

Wynter stuck her painted pink lips out in an obnoxious pout as I wiped at my mouth, trying to erase the poisonous taste of her off my lips. As soon as she threw herself at me, I clamped my jaw shut and pried her off as fast as possible, but the woman was like a damn octopus. She'd wrapped herself around me so tight, digging her claws into my arm, that it took me a second to shove her off.

And that second? It might've cost me the best thing that'd ever happened to me if the look in Magnolia's eyes was anything to go by.

I didn't blame her for running. Considering everything she'd been through, jumping to the worst conclusion possible was to be expected. I was mad as hell that I'd been the one to give her a reason to doubt my feelings, even if it wasn't intentional. I had to fix this, but first, Wynter had to get the fuck out.

Movement over her shoulder grabbed my attention, and I didn't realize it was possible, but I got even more pissed off when her shifty assistant, Ross, squirmed in the shadows. Naturally, he'd be here with her. I slid my gaze back over to Wynter. "Answer. Me."

"I missed you," she tried, her voice going all simpering and soft in a way that made my skin crawl. What had I ever seen in this girl?

Folding my arms across my chest, I glared down at her. "Try again."

She dropped all pretense of sweetness and looked me over shrewdly, like something she'd like to own and carry around in her obnoxiously large handbag so she could use it whenever she saw fit. "I left because I thought my followers got tired of our relationship, but I was wrong, okay? Once we were officially over, I dropped a massive amount of subscribers. I'm trying to figure out what the problem is, but to stop the hemorrhaging, I need you back."

She was all business now, but I knew exactly what the problem was. Wynter had no substance whatsoever. She was all surface, ambition, and a pretty face with nothing underneath that people could grasp onto or relate to.

I laughed, but it wasn't a nice laugh. It was sharp and a little too loud, and she cringed when it rolled over her. "Not a chance in hell. Now kindly get the fuck out and never come back."

Her eyes narrowed, and her spine straightened. "Excuse me? No. I'm not going anywhere. You haven't even heard my proposition yet."

"I don't want to hear anything you have to say, but hear this. I don't want you. I will not be participating in any way in your life from here on out, and if you don't get the hell out of here in the next three seconds, I'm going to have security escort your ass out." I was not playing games, and every second it took to get Wynter out of here was another that Magnolia was convincing herself of things that just weren't true.

The longer this took, the harder it'd be to pull her out of her destructive thoughts.

Wynter stomped her foot and huffed. "You're making a mistake. If I-"

I held up my hand and reached into my pocket, bringing my phone out and finding the right contact. It was already ringing, and I brought it to my ear and called in Connor. He was just in the other room, so it took him less than thirty seconds before he was standing in the hallway with us, his imposing form taking up a lot of the space, and the rest was taken up by Indy on his right.

Wynter's eyes widened before she tilted her chin in the air and spun on her heel. Connor looked at me with a raised eyebrow, and I nodded toward where Ross was lurking in the shadows. Indy stepped over and corralled him toward the exit. "Please make sure neither of them are allowed backstage for the rest of the tour," I requested, and Connor nodded, a menacing grin taking over his face. He'd always hated the pair of them. "Oh, and make sure you get a picture of them getting tossed out. I think I might need to update my Instagram account."

"My pleasure." I didn't doubt he'd get some enjoyment out of keeping Wynter and Ross away, and seeing them publicly humiliated would be the icing on the cake if I went through with it. Neither one of them had endeared themselves to anyone in my life, and I was so damn glad my eyes were open now, and I saw reality as it was and not some weird twisted version that Wynter had created and spun.

Once they were out of sight, I raked my fingers through my hair and turned in the direction Magnolia took off in. My hurried steps echoed off the empty walls as I turned down corridor after corridor, finding each one missing the one person I was desperate to find. My phone vibrated from where I'd slid it into my pocket, and I pulled it out, checking the message.

The picture Connor sent me made my lips twitch, but I couldn't smile until Magnolia knew the truth and was back in my arms.

My phone started vibrating again, but I ignored it. I was pushing it time-wise. I'd already missed the last of the meet and greet, and I'd need to change and get ready to play soon. None of that mattered, though. Nothing was more important right now than Magnolia.

She was somewhere in this building—just out of reach—hurting because of me. There was no way I'd be able to focus until I made it right. Knowing I hurt her made my stomach twist. I never wanted to be the person that caused her tears. I wasn't perfect, and I knew it. There would be times in our life together that we might not get along perfectly, or we might have disagreements, but damn, I'd fallen *hard* for that sweet Southern girl, and losing her over a stupid misunderstanding was *not* an option.

The sound of her despair hit me before I saw her, and my insides twisted painfully. I rounded the corner and moved to stand in front of her, where she was sitting against the wall curled protectively around herself as if using the outer part of her body to shield her heart away from the world. It killed me to see her like that, and I fell to my knees in front of her and watched helplessly, unsure if she'd reject me if I tried to reach out and comfort her.

She hadn't seen me yet, but the quieting of her tears and the stiffening of her shoulders let me know she was aware I'd found her. "Mags…"

It was as if my voice broke her on a whole new level as the floodgates opened and sobs wracked her body. I didn't care if she pushed me away or not, the need to wrap her up in my arms was overwhelming, so I did. I pulled her against my chest, and at first, her body stiffened, but little by little, she gave in until she was leaning against me with my shirt wrapped in her fists and her hot tears soaking through the fabric.

I stroked her hair and whispered comforting words and promises I had every intention of keeping into her ear as I held her, and when her cries finally died down, she sat back and looked at me with red-rimmed eyes puffy from her anguish. I hated myself for doing this to her.

"Is this the part where you tell me it wasn't what I thought?" she asked in such a broken voice, I almost wanted to cry myself.

I reached out and dried the tears from her cheeks with my fingers, but more fell and took their place. "It sounds cliche, but it's the truth. I had no idea Wynter was coming here. I hadn't seen or talked to her at all since she broke up with me, and I didn't want to. I stepped outside the room to find the bathroom, and she threw herself at me before I could even ask what the hell she was doing here or how she got backstage. You walked into the hall the second after she kissed me in what has to be the worst timing in history."

My lame attempt at a joke fell flat as she stared up at me, but her tears had stopped. "I want to believe you."

I pulled out my phone and unlocked it, holding it out for her. "Look through it. You can see the last messages she sent me were from weeks ago."

She hesitated a couple of seconds before giving in and grabbing it.

I didn't mind letting Magnolia into every aspect of my life if it meant she'd trust me. Sometimes when someone was broken, you had to go beyond what other people considered *healthy boundaries* to show them they could trust you. If Magnolia needed to go through my phone or my email or my laptop to see that I had nothing to hide from her, I'd let her in the blink of an eye.

She clicked and scrolled, but it didn't take long for her to realize I'd been telling the truth. She held the device back out for me looking embarrassed, but I wanted none of that. I pushed my phone back toward her. "Take a look at the last message from Connor."

Her eyes widened, and then she cracked a smile, and it was like the sun broke through the clouds, and I could breathe again. "Is Wynter on the ground?" she asked, squinting at the screen to get a better look.

I nodded. "Right after you ran off, she refused to leave, so I called him and had him toss her out. Not my fault he took my words literally. Her and her annoying assistant. Just so you know, she's not allowed to step even a single cloven hoof near this tour again. I made sure of it."

Magnolia actually chuckled as she handed me back my phone, and I pocketed it, ignoring all the missed calls and messages piling up. The guys could wait. They'd understand, and if they didn't, well… I'd deal with the fallout later.

Tonight's show wouldn't be the first concert a rock band had ever started late, and I sort of thought it added to the band's legendary status if we kept people waiting every now and then. Okay, maybe just this once.

"You did that for me?" She looked up at me through eyelashes wet with tears I'd caused and my chest clenched.

"I'd do anything for you, Mags, but this I did for both of us. As much as you didn't want her around, I probably wanted her here less."

"I'm sorry, I assumed you did somethin' wrong and ran off. I should've known you wouldn't do that to me, and I should have stayed to let you explain." She looked away and wrung her hands together, and I wasn't having any of that bullshit.

I reached out and tilted her chin up so she was looking at me again. "You don't have anything to apologize for. If I'd seen you kissing another guy like that, especially your ex, I'd have lost my shit, too." She gave me a small smile, so I kept going. "I know we haven't been together that long, and things are complicated as hell, but I'm so in this with you, Magnolia. I've fallen so damn hard, I'm surprised I didn't break every bone in my body."

Her eyes got wide, and her perfect pink lips fell into a surprised *O* that made me want to kiss her stupid. I chuckled and reached over to close her mouth with a finger under her chin. "I would never, and I mean *never*, do something to hurt you if I had any way to help it. Life's messy, Mags, but I'm not going anywhere because…" I swallowed hard. "I love you."

My heart thundered in my chest. I hadn't meant the words to slip out like that. I figured I'd wait a while until things were more resolved with her past, and we were more settled, maybe after the tour was over and I could integrate her into my life at home. But my brain and heart? They weren't on the same page *at all*, and my heart won out every damn time when it came to Magnolia.

I watched as she bit her lip, absorbing what I said. I wouldn't take it back, and I sure as shit wouldn't regret it because the truth was I *did* love her. I loved her more with every beat of my heart or breath that filled my lungs. My love for her felt endless like it could grow and grow for eternity and never be enough because it couldn't be contained or held within boundaries. It was infinite and all-encompassing, and if she didn't feel the same right now, I'd be okay waiting until she did.

The time would come where she'd realize we were a foregone conclusion from the moment we met. If that wasn't today, it would be someday, and that was enough. The parts of her that needed to be healed fit exactly with the parts of me that needed someone to love, like a set of Legos that clicked together just right. She might need time to see it, but I had no doubt she would.

I was so buried in my own thoughts, I almost didn't hear her whispered words. "I thought I was in love with Winston, but it turns out I never really knew what love was. At least not until you showed me."

Hope sprung up in my chest. Was she saying what I thought she was saying? I kept my damn mouth shut, waiting for her to gather her thoughts because there was no way in hell I was about to interrupt her.

She took a deep, shuddering breath, and I grasped her hand in mine, weaving our fingers together and rubbing my thumb across her palm. "I've never had someone I could lean on before, not really. My grammy was there for me but also raised me to be independent and not need anyone else. She never coddled me. I'm scared," she admitted, dropping her head back down on her knees and taking a few breaths.

"I'm scared because once I say the words, once I speak it into existence, I give you the power to break me. More than Winston, more than anyone, you could wreck me in a way I'd never recover from. I'd never be whole again, just a fractured piece of the girl I once was. Givin' you that power..." she lifted her head so we were staring at each other. "It's terrifyin'."

I nodded. "I know, and you don't have to until you're ready. I'll never push you, but now you know where I stand and how I feel. I'd rather jump off a cliff than make you cry, Mags. God, seeing your face streaked with tears made me want to hurl myself off the damn building."

She let out a little laugh. "Please don't do that. They'd fire me for sure."

"Speaking of... I'm running so damn late they're probably at the torch and pitchfork stage of anger. Ready to head back to the real world?"

When she nodded, I stood and tugged her up with me. "No matter what comes next, Mags, it's you and me, okay?" I kissed her temple and felt her nod against my lips. I wrapped my arm around her waist, and we started the trek back through the winding basement of the arena. The closer we got to the dressing rooms, the louder everything got.

Tuesday Told a Secret was wrapping up their set, so I was really, *really* late. I probably had all of two minutes to change and warm up my muscles before I had to run onstage. I dropped a quick kiss on Magnolia's soft lips before I let go and pushed into the dressing room. I looked back one last time, and she gave me a small smile that settled everything inside me and let me turn my focus to the show.

"Where the *fuck* have you been?" Maddox demanded as soon as I closed the door, but I didn't have time for a long explanation as I crossed the room and yanked my shirt over my head.

I pulled the hanger with my name on it off the metal rack stuck in the corner and pulled the shirt on while I figured out how to give a condensed version of the past hour. Three sets of eyes watched as I stripped out of the rest of my clothes and into my stage gear, waiting for my explanation. "I'm sorry, alright? Wynter showed up and kissed me. Magnolia saw, and I had to clean up the mess."

"Shit," Zen grunted, and the look on his face told me all I needed to know. He knew what it was like to be in a shitstorm with the girl you loved, and he'd do the exact same damn thing I had.

"Is she okay?" True asked, pushing off from where he'd been leaning against the wall.

"Yep. Connor had to haul Wynter's ass outside to get rid of her," I added, pulling my black boots on but leaving the laces untied.

"Can you at least text us next time? We didn't know what was happening, and we were stressed," True requested, and I nodded my agreement.

A knock sounded on the door just as I finished pulling my belt through the loops on my jeans, and I snagged a bottle of water on the way out the door, chugging it as we climbed the stairs to take our places on stage.

It was dark as shit on the stage, but that wasn't new. It'd surprised me how fast I adjusted to playing in front of such huge crowds. I figured there might be some stage fright or something on my first night on tour, but there was only ever excitement and the music. Once my fingers grasped the rough wooden sticks, and my foot rested on the kick drum pedal, my mind emptied, and I waited for my cue to play us in.

A video started overhead, playing our intro, and the arena erupted in screams and bright flashes from people bringing out their phones to record the show. I took a deep breath and relaxed my muscles as Zen's deep, raspy voice wrapped around the crowd in a dirty caress that assured wicked things to come with every word. They ate that shit up, and the screams almost drowned out his voice.

That was my cue, and I lifted my arms and swung them down in time with the frenetic beat of my heart—a heart that no longer belonged to me. Sweat dripped down my back and my hair, and I shook my head to keep it from running into my eyes and making them burn.

Time flew by as song after song poured out of us, the notes erupting into the atmosphere like a living, breathing entity of their own brought to life by the four of us. The music was like some melodious beast set forth to wreak havoc on the crowd.

They went absolutely batshit crazy, but no matter how many notes I played or how loud the shrieking crowd became, I was still consumed by Magnolia, and I wouldn't have it any other way. When I closed my eyes and leaned into the music, her face was all I could see. We hadn't had nearly enough time before I had to jump on stage tonight, but I had a sneaking suspicion no amount of time would ever be enough with Magnolia.

No, every second was precious where she was concerned, and I didn't want to waste any more worrying about the past. It was time to look toward our future, one I fully intended to spend with her. Today had been a lot, my confession of love the cherry on a fucked up sundae, but even if I wasn't sharing them with her, I was busy filling my head with plans—plans that involved me, Magnolia, and a future filled with family, love, and all the flowers she could ever want.

EIGHTEEN
MAGNOLIA

When had my life gone from nightmare to fairy tale? As far as I could tell, the minute Griffin Spencer walked into it, everything changed. Last night, I was so sure I'd made a mistake trusting him, but then he opened his mouth, and the most beautiful words I'd ever heard poured out and soothed all the hurt away.

It was blissful, really, the way he made me feel.

I love you. I love you. I love you.

I still couldn't believe he'd said those three little words—the ones I'd always longed to have someone feel toward me strongly enough to say them aloud. The best part was he knew me well enough to realize I wasn't ready to say them back yet. He gave me the space to figure out my thoughts and feelings without putting pressure on me or guilting me into reciprocating.

I snuggled further into his body, which was wrapped around me in the tiny bunk we now shared. Since that first night he'd crawled inside with me to comfort me from my bad dream, he'd never left, and that was just fine with me. I never wanted him to.

There was a constant buzzing noise that we'd both now gotten so used to that it barely registered—Winston calling and texting all night long. Now, his phone buzzed a few times in between mine vibrating, and he groaned, tightening his grip on me. "Go back to sleep," he ordered, his voice gravely as he ignored his phone.

We were on our way to Houston, and based on the rocking of the bus underneath and around us, we hadn't gotten there yet. That meant there was no real reason to leave the warmth, comfort, and safety of our little cocoon just yet. The sun was already up if the brightness leaking in underneath the curtain was any indication, plus I could hear one of the kids giggling somewhere in the distance.

It didn't matter. Here, in Griffin's arms and wrapped up against his body, was the only place I wanted to be. I closed my eyes and gave in to the pull of sleep, the exhaustion of the past several years of my life seeming to catch up to me all at once in the safety Griffin offered, so I happily gave in, sinking into the contentment of right now.

Soft kisses brushed across my face mixed with the roughness of day-old stubble, and my eyes fluttered open at the contrast. "Wake up, gorgeous."

Griffin's husky words were practically a whisper against my skin, and along with waking up my body, it started to heat up, too. It didn't take much from him to turn me on, and a few words between us in that quiet, vulnerable space when you wake up next to someone in the morning was the perfect setting for my libido to take off like a rocket.

Like he could read my mind, I watched as Griffin's already dark eyes darkened further as he watched the emotions play across my face, but he had more self-control than I did and shook off the temptation. "Nice try, Mags," he chuckled. "Lucky's dying to get outside, and we both need breakfast before you check in with the crew. Time to get up."

He leaned back and pulled on my favorite grey sweatpants and a white t-shirt that hugged his chest and biceps in an incredibly distracting way. He grinned—because he knew exactly how his clothing choices made me react—before he climbed over my body and out of the bunk, reaching back in to grab Lucky and cradle the pup against his chest.

At this point, was Lucky even mine? Or was he ours? My traitorous dog seemed to like Griffin more than me, so it seemed the answer was the latter. Not that I could blame him. Griffin had this relaxed energy about him that made you want to get closer.

"I've got the little dude. You've got ten minutes to get your sexy butt downstairs so we can eat, and you can get to work. I've got somewhere I want to take you this afternoon, so get movin'." He disappeared down the hall, leaving me to get ready.

It only took me a few minutes to toss on some cutoff shorts, a tank top, and brush my teeth before I was finger-combing my hair and jogging down the stairs. It didn't take much to get it to fall under control.

Griffin hadn't come back onto the bus yet, but a glance at my phone before I slid it into my pocket said I had about twenty minutes before I needed to check in with the stage crew and equipment guys to make sure we were on schedule and put out the inevitable fires that'd sprung up this morning. When I peeked out the window over the sink as I made my cup of tea, some of the crew already was unloading gear from the semis, which meant they would hopefully be ahead of schedule today.

"Morning, Magnolia," Maddox drawled as he joined me at the counter near the coffee maker. I moved out of the way so he could get his cup.

"Good mornin'," I replied, taking my first sip of spicy tea, glad I'd spiked it heavily with milk and sugar.

I sat down at the table to wait for Griffin, and Maddox slid in across from me. I looked behind him for Ryan, and he must've seen where I was looking because he answered my unasked question. "Ryan jumped off the bus the second it stopped moving to meet up with Connor." I was surprised he didn't seem bitter at all. Maddox seemed like an intense guy, like the kind of guy who'd want his wife by his side twenty-four-seven rather than having her own career, but that wasn't how he acted toward Ryan at all. Their dynamic was one I'd probably get to know a whole lot better if I ended up with Griffin long-term.

My stomach fluttered at the idea, a whole flock of pelicans taking flight at the same time and swooping down into the ocean to scoop up their breakfast. It wasn't just nervousness and vulnerability—it was a healthy dose of excitement at the prospect of a future with Griffin, too.

The bus door flung open, and Griffin moved inside with Lucky on his heels as he hopped up the steps. My little ball of fluff was getting so much bigger and could now move up them on his own, not exactly easily, but he could do it.

A scowl marred Griffin's beautiful face as he slid into the booth next to his brother, running a hand through his hair as Lucky flopped down across his feet. "Wynter won't leave me the hell alone. You'd think me telling her to stay away, having her tossed out on her ass, *and* updating my Instagram for the first time in a month just to post a picture about our breakup would've given her the hint she needed, but no. She's been blowing up my DMs for two days straight, begging me to reconsider. I blocked her, and she switched to texting, so I blocked her again, and now she's having her assistant message me."

He sighed and leaned across the table, swiping the mug from between my hands and taking a long sip. Maddox eyed Griff thoughtfully. "Pass it off to Montana and Harrison. You know they've got ways to ruin her socially. You weren't around yet, but this chick, Lexi. She fucked with True, and Harrison blacklisted her. She hasn't worked since. It didn't help that she was an attention whore and a nut job, but still. Hand it over to them and let them work their voodoo on her."

Griffin looked over at me. "What do you think?"

I shrugged. "This isn't really my area of expertise, but it sounds like you've tried everythin' you can. Maybe it'd be better to let the professionals handle it. Isn't that what they're there for?"

Maddox laughed almost gleefully and rubbed his palms together. "I hated that Wynter chick and you guys know Montana. She's going to have a fucking field day with this. It'll be like Christmas came early." His eyes lit up. "Oh shit, please let me tell her," he begged, turning to his brother with pleading eyes, and I couldn't help it; I giggled.

A smile even tugged at the corner of Griffin's mouth before he relented. "Fine, you can tell her."

Griffin hadn't even finished the sentence before Maddox's phone was in his hand, and he was dialing Montana's number. "It's your lucky day…" he started, and Griffin motioned for me to follow him out of the booth and outside, Lucky gnawing on his leash happily as he jogged beside us.

Griffin led us over to a shady spot under a tree away from the arena where it was quiet, and the chaos of the tour hadn't taken over. He turned to face me, vulnerability painted all across his face.

"You know I grew up in this area, right? Just south of here, actually."

I nodded because it'd never been a secret that both he and Maddox were from Texas, but it was a huge state. As far as I knew, Maddox and Ryan were from a tiny town up north, though.

"Well, we have some free time this afternoon, and I want you to come with me to see my parents."

All the air whooshed out of me, and I could feel my pulse in every inch of my body as my heart pounded. "You do?"

"I do. I love you, so they're going to love you. Trust me, okay?" He reached out and grabbed both of my hands in his, his gaze so open and hopeful. How could I possibly turn him down? Winston's parents were pretentious and hated me from the start, so the idea of meeting Griffin's family had a cold sweat breaking out across my skin, but I reminded myself this was a completely different situation and Griffin most definitely wasn't Winston.

Finally, I nodded my agreement. "Okay. I'd… like to go with you." My words were hesitant, but I meant them. Griffin talked about his parents like they were his heroes. You didn't meet many adults who still thought about their parents that way, and his relationship with them was so foreign to me I couldn't even picture what it must be like to see them interacting with each other in person.

One thing was for sure—I was going to get my chance later today.

I left Lucky with Griffin and took off to get started on my list for the day. The sooner I could get through everything, the sooner I could get ready to meet Griffin's parents. I was so busy all morning I hardly had time to think about it, let alone get nervous. As soon as the last item was checked off, though, the nerves hit me full force, and my stomach felt like it dropped to my toes.

I found Griffin waiting for me in the bunk with Lucky snoring curled up at his side. The show wasn't until tomorrow, but we were staying on the bus tonight, so there wasn't a lot of room to get ready, and right now was one time I'd be thankful for the insane humidity of the south because there was no other way to get the wrinkles out of my sundress. Living out of luggage all the time wasn't great on what little fashion sense I managed to have, but at least if I stood outside for a little while, I wouldn't look like I'd just crawled out of bed with their son.

I grabbed my camera bag and purse and met Griffin downstairs. When we stepped off the bus, Lucky's leash wrapped around Griffin's wrist, there was a rental SUV waiting for us with Maddox behind the wheel. Ryan was up front with him and gave me a warm smile. "Climb on in."

I turned to Griffin, and he looked sheepish. "Sorry, I forgot to tell you my brother and Ryan were coming along."

I wasn't upset, though. Actually, I was relieved to have more familiar and friendly faces along for the ride. It would take some of the pressure off me. I shifted up onto my toes and kissed his cheek before murmuring, "I'm glad they'll be there," in his ear.

He shivered, and a small smile of satisfaction formed on my lips at the effect I had on his body. "Hold that thought until we get there. You've never ridden in a car while Maddox is driving."

"I heard that, asshole," Maddox laughed, and even I was chuckling as I climbed into the back seat and buckled up.

When Griffin picked up Lucky and then climbed in after me, he slid all the way across the bench until our thighs touched and then grasped my hand in his, kissing the back. "Thank you for doing this."

The smile he gave me was capable of dropping panties and breaking hearts all over the world, but it was just for me, and something inside me shifted. I wanted him to know exactly how much he meant to me. The thing was... Griffin had become *everything*.

That was why meeting his parents was so scary. I wanted—no, I needed—them to like me. If they didn't, he might not want to be with me, and the thought of losing him was beyond my ability to deal with.

Maddox and Ryan carried on a quiet conversation up front, but I sat silently watching the scenery fly by the window at breakneck speed. My nerves were growing every mile that passed until my palms were sweaty, and my breathing was erratic. Griffin leaned closer, plopping Lucky into my lap. "They're going to love you, Mags. You don't need to worry, and even if for some reason they don't, which won't happen," he rushed to say as I opened my mouth to argue.

"It won't change a damn thing. I *love* you, Magnolia. That's not just going away no matter what anyone else thinks."

"Okay," I agreed quietly, resting my head on his shoulder. I didn't know what else to say, but his words quieted some of my nervous energy, and I stroked Lucky's velvety ear, closing my eyes and letting Griffin's heartbeat lull me into almost a meditative state.

The car shifted as it turned onto a residential street and then made a few quick turns before pulling into a driveway. I peeked out the windshield, and the house was made of bricks and much bigger than the one I grew up in, but it wasn't a mansion or anything. More like upper-middle class. "Was this where you grew up?" I asked, and Griffin grinned.

"Yep, after we realized the neighbors were cool with my drumming. Spent most of my formative years right there," he pointed to the furthest window to the right on the top floor. It was partially hidden by a huge oak tree that sat shading half of the front yard.

Maddox snorted. "How many times did you sneak out with that tree right there? I can't believe mom let you have that room."

I wondered if Maddox had ever been here before, but I didn't want to ask. The boys' history wasn't my business unless they wanted to talk about it, but I knew they hadn't found out about each other until a couple of years ago or so.

"I was a good kid," Griffin shrugged. "She never suspected a thing."

Maddox cracked up, and Ryan shook her head at me and mouthed *boys*, and I grinned back. Their easy joking relieved some of the tension I'd been carrying around.

A pretty woman with an easy smile stepped up next to the driver's window and knocked on the glass. Maddox turned and rolled it down, and her smile widened. "Are y'all going to come in or stay out here baking in this heat? I made cookies." She swept her gaze over all of us and stopped on me, appraising me with one look before she gave me a small smile and winked at me before she turned to go inside.

What did that wink mean? Was it a good thing? My mind was spinning in circles as I let Griffin pull me out of the car.

We walked up the driveway, and I leaned over to whisper, "Are your parents gonna mind Lucky bein' in their house?" I hadn't stopped to think that not everyone was a dog person and wanted fur on their stuff.

"My parents love animals, but my dad has to travel a lot for work, so they don't have any right now."

We walked in the front door behind Maddox and Ryan straight through the entryway to the kitchen toward the back of the house. It was huge and gorgeous, obviously a place of pride for Griffin and Maddox's mom, who was pushing a platter of cookies across the island before she turned to pull a pitcher of sweet tea out of the fridge.

Maddox and Griffin both stepped around the island and took turns hugging their mom before grabbing cookies and a glass each and plopping down on two of the barstools on one side of the counter. She turned her attention to where Ryan and I stood together on one edge of the counter, and my heart thudded in my chest. "Come over here, girls. I won't bite," she laughed, and I followed Ryan closer.

"It's good to see you again, Monica," Ryan said cooly. I didn't know much about Maddox's childhood, but Ryan had been there for a lot of it, so maybe that was why. All I knew was Ryan was just as protective of Maddox as he was of her. Maybe even more so.

"You, too, honey. And you," she turned her sweet smile on me. "You must be Magnolia. Griffin talks about you non-stop."

"Mom!" Griffin looked mildly embarrassed, which made me smile. He talked to his mom about me?

"That's me, ma'am. It's nice to meet you." I held out my hand for her to shake, but she ignored it and wrapped me up in a hug. "Please call me Monica."

"Okay… Monica. Thank you for havin' us." My grammy taught me manners, and I was sure as heck gonna use 'em.

She brushed me off, letting me go so she could look me over before she settled her attention back on Griffin. "I like her," she announced, and Griffin shot me a smug look as the tension melted out of me. Monica Spencer was the complete opposite of Winston's mother, and I'd never been more thankful for something in my life.

Well, that wasn't true, but it was at least second or third on the list.

"Where's dad?" Griffin wondered, looking around.

Monica waved her hand in the air. "He'll be home in a little while. He had a meeting he couldn't get out of." She led us into the back yard where there were a pool and comfortable patio furniture.

As Griffin took the seat beside me, with Ryan on my other side, he bent down and let Lucky off his leash so he could run around the yard. My poor pup—our poor pup? We really needed to have a discussion about that—didn't get enough time off the leash, so I welcomed this break for him.

Maddox and Griffin spent the next half hour catching up with their mom, filling her in on where we'd been on tour and showing her pictures on their phones. It was cute how they suddenly turned into little boys again when they were around their mom, and I could only imagine how their dynamic would've been between them if they'd grown up together.

Ryan was watching intently, too, and she leaned over to whisper into my ear, "This is why I get so pissed off whenever I see Monica. She ran, and she didn't take Mad along, and he missed out on so many years of knowing his brother and knowing what it was like to have a parent who loves him. She did damage that didn't have to be done, and I'm struggling to forgive her for it even if he already has."

I reached down and squeezed her hand in understanding. "I can't imagine what he went through, but if it was anything like what Winston did to me, I could never leave my child in that situation. You have every right to be mad at her for it. Hell, *I'm* a little mad at her for it, and I don't know much. All you can do is support him and know that you'll do better when you have kids. Both of you."

She gave me a small, grateful smile but didn't let go of my hand. I had a feeling she needed my support just as much as I needed hers. We sat like that a few more minutes before a tall man with dark hair like Griffin's and broad shoulders like his, too, stepped onto the patio and walked over to Monica, dropping a kiss to her cheek as she smiled lovingly up at him.

He turned toward us with kind eyes and a soft smile as he pulled Griffin into a hug and then held out his hand to shake Maddox's. I didn't know what kind of a relationship he had with his stepdad, but they seemed to at least tolerate each other.

When he was done with the boys, he turned to us. "Hi, Ryan," he smiled at her, and she smiled and waved back.

"Grant."

Finally, he got to me. "And you're Magnolia, right?"

I nodded and stood, holding out my hand to shake his. "I'm Grant, Griffin's dad. It's nice to finally meet the girl who has our son's heart."

My smile froze on my face. How much did Griffin tell his parents? My gaze slid to his, and he had the decency to look at least a little bit sorry. I snapped my attention back to his dad.

"It's nice to meet you, sir, and I promise I'll take good care of it."

He laughed and patted my hand before letting it go. "I'm sure you will."

I sat back down, and he took the spot beside Monica, wrapping his arm around her shoulders. They asked us all questions, and with Grant there, the environment was a lot less awkward. He was outgoing and calm, making us all laugh with stories from work, but he smartly kept the conversation on current things, never bringing up Griffin's childhood or the past.

We stayed for dinner, Grant grilling burgers with the boys and Ryan and I helping Monica in the kitchen with the sides. It wasn't until we were all full sitting around the table on the patio with the sun setting that I mentioned something that'd been on my mind since Griffin asked me to come here this morning.

"Would y'all mind if I took some photos of the family? I brought my camera, and the light is perfect." It was the golden hour, that last hour of daylight where the shadows had gone all soft, and the light from the sun had a golden tint to it that made pictures look magical.

Monica looked at me like I wasn't quite real before a sheen moved over her eyes. "I'd love that if the boys are okay with it."

Griffin nodded, shooting me one of his crooked grins, the ones that made my heart flutter and my panties damp. That grin of his meant nothing but trouble, but the kind of trouble I'd always run towards with him instead of away.

All eyes turned to Maddox, but he was watching me. "Why would you do this for me, for us, Magnolia?"

I shrugged. "I know what it's like not to have anyone. When you find the people in your life who love you—your family—no matter how long it takes, those are the moments to remember. A picture can freeze time and can remind you of what's important in life. If I can give that to you, I want to."

He stood up and walked over to me, bending down and pulling me into a hug. "Thank you," he whispered in my ear, and I bit back my shock. Maddox Everleigh had officially surprised me.

"What are we waiting for? The light's not going to last long," Maddox declared, straightening up into his usual boisterous self.

"Let me grab my camera." I ran out to the SUV and grabbed my bag, pulling out the body and attaching the lens I wanted to use. I stepped back into the yard and took a couple of test shots to adjust the settings before I unfolded the reflector I brought along. I found a spot in the back corner of the yard near an old tree and started taking pictures with Ryan as my assistant. She maneuvered the reflector exactly how I told her as we used every minute of the remaining daylight to capture not only Monica and the boys, but Spencer and Monica, Griffin and Maddox, Maddox and Ryan, and everything in between. I wanted to make sure I had the perfect family shot.

When the sun was almost gone, Ryan reached for my camera, pulling the strap from around my neck. "Tell me what to do. I want to take one last one of you and Griff."

My cheeks heated, but I guided her through the process. The settings were already right, so all she had to do was focus and push the button. I stepped up beside Griffin and looked up into his eyes. He rested his hand on my hip and leaned down until his forehead was touching mine. "You're so beautiful," he murmured as we stared at each other.

I wasn't even aware of the clicking of my camera in the distance; I was so lost in Griffin as he bent down and kissed me softly. When he pulled away, it was too soon, but the light was nearly gone. The first fireflies blinked into existence beside us, and I watched them in wonder. There was something enchanting about fireflies, like stars that lived here on Earth.

"Hey," Griffin murmured, drawing my attention back to him as the fireflies reflected in his eyes. "I love you."

I sighed, brushing my lips against his, finally ready to jump in with both feet to this thing with him. "I love you, too," I whispered, afraid the confession would tilt my world on its axis, but all that happened was Griffin tightening his grip on me like he never wanted to let go as everyone else retreated to the house to give us our moment alone.

My arms wrapped up around his neck, playing with the soft hair at the back of his head as we swayed back and forth, dancing to music neither one of us could hear under the soft glow of the moon and the twinkling of the fireflies. If a moment could be perfect, that was it.

NINETEEN
GRIFFIN

"**M**eeting the parents, bro? That's kind of a big deal," Maddox pointed out as we hung out down in the lounge on the bus after our Houston show. We were on our way to New Orleans, and all the other guys were in bed or upstairs in the other room. Magnolia had been exhausted and passed out pretty much as soon as I stepped foot on the bus, but I was still wired, so Mad and I were throwing down on some Madden on Xbox.

"Yeah, well, I'm pretty damn serious about Magnolia," I admitted, picking a blitz play and sitting back while I waited for Maddox to pick out his offense.

"I can tell. Does all that shit with her ex freak you out?" He stared at the screen as we both mashed buttons, trying to get the upper hand, but I smacked him down, and he growled, tossing his controller onto the table as I smirked in his general direction.

"It probably should, but nah. He's quieted down after the restraining order, so maybe he'll finally back the hell off." It was true. Winston still called a few times a night, but there'd been no sign of him otherwise. We were both sleeping better because of it, and Magnolia had started to relax little by little again, the way she had when he'd been in jail. "I'm ready to put that chapter behind us and move on."

Maddox shook his head. "I don't think it's going to be that easy, and I know what I'm talking about." He shivered a little, and I wondered if he was thinking about how everything went down with Ryan's sort-of ex, Yates. "The dude is unhinged. You're not indestructible, Griff. I'm relieved as fuck you brought Ryan and Connor in to help."

My fingers wrapped around the beer I was nursing, and I took a long sip. "I know, me, too. I'm just ready to move on, you know? That's why I wanted her to meet mom and dad. I want a future with Magnolia."

Maddox got a far off look in his eye before blinking to clear it and nodding. "If I could've, I would have hauled my ass back to Texas and kidnapped Ryan when I was your age. It's good to know what you want."

He was right about one thing—I knew *exactly* what I wanted. Me and Magnolia and the rest of our lives spread out ahead of us without the threat of the past creeping in to steal it away. I didn't know how long the band would keep putting out new music, but I wanted to be along for the ride until they called it quits, and they showed no signs of stopping anytime soon. Would Magnolia want this for her life long-term?

Only time would tell, but first, we had to put Winston behind us and get through this tour. With Maddox and the other guys surrounding us, plus security, I had no doubt we'd be just fine and come out better for it on the other side.

"What the hell is this?" I demanded as I approached what looked like it might have once been my drum kit but now was a mess of twisted metal and shredded plastic. It looked like it'd been run over by a car and then backed over again and again just in case it wasn't broken enough the first time.

And there it sat at the back of the stage as if nothing was wrong with it. What the fuck?

The other three guys moved behind me; I could feel them over my shoulders and at my back. "How the fuck did that happen?" Zen asked, expression hardening as he looked over the mess that used to be my drums.

"Are you okay?" my brother asked as he gripped my shoulder. If anyone understood how much our instruments meant to us, it was these guys. My drums were an extension of who I was.

This was the set I practiced on for hours once I moved to LA, the set I used when we recorded our first album, and it meant more to me than almost anything, even if it was just an object.

I clenched my jaw, and my hands curled into fists. Was I okay? I was pissed the hell off. "I'm fine," I snapped, not angry at any of them but at the situation.

"Where's Magnolia?" True asked, looking around but not spotting her. He raised his voice to a yell. "Someone get Lucas." There were enough people around us that he must've figured someone would hear him and make it happen. Maddox pulled out his phone and sent a text at the same time.

"I asked Magnolia to meet us up here," he filled in, tucking his phone back into his pocket as he turned back to my ruined drums.

I tucked my hands into my pockets, taking a few deep breaths and trying to calm my thundering heart. Magnolia was skittish at the best of times, and me being all pissed off and worked up over a set of drums wasn't worth causing her stress, but it was hard as hell to stuff the anger and irritation flaring up inside me down.

Still facing the back of the stage, the skin on the back of my neck prickled with awareness as Magnolia moved up onto the stage, so I wasn't surprised when she stepped up beside me, and a gasp fell from between her soft pink lips. "What happened, Sugar?"

She looked up at me with wide eyes, searching for answers I couldn't give. I shrugged. "Found it like that when we came up here for soundcheck."

Magnolia watched me carefully before she reached up tentatively and wrapped her small hand around my bicep, gently squeezing, and I found myself leaning into her touch. "I'm sorry," she murmured, her eyes full of compassion and hurt on my behalf that had the anger melting away. I loved that she cared enough to get upset, but I simultaneously hated that she was distressed at all.

We were human, and I couldn't keep her in a bubble and shielded from any emotion but happiness for her entire life. Logically I knew that. The illogical part of my brain—the more feral, animal part—didn't give a shit about reality and wanted to tuck Magnolia away from the world and keep her perfectly happy forever.

The end.

Sighing, I gripped her wrist lightly and tugged her toward me, wrapping my arms around her and holding her against my chest. She melted into me and squeezed me just as hard as I was squeezing her as for a few minutes, we just clung to each other out in the open, not caring who saw or what they thought.

Just having her close to me like this, breathing her in, and feeling her body against mine had me calming down. It wasn't until I heard a whispered, "Holy shit," that I pulled back.

Lucas, the equipment manager, stood there with a mix of shock and anger on his face. "What the hell happened?"

"We were hoping you might be able to tell us that," True replied, watching Lucas carefully.

The guy shook his head, his dirty blonde hair falling over his forehead. "It was fine when we put it up here this morning. I was restringing a guitar right after and haven't been up here since."

Magnolia straightened, and I could see her snap into boss mode. She shifted slightly away from me but didn't let me go. Even when she was being professional, she knew I needed her touch, and my lips turned up a little at how in tune with me she was.

It was the same for me with her.

She faced Lucas, a *don't mess with me* expression on her face. "Who's had access to Griffin's drums since you set them up?"

Lucas looked around, his hazel eyes flitting over the entire arena and his arms moving out wide to either side of his body. "Um, everyone here? They're not off-limits once they're set up on stage. Anyone with access to the backstage area can get to them."

Magnolia chewed on her lip while she considered that. "Get this moved out, and the backup set up, and keep your eyes and ears open. If you hear anythin', I wanna know about it immediately."

Lucas nodded, looking sadly over at me and then at the drums. He was a young guy, probably close to my age, and loved music as much as the rest of us even if he didn't have the talent it would take to go pro. It probably hurt him to see my instrument decimated like that, too, just like the rest of us. "Yeah, you got it."

Magnolia turned those stunning icy blue eyes back up to me. "Do you want to try and salvage them? Do you think it's even possible?"

"I don't know, but I want to try." I hadn't even thought about what to do next, but the words felt right. I wasn't ready to let go of this piece of myself just yet if I didn't have to.

She nodded and then brightened. "Hey, I know this is bad timin', but we're in New Orleans. I've always wanted to visit, and we're actually here." I chuckled at her enthusiasm and leaned down to steal a quick kiss. Her cheeks turned pink, and my whole chest flooded with warmth at the way she responded to me.

She looked a little dazed, and I brushed some of the long, silky strands of her hair behind her ear. "We're in New Orleans, and..." I prompted with a smirk on my face, my drums almost forgotten as I wrapped myself in all things Magnolia.

She blinked a few times before a mischievous smile crossed her face. "And I want to explore, so... Will you go on a date with me tonight? After the show?"

She was so damn cute. "A date, huh? I think that could be arranged."

Magnolia stepped into my arms again and pressed her body against mine. I lowered my head so my forehead touched hers and breathed her in with my eyes closed. "I love you," I whispered, and she tightened her grip where she had her arms wrapped around me.

Her phone chiming interrupted our moment of peace in the chaos, and she gave me an apologetic look before pulling back and tugging it out of the back pocket of her jeans. She frowned down at the screen before turning it around and showing the message to me.

Unknown: Next time, I'll break more than just the drums.

A chill swept over me that was quickly replaced by a raging inferno of fury. Magnolia watched me with a sort of sad resignation on her face. "I'm so sorry, Griffin. I'm sorry I dragged you into my mess and that now he's taken somethin' you love from you. It's what he does, and maybe-"

I pressed my finger over her lips, stopping her destructive train of thought. "No. There's not a chance in hell I'm letting you walk away from us because of your asshole ex. Not happening. I don't care what he does to me or what he takes, as long as he doesn't take you."

Her whole demeanor shifted, and she sagged against me as I slipped her phone into her back pocket after forwarding the message to Ryan and Connor. "I don't understand why you'd stick with me through this when you don't have to," she mumbled where her face was buried in my chest, and I pressed a kiss to the top of her head before resting my cheek there.

"That's the thing, Mags. I *do* have to. Someday you'll believe me when I tell you I love you. That means something, and it sure as hell means I'm not going anywhere when things get tough. I knew what I was signing up for when I started this thing between us. You can even ask my brother since I talked to him about it first. I'm in this with you for good." I made sure to project nothing but confidence and sincerity in my words, leaving no doubt about how much I meant every single one.

"Magnolia!" one of the stage crew called, and she lifted her head reluctantly away from me to look over my shoulder.

"I've gotta go." She loosened her hold on me and stepped back. "Don't forget you're mine after the show tonight."

"I'm always yours, Mags." I was relieved she wasn't shutting herself off from the world again with the latest Winston development.

She started walking across the stage, and I watched her go, hungry for every little bit of her I could get, and she turned back and shot me a playful smile. "Oh, and I love you, too." Then she blew me a kiss, and at that moment, I imagined I looked like some lovestruck fool with cartoon hearts floating around my head because that was how I felt.

I was bummed about the drum kit and pissed that it wasn't just an accident, that Winston had intentionally fucked with me, but it wasn't the end of the world. I had the girl of my dreams by my side, and nothing was going to ruin that.

Not a single damn thing.

"I wish it weren't so late," Magnolia sighed when it wasn't quite midnight yet, and the city around us seemed like it was just getting started to me. There were tons of people on the streets, and as we strolled down the sidewalk with our fingers interlaced, we were constantly having to dodge out of the way of people walking in the opposite direction.

"And if it weren't so late, what would you do?" I wondered as I let go of her hand and slung my arm over her shoulders, my fingers playing lazily in her hair.

She moved closer into my side, sliding her hand into the back pocket of my jeans. "I've always wanted to try a beignet, but they don't serve them this late."

My answering hum was noncommittal as I watched her take in the sights and sounds of the French Quarter. She wasn't paying attention where we were headed, content to be tucked under my arm and watching all the colorful displays of human creativity happening on every street corner—and sometimes in the middle of the street itself.

She giggled at a pantless drag queen directing traffic with thrusts of her hips and shimmies of her chest, and tossed dollar bills in the open containers of street performers as we strolled like we had all the time in the world. The city was alive, and experiencing it for the first time with Magnolia felt right. At that moment, my inexperience with travel felt like a gift.

I steered us off the busier street toward the riverfront, and Magnolia looked up at me as we walked, finally noticing the change in our surroundings. "Where are we goin'? I wanted to get some dinner."

"Funny you should ask…" I teased as we turned a corner, and Cafe Du Monde stood like a beacon in the night, its lights shining brightly on the darkened street.

Magnolia's eyes brightened, and she looked back up at me again, moving her gaze away from the historic building. "You didn't."

"I did."

She shook her head but laughed. "How?"

I shrugged, keeping my secrets to myself. It hadn't been hard. One call to Montana, and they were more than willing to open their doors special for us tonight. "Do you want to try a famous donut or not?"

She gasped in mock horror. "*What* did you call them? Blasphemy!" She poked me in the ribs, and I laughed, grabbed her hand before she could do it again, and kissed her finger.

"How about you show me what all the hype is about then?" I held open the door for her, and she moved into the cafe, stopping inside the door so that I almost ran into her back.

"It's just like all the pictures online," she observed, her voice all breathy and wistful, sort of like she sounded after I made her come, and she was relaxed and happy. The comparison made my dick thicken, and I wrapped my arms around her and pressed my front to her back, needing to touch her. I *always* needed to touch her, just sometimes, I was better at holding back than others.

The manager behind the counter smiled at us, and, keeping my arms wrapped around Magnolia's waist, I nudged her forward. She rested her head back on my chest and looked up at the menu. "It's way too late for coffee, but I've gotta have the full experience." She ordered enough donuts—sorry, *beignets*—and coffee for at least six people, and we sat down to wait for our order.

I'd have paid all the money I had to listen to her make the sounds she did when she took the first bite of the fluffy dough covered in powdered sugar. She groaned, and her eyes rolled back in her head, and I had to adjust my quickly hardening cock, so it didn't press uncomfortably against the zipper of my jeans. Everything about Magnolia turned me on, but when she looked like she did right now, I was completely captivated.

"You've gotta try one," she mumbled around a bite so big her cheeks puffed out a little, and I laughed at the sight of her, lips covered in powdered sugar and eyes closed in complete bliss. The chair scraped as I pushed back and stood up, moving to the other side of the small table and bending down to kiss the sugar off her lips.

"I can't imagine it's better than you," I murmured before sucking her bottom lip into my mouth. I dropped one last kiss on her lips before I moved back and let her finish chewing, swiping my own mouth to get rid of any lingering powder.

"Thanks for this." She dusted her hands off and lifted her coffee to take a small sip. "I didn't think after this afternoon you'd be up for much with, you know..."

"Winston beating the hell out of my drums?" I finished, my lips tilting up into a small smile. I'd played the show with the backup set and managed, and it wasn't as bad as I thought it'd be. Tomorrow I'd need to get in some practice to get used to the quirks of this set, but I could do it.

She winced and nodded, and I moved over to drag my chair beside her. I wasn't sure why I'd even taken the spot across from her in the first place. "Not gonna lie, it sucked that he did that. I've had those drums since I was sixteen, and every bad day I've had since then got worked out on that kit. Every song I've learned or recorded, every show I've played in front of an audience all happened on that set. I hope they can fix it, but if not," I shrugged. "At the end of the day, it's still just a thing. It's replaceable. I'll get over it."

She looked down at her lap, and I reached out and gripped her hand. "It's not your fault."

"But-"

"Nope." I swooped down and kissed her to punctuate my point. "Anything that happens is Winston's fault. Period. I won't hear you apologize again. Winston's the one doing all of this and using you as an excuse to let his crazy out. If it weren't you, it'd be someone else, Mags, because you're not the problem here. He is."

She deflated a little and looked up at me with what could only be described as hope shining in her eyes. "You really mean that?"

I nodded. "I do. So, no more Winston talk. Let's not let him ruin our date, okay?"

She gave me an innocent smile then and reached out, plucking the rest of her fancy donut up off the plate and smashing it right into my face. I coughed a little on all the powder but smiled at her through the mess as she giggled so hard she couldn't breathe. Then I pulled her into my side while she was still laughing, and my face was still covered in bits of fried dough and white sugar, and snapped a picture. I didn't want to forget how happy she looked at that moment.

After we finished and I cleaned up my face, the manager bagged up a few more beignets for Magnolia, and we headed out back toward Bourbon Street, my arm around her shoulders and hers snaked around my waist. The streets had only gotten busier since we'd been in the cafe, and when we got to our destination, the music and sounds of glasses clinking and people having a good time filtered out the front doors that'd been thrown open to entice people on the street to come inside.

"The Nightcrawler?" Magnolia asked, looking up at the beat-up old sign hanging over the front door.

"Last stop of the night. This place is famous for their hurricanes. You can't come to the Big Easy and not try one."

She got that adorable wrinkle between her eyebrows. "A hurricane? Like a tropical storm?" Her gaze shifted from the sign to the sky, and I chuckled.

"Like the drink. C'mon." I guided her inside where a live band played, and I was grateful it was something other than jazz. I could appreciate jazz's musical composition, but it was sure as hell not a genre of music I enjoyed listening to, and there seemed to be nothing *but* jazz down here. It felt like I'd never escape it when we wandered the streets outside.

We pushed through the crowd and ordered a couple of drinks, and when the bartender slid them across the faded wooden surface of the bar, I shot him a look, and he nodded his head toward the dark back corner. Not only had I arranged the beignet surprise for Magnolia, but I had one last trick up my sleeve.

"How about we drink these somewhere a little quieter?" I murmured against her ear, and then I watched as a shiver rolled through her entire body. She looked up at me with questions in her eyes but didn't ask them, choosing to follow me instead as I led her toward the back and through a door marked *private.*

Behind the door was a steep set of stairs that looked old as hell and creaked as they took us to the second floor of the building. There was a hallway full of locked doors except one that led out to a small patio with an iron railing that overlooked Bourbon Street.

Magnolia spun to face me as soon as she saw where we were headed, her eyes lit up like fireworks on the Fourth of July. "Do we really get to hang out up here?"

I nodded, pushing open the door and waiting for her to follow me out. She hurried through the doorway and leaned against the railing, looking down at the street below with fascination. "I've always wanted to be able to come up here and hang out, maybe toss some beads during the parade."

I moved up beside her, pushing her hair away from her neck and peppering it with kisses, never able to keep my hands off her for long. She spotted the table in the corner of the patio and set her glass down as a drip of condensation slid down the stem. I did the same before turning to face her.

I pulled a strand of shiny cheap beads out of the pocket of my jeans and dangled them in front of her. Her eyes widened and she reached for them but I tugged them back, a wicked smile on my face. "Nope, that's not how this works. You have to give me something for them."

She looked around the small balcony before shoving the bag of leftover beignets in my direction. I laughed and shook my head. "No, I was thinking something more of the *naked* variety," I purred, stepping closer to her and running my finger across her exposed collarbone and down her chest between her breasts.

Magnolia shivered under my touch but dropped the bag she was holding onto the tiny cafe table beside us, a naughty twinkle in her eye. She reached for the hem of her tank top and pulled it up an inch, exposing a sliver of her flat stomach. My gaze dropped immediately to watch, my attention fully on that tiny strip of skin that had my mouth already watering.

"How about this? Is there enough nakedness to get the beads?" she wondered, her voice syrupy sweet, and I shook my head, unable to tear my eyes away from where I was willing the fabric to disappear off her insanely hot body.

She inched the fabric up higher until it was bunched just under her tits, and I was forced to exhale when I started to feel a little dizzy from lack of oxygen. Her back was to the street, and up here, we were tucked into the shadows, the street lights blazed down onto the cobblestones below us, so no one was looking up in our direction.

Still, it made me feel better that her back was to the crowds.

Magnolia raised an eyebrow at me playfully, and I shook my head, curling my fingers into fists to keep from reaching out and running my fingers along the silky skin of her flat stomach. She arched her back and slow as fucking molasses lifted her shirt over her head and tossed it onto the table. She wasn't wearing a damn bra, and I couldn't stay back anymore.

Nothing else was on my mind but tasting Magnolia's skin, sucking one of her perfect pink nipples into my mouth, but she stepped back, pressing her back into the railing as she shook her head and held out her hand. "I'd say I earned my beads."

I'd forgotten all about the damn things that were still dangling from my fist, so I reached up and dropped them over her head, watching as the shiny purple plastic balls settled in the space between her tits. I ran my fingers up her side, and she squirmed under my touch, and then I lowered my mouth to pull her nipple inside, circling it with my tongue and scraping it gently with my teeth.

Her fingers sifted through my hair, and she gripped the back of my head, pulling me closer as she threw her own head back and whimpered. Both of my hands and my mouth were full of Magnolia, but it wasn't enough. I didn't think it could ever be enough.

I reached down and flicked open the button on the front of her cutoff shorts and slipped my hand down inside her panties, wasting no time in finding her entrance slick already and sliding a finger inside. Her whimpers turned into moans as I slowly moved my finger in and out a few times before using her wetness to circle her clit. Her hips moved in time with my strokes, and I moved up to capture her lips. The noises she was making were probably carrying down to the street below, and while it was noisy, I didn't want to take the risk of anyone looking up here and seeing my girlfriend about to come all over my hand.

She opened for me and kissed me like the world was on fire, like it was our first time and our last time, and like she was desperate to have as much of me as she could. A kiss had never turned me on more than this one, but I said that every time with Magnolia.

Every single time was better than the last.

We tore our lips apart, both of us panting and her cheeks flushed. "Turn around," I growled, and she spun, pushing her hips back against me. My dick was so hard it was throbbing, and I ripped her shorts down just far enough that

I could get inside her. My hands shook as I unbuttoned my own jeans, sliding them and my boxers down my hips far enough to free my cock, and I wasted no time in pushing inside her.

Magnolia gasped, gripping the black iron railing in her white-knuckled grasp as we moved together, taking what we needed most from each other. The beads rattled against her skin as I pounded in and out of her. I wasn't fucking her soft or easy; it was raw and needy and possessive.

She started to cry out, and I reached out from where my hands held tightly to her hips and covered her mouth with my palm, pulling her back against my chest so I could whisper in her ear. "Shh, baby. You don't want all of Bourbon Street to hear you come all over my cock, do you?"

She clenched around me at my dirty words, and I groaned. She nipped my fingers where they covered her mouth, and I cursed as my dick pulsed inside her. She was playing with me as I fucked her, and I loved her for it. "If I let go, do you think you can be quiet?"

She nodded, so I slowly removed my hand; the only sound for a few seconds was our heavy breathing, bodies slamming together, the distant crowds below, and the plastic beads jingling as we moved. I slid my palm down her stomach and found her clit, circling and rubbing it to the rhythm of my thrusts until she threw her head back and tightened around me, ripping my orgasm straight out of me as she came.

Her inner walls squeezed rhythmically until she'd stolen every last drop from me, and we stood there still connected and completely out of breath. I was dazed and overwhelmed by everything I felt for Magnolia, and when she looked back at me with the same relaxed grin I wore, I knew she felt the exact same way.

TWENTY
GRIFFIN

The bus ride from New Orleans to Phoenix was so damn long, if it wasn't for the breaks at random truck stops along the way, we would've had a real problem. Lucky was still a small puppy, and he definitely would've pissed all over the bus.

After yet another stop where we'd all piled out to stretch our legs and grab snacks, Magnolia and I were lounging back in our bunk, and Lucky was curled up on my stomach snoring. His fur was still downy and soft, and my fingertip traced a pattern up his little nose and over his head over and over while he slept.

"I've been meaning to ask you," Magnolia started, looking up at me from where she'd cuddled up to my side with her head resting on my chest.

"Mhm." The rumble from my voice made Lucky jump, and we both chuckled at his confused expression before he settled back into his nap.

"Lucky seems to have adopted you." I snorted because she wasn't wrong. The dog was completely attached to me. As soon as I stepped foot in his vicinity, he was glued to me like he was afraid I'd disappear if I moved out of his line of sight.

Her smile was soft as she watched me. "I've always called him my dog, but the truth is, I only got him a day or two before we met you. He's just as much yours as he is mine… if you want him to be." Her voice was hesitant, like she didn't think I'd want to claim him—or her. Nothing was further from the truth, and I planned to fix that little misunderstanding right the hell now.

"Listen to me very carefully, Magnolia." I waited until I was sure she was focused completely on me and ignoring the constant buzzing of her phone that'd started up again last night. "You and Lucky? You're a part of my life now, a part of my family. I'm not going anywhere. So, yes. He's mine just as much as he's yours, but you're mine, too."

Magnolia leaned up and kissed me thoroughly before burrowing back into my body like it was her own personal pillow. She was quiet after that, but I didn't blame her. We'd been up most of the night with her damn phone going off, and I'd finally given up around three a.m. and answered, telling Winston to leave her the hell alone and then putting it on *do not disturb* for a couple of hours so she could sleep.

I didn't think he'd listen, but I had to do something because he sure as hell wasn't giving up like I thought he would. It seemed like he was escalating instead. We needed to report it to the police, but the question was what police did we talk to? We were all over the place, and each incident happened in a different state, a different jurisdiction. I really needed to talk to Connor about all of it and see what could be done.

With so many people coming and going on this tour and having access, it was hard to lock everything down as tightly as we needed to to keep Winston away. I never thought I'd say it, but I'd be glad when the tour was over, and we could have a lot more control over who had access to Magnolia. Then we'd be able to work with the local police to deal with the threat that Winston posed.

Now that we'd settled what she meant to me, all the tension poured out of Magnolia, and she dozed while I held her, content to spend the next couple of hours doing nothing but this where no one could touch us, and we had this little reprieve from the real world.

𝄞

"How is it that a hundred degrees in Arizona feels so different than a hundred degrees in Texas?" I wondered, pushing my sunglasses up onto my face as we stepped off the bus and jumped into the waiting SUV to the hotel.

"Humidity's a bitch," Jericho supplied, climbing into the back seat and reaching out for Moon to hand over their son so she could climb in after him. "Makes it so your body has a harder time cooling down with sweat since it doesn't evaporate."

We all looked at him like he'd lost his damn mind, and he scowled. "What? I read."

Maddox scoffed. "With all your new free time?"

Jericho held up his middle finger, and I turned back to watch Mags. Lucky was sitting in my lap, his sharp razor puppy teeth cutting a hole in my t-shirt where he was chewing on it, but I let him because I didn't have anything else for him to play with and better my shirt than my skin. Magnolia was the last one to get in the car, and once she closed the back door and took the seat beside me, we were on our way to the hotel.

I couldn't wait.

Being confined in a close space with the girl I loved wasn't exactly a hardship, but having to be quiet—and worse, keep her quiet—while making her come was a real pain in the ass.

It was still early morning, and I hadn't even had coffee or food yet, so when we pulled into the hotel, I beelined to drop our stuff and Lucky off in the room Magnolia arranged for us before dragging her down to the restaurant in the lobby.

"You've gotta eat, Mags. I won't take no for an answer."

She huffed but let me take her hand and guide her into the restaurant. "Fine, but only because I smell bacon, and you'd have to be a monster to say no to bacon."

"Facts," I laughed, pulling her chair out for her as we sat at the table the host led us to before I moved my seat closer to hers and sat down.

She had a busy schedule today making sure everything was not only set up for tonight's show, but we were going to meet up with Connor and his team again this afternoon to see what we needed to do next about Winston and his escalations.

Luckily, we had two shows back-to-back in Phoenix, so we'd get to stay here for a couple of days, which meant we had a little breathing room.

"What are you up to this mornin'?" Magnolia asked, sipping her iced chai latte.

"I'm gonna see if Lucas can get the new kit set up so I can get in some time on it, and then I thought I'd find Connor and see about setting up a meeting for all of us about Winston. Oh, and don't forget hanging out with our furry little guy."

She nodded. "I'll talk to Lucas, and we'll find a space for you that's not on stage to practice. Give me an hour?"

I smiled at her because she got how important this was to me. "Thanks. Now let's talk about what I can do for *you* today." The smile I gave her was downright wicked and full of all sorts of dirty intentions that I didn't even try to hide. Her cheeks tinted pink, but she leaned closer like her body was making the decision for her, and it wanted to be closer to mine.

My fingers crept up the smooth skin of her bare thigh, right up until I hit the hem of her cutoff shorts. I stopped there for a second, moving my fingers back and forth over her skin across the hem but never maneuvering beneath the fabric, not yet.

Back and forth, back and forth, I dragged the tips of my fingers until she shivered, and I slipped my fingers into her shorts, inching higher. "What are you doin'?" she whispered, and my smile widened as I watched a flush creep up her chest and neck.

"Do you want me to stop?" I countered, leaning over and dropping a kiss to her shoulder and watching her skin erupt in goosebumps.

Her eyes fluttered closed, and a soft sigh escaped her lips, one that had me watching her mouth intently. Oh, the things her mouth could do…

"Want to go back upstairs for a minute?" What I had in mind would take a whole hell of a lot more than a minute, but if that was all she had to spare, I'd make it work.

Magnolia opened her eyes and glanced down at the watch on her wrist. "I've got twenty minutes before I'm meetin' Lucas." She looked back up at me and her gaze darkened as she watched me. "Think that'll be enough?"

"Baby, no amount of time will ever be enough with you, but I'll do what

I can." We pushed back from the table and hurried back upstairs, kissing and touching each other while we waited for the elevator, and once we were inside. Neither of us could wait to get up to our room.

Her warm giggle made my heart pick up its already frantic pace. Damn, I'd do anything to keep that smile on her face, but I watched almost in slow motion as it dropped off almost as quickly as it'd come when we approached our room.

I turned and followed her gaze to the partially opened door to our room. "Shit."

She hurried forward, but I grabbed her arm, pulling her back. "Let me go first; you text Connor." There was no damn way I was letting her step foot in that room before me. Anything could be lurking in there, and from where I was standing, there was no way to tell what could be waiting for us inside.

Her hands shook as she pulled out her phone, and I stepped around her, moving toward the door and nudging it open with my foot. I looked tentatively inside but didn't see anything. It wasn't a huge suite, but there were a couple of rooms, so I moved through them quickly. There was no one there, but someone missing.

I stepped back into the hall and ran my hand through my hair, the breakfast we just ate settling like a brick in my stomach. "No one's in there, and none of our stuff's missing, but…"

Magnolia looked up at me with worry clouding her eyes. "But?"

"Lucky's gone."

"What?" She pushed past me into the room and started frantically searching, and I didn't stop her. If she had to see for herself, I'd let her.

"No." She moved to stand in front of me, and I tucked her into my arms, holding her tight while her whole body shook. I had a feeling she was crying, but I couldn't see her face to know for sure. My whole heart hurt, and I was mad as hell.

How had someone gotten in our room?

Security was seriously not doing their job, and Connor and me? We were going to have words. Right now, I kinda wanted to punch a hole in the wall, but instead, I held my girlfriend while she cried over our kidnapped puppy and tried to push my temper aside to think through things logically while we waited for Connor.

We hadn't been at breakfast that long, and if someone—more than likely *Winston*—wanted to hurt Lucky, he'd have done it here and left the evidence for us to find, but he didn't. Which meant he wanted something else.

A soft knocking sounded on the door before it pushed open, and Connor and Julian stepped inside. Connor stopped near Magnolia and me, but Julian continued into the room, checking the entire space. Connor looked us over as if he was checking for injuries. "What happened?"

I glared at him. He wasn't doing his damn job as far as I was concerned, and Magnolia's asshole ex was good at getting access where he shouldn't. "Someone got past your security. *Again.* Our door was open when we got back from breakfast, and Lucky's gone."

"We're doing the best we can to lock everything down, but there are a lot of variables-"

"I don't want to hear any more fucking excuses, Connor. This is unacceptable. Hire more guys if you have to; I really don't care. But already this week, we've dealt with my ex-girlfriend getting backstage, my drums being destroyed, and our room being broken into, and our dog stolen. It's like there's no fucking security at all!" I was breathing hard by the time I was done with my rant, and my voice had risen to the point I was yelling at him, but shit, I was pissed the hell off.

Connor's jaw ticked, but he wisely kept his mouth shut. What could he possibly say? He'd let me down, and I didn't trust him to keep Magnolia safe anymore. Maybe I needed to hire someone else. "I want to hear what the hell you're going to do to fix this moving forward."

Julian joined our little group, and Magnolia pulled away from me enough to wipe her eyes before she turned to face the two of them, too, leaning her back against my chest. I glared at Connor over her head.

"I asked Sebastian and Ronin to fly out, so we have more bodies to keep watch."

"That's it?" Forgive me if I didn't think that would be enough, especially considering Sebastian was more of a behind the desk sort of guy.

"I've got Ryan and Indy out looking for Lucky, too."

"And what are you going to do about Winston? We all know that's who did this." Magnolia tensed at the mention of his name but didn't say anything, and really, what could she say?

"When Ronin gets here, he's going to rendezvous with the local PD and fill them in. We'll be here the next couple of days, and if he did do this," he gestured around the room, "I'll ask Sebastian about getting footage from the cameras in the halls and lobby. Hopefully, they caught something, and we can get him taken in."

"When does Ronin get here?" Magnolia wondered, her voice quiet and raspy from crying.

"They're in the air now. Sebastian will deal with getting the footage." Connor sighed and nodded at Julian, who gave Magnolia an apologetic look before stepping out of the room. "Look, I'm sorry this happened. We've handled tour security before and stalkers before, but sometimes it gets a little chaotic. I'm not trying to make excuses," he hurried to say when he saw the thunderous expression on my face, "but I'm trying to explain. I can't promise you Winston won't get through again because he's sneaky as fuck, and with the way the band and their families are growing, I don't have enough people on my team to cover every possible outcome."

He blew out a breath. "I'm going to bring more people in, but it's not that simple. I can't just hire anyone off the street. They require vetting, and I usually only accept people who get a personal recommendation from someone I trust. That shit takes time."

He and his team were overwhelmed. I could understand that even if I hated it because it meant Magnolia was in more danger than I thought. The guys always spoke so highly of Connor, like he could handle anything and fix any problem. Now I knew that wasn't the case, so I needed to step up watching our backs myself. "Should I hire more outside security?"

"I want to say fuck no because admitting I can't handle something goes against every instinct I have, but I honestly don't know. I think we should search for the dog while the guys are in the air and re-evaluate when they land, and I have a more complete picture of what's going on. Having Ronin touch base with the local PD and Sebastian pull the footage will help."

I looked down at Magnolia and waited for her to meet my eyes. "What do you think? Do you want to wait? Because I don't give a shit. If you'd feel safer with me hiring every bodyguard in the state of Arizona, I will, and I'll do it right now."

She nibbled on her lip for a few seconds before shaking her head. "No, I think we should do what Connor says. At least he knows the situation, and I trust Ryan." Connor winced at how she obviously left him out. "I have a restraining order, but I know Winston's not going to leave me alone. He never has. We have to catch him breaking it and get him arrested. Even then, I don't know how long he'd go away for." Her tone was hopeless; her body language screamed dejected.

At that moment, I was lost. I had no idea what to do to fix this short of killing the guy, and I wasn't willing to be locked up for a life away from Magnolia to make him go away. Maybe that was selfish of me, but the way she looked at me? I got the feeling she wouldn't be happy with me going away, either, and I lived to make Magnolia happy.

I craved it. I'd do almost anything for it—anything short of murdering someone. If he hurt her again, though? All bets were off.

"If that's what you want, Mags." I turned my attention back to Connor. "The other guys, they might be okay forgiving screw-ups when everything turns out okay in the end, but I'm not them," I warned. "If Magnolia gets hurt on your watch, I'm going to be out for fucking blood."

Shadows crept into his eyes before disappearing again. "I get it, and I'll do my best not to let you down." He was speaking to Magnolia, and she gave him a nod. "I'm going down to help look for Lucky, and I'll text you when Ronin and Sebastian land, and we've got something to share."

"Fine." My tone was frosty at best. I was still pissed, and I didn't see it going away anytime soon. We watched him go and didn't say another word until he was outside.

"You okay?" I finally asked Magnolia after turning her in my arms so I could see her face. She had tears streaming down her cheeks, and her lip wobbled a little. Her eyes were red and glassy, and her nose was a little bit pink.

Even devastated, she was beautiful.

"I just want it to stop. I want Lucky back, and I never want to have to think about Winston again." She looked up at me despondently, tears continuing to leak from her eyes, and I hugged her tighter. "I don't see how it's possible, though. He's never gonna go away. He's never gonna stop. Even if he goes to jail, it won't be for life. What's to stop him from comin' after me once he's out?"

The hopelessness in her eyes shredded me. "Baby, I'll get us a damn bunker if I have to to keep him away. I'll hire every security person in the state. I'll do whatever it takes to keep you safe and able to live your life without his interference. I promise." That was a promise I damn sure planned to keep.

She reached up and ran her palm along the stubble on my jaw. "Thank you." It was almost a whisper, but I got lost in the depth of gratitude in her gaze, practically falling into the clear, blue depths of her eyes before she finally pulled away. "We need to help find Lucky."

"Right," I agreed, releasing my hold on her and taking her hand instead. I was just as upset as she was at the loss of our puppy. He'd quickly become my little sidekick, always at my side if I wasn't at rehearsal or soundcheck. He even came to the fan meets with me sometimes, and he ate up the attention from everyone. If Winston hurt him, I didn't know what I was going to do.

We left the room, making sure the door was securely shut and locked. I needed to request a new room because that one didn't feel safe anymore. It didn't matter that the locks on the doors were the same in all the rooms. What was important was a new room wouldn't make Magnolia feel like she'd been violated.

Maybe we'd just sleep on the bus and skip the hotel altogether.

For the next few hours, we scoured every inch of the hotel and the businesses on either side. The rest of the guys in the band and their wives and kids even helped, but we didn't find him. We had a meet and greet before tonight's show and soundcheck to get to over at the arena. Magnolia needed to deal with a couple of issues that'd cropped up with the stage crew today, so we reluctantly all headed over to the arena.

Magnolia's mood got worse and worse as we drove away from the hotel. She was closing in on herself, something I noticed she did when shit got bad with her ex or she felt out of control. If anything, it only made me hold her hand tighter. I wouldn't let her get lost inside her own mind or give up on life. Did we have a lot of challenges coming up in getting rid of Winston? Yup, but she was worth it.

Our future was worth it, too.

We pulled up beside the buses, and Magnolia perked up, squinting out the window and pressing closer to the glass. "Oh my god," she breathed, and she was out the car door before it had even fully stopped, yanking her hand out of my grasp and running toward the bus.

It took a second for my brain to catch up, but then I took in the tiny, grey puppy shivering despite the blistering heat where he was tied to the door handle of the passenger side of the bus. I unbuckled and followed her, jogging over to where Magnolia had Lucky wrapped in her arms and was crying—hopefully, happy tears this time—all over his fur.

I wrapped my arms around them both, filled with a mixture of relief and anger. Winston wanted to show us exactly what kind of power he had and how easy it was for him to gain access to our lives. He could've hurt Lucky today, and he wanted us to know it. Thankfully he hadn't, but he could have, and that was so damn unsettling, I found my gaze searching for Connor.

He watched us from where he stood near the driver's door of the SUV we'd ridden over in, and when we locked eyes, the determination in his settled something inside me. Of all the shit the guys had been through before and everything since I'd joined up, Winston might be Connor's greatest challenge.

I hoped like hell he was up for it.

TWENTY ONE
MAGNOLIA

"What time are they gonna be here?" I called out across the suite, watching Lucky as he jolted out of sleep from where he napped at Griffin's feet by the couch. Neither one of them had spent even a minute apart since we found our little ball of fluff yesterday afternoon.

My stomach flip-flopped at the memory of finding the room empty. Winston almost took something else from me. I thought he was done with that, that I'd walked away and drawn that line in the sand that said I was done letting him take anything from me.

Apparently, I'd been wrong about the level of control he still had over my life. Right now, I didn't want to think about that. Not with my boyfriend's parents coming into town to see him play with the band for the first time ever. It was a big deal, and despite Ryan's reservations about Grant and Monica, I liked them well enough.

Griffin had been bouncing off the walls all day, so I knew he was excited for them to watch him play. Why they hadn't seen him when we were in Texas, I didn't know, but they were coming tonight, and I was looking forward to seeing them, too. I was in the bathroom pulling my hair into a messy side braid when my phone vibrated.

I'd gotten so used to ignoring it, I almost didn't check it, but the guilt started to eat at me, so I peeked.

Ryan: Ugh, the in-laws. Stick with me tonight? I'm willing to bribe with donuts.

I turned around and shot Griffin a look. "Did you tell your brother how much I love donuts?"

He flashed me his crooked smile, the one that made my stomach flutter, and my heart beat faster. I wouldn't even mention what it did to my panties. "I might've mentioned our date in New Orleans."

"Ryan's trying to entice me to be her shield from your mom tonight with donuts."

His eyebrows furrowed. "Shield?"

I walked across the room so I wouldn't have to yell and plopped down on his lap, wrapping my arms around his neck to play with the hair at the back of his head I loved so much. It tickled my fingertips. "You didn't know that Ryan isn't the biggest fan of your mom?"

"What? No, I didn't." He looked genuinely confused, and I smoothed the wrinkle in his forehead with my finger.

"She's pissed Monica walked away and left Maddox behind with his dad. Ryan was there for everything Maddox went through, and she blames Monica for most of what happened after she left."

Griffin ran his hand along my thigh almost absently, like he was lost in thought, and I took a second to reply to Ryan.

Magnolia: I've got you, girl, no bribe needed.

Magnolia: But bring the donuts just in case.

Ryan: You're the best x

"I can see where she's coming from," he finally admitted, "but she doesn't know what it was like for my mom. I think the person who can best understand what she went through is you. Maddox's dad… he almost killed her more than once."

"Yeah, but I would never—and I mean *never, ever* leave my child behind to face that on their own. I can't pretend I know what was goin' through your mom's head, and maybe mentally, she broke and wasn't capable of makin' great decisions at the time. The only one who knows is her. But I can tell you I've walked through a hell like that, and I wouldn't leave my dog behind, let alone my child."

I hugged him closer to me, sensing he needed the reassurance. Griffin was close to his mom, and I doubted he enjoyed the turn this conversation had taken. "I'm not sayin' your mom's a bad person, and when I met her, she seemed sweet and like she really loved both you and your brother. All I'm sayin' is I can see where Ryan's comin' from. She's overprotective when it comes to Maddox, and if you'd gone through the same things he had, I'd probably be upset, too."

The corner of his lips quirked up. "I love that you care about me."

I rolled my eyes but laughed. "I even kinda *love* you, Sugar."

"You'll love me even more in a second," he growled, flipping me, so I was underneath him on the couch and showing me with his tongue exactly how he felt about me, too.

"Thank you for this," Ryan leaned close to me and whispered as we stood side by side, just backstage. She passed me a bag that smelled deliciously like sugar and deep-fried dough. I'd met Griffin's parents at the gate to get in and handed them over all-access passes so they could be back here with us, and they'd stuck by either Ryan or me since they'd gotten here because the boys were busy getting ready for the show.

Ryan and I both had jobs to do, but I tried to keep them distracted and away from Ryan as much as possible by introducing them to Lucas and showing them how the tour worked behind the scenes. We went up in the audio booth, and they spent some time with Jericho, and then I gave them a tour of the bus.

By the time I'd crossed everything off my to-do list, we only had about fifteen minutes until the guys took the stage, and Grant and Monica had wandered off to get drinks from the makeshift bar backstage while Tuesday Told a Secret played their set.

"I get it," I assured her as the tiny hairs on the back of my neck stood up, and I turned to find Griffin moving through the crowd of people backstage, eyes locked on me. His brother was right behind him, and Griffin practically tackled me before he kissed me until I couldn't breathe, a huge grin on his face.

"What was that for?" I wondered, trying to catch my breath as his parents made their way over to us. He looked so damn hot in his ripped black jeans and black t-shirt that hugged his chest and arms like it was custom made. All his tattoos and piercings were on display, and I marveled at how turned on I got just from looking at him. My attraction to Griffin was intense, and I hoped it would never change. One look from him and I wanted to climb up his body and never come back down.

"Because I couldn't stand the thought of not touching you for the next ninety minutes without doing that to hold me over." His smile was wicked, and I shivered. His grin only got bigger, and my panties only got wetter the longer we stood there staring at each other, a silent communication building anticipation for later, making the air between us charged and almost electric.

"Well, this isn't awkward at all," Griffin's dad, Grant, chimed in, breaking the spell, and we all chuckled. Even Maddox, who had his arm thrown around Ryan's shoulders. She was looking at me instead of Monica.

"We can't wait to see you boys play," Monica gushed, maneuvering into the space between Griffin and me, which wasn't a lot, and hugging him and then Maddox. When Maddox let her go, Ryan moved closer to me, almost behind my back.

Monica looked genuinely excited, and her whole face was lit up. I wondered if she'd ever seen her boys on stage together. There was a reason Shadow Phoenix was as popular as they were—they made magic up on that stage. She was in for a serious treat.

The guys said their goodbyes as Tuesday Told a Secret moved off stage. They had to get in place, so we watched them go, an awkward sort of silence settling in around us. Once the guys moved on stage, there was more space to work with. The crews shuffled around, and there weren't as many people just hanging out.

"Do y'all want to watch from back here at the side of the stage, or do you want to go out in front?" I wondered, eyeing the view we'd have if we stayed back here. They'd get to see Maddox's back and Griffin from the side. If we went out in front, the crowd would be more intense, but they'd get to see the show as the guys intended it.

"My vote's for the front," Grant told us, and I turned to Monica, who was nodding along.

"We won't be able to see everything from back here."

I turned to Ryan. "What do you think, safety-wise?"

She considered for a second before nodding. "We'll stay on this side of the perimeter fences and in front of the venue security. It should be fine."

Decision made, I led everyone around to a spot just in front of the metal fences that'd been put up to keep people from climbing on stage and nodded at the security guy standing guard. Coordinating with venue security was part of my job, so I'd met this guy before the show, and he didn't bother trying to tell us we couldn't stand there.

We took our places as Zen started his opening monologue with the crowd, but my eyes were locked onto Griffin the whole time like they always were. I couldn't help myself. He was magnetic and drew me in, and it was impossible to resist watching him play. The energy that poured off him was contagious, and the other guys fed off it.

Ryan danced on one side of me, and Monica bounced around on the other as they guys played through song after song. When there was a short break in between songs, my ears rang from the deafening sounds of the audience. Tonight's show was one of the best I'd seen so far, and I had to wonder if that had to do with Monica and Grant being here to watch.

Ryan stiffened beside me when the guys started in with some of their older stuff, and Maddox dedicated a song to his mom. I took her hand, squeezing it to let her know I supported her. Her issues with Monica weren't going anywhere, but I hoped she could put them aside for this visit. The guys seemed so happy with their mom here—and Griffin with both parents—and with all the drama that'd been happening on the tour, the last thing we needed was to start fighting amongst ourselves.

The energy between us had been weird and uncomfortable for most of the show, so I hadn't even gotten to do my usual ogling of my super hot boyfriend and the way his body commanded the instrument he played. Watching him on stage usually meant by the time the show was over, I was so turned on I could barely stand it. Griffin would drag me off into some tiny corner somewhere or our hotel room and make me come until I couldn't remember my name.

Unfortunately, tonight wasn't going to go that way, so I guessed it was a good thing I wasn't ready to jump his very sexy bones. I reserved the right to pout about it, though, and a quick side-eye at Ryan told me she was having similar thoughts.

"Is it just me, or are the 'rents totally cockblockers?" she leaned in and basically shouted into my ear. I cringed and looked to see if Monica heard her, but she was oblivious as she started up at the stage with pride shining in her eyes.

Cracking a smile, I leaned back toward Ryan. "It's not just you… but if we don't have cocks, is it still cockblockin'?"

She cracked up, and I was happy to see the tension melt off her, at least for a little while. We danced and sang along as a group, and even Grant got in on it. Being between Ryan and Monica could be a little bit uncomfortable sometimes, but I liked both of them, and I was in a unique position to see the situation from both of their points of view.

For both of their sakes—and Maddox's—I hoped they could get past their issues. They were fortunate to have each other as family, I would know. Now that I was on the verge of gaining the family I'd always wished for, I didn't want there to be fighting and anger. Call me crazy, but I wanted everyone to love each other and get along, and I'd do whatever I could to make it happen.

The guys wrapped up their show with one last song and a bow to thunderous applause. As they left the stage, we did, too, making our way backstage. As soon as we stepped foot behind the stage, I was pulled against a sweaty chest, and Griffin's arms wrapped around me. I breathed him in because there was something about his scent mixed with the sweet smell of fresh sweat when he played a show that did it for me. I could bottle it and sell it; he smelled so good.

His chuckle vibrated through his chest, and I smiled in response and reluctantly let him go since his parents were standing right next to us. All I really wanted to do was lick him, but I kept my tongue to myself.

"Incredible show, son," Grant praised, and then amended, "both of you."

Maddox grinned, and Griffin moved to hug his mom, and she scrunched her nose and swatted him away. "Magnolia can have all your gross, sweaty hugs.

I'll take a rain check until after you shower." She laughed as Maddox came around behind her, and the brothers trapped her in a sweaty hug sandwich, and I couldn't help the giggle that bubbled up. Even Ryan's lips curved up into a reluctant smile as she watched. Grant finally gave in and said, *screw it*, throwing his arms around them all.

"Okay, I've gotta wrap up here and make sure everyone's on schedule. The guys need to shower, and Ryan..." I raised my eyebrow, and her eyes flashed with gratitude.

"I've got to check the buses and meet with Connor."

I nodded. "How about we all meet back at the hotel in an hour? If you guys are up for it, can we grab a late dinner? Maybe some drinks?"

They all agreed, and we parted ways, Ryan staying by my side while everyone else moved to go clean up. She looped her arm through mine while we made the trek to the equipment room. After a show, my first stop was always with Lucas to make sure he didn't need anything extra from me. If anything happened to the instruments during the show or he needed to order anything, making sure it got to the next stop was a logistical nightmare, so that was why I stepped in.

"Thanks for having my back with Monica," Ryan sighed. "I know you could just as easily take her side in this because of your history."

"I could, but I also understand how it feels to love someone so much you want to hurt anyone that causes them pain," I confessed, and she smiled knowingly.

"You do, hmm?" she teased, and I blushed as we turned down another corridor. "I'm happy for you. If anyone deserves a good guy, it's you, and Griffin is one of the best."

"You know I'm thankful for you, too, right?"

She looked at me, studying me for a second before her head dropped onto my shoulder. "I know, and I'm beyond grateful Griffin got his head out of his ass and picked you because you're awesome, and I already think of you as a friend. I hope you know that, Magnolia."

My eyes pricked, but I blinked away the tears. I couldn't remember the last time I had an actual friend. Maybe never. "I hoped."

We walked arm-in-arm until we got to the equipment room, and she stood up, letting me go. "This dinner is going to be a shit show," she complained, and I laughed.

"It doesn't have to be. How about you sit next to me, and any time you want to lash out at Monica, you squeeze my hand? Maybe we could make it a drinkin' game. If we get tipsy, that might make it more fun, right?"

She snorted. "Or it might erase what little filter I have completely. Besides, do you even drink?"

I bit my lip. "I could start." She raised her eyebrow, and I amended, "I want to try it."

She looked up at the ceiling while she considered. "How about every time I want to punch Monica, we take a sip?"

"Am I about to get alcohol poisonin'?" It was a legitimate concern if her mood anytime we were around her mother-in-law was any indication.

She laughed. "Maybe, but if not, it'll be fun."

"If you say so." I moved to go into the room Lucas was using for equipment storage. "See you in a bit?"

She nodded, and then I got to work, trying to ignore the excited butterflies bouncing around my stomach at the idea that I had a friend and not only that, but she was leaning on me for support. It made me feel stronger than I had in a while. If I was strong enough for her to lean on me, that meant I must be healing from the damage Winston did, right?

It took less time than I thought to do my rounds and check in with everyone. Everything was running smoothly for once. The buses were leaving tonight—or should I say early tomorrow morning—and heading for Vegas, so the stage crew was already breaking down the stage by the time I grabbed a ride with Ryan over to the hotel.

A quick Google search for restaurants not only open at this hour but also that had food we'd want to eat narrowed our options considerably, so it didn't take us long to decide where we'd go. We piled into one of the black SUVs that traveled along with the tour, and Maddox slid behind the wheel with Ryan beside him. Griffin and I took the very back seat so Monica and Grant wouldn't have to maneuver back there, and he didn't waste any time pulling me across the seat, so our bodies were plastered together.

His warm palm settled on my inner thigh just below the hem of my shorts, and he traced maddening circles along my skin that had me shivering under his touch. He leaned in, his lips brushing the outside of my ear as he whispered, "I've been hard since that kiss before the show, and if I have to wait until after this dinner to sink into you, I might lose my mind."

He pressed a kiss to the sensitive skin behind my ear, and a spark shot straight down to my core. He smirked as he pulled back, knowing full well how much he turned me on. His gaze dropped to where my nipples had tightened under my tank top like he could see straight through the fabric and into my bra, and I squirmed as his fingers crept higher at the same time.

By the time we pulled into the restaurant parking lot, I was so turned on I couldn't think straight. Griffin had to adjust himself before he climbed out of the car behind me, so at least I wasn't the only one suffering.

The restaurant wasn't crowded, and we were shown to a table right away. I briefly considered making a break for the bathroom to relieve some of the tension Griffin built up on the ride over here, but Ryan tilted toward me before whispering, "Girl, I know that look, but if I have to suffer, you do, too."

I scowled at her, but she just laughed. Everyone at the table looked at us with questions in their eyes, but we both ignored them and went back to looking at the menu. "What kind of drink should I get?" I asked Ryan and Griffin perked up.

"You're drinking?"

I nodded and then shrugged. "I thought it might be fun to see what all the fuss is about." It wasn't like I hadn't had alcohol before, but it was just a couple of sips here and there. I'd never even been close to getting drunk.

"A drunk Magnolia? This I've gotta see," Maddox chimed in, clapping his hands and rubbing them together like he couldn't wait. I didn't think I'd really be that much different, would I?

"How about mojitos? They're yummy," Ryan suggested, and I looked to Griffin, who shrugged.

"That sounds as good as anything. You're not going to know what you like until you try different drinks." He leaned closer. "Don't worry about letting go tonight. I'll stick with water so I can make sure nothing happens."

"Thank you," I breathed, and then he kissed me, but it was too quick, and I chased his lips with my own when he pulled back. He just laughed and draped his arm across the back of my chair. Of course, it wasn't as innocent as it looked because his fingers worked their magic into my skin as he ran them back and forth that set off fireworks all the way down to my toes.

When the waitress dropped off our drinks, Ryan lifted hers and clinked it with mine before she took a sip. I followed and took a small sip, not knowing what to expect, but I was pleasantly surprised when the drink was light and sweet and refreshing. I set it back down while I tuned back into the conversations around me.

Monica was retelling a story from when Maddox was little. "You were about five and decided you were big enough to climb onto one of the horses all on your own. I'd been in the kitchen doing the dishes, and you snuck out the back door. By the time I found you, you were in the bar with one leg lifted above your head and tangled in the stirrup, and you were crying because you couldn't get it out." She was laughing, but Ryan grabbed my hand and dug her nails in.

I took that as my cue to take a drink, and she followed suit, gulping her drink. I eyed her but didn't say anything. I didn't plan to gulp mine, but I took a healthy swallow before setting it back down.

Monica turned to Ryan. "I've got so many stories of the two of you when you were little. It's a shame you grew apart, but I'm glad you found your way back to each other."

"Yeah, I bet," Ryan muttered under her breath, and Maddox turned and watched her curiously. In all the time I spent around the guys and their wives, I didn't think I'd ever seen Maddox get upset with Ryan about anything. I found myself holding my breath to see what would happen because, at the first hint of violence or anger, I was probably going to bolt.

It brought up too many painful memories of my own. Maybe I had PTSD.

"What do you mean by that?" Monica asked, genuine concern and curiosity in her eyes.

"Nothing, it's fine. Let's just let it go." Ryan lifted her glass and took another sip, but this time I didn't bother. If I had to get out of here, I didn't want to be inhibited in any way.

"No, I want to talk about it. I didn't want to say anything, but I've noticed how you look at me," Monica supplied, and Grant murmured his agreement, and then all bets were off.

"Okay, I guess we're doing this." Ryan lifted her glass and finished her drink, and I slid mine in her direction in case she needed more liquid courage. Maddox was still watching his wife like he didn't know what to do. I figured she'd at least have talked to him about her feelings in private, but the way he watched her now, I wasn't so sure he had any idea what had been eating at her.

"I think it's incredibly messed up that you left, Monica. You left, and you didn't take Maddox. Do you have any idea what he had to endure at the hands of Russell? I was there. I saw everything. I was the person he ran to, the one whose bedroom window he climbed into after he'd been used as a human punching bag." She was breathing hard, and Maddox took her hand, pulling her closer. At least it didn't look like he was about to lose his temper.

I glanced across the table at Monica, and she'd stilled and gone pale. "If you didn't think I knew what his father was capable of, you're wrong. I knew."

If looks could kill, Ryan would've just murdered Monica at the dinner table with the glare she shot her. "You knew, and you still left him. What kind of mother *does* that?"

"One who's trying to protect her son," Monica countered, her shaky voice getting stronger.

Ryan reared back like she'd been slapped. "*Protect* him? How the hell does leaving him with his unhinged father protect him?"

Griffin reached for my hand under the table, and I gripped him like my life depended on it. My heart was beating so fast in my chest, it was hard to breathe. Monica reached for her glass of water and took a sip, her hand trembling the whole time. "When I was packing to leave, Russell came home unexpectedly. He told me if I took his son, he'd hunt me down and kill him. Not me, Maddox. He said he'd never let him go, and he would never stop, and that when he found us, he would make me watch while he killed our son before he killed me, too."

The silence around the table was deafening. No one knew what to say, but Ryan looked like she wanted to throw up. "So," Monica continued, her voice completely flat. "I had nothing when I left but a small suitcase. I lived in a women's shelter and went to therapy and did what I could to survive and turn my life around, but I knew when I left, I couldn't take him. How would I have hidden Maddox? I couldn't. I figured I would get on my feet and come back for him, but it took longer than I thought, and when I tried to reach out, Russell wouldn't let me get near him."

She sniffled, and Grant handed her his napkin. She gave him a wobbly smile and wiped at her eyes before she turned to Maddox. "I never wanted to leave you behind, and not a day has gone by since the day I left that I didn't wonder if I should've done something different. I'm so sorry, Maddox. So, so sorry I left you with that monster."

Maddox pressed a kiss to Ryan's forehead before he stood up and wrapped his mom in a hug. Despite the drama, I suspected they all needed this closure, and maybe I needed to see it, too. Maybe I needed to forgive myself for feeling weak or wondering what I could've done differently because I did the best I could do in a shitty situation.

Ryan pushed out of her chair and went over to join the hug with Maddox and his mom. They'd needed to get everything out in the open, and now it looked like they'd heal and be okay.

Griffin squeezed my hand like he knew what I was thinking, and I smiled at him gratefully. After that conversation, the discussion turned to the guys and the tour and what we'd all seen and done so far, which was much safer territory. None of us seemed to want to linger long after dinner was done, and I hadn't managed even to finish my first drink, let alone get tipsy like I'd gone into the dinner thinking I would.

When we stepped out of the restaurant, I did the typical scan of my surroundings, and my breath caught when I saw a familiar figure underneath a street light across the parking lot. Griffin noticed me tensing up and looked at me with concern. "What's wrong?"

"Winston," I choked out, the adrenaline kicking in and making my whole body tremble.

"Where?" Ryan bit out, and I pointed him out. He turned and started walking briskly away, and she took off with Maddox on her heels. I didn't want her to get near him. Who knew what he might do to her if she cornered him. The thought made me shudder.

Monica stepped up beside me and rubbed my arm where she could find space. Griffin had wrapped himself around me and was holding me protectively against his body like he was my shield against the world. Maybe he was.

"What's going on?" Monica asked, looking between Griffin and me while Grant stared out in the direction Ryan and Maddox took off in with a frown.

"Magnolia has a lot in common with you, mom," Griffin answered for me, brushing the hair out of my face. "Her ex was a lot like yours."

Monica's whole expression changed to one of understanding and sympathy. "Oh, sweetheart. I'm so sorry. Was that him?"

I nodded, not really sure I could get actual words out of my mouth right now. "He's been following her," Griffin added.

"If you ever want to talk about it, you can call me. Trust me when I say I know what you're going through, but it'll be okay. Just look at Grant and me. He's my second chance. You'll get yours, too." She turned her attention onto her son. "Will you make sure you give her my number?"

Griffin nodded, and I felt his chin move against the top of my head where he had me tucked up against him. When he spoke, his words vibrated his chest in a way that comforted me and helped calm my fight or flight response down. "Yep, I can do that."

We had to wait for Ryan and Maddox to come back because Maddox had the car keys, but when they did, they were both breathing hard but empty-handed. "He got away," Ryan panted. "Again."

"But we saw him, Magnolia. It was definitely Winston," Maddox added, pacing back and forth a bit to catch his breath.

"Can we go back to the hotel now?" I asked, suddenly completely worn out and over all of Winston's games.

"Yeah, Mags. We can do that." Griffin held me all the way back to the hotel, but I couldn't shake the desolation creeping into my thoughts. Monica was proof there was good on the other side of a situation like mine, yet right now, it didn't feel like I'd ever be free of Winston's obsessive grip.

TWENTY TWO
MAGNOLIA

"It's so much different than I thought it'd be."

"How'd you envision it?" Griffin wondered as we drove into Las Vegas in the middle of the day. Maybe it was because it was mid-afternoon and not night, but it looked like any other city to me. Maybe a few more tall buildings, but it wasn't as glittery or fancy as I expected.

Scrunching my nose up, I watched discarded papers blow along the sidewalk. "More... sparkly? Gold? Fancy?"

He laughed and stopped petting Lucky where he was curled up in Griffin's lap so he could thread his fingers through mine. "It's like anywhere else. It has its shiny parts and its tarnished parts."

"Maybe you can show me some of the shinier bits while we're here."

He pressed a quick kiss to my lips and then grinned. "We've got two days here. In Vegas time, that's forever. We can get lots of fun stuff in, but tonight the guys want to go out."

"Out?"

"Yeah, dancing, drinks. There's a club here they like, we went last time we were in Vegas, and it was fun. I think you'll like it." His phone buzzed, and he looked down at it.

"Shit. We've got to hit up a couple of radio stations this afternoon for interviews before the show. Maddox says Ryan's going to stick with you while we're gone so you won't be alone." He gave me an apologetic look, but I leaned into him, laying my head on his shoulder. Sometimes I just wanted to be close to him for no reason at all other than I loved him.

"That actually works out because I've gotta talk to the arena staff and get the stage crew situated, so I'll be busy until later tonight anyway." He pressed a kiss to the top of my head as the bus pulled into the arena parking lot. I moved away from him reluctantly, steeling myself for the day ahead. Neither Griffin nor I got much sleep last night after the incident with Winston at the restaurant.

There were only three shows left on the schedule, and it was hard to believe we'd made it a whole month on this tour and through almost every stop already. It'd flown by.

When we got off the bus, Griffin kissed me goodbye and followed the rest of the guys off to do their promo. Their PR guy, Harrison, had flown over from LA for the day, so he was with them, and Jericho looked like he was going to tag along, too, even if he didn't have to anymore. I sometimes wondered if he missed being on stage with the guys, but he seemed happy with his decision to step back and stick to the booth. He spent most shows up with the audio engineer making sure the music sounded how the guys wanted it.

I checked in with all the different equipment, stage, sound, and lighting crews before pulling my phone out and finding the radio station the band was interviewing with this afternoon. I tucked in my earbuds while I sat in a shady spot with my laptop going over the tour financials. The interview was already half over by the time I tuned in.

"Everyone knows it's been a whirlwind couple of years for you guys. While your fresh music has been climbing the charts, you've all made some huge changes in your personal lives, getting married, and having kids. All except your newest member." I could hear the shift in her voice as the host paused before the next part. I held my breath while I listened.

"Griffin. Last we checked, you were all over Insta with your girlfriend Wynter, but according to your account, that's been done for *weeks*. Does that mean you're on the market?"

His voice was deep and rich, and the sound of his laugh made me shiver. "Wynter was just a horrible mistake I wish I never made. We all have one of those, right?" The guys all agreed, and the host laughed. It seemed like he was trying to change the subject, but she wasn't letting him off the hook that easily.

"So, Wynter Mattison's definitely out of the picture. Got it. Can you make all my listener's dreams come true and let them know you're back on the dating scene?"

"Sorry, Sasha, but no. I'm taken." My stomach was doing full-on somersaults at his words. There was something so hot about him claiming our relationship publicly, even if he hadn't told anyone who I was.

"Already? Oooh, juicy," she purred. "Who is she?"

"While Griff's love life is *truly fascinating*," Maddox's sarcastic drawl cut in, "I think we've got some tickets to give away to tonight's show."

The host—Sasha—wasn't going to be deterred, though. She was like a dog with a bone. "Yeah, we'll get to those in one sec. Tell us about this mystery girl, Griffin."

"She's not much of a mystery," Zen chimed in, and the guys all chuckled.

"Yeah, we see her every day," True added.

"And that's probably enough of that," Griffin shut them down.

"Okay, okay. Let's give away those tickets…" My heart was racing as I pulled my headphones out of my ears—holy crap on a cracker.

It was out there now, and while no one knew who I was yet, it was probably only a matter of time until they did. Griffin was really serious about this thing we were doing, wasn't he? Otherwise, he wouldn't have said anything. My heart felt like it was taking flight in my chest.

If I hadn't gotten distracted by having to find an alternate cooking space for the caterers, I would've been able to dwell on what it meant for our relationship now that it was more out in the open, but as it was, I didn't. It took every ounce of my concentration to get through the rest of the day without overthinking every situation that might come from Griffin's words on the radio.

I didn't get a chance to see Griffin again until he was on stage, and even then, I was so busy I only got to watch for a few minutes. It didn't stop me from pausing for a minute and taking him all in as he played; his skin slick from sweat glistened underneath the stage lights, and I craved the salty taste of him on my tongue.

Was it weird I wanted to lick him?

Once the show was over, the guys did their post-concert thing, and I ran around like a chicken with my head cut off to make sure everyone was on task. There wasn't even close to as much work tonight as there was on a night where we were traveling, so it didn't take long before I was catching a ride over to the hotel to change into something worthy of a Vegas club.

Too bad I had nothing like that at all in my wardrobe. The dressiest I got was cut off jeans and tank tops, so when I stepped into the room, and Griffin pointed me toward the closet with a glint in his eye and a smirk on his lips, I knew he'd done something.

"What'd you do?" I asked as I stepped into the closet and found a wardrobe bag hanging by itself.

"Go see." His voice came from right beside my ear. He'd moved up behind me and stood so close I could feel the heat radiating off his body. It made everything inside me spark to life, and the last thing I wanted to do was step away. I wanted to move closer, turn around maybe, rip his shirt off his freshly-showered chest, slide my hands into his still-damp hair…

"I can feel the dirty thoughts bouncing around in your head, Mags, and if you don't stop, we'll never get out of this room. Don't you want to experience Vegas?" His voice was all growly and did absolutely nothing to help how worked up I was.

I pushed off him, needing to put some distance between us before I gave in to every fantasy currently rolling through my mind, but when I looked back at him, his tongue ran along his lower lip, and the piercing in his tongue glinted in the light as his dark eyes glittered in my direction and I had to tear my gaze off him. "Right, Sin City."

His dark chuckle wrapped around me like a caress, and I shivered, but I tried to ignore it as I stepped up to the garment bag and tugged the zipper down to reveal a tiny white dress. I looked back at him over my shoulder and raised my eyebrow.

"Just try it on, please?" Griffin's hungry gaze was almost pleading. "I saw it in the store window on our way back to the hotel and made Connor stop so I could go in and get it. The guys gave me tons of shit, but I had to see you in it.

I've been picturing it all afternoon."

"Fine, but you have to go wait out there," I pointed to the bedroom behind him. "You don't get to see until the big reveal."

His heated gaze swept up and down my whole body, leaving nothing but fire in their wake, but he did what I asked and went back out to the bedroom with Lucky on his heels. I blew out a breath and looked at the dress, wondering how I was going to pull it off. I wasn't ashamed of my body exactly, but I didn't typically show it off. This dress?

Yeah, it wasn't going to leave much to the imagination.

There was no way I could wear a bra with it, so after pulling my shirt off and my shorts down, I unhooked my bra and tossed it aside. I let out a breath of absolute relief the moment my bra fell away and took the dress off the hanger. It was tight and would hug every curve with spaghetti straps and a slit up the right thigh, even though the skirt already hit at mid-thigh as it was. When I maneuvered my way into it, I could still see the line of my thong, so I slipped it off, saying a little prayer that the skirt would stay in place and nothing would be exposed.

I'd never felt more naked while wearing clothes before.

On the floor underneath the garment bag was a matching pair of heels, and I slid my feet into them. Everything fit perfectly, and how Griffin had managed that was beyond me. I ran my fingers through the waves of my hair but left it down otherwise. I considered it my best feature, and the dark strands against the ivory dress really popped.

When I stepped out of the closet, it took no time at all for Griffin's jaw to fall open and his eyes to turn a little wild and possessive as he scanned me from head to toe like he had before. This time, it looked like a fire had ignited in his eyes, and I had to look away before I fell into the intensity of it.

He stood up and pulled me into his arms, raking his fingers into my hair and angling my head so that when he kissed me, it was deep and intense right off the bat. His hands wandered up and down my body, and mine gripped him just as hard, holding him as close to me as I could get him. His erection pressed into my belly, and then he slowed down the kisses and pulled away with a groan. "Damn, you look good enough to eat, but I don't know if I can handle a whole night out with you looking that good. I'm going to get into a fight for sure."

I laughed and patted him on the chest. "You bought the dress; now you have to live with the consequences, Sugar. Did you walk Lucky?"

He blew out a breath and adjusted himself before nodding. "Yeah, he'll be good here for a few hours."

He knelt in front of Lucky's dog bed that looked more like a super fuzzy pillow, and our puppy flopped over onto his back and presented his belly for Griffin to rub. Griff obliged with a laugh and then stood and straightened his black jeans and a white t-shirt. It wasn't fair he got to look that good in just jeans and a t-shirt while I wore a dress that was like a second skin, but the way he looked at me while I wore it made up for the discomfort of possibly having my bits on full display.

Kind of.

Griffin looked at his phone before slipping it into his pocket. "Ready?"

I nodded and took the hand he held outstretched for me. "Where are we going first?"

"Lobby to meet everyone, then Dusk." His arm found its way around my waist, and he rested his hand on my hip. The warmth from his skin seeped through the thin fabric of my dress and shot straight to my core. The fact I wasn't wearing underwear was suddenly becoming a problem as my thighs got a little slick.

He stopped and studied me as I tried not to squirm. "Are you wearing panties under that dress?"

I looked around the empty hall of the hotel before shaking my head. He swore and pulled me close, kissing me like his life depended on it before letting me go, and when he did, we were both sucking in air like we'd climbed ten flights of stairs. Now the problem between my legs was much, much worse.

"You can't kiss me like that," I told him, tugging the hem of my dress down a little, and his lips curled up into a wicked smirk.

"Why not?" His fingers danced across my thigh and up under the hem of my dress while his other arm moved across my back and held me up. He nuzzled into my neck and pressed kisses along the skin of my shoulder that made me shiver. His fingers moved higher and higher before his phone buzzed in his pocket. I felt it where his body was pressed up against mine, but he ignored it. His fingers crept higher until they brushed against my slit, and I jerked at the contact, but his phone vibrated again.

His frustration matched mine when he growled and took a step back, leaving his arm around me because my legs were a little wobbly. "What?" he snapped, lifting his phone to his ear. He rolled his eyes at whoever was on the other end of the call. "We're on our way."

He hung up and put his phone back into his pocket, dropping one last, and way too fast, kiss to my lips before taking my hand. "They're all downstairs waiting on us." We started moving toward the elevator again, and when we stepped inside, he closed in on me again, pinning me to the wall with his chest and leaning close, so his lips just brushed mine, but he wasn't quite kissing me.

"I'm not going to kiss you because if I do, I won't be able to stop," his eyes blazed like he didn't want anything more than to do what he just said he wouldn't, and I was sure my gaze mirrored his. "Later," he murmured, letting the promise hang in the air as he stepped back and my nipples pebbled from the sudden loss of his warmth.

I was sure it had nothing to do with how worked up he'd managed to get me on the short trip down to the lobby.

When we stepped out of the elevator, he wove our fingers together, and we joined up with the rest of the group. Ryan shot me a knowing look, and when I looked her over, the flush of her cheeks and her disheveled hair looked about right, and I gave her a smirk right back. Kennedy's eyes were bright as she waved at me, and Amara grinned from where she was tucked under True's arm. Moon winked in my direction, and that was apparently all the communication we needed for now.

"You off duty tonight?" I asked Ryan, and she nodded.

"Ronin and Sebastian are covering because Maddox threatened to fire all of them if they didn't let me come out tonight as—*and I quote*—just his wife." The look she gave him was one of equal parts complete adoration and exasperation. I laughed, and Griffin tightened his grip on my hand.

"Have you been to this Dusk place before?" I wondered, and she shook her head.

"Last time we were in Vegas together, we were supposed to go, but we got a little sidetracked."

Moon snorted, and Kennedy practically cackled. "Is that what we're calling it?"

"Hey, it's not my fault Vegas is the best place to get married. When the opportunity presented itself, we had to take advantage," Moon explained, and Jericho pulled her close and dropped a kiss on her temple. She looked perfectly content to snuggle in further to his body while True eyed Griffin.

"Dude, we're in Vegas. Connor's here…"

Zen and Maddox both laughed at the same time, and I looked between them, wondering what the hell they were talking about. "What does Connor have to do with anything?"

"They're just wondering if you two are going to pull a Maddox and Ryan or Jericho and Moon type of situation tonight where we're finding ourselves standing in the Little White Wedding Chapel at one a.m. watching Connor marry you," Amara supplied, and True raised his eyebrow.

"We're not getting married in Vegas," Griffin's firm response left no doubt about that, and he glanced down at me, and I nodded. We hadn't talked about getting married, but when he talked to me, he always did it with the future in mind. Now that he'd carved out a place in my life, I couldn't picture it without him, but getting married felt like a *really* big step, especially after only being together a month.

I loved him, but I wasn't ready.

Besides, I didn't want to get married in Vegas. I hadn't given a whole lot of thought to what my wedding would be like, but now that I was thinking about it, I knew Vegas wasn't what I wanted.

"Now that we got *that* out of the way, can we please get out of here?" Griffin asked the group, tucking me under his arm and pulling me close.

We moved as a group out of the lobby and into the waiting cars. It took two huge black SUVs to get us all to the other side of the Strip where we moved into a swanky hotel. I was never more happy than at that moment that Griffin bought my dress for me because not only did I fit in with all the rest of the girls in our group, but I'd look like I belonged inside the hotel. "I thought we were goin' to a club?"

Griffin grinned down at me. "We are. It's on the roof."

When we stepped off the elevator on the top floor, my eyes went wide. The music was pulsing, and between the clear glass walls around the edge of the building, the open roof with stars shimmering above our heads, and the mirrored bar and accents everywhere, it was like a wonderland of glitter and magic that wasn't like anything else I'd ever seen. "Wow," I breathed, and Griffin pulled me a little closer by the hand he had resting on my hip.

"Isn't it pretty?" He let me go long enough for the rest of our group to shuffle in behind us.

"We're starting with shots," Maddox declared and started moving toward the bar.

"I'll go help and keep him in check," True added, following behind his friend.

Amara grabbed my hand and pulled me away from a grumbling Griffin. "Us girls are going to hit the dance floor. Feel free to watch."

She pulled me along with her, and Kennedy wove her arm through mine. Moon and Ryan were on the outside of our little girl group with me in the middle, and we walked across the club to the dance floor. The five of us formed a little circle and got lost in the music, shimmying our hips and moving to the beat. No one approached us or tried to break into our circle, and when I glanced back at Griffin, I found all the guys not far away watching with all sorts of expressions on their faces—everything from possession to heat to wonder.

Not long after, hands came around and gripped my hips, and I leaned back into Griffin's chest, swaying as he wrapped himself around me. "You look so goddamn sexy," he murmured right into my ear so I could hear him over the music and heat coiled in my belly.

The bass rattled up through the floor, and my body, the vibrations doing fantastic things in combination with Griffin's body pressed against mine. We danced with the group, drank a little too much, and I couldn't remember ever having a night where I felt more carefree than I did tonight.

By the time we left, I was dazed and happy, and all the weight I'd been carrying around for weeks—or really, years—was blissfully absent. I leaned heavily on Griffin while we rode the elevator down to the lobby, and as soon as the doors slid open, lights started flashing. I threw my arm up to shield my eyes, and all the guys, Griffin included, moved almost as one to step in front of every one of us girls.

"How the fuck did they know we were here?" Zen yanked his phone out of his pocket as Maddox rolled his eyes, but the tight set of his jaw showed just how pissed off he was by the crowd of photographers waiting for us right outside the lobby. It was an overwhelming amount of people with cameras pointed right at us, and suddenly the weight of the world crashed back into reality.

"Dude, we weren't exactly discreet. Anyone upstairs could've tipped them off." Maddox was looking at his wife with concern, probably because he knew she would do what she did next.

Ryan snapped right into bodyguard mode and addressed all of us. "The cars are outside, and Connor, Julian, and Indy are clearing a path. You guys know the drill. Heads down, don't answer any questions, and no matter what they say, do not stop walking."

Everyone looked more annoyed than anything, but this was my first time dealing with the madness that came along with hanging around celebrities, let alone dating one. A shiver rolled through me and not the good kind. "It's going to be okay, Mags," Griffin promised, turning back toward me and pulling me into a hug that I really needed at that moment. "You trust me, right?"

I nodded, breathing him in and trying to ignore the lights still flashing around us.

Kennedy moved up beside me with Zen keeping his body in front of her like a shield. She smiled up at him before focusing on me. "I know those ass munchers out there are a lot to deal with, and my first time was a lot like this where they ambushed us, but you've got all of us with you. I doubt they'll even focus on you honestly, not with so much man candy in one spot." She winked at me and then laughed when Zen wrapped his arms around her and dropped a wet kiss on her cheek that she promptly wiped off. He looked immensely proud of himself, and it helped break the tension as we all laughed.

"Everyone ready?" Ryan called out, looking at her phone and everyone gathered closer to her. "Straight to the cars," she reminded us, and Jericho snapped.

"We're not fucking new, Ryan. I think we can handle walking fifty feet without fucking it up."

Maddox glared at his friend. "Watch your tone with my wife."

Jericho flipped him off, and I thought they were going to go to blows, but instead Moon distracted Jericho and Maddox was too busy focusing back on Ryan to keep tabs on what Jericho was doing, so the rest of us got ready to step out of the relative safety of the hotel lobby.

Ryan stepped through the doors first, and Maddox stuck by her like glue. We all followed, Griffin and I somewhere in the middle of the crowd, but when the photogs started shouting out crap about Wynter and his new mystery girl, it felt like a thousand eyes were on us all at once, like a spotlight had suddenly illuminated from overhead. My heart pounded in my chest like it wanted to escape.

When we got to the cars, no one hesitated to dive inside, and when the doors were finally shut, I was a sweaty, shaky mess with adrenaline pounding through my system. Griffin pulled me onto his lap and buckled the seatbelt over us both, his grip on me so tight it was almost painful. "See? Not so bad," he joked, and I barely cracked a smile.

What the hell was I doing dragging Griffin into my mess? It was only a matter of time before some over-eager reporter dug into my identity and found out about Winston and everything that came of that. There was a big enough paper trail between the restraining order and the medical records to paint quite the picture. Did I want all of that splashed across the headlines?

Did Griffin?

I bit my lip as tears threatened, but I didn't let them fall. Not yet. I wanted the quiet of our hotel room and—damnit—to curl up in the safety of Griffin's arms and fall apart. But was that fair to him?

"Whatever you're thinking right now, stop it," Griffin whispered against my ear. "I can feel you pulling away from me."

"I'm not-" I started to protest.

"You are, and if I haven't done enough yet to show you that I don't care what the world thinks about our relationship because all that matters is me and you, I clearly need to step up my game."

"You just started with the band, Sugar. I don't want to mess it up for you." It all really boiled down to that. I was ashamed of my past, of what I'd let happen to me. It didn't feel like a choice at the time, but looking back now, I hated that I let the manipulation and abuse continue as long as I did. Griffin tying himself to me publicly could hurt his career, and I didn't know if I could handle being responsible for that.

But I didn't think I could let him go, either. He'd quickly become the best thing in my life, and the idea of leaving him behind made my heart feel like it was being torn from my chest.

What the hell was I going to do?

TWENTY THREE
GRIFFIN

Magnolia had been quiet since everything went down last night at the club. Wynter started blowing up my DMs again with gloating messages about how I would need her back now that my relationship with Magnolia had been exposed and how I'd see that she was right about us needing each other.

Wynter could go jump off a damn cliff.

I blocked her as soon as the messages started flying in. "What does your shrew of an ex-girlfriend want?" Magnolia yawned, stretching her body so that I became very aware of every place her skin touched mine. We were curled up in the bunk streaming a movie on her laptop, alone for the moment while Nico and Phoenix had Lucky.

"Nothing new, just to tell me how right she was about everything, which, to be clear, she wasn't." I brushed Magnolia's hair away from her face. "I thought I blocked her already, but I hadn't, so I went ahead and fixed that little oversight. Please don't even give her another thought. I know I won't."

She let out a soft sigh as I ran my fingers through her hair. "Griffin?"

"Hmm?" My eyelids were heavy as the rocking of the bus lulled me into an almost-sleep while we made our way to the last stop on the tour—Los Angeles.

Home.

"Where do you see this going?" she asked softly, almost a whisper.

"What, us?"

She nodded, and I reached out and closed the laptop, so I had her full attention. "I thought it was obvious."

She moved away from me a little so she could see my face, and hers could only be described as unsure. Her eyes were clouded, and she was nibbling on her lower lip. "I don't want my problems to hold you back or get in the way of what you're doing," she finally confessed.

I tugged her back so she was nestled against me again, and she burrowed her head into the space between my neck and shoulder. "Making music was always one of those things that was a dream, but it wasn't what I figured I'd do with my life. I'm content for it to be whatever it's going to be, and it's fun as hell getting to spend time with my brother and the other guys and be a part of this crazy thing. I just happened to fall into this insane opportunity, and if it ends tomorrow, I'll be content in the knowledge I enjoyed the hell out of it."

I ran my fingers down the smooth skin of her arm, and she shivered, making a grin tug at my lips. I loved how sensitive Magnolia was to my touch, and I hoped it'd never change. "You've never experienced it, so I don't expect you to know what I mean when I say this, but I love you unconditionally, Mags. It hasn't been that long yet, so I understand that I haven't had the chance to fully prove it to you yet with my actions, but you'll see. Your past would never scare me off, and if you go through something shitty or difficult, you won't be alone. Not only will I not run, but I'll stand by your side. So, stop the destructive thoughts running through that big, sexy brain of yours and try to accept that I don't give a damn what ends up in the news or what people say about me or you or your past. It does. Not. Matter."

She moved up to kiss me, and I could feel the relief in it. With every sweep of her tongue against mine, her body relaxed more and more until she was completely pliant and had shifted so she was lying half on top of me. I moved to grip her hips and tugged her until her knees landed on either side of my hips, and she was straddling me without ever breaking our kiss.

The languid kiss started to turn into something else the longer it went on and the air charged between us. We had almost no space in the bunk made for one person, but we didn't need space. I needed her as close as she could get, and based on the way she was yanking my shirt up and grinding herself on my hard as fuck cock, I'd say she felt the same.

We pulled apart long enough for her to get my shirt over my head, and then our lips collided again, and the kiss was hot as hell. "This has to be quiet and quick," I whispered against her lips.

"It will be," she agreed, reaching down to push my pants and boxers down just enough to free my dick before she tugged her panties to the side and slid down on me. I hissed at the feel of her body enveloping me, all tight and warm and mine.

My fingers dug into her hips as I gripped her, urging her to rock against me. We were practically chest to chest in the tiny bunk as we fucked, her tits rubbing against my bare chest with every movement. A familiar tightness in my balls had me thrusting myself into her harder and faster in the little space we had, chasing my release and bringing her along with me.

I swallowed her cries with sloppy kisses as she came around me, gripping me so tight with her walls I couldn't help but fall over the edge with her. She went boneless on top of me, and I stroked my fingers down her back while we enjoyed being connected a little longer. Neither one of us seemed to want to move, but eventually, she rolled off and cuddled up beside me. I reached down and tucked my still semi-hard cock back into my pants.

"Where do you see yourself in five years?" she wondered as her fingers danced across my chest and abs, and a small smile tugged at my lips because I'd caught her looking at me enough to know she couldn't get enough of my body just like I couldn't get enough of hers.

"Hard to say," I admitted, playing with her hair while I stared at the dark space above me. "I doubt the rest of the guys are going to want to keep doing this for five more years. It's already been more than a decade, and their kids will all be getting older so it'll be harder to tour."

"Would you want to join up with another band or try to make one of your own?"

"Nah. I think whenever this thing with Shadow Phoenix ends, I'll be ready to do something else. I love music, don't get me wrong, but the whole fame and traveling all the time thing? I think it'd get old fast."

"Well, if you weren't doin' this, what would you be doin'? Or what do you want to be doin'?" she wondered.

"You know, before I found out about Mad, I was sort of lost. I worked a shitty job and lived in a shitty apartment with no direction other than I loved playing the drums. Now that I've done this and will probably keep doing it for a while, it's more clear than ever I'm doing exactly what I'm supposed to be doing. That sounds cheesy as hell," I laughed, and she did, too.

"No, I get it, and maybe you're wrong. Maybe the guys'll keep makin' music and tourin' forever. They don't seem like they're tryin' to stop, and they really love what they do. Most of all, they're like a family, and as long as people are still listenin' to their music, I bet they'll keep playin' it."

"I hope you're right. I don't ever want to stop doing this, but it'd also feel wrong to play with anyone else. So, in five years, if I'm fantasizing about what I want my life to be, I want to be able to call you my wife, I want a house of our own where you can have as big of a garden as you want, and I want to still be making music." Those were definitely my top three must-haves.

"Do you want kids?" she asked, kicking her leg over mine so our limbs tangled together, and I dropped a kiss to her forehead.

"At least two, but I'm not in a rush. How about you? What do you want your life to look like in five years?" I turned her question back on her.

She was quiet for a long time, so long I wondered if she fell asleep. "You know, I never really gave a lot of thought to my future beyond survivin' the now. It always felt so far off when I was just tryin' to figure out how to get through the day. I still don't know what's gonna happen with Winston and everythin', but if I could have anythin' I wanted? It would be you and me wherever we end up, with lots of close friends and maybe startin' a family of our own. I don't mind tourin' and travelin', but I want a place to call home that we can make our own and put down roots, and I want to spend more time on my photography."

"And kids?" I prompted, closing my eyes and breathing her in. Her sweet scent filled my lungs as I waited. If she didn't want kids, I'd deal with it, but I'd be bummed. Kids were something I always wanted, a family like the one I grew up in except with a sibling close in age. Maddox and I weren't that far apart, but we hadn't known about each other until we were adults.

"I love kids," she finally answered, and the tension that I hadn't noticed wracking my body seeped away. "When I was little, I didn't have anyone other than Grammy. No friends and my parents were already dead, so I'd pretend that my stuffed animals and toys were friends or brothers and sisters I could play with." Her tone was almost wistful as she got lost in the memory she was sharing with me.

"I always thought that if I ever did have kids someday, I'd want at least two, too, because I hated growin' up with no one and always wished I had a brother or sister."

"Yeah, same," I murmured, kissing the top of her head as she burrowed further into me. I pulled the blanket up over us. Now that we'd relaxed, I could feel just how cold it was on the bus. They must've had the AC down lower than usual.

How perfect was it we were on the same page with kids and our future? It wouldn't be that difficult to make this thing between us work long-term. One lesson I learned from my relationship with Wynter was that whoever my partner was going to be should be on the same page with our life goals.

Magnolia and I might as well have been the same person; our goals and visions for the future were so closely aligned.

She let out a heavy sigh. "None of that matters if Winston doesn't lay off, though. I refuse to bring a child into the world so that Winston can terrorize them or use them to threaten me."

Anger bubbled up inside me at the idea because those hypothetical future kids of hers? Yeah, they were going to be mine if I had any say in it and the idea of Winston still being an issue then was enough to make me want to hit something.

Preferably Winston's face.

"He's not going to be a problem much longer. Connor and Ryan are working on a plan," I assured her. Ronin and Sebastian had been digging into every security feed they could, compiling evidence of everything he'd been doing on tour and building a case to hand over to the police. Despite how much Connor pissed me off, he was a professional, and I was trying to trust he'd take care of Winston.

Still, I'd asked Ryan to keep a copy of everything they found just in case I needed to bring in outside help. I hadn't told her that last bit because if I hurt her feelings, I'd be staring down a very pissed off Maddox, and I wasn't kicking that particular hornet's nest unless absolutely necessary.

"I hope so," she murmured, her voice all soft and sleepy. When she sounded like that, and I got moments like this with her that were quiet and felt like we were the only two people in the world, they were my favorite.

Humming one of my favorite old Shadow Phoenix songs, I closed my eyes and stroked her hair until we both passed out.

"What do you mean you don't know?" I questioned, frowning at Magnolia as she stepped off the bus with Lucky in her arms.

She shrugged. "I haven't figured it out. I thought I'd probably stay in a hotel until I figure out what to do next."

"You're fucking kidding me, right?" I tried to keep the anger out of my voice, but she still flinched, and internally I kicked myself for being an asshole. I took a deep breath and tried again. "There's no way I'm letting you go and stay in a hotel alone. You're coming home with me."

Yes, I knew I was being demanding as hell, but this was a hill I was willing to die on.

Her cheeks turned pink, and she wouldn't quite meet my eyes. "I didn't want to invite myself along or assume." Of course, she didn't. Magnolia had been on her own and taking care of herself almost her entire life. She wasn't used to leaning on anyone, but that was one of a long list of things that were going to change now that I was in her life.

I softened my tone even more and stepped closer, right up into her space so I could run my knuckles along her cheek. She leaned into my touch, and I sighed. "I just got to spend the last month spending every night sleeping next to you, waking up to your gorgeous face, and having you any time I wanted. Do you think I'm going to give that up now that we're home? Not a damn chance."

A sweet smile tilted her lips up, and I leaned down to capture them in a too-quick kiss. "I've been staying with Maddox since I got to LA, but after tomorrow's show, we'll start looking for a place of our own. Okay?"

I hoped like hell she wouldn't argue with me on this. I had this deep-seated need to be around her. It wasn't violent or sick, like Winston. It was more she fascinated me and made me feel like I could do or be anything. Magnolia made life brighter and more fun, and experiencing everything with her was a gift I didn't want to let go of. I thought she felt the same—she told me she loved me, and the way she looked at me like I hung the stars said everything else she'd never put into words.

"Okay," she finally breathed, and I exhaled loudly. I hadn't even realized I was holding my breath until she gave me the answer I hoped she would. I wasn't sure what I would've said if she didn't want to keep going like we had been, except in real life.

The tour hadn't really been real life. It was a sort of bubble we'd existed in for the past four weeks where anything outside the next stop or the next problem or the next show didn't exist. The only thing that'd managed to pierce that bubble was Winston, and I hated him for it.

Here it would be different. We were on our home turf, and after tonight's show, Magnolia and I could start to figure out what our lives together would look like. Did she want to find a job managing another tour after this one? Or could I convince her to stick around with me?

I wanted her to go on tour with another band about as bad as I wanted my teeth kicked in.

Scooping her up into a hug, Lucky nipped at my chin, and we both laughed at him. He'd gotten a lot bigger over the course of the tour, and I was happy we weren't going to be cramped in that bunk together anymore. He needed room to run and play, and a tour bus and endless stream of hotel rooms weren't going to cut it.

"I've got stuff to wrap up here, final checks and everythin', but I can tell people are happy to be home. Everyone seems more relaxed, and it'll be bittersweet when the show ends tonight, and we move on from the tour. A lot of my favorite memories happened in the last four weeks," she confessed, and her eyes looked a little misty.

I kissed her forehead and took Lucky out of her arms, setting him on the ground, pulling his leash off her wrist, and looping it around mine. "Go do whatever you need to. I've gotta meet up with the guys for practice and then soundcheck. I'm going to run home if I have time and drop Lucky off, too, so he can play in the yard if he wants."

There was that look like she couldn't quite believe I was real again. "You're the best, Sugar. I probably won't get a chance to see you until after the show." Her voice was dripping with disappointment, and I felt the exact same way.

"Meet me backstage after? Then we'll go home?"

She hummed. "Home." She said it like she was testing how the word tasted on her tongue before she gave me this bright smile that made everything around her look dim in comparison. "I like that. Knock 'em dead tonight, and don't forget I love you," she sing-songed as she walked backward a few steps before turning around and throwing me one last look over her shoulder before she walked off into the crowd of road crew bustling all over the place.

"What do you say we get you home?" I looked down at Lucky, who was sitting on his hind legs and staring right back up at me with his head cocked to the side. I swooped down to pick him up, and when I stood up, an SUV pulled up beside me.

"I'm headed home. You coming?" Maddox asked through the rolled down passenger side window. I nodded and opened the door, sliding inside. I held Lucky in my lap and put the seatbelt around both of us. Riding in a car Maddox was driving was scary as hell, and I was man enough to admit it.

"Last show tonight," my brother mused, and I grunted a response as he floored the gas to race through a yellow light right before it turned red. I reached over and gripped the side of my seat.

"It went by quick." My stomach lurched when he cut across three lanes of traffic and darted between two semi-trucks to merge onto the freeway.

"It always does. What are your plans after?"

Instead of watching out the windshield at my potential forthcoming death, I studied Maddox instead. "Sleeping for two days straight. Then getting back in the studio whenever the guys are ready to go again."

Maddox hummed. "What about Magnolia?"

"I'm not leaving her behind. I'm bringing her home with me—with *us*—until we can find our own place."

His eyebrows furrowed. "You're moving out?"

I chuckled. "It almost sounds like you don't want me to."

"That's because I don't. It's been—fuck." He took one hand off the wheel and ran it down his face, and I had to close my eyes and take deep breaths to keep from freaking out about his driving. "It's been really nice having you close." He said the words like they'd been torn out of him, like he was embarrassed to admit he actually had feelings.

I didn't care—my long-lost brother actually *liked* having me around. It was exactly what every little brother everywhere wanted to hear, and my heart suddenly felt full to the point of exploding.

"It's been awesome for me, too, but you're married, and you and Ryan deserve some privacy, especially if you want to start a family." That'd been a point of contention between them for months. Maddox wanted to have kids right now; Ryan loved her career and wasn't ready to take time off just yet. They loved each other too much not to figure it out.

"Besides," I added. "Magnolia and I deserve our own space, too. It's still really new between us, and I don't want to mess it up."

"And you don't think moving in together after a month of dating is going to mess it up?"

I shook my head. "If anything, after spending the past month practically glued together, I want more time with her, not less."

Maddox grinned. "I know exactly how that feels. That's what it's like with Ryan, what it's always been like. I'm happy you found someone like that, bro. Seriously."

"Thanks, Mad. I'm happy for you, too." I clapped him on the shoulder, and he shook me off, clearing his throat and turning up the music.

"Enough feelings bullshit. If you're moving out, you've gotta stay in the neighborhood. Text the guys and tell them to keep their eyes open for properties that could work."

That was a conversation I needed to have with Magnolia first. Part of my family was in Texas, and the rest were here, but Magnolia deserved to have a say where we ended up, too. But I'd humor my brother and send out a group text. Since they all lived in the same neighborhood, I didn't think it'd take long for them to come up with something.

I could worry about that tomorrow, though. For tonight, we had a show to get ready for.

"What's up, LA? You ready to get *wild*?" Zen's gravelly voice purred across the industrial sound system of the arena as it was quickly drowned out by screams and cheers. There was something about the energy in the building tonight that was electric.

Maybe it was being back home, or maybe it was because this was the last stop on the tour, and we were all excited to put everything we had into one last show. I wasn't sure, but my heart was kicking a staccato beat against my ribs as I pounded on my drums. My custom earbuds were in that let me hear the music we were playing but drowned out a lot of the crowd, and I lost myself in the rhythm of it all.

Sweat poured down my entire body, and it ran into my eyes, making them sting. In between songs, while Zen whipped the crowd into a frenzy with his sultry words and cocky smirk, I reached down and grabbed my bottle of water and took a healthy swig. It wasn't until I sat back up and reached for my sticks that I registered that there was a problem.

Zen, True, and Maddox were all rushing off the stage, and I watched in confusion because there hadn't been a cue to change sets or costumes. A faint *pop pop pop* sound rang out, and I yanked out my earpiece to see if I could figure out what the hell was going on. The screams I heard weren't cheering anymore, they were terrified, and if I thought my heart had been beating fast before, it was nothing on what it was doing now.

I ducked down, suddenly very aware of how out in the open I was. The lights came on in the arena, and I scanned the crowd, watching as people rushed to get to the exits, trampling each other in their panic. My head whipped around as I looked for Magnolia, but I couldn't see her in the chaos. When I looked at the side of the stage where huge black curtains cascaded down from the ceiling, Ryan stared out at me with determination in her eyes. She ducked down and ran for me, sliding on her knees, so she was right beside me behind my drums.

"There's an active shooter, Griff. We need to get you backstage." Her words were overshadowed by another loud series of *pops* that rang out, and we both ducked as the sound of metal pinging off metal hit way too close to where we were crouched.

"Shit," Ryan hissed when she looked back, and another shot almost hit her.

"Stay the hell down," I bit out, yanking her back and behind me. Whoever was shooting was getting closer to the stage based on the number of shots I heard ricocheting off the stage and the instruments and equipment around us.

"We can't stay here; he's almost at the stage," Ryan observed, looking over my shoulder since I was blocking her with my body. No way was she getting hurt trying to save me. Maddox would kill me.

"Okay, can we crawl?"

She shook her head. "Too slow." Ryan was making hand signals at one of the guys backstage, and she nodded. "Indy's going to try and lay down cover fire, and we're going to duck and run backstage when I give the signal. Got it?"

"Got it," I agreed. My heart was thundering in my chest, and I was almost out of my mind worried for Magnolia because I had no idea where she was in all of this, but oddly that helped me focus because if I worried about her, I wasn't thinking about the shit I was in right now.

More shots fired around us, and then a second set of gunshots came from further away. Ryan popped her head up just a little and then shouted, "Now!" and we crouched and ran. I made sure to keep her body angled behind mine, and she made it to the backstage area a few seconds before I should've.

Except I didn't quite get there because white-hot agony tore through my body as another round of shots went off, and this one hit their target—me.

My shoulder felt like it was on fire and hot liquid rushed down my arm as I tried to breathe but couldn't. I gasped for air as blood gurgled up my throat, and my knees gave out as I crashed to the stage. Blackness dotted into my vision until all that was left to do was give in to the nothingness.

TWENTY FOUR
MAGNOLIA

Every blink felt like sandpaper rubbing across my eyeballs. I'd lost track of how long I'd been pacing the dingy hospital waiting room while Griffin was in surgery. His blood still stuck to my clothes, but I couldn't bring myself to change.

I was only capable of putting one foot in front of the other until I hit the end of the room, pivoted, and walked back.

Step, step, breathe in.

Step, step, breathe out.

Griffin might die, but I refused to believe it. He couldn't die. He *wouldn't* die. He made me promises that I knew he'd keep, which meant he wouldn't give up. He'd fight for me, for us, like I'd fight for him.

When Indy finally hit the shooter with a couple of bullets in the chest, I'd been numb but not surprised to learn it was Winston. The guilt would be bad when I could feel it, and as it was, it churned in my stomach, but in such a distant way, I couldn't even process it past the numbness and cold that had settled into my bones.

If Griffin lived—*when* Griffin lived—I could let the guilt have its way with me. Until then, I paced.

"I brought you some tea," Kennedy offered, pressing it into my hands and keeping a hold of the scalding cup until she was sure my fingers had securely wrapped around it. The thought of eating or drinking made my stomach roil, but

I sipped it anyway. I didn't taste a thing.

Running onto that stage and finding Griffin unconscious with blood pooling underneath him had been like the worst kind of nightmare I'd ever had, and I desperately wanted to wake up and find him giving me his crooked smile with that sparkle of mischief in his eyes. I choked back the sob trying to claw its way up my throat, and sipped the tea again, continuing to pace.

The room was crowded with all the guys and their wives, none of them wanting to be away from each other in the aftermath of the mass shooting my deranged ex-boyfriend had perpetrated, and in time, maybe I'd come to realize he was sick and this wasn't my fault. Today wasn't that day, and I suspected it would take a long time with a therapist to wade through that minefield.

Today, this minute, this *second* was for Griffin. Every tick of the hand on the old analog clock was one more second Griffin was still alive, that no one had come out to tell us the worst happened. Every second that ticked by meant he had a better chance at living, that he was being healed.

At least that's what I was telling myself.

Step, step, breathe out.

Step, step, breathe in.

The set of double doors I'd been trying not to focus on pushed open, and a tired-looking doctor stepped through, her hair mostly hidden by a surgical cap and a white coat thrown over her blue scrubs. She approached the waiting room with a tablet cradled in her arms. "Are you Griffin Spencer's family?"

My heart leaped into my throat, and my legs threatened to collapse from under me. Amara stepped up beside me without missing a beat and wrapped her arm around my waist, holding me firmly and keeping me upright.

"I'm his brother," Maddox confirmed, his voice raspy like he hadn't said anything in hours. He probably hadn't. None of us had.

"I'm Dr. Arbor. He's in recovery now. The bullet was still inside of him and had ricocheted off his scapula and taken an unexpected trajectory through the subclavian artery, so it took us longer to get out. He lost a lot of blood and was given a transfusion. He was extremely lucky. A couple of inches south, and it would've hit his heart."

"Can we see him?" Maddox wrapped his arm around Ryan as they leaned into each other for support, looking dead on their feet like the rest of us. Kennedy stood to my left, her back pressed against Zen's chest.

"When we get him out of recovery and into a room, a nurse will come get you. He's not out of the woods yet, but I'm hopeful." The doctor gave us a tired smile before she turned and walked back through the doors, and relief washed over me. Tears pricked my eyes, and I let out a shuddering breath.

Amara stayed with me and rubbed my shoulder as we walked over to the chairs I'd ignored up until now. Griffin was alive. That was all that mattered. I collapsed into one of the hard plastic chairs and let the tears fall. I was too exhausted to deal with the emotional storm brewing inside of me, but it didn't look like I'd be sleeping anytime soon.

"You need to get some sleep," Moon gently pointed out like she'd heard my inner monologue as she took the chair on my other side. Jericho stood like a sentinel at the door to the waiting room with his eyes glued to his wife, but I didn't blame him for wanting to stay vigilant. I didn't think I'd ever be able to go into a public place again without fear of someone storming in with a gun and opening fire on the crowd.

"I can't sleep, not until I see he's okay with my own eyes," I choked out, the tears falling freely now. I didn't even care to hide them. If I forced them down and locked them inside, I feared they would still find a way to boil over and escape.

As the hours trickled by, my only awareness of the time passing was the ticking of the clock on the wall and the changing of the cups of tea and coffee between my hands. One minute the cup would be cold, and then it would be hot. There were murmurs of conversation around me, but I didn't tune in to any of it. I couldn't, not until I got to see Griffin.

Finally, after what felt like an eternity, a nurse stepped into the doorway of the waiting room. "Family of Griffin Spencer?"

"That's us," Maddox confirmed, standing up. His gaze settled on me, and he jerked his head to the side in a motion I took to mean he wanted me to go with him. The knot in my chest loosened just a little bit as we followed the nurse back to the room they'd gotten Griffin settled into.

I wasn't ready for what greeted us when the nurse pushed into the room.

A sob escaped me when I took in how pale and lifeless Griffin looked hooked up to all the machines monitoring him. He was breathing on his own, and that was something. Maddox wrapped an arm around me and pulled me to his side, his own breathing ragged like it hurt him as much as it did me to see his brother like that.

"He's strong, Magnolia," Maddox tried to reassure me with an uncharacteristically soft voice. Then he got a bit louder. "He also knows if he dies on us, I'll find a way to bring him back so I can kick his ass."

A watery smile broke through my tears, and I pulled up one of the chairs in the room so I could sit as close to the bed as I could get. I carefully grabbed his hand, avoiding the IV line and the wires while I gripped his fingers. The familiar calluses on his palm had my eyes pricking with tears again, but I blinked them away. While his hand was warm, his fingers didn't move to hold mine back.

I laid my head on the edge of the bed, watching Griffin's chest rise and fall slowly with each breath he took, and it must've lulled me to sleep because I was jolted awake by a voice I would've given anything to hear again. "Hey, Mags," Griffin croaked, and I stared into his rich brown eyes before bursting into tears.

"Shh, don't cry, baby," he soothed, and I laughed through the absolute mess running down my face.

"I should be comfortin' you right now," I chastised, but it lacked any heat as I climbed up in the bed with him when he held his arm out for me to curl up into his side. His other arm was trapped against his chest in a sling, and his face paled a little as I settled in, but when I tried to move away, he tightened his hold on me.

"I'm fine; please stay." He shifted a little, and I pulled the blanket up around us.

"I was so scared that I lost you," I confessed, lying my head on his shoulder and breathing him in. I rested my hand on his chest over his heart and closed my eyes, letting the steady beat relax my exhausted body.

"It'll take more than a little flesh wound to take me away from you," he joked, and I lifted my head to scowl at him.

"A *little flesh wound?* You almost bled to death!" My breath caught, and my eyes were burning again. I wasn't sure how many more tears I had to cry.

"Maddox told me Indy took out Winston," Griffin finally sighed, pulling me tighter against his body as his thumb drew circles on my upper arm. "Does it make me a horrible person that I'm glad?"

I shook my head. "Not unless I'm a terrible person, too. I'm not sure what other kinds of havoc Winston wreaked because all I could focus on was makin' sure you were okay. I probably should find out." I was thinking out loud, and Griffin pressed a kiss to my forehead.

"We can ask the guys later," he reassured me.

"Oh," I sat up. "I should probably go let them all come in and see you. Everyone's been waitin' for... well, I'm not really sure how long it was. I wasn't exactly payin' attention."

He tugged me back against him. "Later. We're both exhausted." His eyelids were heavy, and it looked like he was fighting to keep them open. "Sleep with me for a while; then you can let them in."

Now that he was okay, my body felt like it was on the brink of shutting itself down whether I wanted it to or not, so I closed my eyes, reassuring myself he was here, and everything was going to be okay. There'd be time for thinking through everything that happened later, but for now, Griffin wasn't going anywhere, so I let myself drift into a deep, dreamless sleep.

"I didn't get shot in the damn leg," Griffin grumbled as his brother wheeled him out of the hospital.

"Just shut up and let me push this fucking thing outside. Hospital policy," Maddox smirked, liking giving his brother crap a whole lot if the look on his face was any indication.

Ryan rolled her eyes and mouthed *assholes* at me before she moved around to get in the driver's side of the waiting car. Once we were out of the hospital's sliding doors, Griffin stood up out of the wheelchair with ease and glared at his brother before breaking into a little dance and then throwing his good arm around my shoulders. "Told you my legs worked, dickhead," Griffin tossed over his shoulder at his brother.

After a few days in the hospital with people in and out of his room constantly, we were all ready to get out of there and go home. None of us had been eating or sleeping well, but I hadn't left the hospital once in four days. I was more than ready to get out of here and start our new normal.

Griffin would have to start physical therapy, but not yet. For now, we planned on laying low and relaxing. Looking around the hospital entrance, I was surprised there weren't more media here, but then over at the parking lot entrance, I noticed the blockade that'd been set up by Connor's security guys with all of them lined up like big, hulking impenetrable walls keeping the cameras away.

My stomach flipped over when I let myself think about the headlines over the last several days. Winston had thankfully not managed to kill anyone else, but he'd hit a dozen people with his spray of bullets in his attempt to get to Griffin. They were all going to heal physically, but knowing something about the emotional scars they were going to have, the guilt welled up in me again.

It'd been a struggle to keep it at bay, and when the hospital's caseworker came in to check on Griffin and offer him some recommendations for therapists if he wanted them, I asked her for some of my own. I'd been avoiding dealing with my trauma for too long, and now that Winston was gone, I had a lot of conflicting thoughts and feelings I needed to deal with.

I couldn't shake the thought that all the people that got hurt? That was on me. Griffin reminded me over and over that it wasn't my fault, that Winston was the one who decided to pull the trigger. In my mind, Winston wouldn't have been there, though, if I hadn't taken the job on the tour. If I'd stayed away, Griffin wouldn't have been shot, and neither would any of those other innocent people who just wanted to see a band they loved play and enjoy the music.

"It wasn't your fault," Griffin reminded me like he could hear my thoughts. It always startled me when he did that, like he was so in tune with me he knew what I was thinking without me having to say anything. He'd taken to reminding me all the time that Winston was the one to blame, and the media and the police apparently agreed with him.

I did, too.

I just also thought it was partly my fault. I wasn't sure anyone could convince me otherwise. Two days ago, when the police declared Griffin was healthy enough to talk to them, we'd all been there crowded into his hospital room while we spent hours answering questions. Connor showed up and handed over everything he'd collected on what Winston had been up to on the tour. All the video Sebastian collected and the police reports that'd been filed that Ronin managed to get copies of were given over to the cops, and we washed our hands of it.

Connor hadn't made eye contact with me since the shooting, and he'd barely mumbled two words to Griffin—the two words being *I'm sorry*. I knew he blamed himself for everything that happened, but it wasn't his fault. Winston was determined, and nothing was going to stop him on his quest to make me his.

Griffin watched me with concern as we drove through LA toward Malibu, heading back to the house I'd never stepped foot in before but was about to become my home. The shooting had brought us all closer together, and the idea of living with Maddox and Ryan while Griffin healed up wasn't nearly as uncomfortable as it'd been a week ago.

Having extra hands around to make sure he had everything he needed to get better was the best scenario I could think of.

"I've been stuck inside for days," Griffin complained. "What do you think about a beach day? We don't even have to go far; how about the stretch behind the house? Lucky can run around and go crazy, the guys can bring their families, and we can soak up some sun."

I had to admit it sounded fun. "You just got *shot*. The doctor said you're supposed to rest," I reminded him.

He flashed me that crooked smile I loved so much. "What's the difference between laying in bed resting and laying on a blanket on the warm sand?"

He had a point, so I didn't argue. Maddox and Ryan exchanged a glance before he pulled out his phone and shot off a text. Thankfully, Ryan was driving. "We're in. I texted the guys, and you know Kennedy will make a whole fucking production of it. Prepare for a full meal and bar, especially if she calls Grayson."

"Who's Grayson again?" I wondered, not recognizing the name.

"Her twin. He's a chef, and his food is to die for," Ryan supplied, meeting my eyes in the rearview mirror.

"Oh. Well, I hope she calls him because I'm starvin'. I feel like I haven't eaten anythin' but crappy hospital food in forever." I realized I sounded a little whiny, but who wouldn't be after everything I'd been through this week? I would give almost anything for a delicious meal, a hot shower, and a comfortable bed where I could curl up with Griffin for a solid eight hours.

Ryan's lips twitched. "Mad can text and let her know to ask him to come along if he's free."

"On it," Maddox added, fingers flying across the screen of his phone.

We settled into a comfortable silence after that, and it didn't take long before we'd pulled up in front of a gorgeous house with tons of windows. When we walked through the front door, Lucky was there waiting and pounced on us as soon as we were inside.

"I think someone missed you," I mused while Griffin flopped down on the ground and let Lucky climb all over him while ruffling his fur with his one good hand.

Maddox and Ryan both laughed as they stepped over and around the pile of limbs and fur right inside the front door. "Everyone's meeting out back in an hour," Maddox told us before the two of them walked off deeper into the massive house. I had to wait for Griffin to show me around since I'd never been here and had no idea where I was going.

He sat up and tucked Lucky up under his arm. "I swear he got bigger while I was in the hospital."

I looked at our puppy, who had his tongue lolling out of his mouth and his tail thumping furiously against Griffin's side. He *did* look a little bigger. "He's growin' like a weed," I agreed before I reached my hand out to help Griffin up off the floor.

"I'll show you where our room is first," he offered, and I closed the door and turned to follow him through the house. It was bright and airy, and I instantly loved it. The view out the wall-to-wall back windows was all blue sky and soft sand, and a contented sigh escaped me. I couldn't believe I was going to be staying here with Griffin.

It seemed like all my horrible luck was finally turning around.

"Here we are," Griffin pushed into the room and stood back to let me pass by. He set Lucky down on the plush carpet, and the puppy followed me around while I checked out the space. We had an en suite bathroom, and a huge bed sat in the middle of the room. There was a set of French doors at the back of the room that opened to a huge balcony that overlooked the Pacific ocean, and when I stepped inside the closet, I gasped. It was the size of another bedroom, but there wasn't much in it.

"There's plenty of room for you to fill it up," Griffin offered with a grin as he stepped inside behind me, wrapping his arm around my waist so I could lean against his back. I'd need to go get all of our bags out of the car since we'd loaded everything from the tour bus into the SUV and mostly forgotten about it while we'd been at the hospital.

I laughed. "How much stuff do you think I own?"

He shrugged. "Doesn't matter; we've got room for it."

Spinning in his arms, I lifted onto my toes and pressed a kiss to his plush lips. "Thank you."

His eyebrows furrowed. "For what?"

"Bein' you and lovin' me." I never imagined in my wildest dreams I could be as in love with someone as I was with Griffin. Him loving me too? That was practically a miracle.

"You never have to thank me for that, Mags. Loving you was inevitable. I couldn't have fought it if I wanted to." His crooked grin had my insides turning to mush and heat spiraling through my body and pooling in my core.

His eyebrows lifted while he took in my expression. "What's that look for?"

"I think we need a shower before we hit the beach," I declared, giving him my best devious smile.

His gaze darkened, and his grip on my hip tightened. "We?"

"Mmhmm."

He let me go and backed out of the closet, never breaking eye contact when he flicked the button on his jeans open, exposing the band of his black boxer briefs. "You're going to have to strip me down if you want to get me naked."

"Somehow, I don't think that's gonna be a problem, Sugar." Having control over my strong, ink-covered, sexy-as-sin rockstar boyfriend was something I was going to enjoy.

Immensely.

"Can someone grab me a platter?" Kennedy's twin brother, Grayson, yelled out into the group from where he manned the huge grill he'd convinced the guys to haul down into the sand. The delicious smell of charred meat carried on the breeze, and my stomach grumbled in response.

"I've got it," Zen was already walking back down from the house a few doors down that he and Kennedy shared. True's house sat in between theirs and Maddox's with Jericho's down a few on the other side. He handed his brother-in-law the dish before clapping him on the back and jogging down to grab Nico, flinging the giggling toddler up in the air.

We were all sprawled on blankets on the soft sand, soaking up the sun and watching the kids run around. Phoenix was tossing a stick of driftwood she'd found for Lucky, and Benji, Moon and Jericho's son, was taking unsteady steps on the blanket while trying to keep up with the other kids. Laughter and shrieks of delight accompanied the ebb and flow of the waves to make the soundtrack of the afternoon, and I sat up from where I was lounging on the blanket Griffin insisted we drag down here.

Griffin smiled softly at me, though I couldn't see his eyes from behind his sunglasses. "You okay?"

I took a deep breath and watched everything going on around me for a minute before I answered. Was I okay? A slow smile crept across my face. "I'm more than okay." I leaned over and kissed him before jumping to my feet and reaching down to help him up. I looked around the beach again, the group of people that'd taken me in and done their best to protect me when they didn't have to.

They were my new family, and as I watched other people—strangers—down the beach, I realized that today, right now, was the first day of the rest of my life. I took off toward the water, my heart suddenly lighter than I could ever remember as I crashed into the waves, and the cold water splashed up onto my skin.

Griffin was on my heels and wrapped me up with his good arm, lifting me and spinning me around while I laughed. "You look happy," he murmured, finally setting me back on my unsteady feet as the waves washed the sand out from underneath them.

"Better. I'm free."

EPILOGUE
GRIFFIN

One year later…

"Today's the day," Maddox was practically hopping around me, and I rolled my eyes.

"No, shit."

My brother punched me in the arm, and I didn't give him the satisfaction of seeing my wince, even though he punched hard as hell, and it hurt. "Asking Magnolia to marry you is a big fucking deal."

I snorted. "Again, no shit." He seemed almost as excited for me to ask her as I was. "You realize she's going to be marrying me and not you, right?"

He punched me again, and this time I glared at him. "You know it's not like that, bro." And he was right, I did know. His six-month pregnant wife would kick his ass if it was, but Ryan loved Magnolia as much as the rest of us.

Well, I liked to think I loved her more than the rest of them, but that was the thing with my girlfriend—you couldn't help but love her. Everyone who met her fell under her spell. "I know, but it's fun to give you shit."

Maddox relaxed but then perked back up. "What can I do to help?"

I looked around at the empty house, the one I'd been working on for months in secret for this exact moment. It wasn't quite on the same street as all the other guys' homes, but that was fine with me because I wanted a little bit more land. If we had to walk a couple of blocks over to my brother's house to use the beach, that was fine with me.

Magnolia deserved the garden she'd always wanted and with a beach house, that wasn't going to work. So, when this little fixer-upper came onto the market, I snatched it up and had been slowly working to make it perfect between hours in the recording studio and rehearsals. "The bed frame needs to be put together. You could do that."

I ran through my mental checklist of everything that needed to be in place before I texted Magnolia to come by later tonight and didn't miss Maddox's knowing smirk. "Making sure the new place has all the important stuff, huh?"

"Shut up," I snapped but without any real anger behind the words. Magnolia and I had been living with Ryan and Maddox for the past year. It wasn't exactly a secret we couldn't keep our hands off each other, but I didn't like my brother talking about my future wife like that.

"Are you nervous she might say no?" Maddox asked while he leaned against the kitchen island, sipping a bottle of water.

Was I? I shook my head. "We've had a million discussions about what we want out of our future and where our relationship is leading."

"How mature of you," Maddox teased, and I scowled at him.

"I like to think so. Anyway, she knows this is coming. She just doesn't know when or how."

"It was good timing that you finished up the house before next week." Maddox pushed off the counter and walked across the kitchen, staring into the backyard. I'd hired someone to design the space and plant a few things so it didn't look barren, but I wanted Magnolia to be able to make it whatever she wanted without having to rip out a ton of stuff to get started.

"Yeah, I'm excited for the album to drop, but not looking forward to all the damn promo that goes along with it. I could never do another interview and be completely happy about it." We'd been in the studio for the past six months working on a new album. I wondered if the guys were going to walk away after this one, but they didn't show any signs of slowing down, and I was happy to be along for the ride. I'd even co-wrote one of the songs on the new album with True. It was crazy the amount of inspiration being in love gave me.

"Fuck, don't remind me. I'm trying to block that shit out until Harrison cracks the whip." Maddox turned back toward me and reached down to pet Lucky where he was curled up just outside the kitchen on the rug I'd laid down in the living room. "You ready for another tour? If the album does as well as Montana and Harrison think it's going to, it's only a matter of time. Only this time, it'll definitely have more stops and probably be international."

"Really? Magnolia's going to freak if we go international this time." I flipped on the water at the kitchen sink, needing to scrub off the dirt from working out in the garden.

"Has she sold any more of her pictures? I still can't believe she quit after the tour. She was the best manager we'd had. You sure she doesn't want to come back for this tour?" He gave me a hopeful expression, and I shook my head while I reached for a paper towel to try my hands.

"No, she'll be along for the ride this tour and not in charge of it. She's all about her photography now, but if we get to go international, the pictures will be incredible. And yeah, she's sold out three times this year. She's sending a new batch to the gallery in a couple of weeks, so she's been stressed trying to pick the best ones." I tossed the paper towel into the trash under the sink.

Okay, so the house wasn't completely empty. There were a few basic necessities here that I'd moved in over the past few months, but there wasn't much in the way of furniture. We couldn't live here yet, but it wouldn't take long to fill it up once Magnolia got to put her stamp on it.

"Ugh, I better get to work on your bed. I swear to fucking god, I must love you because if I wanted to do manual labor, I'd have stayed on the farm in Texas," Maddox complained, but he left to go do what I'd asked him. Since I got shot a year ago, we'd been even closer. Now, outside of Magnolia, I considered Maddox my best friend.

The other guys weren't far behind, and I couldn't imagine my life without them. It was why when Magnolia and I had been having one of our many discussions about where we wanted to settle down and what we wanted our future to look like—the one we were building together—we decided we wanted to stay in LA. Neither of us particularly liked it here, but we couldn't leave all of our friends and family behind.

I clenched my hand around the pocketknife I'd just dug out of my pocket, and a twinge of pain shot through my arm. After months of physical therapy, I'd regained the full use of my limb and my shoulder, but every now and then, I still got shooting pains if I'd been using it a lot. Even a year later, my surgeon reassured me it could still continue to improve if I built muscle and continued to do the stretches and exercise the PT gave me.

There was no way Winston was going to steal my ability to drum from me, so I was religious about it, and it'd paid off. If all I had after being shot was a twinge of pain every now and then, I'd call that a win. Plus, all the extra time in the gym meant my body was more cut than ever, and Magnolia practically drooled every time I took my clothes off, so there were plenty of benefits even if I still mostly hated the gym.

I pushed the patio doors open and stepped outside. I'd had them custom-built for the house since Magnolia loved flowers. A small French door wouldn't work, I wanted it to feel like the outside and inside had a seamless transition, so these doors were almost like a window, sliding into each other in a stacked way until the entire wall was open.

Moving across the grass and to the small garden area that'd been installed, I stopped in front of an orange tree. It had tiny white blossoms all over it, and I smiled, hoping Magnolia got their significance.

Love.

Marriage.

Fertility.

That last one, we weren't quite there yet, but hopefully someday soon. Lucky followed me outside, trotting lazily over to where I stood under the tree, and he plopped down on his hind legs, blinking up at me as I carved the bark with my pocket knife. When I was finished, I brushed off the excess bark and folded up the knife, slipping it back into my pocket.

I checked the time on my phone—three-thirty. I had a couple more hours until sunset, but I still had a lot to do. I had Grayson cater dinner for us because he was Magnolia's favorite chef, and I needed to string fairy lights around the backyard.

Walking down the hall, I found the bedroom where Maddox was cussing enough to make me laugh. He glared at me. "Shut up, asshole. You want to laugh? You can do this yourself." He tossed the screwdriver he'd been holding onto the floor and stood up, and my grin got wider.

"How about we do it together?" I offered, and he sighed.

"Fine, but if you weren't getting fucking engaged today, I'd tell you to fuck off, and I'd be out of here." He sank back to his knees, and we worked to get the huge bed frame that I'd picked out put together and set up before the mattresses got delivered at five.

"Why do you need such a huge goddamn bed?" Maddox panted as we shoved it into place in the center of the room.

I tossed him one of the bottles of water I'd brought back here with me an hour ago, so it was pretty much room temperature, but he didn't seem to mind. "Lucky got used to sleeping in bed with us on the tour bus, and now he whines if we try and make him sleep on his own bed."

Maddox chuckled. "You're totally going to be one of those couples who has like three kids and a dog in bed with you, aren't you?"

I hid my grin with a sip of water, shrugging. "Maybe. That wouldn't be so bad, would it?" The idea of that made my chest warm and full, and there was a big part of me that hoped that was exactly where we ended up.

The doorbell rang, and I cursed. "What time is it?"

"Almost five," Maddox responded after checking his phone. "Bed?"

I nodded. "Do you mind getting it? I need to stick Lucky in the backyard, so he doesn't get in the way."

Maddox went off to deal with the bed delivery, and I shut Lucky in the yard, trying to ignore the pleading look he gave me. Damn puppy eyes made it almost impossible to say no.

Once the mattress was in place, I made the bed and got LED candles set up around the room, and when we stepped back, Maddox clapped me on the back. "This is romantic as fuck, bro. I'm gonna have to do this for Ryan. Now that she's pregnant, she's been all over my-"

"Dude," I interrupted. "I do *not* want to hear about your sex life with my sister-in-law."

"Yeah, but-"

"Nope."

"Fine, but just wait until you have kids. The guys have all talked about what it's like, but I didn't believe them until it happened. Now I'm wondering how many kids I could convince her to have just so she stays pregnant all the time." He rubbed his hands together in an evil plotting sort of way, and I chuckled.

"You forget we lived together for two years. It wasn't like your sex life was bad before."

"Fuck, no. It was great, but now it's like *next level*." He waggled his eyebrows at me, and I decided to change the subject since he was clearly not listening when I said I didn't want to hear about it.

"On that note, I'm going to shower. You mind sticking around a little bit longer? Gray's sending over dinner, and I want to make sure I don't miss it." I moved into the bathroom while Maddox flopped down on my new bed, making himself comfortable.

"Yeah, I'll be here until you text Mags." I rolled my eyes at his use of my nickname for my girlfriend. He'd been calling her that for a year now despite my protests, and now I was convinced he did it just to piss me off, so I ignored him, hoping he'd get tired of it.

After a quick shower and changing into my favorite jeans and a white t-shirt, I called it good. Magnolia and me? We weren't fancy clothes people. We were jeans and bare feet kind of people, and if anyone would appreciate what I had planned, it'd be my love.

We were so alike in almost every way, it was scary sometimes. She knew what I was thinking before I said it half the time, so keeping this huge secret from her for the past however many months had been one of the hardest things I'd ever done.

But it was finally time.

Maddox had met the delivery from Gray and started setting it up in the kitchen and out at the little table I had in the garden by the time I was done getting dressed. The lights were ready, the sun was setting, and the sky was splashed this gorgeous pinkish-purple color with a hint of gold, and I walked back into the bedroom to turn on all the candles and text Magnolia the address.

Griffin: Come meet me here.

Magnolia: When?

Griffin: Now.

Magnolia: Be there in ten, Sugar x

Walking into the closet, I grabbed the little blue box and plucked the ring out of it. The doorbell rang, but it was way too soon for Magnolia, so I panicked for a second before I remembered the photographer I hired. I jogged out and let her in, showing her where to set up before I rushed over to Lucky, kneeling in front of him and slipping the ring onto his collar.

"I'm gonna need an assist from you tonight, bud. Give our girl those puppy dog eyes, and she won't be able to say no, okay?" He licked my chin, and I laughed, as I noted clicking somewhere in the background, but I ignored it until the photographer spoke up—Amy, I thought her name was.

"Just act like I'm not here. That moment was too sweet not to catch," she muttered, moving back to where I'd shown her to hide. I didn't want Magnolia to see her when we first walked out here.

"I'm outta here, Griff. Call me in the morning, let me know how it went," Maddox said, pulling me in for a hug before he left, and then it was just me and my nerves for the next few minutes. I took deep breaths because what did I really have to be nervous about? I knew Magnolia wouldn't say no, but at the same time, did I really know?

She'd been through a lot before me and after. She'd been in therapy for a year, we both had, and she was so much different now than she had been when we'd met, and yet in so many ways, she was still the same girl. I never wanted to be without her, and I was pretty sure she felt the same way.

The doorbell rang again, and I took one last deep breath. "Showtime."

On my way back through the house, I shut Lucky back outside so Magnolia wouldn't catch sight of the ring before I was ready. The photographer volunteered to hold him on a leash until I called for him. Maddox had the food set up, and everything was perfect.

I swung the door open, and Magnolia's eyes widened as she took in the empty room behind me. "What is this place?"

"Come inside and see." I reached for her hand, threading our fingers together as I shut the door behind her.

She was looking around, but there'd be time for a tour later. "Who's house is this?"

"So many questions," I teased. "I should've blindfolded you."

She smacked me in the arm, and I laughed, but then she did, too. "Okay, so… where are we going?"

I hummed but didn't answer as I pushed the back door open again, and she gasped. With the color in the sky and the fairy lights and how the flowers were all in bloom, even only half-finished like it was, the place was beautiful. "I want to show you something," I murmured, tugging her along until we were underneath the orange tree.

I didn't let go of her hand, but I stepped aside so she could see what I'd carved into the trunk of the tree. *M + G* with a big heart around it. A slow smile worked its way across her face as she looked at it. "Whoever owns this house is gonna be pissed you put that in their tree," she noted, and I chuckled.

"Hold that thought." I looked over at Amy hiding away in the bushes, and she sent Lucky barrelling my way. He was wagging his tail and wiggling all over the place because he hadn't seen Magnolia all day, but I somehow got him to sit, and then I lowered down onto one knee.

Magnolia's stunning eyes were wide, and she gasped. "What's happenin'?"

"I love you, Mags." I grinned up at her even as my heart drummed in my chest. Why the hell was I so nervous?

"I love you, too," she whispered, still watching me with wide eyes.

"Since I met you, it's always been you and me. You're a piece of me, and without you, I'm fractured. You get this light in your eyes when life surprises you, and I could spend my entire life just watching you experience yours. You have this almost child-like wonder with every good thing that happens, and I want to be the one who puts that look in your eye. I want to be the one that stands by your side through all those good things, but the bad ones, too. I want to be the one you trust more than anyone else, the one who you run to when things go wrong, the one who shows you you can do anything when you think you can't."

My voice had gone gravely, and Magnolia definitely had tears running down her face. "All that is to say I love you with my whole heart, and I don't want to do this life without you, Mags. So, here, in our new backyard in the house I've spent the last six months making ours, the house I hope we build our future in,

I'm asking if you'll be my wife. Will you marry me?"

I let go of Lucky's leash, and he barrelled into her legs as she fell to her knees in front of me and threw her arms around me. "Is this real?" she whispered through her tears, and I pulled her closer.

"Oh, it's real. I've got the scars to prove it. So...?"

She leaned back, and with cheeks streaked with tears that Lucky was attempting to lick off, she gave me the most blinding smile I'd ever seen and nodded frantically. "Is there even a doubt? I said when you got shot, I'd give up anythin' for just one more day with you, and now you're tellin' me I get to have a lifetime of days?"

Her body was trembling, and I pulled her back into my arms and held her while she cried. "Is this too much?"

She shook her head. "No, it's perfect," she managed to choke out between sobs. "I'm just overwhelmingly happy. If you'd asked me two years ago if I thought I'd ever get my happily ever after, I'd have laughed at you. Yet here I am, with the man of my dreams on his knees in front of me, wanting me in a way I only ever dreamed about. I... yes. Yes!"

I pulled back, brushing her now-damp hair away from her face where it was stuck to her cheeks. "Yes?" I questioned, studying her to be sure I heard right.

She nodded frantically, and I kissed her like my life depended on it, like I didn't know if I'd ever get to kiss her again, except this kiss wasn't about endings.

It was about beginnings.

And Magnolia? She was where my entire life began, and I couldn't wait to see what happened next.

THE END

JOIN MY READER GROUP AND
BECOME A MEMBER OF THE

WILD RIDE CREW

Want to talk about what you just read? Join us backstage in my reader group!

facebook.com/groups/thewildridecrew

NEXT IN THE SERIES:

WICKED GOD

THEY CALL ME LORD. BUT I'M NO SAVIOR.

I never asked to be born part of British royalty. When I left my old life behind, I broke a thousand-year tradition and became the black sheep of my family.

Now I live how I want, free from the weight of the crown. When the guys of Shadow Phoenix throw an unexpected challenge my way, I willingly jump in without hesitation.

UNTIL A TINY SPITFIRE OF A WOMAN THROWS ALL OF MY PLANS INTO CHAOS.

Bellamy Frost's cheeky mouth and soft curves are a recipe for disaster, one I can't let throw me off my game. More than both of our careers are at stake, but keeping things professional with my boss's barely legal daughter may be beyond my capabilities. Freedom comes at a price, after all, and this time the cost may be too high.

Printed in Great Britain
by Amazon

52745920R00162